EXTREME TRUST

X-TREME LOVE SERIES
BOOK 4

KAY MANIS

To my husband, Tony. None of this would be possible without your love and support.
IHUVM!

CHAPTER 1

PETER

I STEPPED off the elevator and scanned the hospital hallway, searching for someone, anyone, who could help me. My head was a mess and my heart even worse. I was worried about my mother's condition and how she'd react to my presence after not seeing me for so long. And I was sick to my stomach, thinking of the awful way I'd left things with Dana.

"May I help you?" a woman asked behind me. I turned and saw a nurse wearing navy scrubs and a stern expression.

"Um, yes, I'm looking for Barbara Fontenot." I glanced at the text my sister had sent me. "She's in room 509 I believe."

"I'm afraid visiting hours are over." She motioned to the huge clock behind her. "It's rather late."

I followed her gaze. It was almost eleven in the evening.

"Are you family?" she asked.

I swallowed back the emotion. Was I? It hadn't seemed like it in a long time. "Yes," I finally said, "I'm her son."

She assessed me with a critical gaze, her eyes holding mine for what seemed like hours. "All right." She finally nodded in approval.

I wasn't sure if I was relieved or scared to death. Seeing my mother, my entire family again after all this time was unnerving to say the least.

"Would you like me to hold your bag here at the nurses' station?"

I glanced down at the duffel bag slung over my shoulder. The material was ripping at the seams, the strap in my hand frayed and worn. Even the once bright Utah Jazz logo was now faded and dirty. I'd had the bag since high school and had taken it on the road with me for years. Somewhere along the way it had become my talisman and I was bereft to part with it.

"It will be safe here," she said, as if understanding my dilemma. "I promise."

I stood, staring at the bag. It wasn't going to protect me from what was coming but still, it was a comfort for me.

"It's really not appropriate for the hospital." Her lip curled. "It's rather…"

Dirty. I silently finished the sentence for her.

She was right, of course. "Um, sure." I slid the bag off my shoulder and handed it to her over the counter.

She grabbed it cautiously and I couldn't help but smile.

"Thank you," I said.

"No problem." She set the bag in the middle of the nurses' station. "It will be right here when you're ready."

"Thanks. And thanks for letting me stay late," I added.

"Peter," someone called from down the hallway. I recognized the voice. My sister.

The sound was like home to me. My heart beat wildly in my chest. Until that moment, I hadn't realized how much I'd missed Victoria.

I turned toward the sound and saw her standing in front of a huge picture window. The streetlamps outside cast a warm light around her angelic face.

God, I'd missed her. I chastised myself for not being a better brother, for not communicating with her more.

She smiled, that glorious, massive grin that always warmed my heart. My sister had always been one of the most forgiving people I'd ever known. Her expression told me she harbored no ill will toward me.

Victoria raced toward me, arms extended.

I engulfed her with my good arm, squeezing her tight. Sinking my face into her platinum blond hair, I inhaled the familiar scent of her strawberry shampoo. Victoria had always been home for me.

She pulled away and stared up at me. Her blue eyes were darker than I remembered. I could see the fear inside, and a pang of guilt hit me square in the chest.

"I've missed you, big brother," she whispered, her voice more unsure than I'd ever heard.

I felt like the biggest jerk in the world for not having reached out to her in the last few months. I was closer to Victoria than any of my brothers despite our age difference.

"I'm sorry," I said.

"Why?"

I studied her face, so different from mine, from all of my brothers and me. Her soft pale skin, light hair, and rounded face were in stark contrast to the rest of the Fontenot boys. Some had often teased that she was adopted.

Her blue eyes reminded me of another pair I was missing.

"Peter?" she asked again.

"Yes?"

"What's wrong?"

"I need to call someone." I reached in my pocket for my phone, surprised when it wasn't there. "Where could it be?"

"What?" she asked.

"My phone."

"I don't know, but can you look for it later?" Her eyes were wide with desperation. "I told Mom you were coming. She's so happy."

"She is?" I reared back, not believing the words.

"Peter." Victoria slapped my shoulder. "Mom loves you. She always has. *All* of us have."

I stared at my baby sister, her eyes seeming to be telling the truth.

"It was you who left, Peter," she said. "Remember?"

Victoria was right, as usual, but her words stung more than I expected.

"So, what's wrong with Mom?" I asked, trying to change the subject. "What have the doctors said?"

I didn't want to care, but I did. Even though I'd blamed her for not supporting me when my father chose to cut me off—financially and emotionally—I knew she'd been trapped by my father, just like the rest of us. The idea that something could be seriously wrong with her scared me to death.

"They're not sure." Victoria's expression fell, tears welling in her eyes. "They're still running tests. It's her heart though." It was clear by her demeanor that whatever was going on with my mother, it was serious. Victoria and our mother were close, best friends really. If anything happened to her, Victoria would never be the same.

"It's all right, sweetie." I drew her in tight for an embrace, trying to comfort her the best I could, given my absence from her life.

She trembled against me, her sobs muffled as she cried. How long had she had to hold it all together?

"I'm sure she'll be fine," I said, kissing her head. "I mean, she put up with Dad for thirty years. If that didn't kill her, a little chest pain won't." I laughed, tugging Victoria close, thankful when light giggles broke through the sobs.

She stepped back and wiped her face. "I'm just so glad to see you, Peter, see that you're healing." She nodded to my arm before her gaze met mine. "It's been too long."

"I'm sorry."

"Don't be. I get it." She smiled and I wondered what it was she "got." She held out her hand. "Come on, let's go see the family."

I cringed, wondering what type of "family" I'd find inside my mother's hospital room.

She laughed and grabbed my hand. "They won't bite."

"I wouldn't be so sure," I said under my breath. I followed behind her as she led me to a closed door. Without knocking, Victoria pushed her way inside.

The incessant beeping of machines brought back memories of my stay in the hospital. Thoughts of Dana flashed through my mind. The way she'd offered to care for me, for no other reason than…she cared.

I need to call her.

"Peter," my mother called from the bed.

My gaze went to the bed where my mother lay. Another familiar face sat next to her. AJ Rhyne, a man I'd admired and esteemed my entire life.

AJ had been my father's business associate, his right-hand man in the day-to-day operations of his software company. He and his wife Gloria were best friends with my parents, long before any of them had children. Gloria died several years ago, and I knew AJ had been devastated.

"What's AJ doing here?" I whispered to Victoria.

She gazed up at me, a small smirk spreading wide across her face. She wasn't going to tell me. This was my punishment. She was forcing me to talk, to ask questions, to get "involved."

I squeezed her tight and nodded.

"Ah, the prodigal son returns," my brother Luke announced from across the room.

My gaze met his, and I wasn't surprised to see a scowl marring his face.

"Shut the hell up, Luke," Victoria said, pulling away.

"Victoria Grace!" my mother exclaimed.

Every head in the room snapped in the direction of her voice.

My mother sat straight up in her bed, cords attached to what looked like every part of her body.

I noted the monitor above her was beeping with a rhythm I assumed was her heartbeat. The pattern looked erratic.

"Mom," Luke said, lunging toward her.

That was when I saw her, really looked at my mother, and my heart squeezed tight. Her hair was grayer, her blue eyes sunken, her skin ashen. Oxygen tubing secured to her nose made her appear feeble and vulnerable, two words I never would have used to describe Barbara Fontenot.

Guilt flooded me. I should have come home sooner.

"What?" Victoria stared at their mother. "He's being a dick, Mom."

My eyes went wide.

AJ coughed, trying but failing to hold back a laugh.

"I don't care if he's being the biggest ass on the face of the earth, he's still your brother," my mother said.

I inhaled sharply at my mother's words. I'd never heard Barbara Fontenot say a curse word, not even darn. What the hell had happened since I'd been gone? First Victoria, now my mother.

"Yeah, Victoria," Luke said, smiling smugly. "I can be an ass and you can't do crap about it." He threw a plastic cup at my sister.

Victoria swatted it away with ease, and the cup went sailing across the room, landing squarely on my mother's lap.

The room fell silent, except for the monitor's incessant beeping, as everyone stared at my mother.

Her gaze moved from Victoria to Luke, one brow raised.

I knew that look. We all did. Someone was about to get a set-down.

I instinctively hunched lower, anticipating her lecture. Instead, one side of her mouth quirked up in a small smile and her whole body shook.

What in the world was going on?

Suddenly she burst into laughter, her head thrown back, eyes closed.

I stared around the small room, dumbfounded when I saw everyone joined in her amusement.

What in the hell was going on with my family? I'd never heard this type of playfulness, never seen them enjoy one another...ever.

My mother finally settled, straightening the sheets on her bed and wiping at her eyes.

AJ reached for a tissue and instead of handing it to her, pushed her hands away and wiped at her cheeks. There was no denying the look of adoration in his eyes.

I shook my head, fearing I might have fallen into the twilight zone.

My mother grasped AJ's hands and held them for a moment before smiling sweetly. "Thank you," she said quietly.

He nodded once as if understanding some silent message.

Her eyes lifted and she stared straight at me, her smile falling. "Would you all excuse Peter and me?" she told more than asked the room at large, her gaze never leaving mine.

And there it was, the lecture I'd been dreading. The speech where she would tell me how much I'd disappointed her, how much I'd cost the family by choosing my own dreams over their needs.

"Ooooh, you're gonna get it now," Victoria said, waving her hands in the air.

Luke pushed off the far wall and walked toward our mother, leaning over the railing to kiss her gently on the cheek. He studied her for a long moment, his brows narrowed. "Call if you need anything, Mom," he said, his voice quieter than usual. "I mean it."

Something was definitely going on. Luke had never been a compassionate person, least of all to our parents.

Luke turned his attention to me. "See ya, bro." He lifted his chin and turned and walked toward the door but stopped when he reached Victoria. "Let's go, Trouble."

"No way," Victoria said, staring between me and our mom, rubbing her hands together. "This is about to get good."

Luke snorted, shaking his head as he shoved her back, pushing her toward the door.

"Hey," she cried.

"Go," Luke said.

"Bye, Peter." Victoria waved over her shoulder as their brother shuffled her out the door.

"Push the button if you need anything, Barb." I turned at the sound of AJ's voice and watched as he stood and leaned over my mother's bed, straightening her blanket before kissing her softly on the lips.

My eyes shot open wide. What in the hell was that?

He'd called her Barb. And he'd kissed her…on the lips.

AJ turned to me, holding out his hand. "Good to see you again, son."

I grasped his palm, surprised when he tugged me in for a brief hug. His display of affection shouldn't have come as a shock. AJ had always been affectionate and free with his feelings, especially with me. He'd always said I was the son he'd never had.

Feelings of guilt washed over me as I watched AJ leave the room.

I'd been a selfish jerk, walking away from everyone, especially AJ, after my father's death. I'd forced him to take on the bulk of the responsibility for my dad's company. Responsibility that should have been mine.

Glancing over at my mother, lying in a hospital bed, it was abundantly clear that I'd deserted a lot of people in my rush to pursue my own dreams.

"Come, sit." My mother motioned toward the chair AJ had just vacated.

I sat slowly, my gaze trained on her, preparing for her wrath.

She reached up and removed the oxygen tubing from her nose.

"Should you do that?"

She shrugged. "I don't know." Barbara Fontenot always knew right from wrong.

I searched her face, not sure where to start. "What happened to you, Mom?"

She drew in a deep breath and released a heavy sigh. Thankfully the machines didn't go ballistic.

"Well," she began, "I was outside, weeding the front gardens. You know I can't stand weeds." She shuddered in disgust.

My mother's gardening skills were renowned in Salt Lake. Her front yard looked like something out of a magazine. She'd had a small greenhouse in the back of our home for as long as I could remember, growing all kinds of herbs and plants. Everything bloomed under her care. Everything except me.

"Yes," I said, laughing. "Weeds are the devil's handiwork." I repeated the words she'd thrown at me hundreds of times, knowing she felt the same way about motorcycles. Apparently, the devil participated in a lot of handiwork.

"My back had been sore all morning," she went on, "but I just wrote it off to being bent over weeding half the day. I had a horrible headache and felt light-headed. My chest felt tight, as if an elephant were sitting on top of me."

I leaned in closer and took her hand in mine. As much as my mother had disappointed me over the years by not supporting me, I certainly didn't want anything bad to happen to her.

"AJ came out and found me," she said, squeezing my hand. "I was sitting in the middle of one of the flower beds, and he said he knew immediately something was wrong. My face was dripping with sweat and it wasn't even warm outside."

"What was AJ doing at the house this morning?" I asked.

She pulled her hand from mine and smoothed out her sheets, her cheeks flushing red.

I realized this wasn't the time to have *that* discussion. "So he brought you to the hospital?" I asked, changing the subject.

"I begged him not to, but he insisted."

"Well, thank God he was there. What have the doctors said?" I held my breath, afraid of what she was going to say.

"They said it could have been a mild heart attack."

"Oh my God, Mom." I reached for her hand again.

"Or could just be indigestion." She waved me away like this was no big deal to be in the hospital, hooked up to machines. "They just want to monitor me for a day or two, as a precaution."

"Well, thank goodness AJ brought you here." I scooted the chair closer. "We don't want to lose you too, Mom."

Her eyes went wide as if shocked by my comment.

"What?"

She shrugged.

"You think I wish you were dead?"

Her gaze fell and she fumbled with the sheets. "No, not dead."

"Then what?"

She glanced up, her blue eyes meeting mine. "I know I'm not your favorite person in the world."

"That doesn't mean I want anything bad to happen to you."

"Speaking of bad things, how's your arm, sweetheart?" She glanced at my elbow.

Her term of endearment caught me off guard. I stared at her, brows furrowed. My mother loved us, I'd always known that, but she lived under my father's rules. One of which was that she not coddle us in any way.

"What?" she asked.

"Words of affection like that don't normally roll off your tongue so easily, *Mother*," I said with no apologies.

"You're right," she sighed. "And I'm sorry for that."

"What's going on here, Mom?"

"What do you mean?"

"What do I mean?" I repeated, laughing sarcastically. "I mean, AJ Rhyne is kissing you on the lips, for starters." She had the good grace to look embarrassed. "My sister is saying curse words, and so are you. And you're laughing about it. This isn't normal Fontenot family behavior."

"I don't know, Peter. I guess this last year since your father passed away has been…." She paused, staring at the ceiling before turning and staring at me. "Freeing." She smiled. "For all of us."

"What does that mean?"

"Your father was a very serious, controlling man."

"Yes, I know." I rolled my eyes, as if her comment was a surprise. "He basically had my life mapped out for me by the time I was eight."

"Yes, yes he did." She squeezed my hand. "And for that I'm truly sorry, Peter. You deserved to be young, to be happy, to choose your own life."

I studied her face. There was no amusement or evidence she was placating me.

"I'm sorry I didn't make him see that," she continued.

We sat in uncomfortable silence. She was right, she'd stood by and done nothing. I wasn't going to let her off the hook that easily.

"It wasn't just *your* life that was chosen for you, Peter."

"What do you mean?"

"Your father and I were betrothed from a young age. From the time that I was a teenager, everyone in the Mormon Church knew that he and I would marry."

That was news to me.

"Our families were powerful. They believed a union between your father and me would make for a stronger branch of the Mormon Church. Which really meant that our fathers would have even more control within the church."

"I don't understand."

She sighed and fell back into her bed as if exhausted.

"Mom, maybe this isn't the time."

She turned and stared at me. "It's past time you know the truth," she said.

I swallowed, not sure I wanted to know now.

"I didn't fall in love with your father and decide to marry him on my own, Peter," she said. "I was forced to."

"Oh, God."

"Well, not forced to, but still. He wasn't my first choice. I guess coerced would be a better word."

"That's horrible," I said.

"It was what was expected of me."

Her words hit too close to home.

"Eventually, I grew to love your father. Having you kids made the sacrifice of true love worth it."

I sank back into the chair in shock. My mother had been forced to marry my father.

She sat straight up, turning to face me. "What I'm trying to say is, I know what it's like to give up your dreams for the sacrifice of your family."

I shook my head, dumbfounded by her admission. "Mom, I had no idea."

"No one did. No one does."

"None of the other kids know?" I asked.

She shook her head. "Only you."

"Wow."

"I was a good little Mormon girl. Did what my father told me."

"You were trapped."

"Some would say. I just looked at it as my duty. My sacrifice for the greater good of God's Kingdom, so to speak."

"You should have told me sooner, Mom."

"Probably. Maybe. I don't know."

I watched her carefully, seeing for perhaps the first time how hard her life had been. Fine lines creased the edges of her blue eyes and mouth. She'd lived a hard life in service of the church, and my father, with no reward.

"Being a Mormon Bishop's daughter and then wife meant you did not go against the fold," she said. "Even though I knew your father was being unfaithful, I still had to be a dutiful wife."

"So, you did know?"

She nodded.

Obviously, she knew. My mother was an intelligent woman.

That was what had hurt me the most growing up. I couldn't help but wonder why she would let my father control her so much. Now I knew. Duty. The same as me. Only she'd fulfilled her obligations. I'd run away.

"I'm sorry, Mom."

"Don't be, Peter. I lived the life I thought I was supposed to. But I wanted you to live the life you deserved." She smiled and I felt the love in her expression.

"I tried to make your father understand that the future he had planned for you would never be the future you would choose." She swallowed hard as tears welled in her eyes. "I'm sorry I failed you," she whispered on a choked sob.

I stood and lowered the railing, scooting in close to her and taking her in my arms. "Please don't cry, Mom. I had no idea. I'm so sorry."

She pulled back from my embrace, staring up at me. "Don't be sorry, sweetheart. I'm so proud of you. We all are."

I peered down at her, not really believing her words.

"Really." She laughed.

I reached around her and grabbed tissues from the side table.

She took several and wiped her eyes. "I'm just sorry you've been at it alone for all this time. I wanted to contact you, I really did." She stared down at the wadded tissue. "AJ and Victoria encouraged me, but I just felt like I'd failed you, as a mother, by not protecting you from your father."

While her words were true, I couldn't help but feel she'd been just as trapped.

She stared up at me, smiling. "I'm just so glad you're here now, Peter." Her face glowed with happiness, her blue eyes sparkled.

In that moment I realized, my mother's unconditional love and affection had been present my entire life, I just hadn't realized it, until now.

She sat back and I let her go. "How are you?" she asked. "How's your arm healing?"

"It's getting better."

She raised her brows. "But?"

How did she know?

"I'm a mother, Peter." She tapped her temple. "I know everything."

"But," I dragged out the word with a long sigh, "it may never heal properly, at least not enough for me to ride competitively again."

"Oh my goodness, Peter." She gasped. "I'm so sorry."

"It's all right. I mean, I love riding, but honestly, I hate competing."

"How long will you be here, in Salt Lake?" There was an air of hopefulness to her question.

"I'll be here as long as you need me, Mom." I smiled.

Relief washed over her face and for the first time since I'd received the call from Victoria, I breathed my own sigh of relief.

"Will you do me a favor?" she asked quietly.

"What?" I knew better than to agree straight away.

"Will you stay at the house while you're here? No hotels?"

Considering the fact that I'd come straight from the airport and had yet to make any reservations, her invitation actually sounded perfect.

"Sure, Mom. There's no place I'd rather stay." And for once in my life, I meant it.

CHAPTER 2

PETER

I PULLED out an empty chair next to AJ and sat at the table inside the hospital cafeteria.

"I'm so glad you're here, son," AJ said, squeezing my shoulder.

"Me too," I said, surprised by my admission. I took a drink of my soda, wondering how to start this conversation. "So, what really happened to my mom?"

AJ cocked his head. "She didn't tell you while you two were alone?"

"She told me how she got here, that you forced her, but she never told me what the doctors have said."

AJ shook his head as if exasperated. "Of course, she hasn't told you."

I raised a brow, waiting, but not patiently.

"So far they've ruled out a serious heart attack."

"Thank God." I exhaled, my hand covering my heart in relief.

"But," he continued, "she may have some blockage that she'll need to take care of as soon as possible."

"Would they do that here?"

"The doctor said they could. This hospital has a state-of-the-art cardiac unit. Your mom is in the best possible hands."

"And that would fix it? Her heart problems, I mean?"

"For now." He sighed.

"What does that mean?"

"Your mom is going to have to slow down, change her lifestyle."

"Lifestyle?" I laughed. "What? She won't be able to plant as many roses this fall?"

AJ's concerned expression fell, anger replacing his usual happy countenance. I'd never seen the man look so furious.

"What?" I asked, somewhat affronted by his glare.

"You really have no idea, do you?"

"I guess not," I shook my head, "because I have absolutely no clue why you're so upset."

He carefully placed his cup down and pushed back in his chair, crossing his long arms across his chest. "Just who do you think has been running your father's company since his death last year?"

"You," I stated flatly. "The board voted unanimously, didn't they?"

His eyes narrowed and instantly my stomach clenched. "You've never read the bylaws for your father's company?"

"No, why would I have? You know I've tried to distance myself once I realized his true intent of my involvement with IP Software."

He studied me for a moment and the knot that had formed in my stomach earlier tightened.

"It stipulates that one member of the Fontenot family must serve in some capacity on the board during the term of the incorporation."

"What are you saying?"

"You hold an MBA, Peter, you know exactly what I'm saying," he said sarcastically, his tone so unlike the man I'd grown up with.

"Wait." I sat up straighter, confused by his earlier question. And more than a little afraid. "Are you trying to tell me that since my father passed away, and I left, my mother has been serving in that capacity, as a board member?"

"Yes." His word was succinct, his disappointment ringing through the room.

"Are you serious?"

"Completely," he said with a curt nod.

I fell back into my chair with a sigh, staring up at the ceiling. How had this happened? "But she has absolutely no business background," I said, more to myself than to anyone.

AJ chuckled. "You'd be surprised just how savvy that mother of yours really is."

Instinctively I knew he wasn't just talking about my father's company. AJ obviously appreciated my mother for much more than her well-crafted business skills. It was becoming increasingly more obvious that he and my mother had started a relationship far more intense than I'd assumed.

"She's been working at least sixty hours a week," AJ continued, "either in the office downtown or at home, trying to satisfy the corporation's requirements. And that's in addition to the hundreds of hours she'd already committed herself to for volunteer work."

"You're kidding?" I sat dumbfounded. My mother had held one job my whole life and it involved diapers, bottles and pot roast. I knew that sounded chauvinistic, and it was, but it was the truth.

"I wish I were kidding," he said.

I turned at the fear in his voice. He wasn't just worried, he was frightened for my mother, and that frightened me.

"I'm afraid all of this stress has finally taken a toll on her physically," he said. "I've warned her repeatedly to slow down, but she's stubborn and hard-headed." His eyes cut to me and I knew what he was inferring. I was just like her. "She has to step down from the board before it kills her."

Pain speared my chest as I watched AJ's face go ashen. He was distraught over my mother's physical health. Without warning, a massive wave of guilt washed over me, nearly drowning me.

"So, someone needs to take her place?" I asked, my head reeling with the realization that I may have to return to Utah despite my own desires.

"Calm down, Peter." AJ smiled. "She's not going to ask you to come home and take over the family business, if that's what you're thinking."

That was exactly what I was thinking.

"What then?" I asked.

"She wants to sell the company."

My mouth fell open as I stared at AJ. "Are you serious?" I couldn't believe his words. Sell my father's company? If my father wasn't dead already, he would be now.

"Very." He held my gaze for several moments and I felt myself squirm. "If one of you boys or Victoria don't take over her position within the board, your mother won't have a choice."

"AJ," I shook my head, "I just can't. I mean, I don't want this to kill my mother, but…." I couldn't go on. I was being a selfish ass, again.

"Peter, don't ever be sorry for lassoing your dreams and letting them take you for the ride of your life, son." He patted me on the back. "Just make sure you never forget which hitching post you tied your horse to."

"Lassoing my dreams?" I chuckled. "Hitching post? I think you've been watching too many westerns, my friend."

"You have no reason to feel bad for pursuing what you want out of life, Peter."

And that was why I loved AJ. He'd always let me dream.

"All I'm saying is," he continued, "don't forget about your family. Just because you're living the life you've always wanted doesn't mean they don't want to be a part of your adventure."

And that was another reason I loved AJ. He always kept me tethered.

"We all have dreams, Peter, even your mom. I think hers has been watching you reach yours. Maybe it's time for your momma to stop watching and start pursuing her own."

I leaned back and rubbed my neck. I'd really never stopped to think about my mother having her own dreams. I mean, how many kids actually think about their parents wanting more than the life they already have?

I recalled the conversation she and I had earlier in her room. She was trying to tell me she was ready to move on, to become something more than she had been forced to be. I knew how suffocating that feeling was and I never wanted anyone to feel that way, especially my mother.

"So, what are the options?" I asked.

"Well, the doctor said if she rests for a few weeks she can probably—"

"No," I interrupted, "I mean, what are her options, what are my mother's dreams? How can we make them happen for her?"

AJ's brows furrowed, obviously surprised by my question.

I could understand. I'd walked away from my mother, from my entire family. Why would I care about their future now?

"You're right, AJ, it's my mom's turn now. Getting rid of this company won't be a problem for me, especially if it means my mother's health."

"I'm glad to hear you say that, son." An enormous smile spread across his face. "I think it's safe to say that anything having to do with plants is a start."

I nodded and we both laughed.

"She's talked about opening up a greenhouse in town," he said. "Maybe starting a training program with the kids at the school. Apparently, gardening is very therapeutic."

"Apparently not if she had a heart attack." I laughed.

"The doctors think that it's come from years of built up plaque, something that can be corrected with medication and diet, but removing as much of her stress as possible will definitely help."

"So, does she have any plans for her future dreams?"

"Oh, yes." AJ smirked. "She's already picked out a small parcel of land that she'd like to build a gardening center on, and she's about halfway through with her business plan."

"Business plan?" I teased.

"Peter, your mother's a highly intelligent woman. There's much more to her than raising kids and teaching Sunday school."

AJ's words were a reprimand of sorts, reminding me of how naive and selfish I'd been.

"She doesn't enter into anything lightly. Unfortunately," he said under his breath, his smile fading.

"What are you boys talking about?" Victoria asked, sliding a chair next to me and plopping down. She opened an oversized candy bar and shoved a third of it into her mouth.

"Still addicted to sweets?" I grabbed at the candy but she drew back as if I were trying to take her newborn child.

"Yes," she mumbled through her mouthful of chocolate, clutching the candy bar to her chest.

"Sorry," I dragged out the word, laughing as I watched her chomp.

She finally swallowed and wiped her mouth with the back of her hand. "Taking a girl's candy is a federal offense, Peter." She batted her lashes at me. "I could have you arrested and fined, maybe even jailed."

I waved my hands in the air as if I were living in great fear of her ominous threat.

She pointed at me, eyes narrowed. "Watch it, brother." Reaching around me, she grabbed my cup. "Is this yours?" Before I could say yes, she sucked down the rest of my soda.

"Um, I think it's empty, Victoria."

She held up the cup and shook it in the air, as if it would magically refill itself. Bringing it to her mouth, she tried again, shrugging her shoulders in defeat when she found nothing left.

I couldn't help but laugh. I'd missed my baby sister. A lot.

"So." Victoria scooted in closer, leaning halfway into my lap.

"Has AJ told you he's trying to make Momma an honest woman?" She grinned.

"What?" I half shouted, rearing back. "Are you guys living together?" I stared at AJ, my voice a full octave higher. My mother living with a man was about as likely to happen as the moon dropping Skittles into Victoria's bed tonight.

"Mmm, hmmm," Victoria murmured, leaning back and shoving another third of her candy bar into her mouth.

"Is she serious, AJ?" I stared at the man who I'd wished could be my father for years.

He smirked, his face washing red.

That was the only proof I needed to confirm AJ Rhyne was indeed living in sin with my mother. I didn't know whether to be ecstatic or disappointed in him. "AJ," I exclaimed like a petulant child, "that's our mother."

"We're not living together." He tried to explain, but the twinkle in his eye revealed there was definitely more to the story than I wanted to know about.

"You may not be living together, but you're definitely doing something together." Victoria giggled.

"Tori," AJ admonished, "you don't have to tell everything you know."

"You know, that's funny, AJ," she smiled, "because my mother says the exact same thing, that you two aren't technically 'living in sin.'" Victoria used quotes, teasing him relentlessly. "You still haven't addressed the real issue."

"What's that?" he asked, his voice filled with apprehension.

"When are you going to make my momma an honest woman and ask her to marry you?"

My mouth fell open. What in the world was Victoria talking about?

"Tori," he said, sounding just as exasperated as I felt. "You and I both know I've already asked your momma multiple times."

"What?" I shouted. "What the hell is going on? You asked my mother to marry you?"

"Please, Peter." Victoria rolled her eyes and waved her hand in a dismissive gesture. "It's not like they're not having sex already."

I choked out a cough.

Victoria reached for my drink but set it down. "Sorry, sweetie, it's all gone."

I bent over, wheezing as I tried to catch my breath.

"Tori, stop," AJ chuckled, "you're going to kill the man." He pounded my back.

I sat up straight, staring at AJ. "So, let me get this straight. You've asked my mother to marry you, multiple times," I said, raising my brow, "but she said no?"

He nodded.

"So instead of waiting for her to say yes, you decided to live with her and ruin her reputation?"

"Yes and no." AJ shrugged.

I raised both brows and for some strange reason, felt like a protective father, interviewing his daughter's potential suitor.

I leaned back and crossed my arms over my chest. "What's the yes and what's the no?"

"Yes, I've asked her to marry me."

"And the no?"

"The no is," Victoria answered for him, "AJ is shagging our mom every night, one night at her house, one night at his. So technically they're not living together, just sleeping together, right, AJ? Although I'm assuming there's not much sleeping going on." Victoria giggled.

My head spun as visions I didn't want began flashing through my mind. The idea of my mother and AJ home alone, in bed, naked, was enough to make me vomit. I bent over, holding up a hand to stop my sister. "Just...no."

No kid wanted to think of their parents having a sexual tryst with anyone, let alone a man who was like a brother to their own father.

"Oh, Peter, come on." Victoria slapped my shoulder. "It's not like you're a virgin, either."

I sat up straight and stared at her.

Her mouth spread into a knowing grin that looked all too familiar. When had my nice, sweet, innocent Victoria turned into this… this…Dana Di Grazio?

Oh, no. "Shit!" I exclaimed. "Dana!" I reached in my pocket for my phone.

"Oooh, the prodigal son curses." Victoria poked me in the ribs.

I remained silent, patting down my body for my phone.

"What is it?" she asked. "What's wrong?"

"I was supposed to call someone as soon as I landed. She probably thinks I'm the most awful person in the world."

"So, call her," Victoria said as if it were the simplest thing on earth.

I shivered at the remembrance of how I'd left Dana. How could I explain that a simple phone call to Dana wouldn't be nearly enough to settle things between us?

"I can't find my phone," I said, panic-stricken.

"So, what's the deal?" she asked. "You're white as a ghost."

"I, uh." I didn't want to say more.

"You messed up?" Victoria asked.

I nodded.

"How?" AJ asked.

"I've met someone," I confessed.

Victoria nodded. "We already know."

"How?" I stared at my sister, then AJ.

"Peter," she said, "you're still in the news sometimes, especially since your accident. You told me you weren't coming home because someone was going to take care of you in Austin. I saw photos of the two of you on the internet. You guys looked pretty cozy."

"I'm sorry, Victoria," I said.

She shrugged, her once playful expression falling.

I'd screwed this up, royally. With everyone apparently. "I should have called and told you about her." I squeezed her arm. "I should have told you I was doing okay."

She stared down at her lap, her bright blue eyes averting mine. "I just figured no news was good news, you know?" She shrugged.

"Victoria," I pleaded, squeezing her tight.

She lifted her head, her gaze meeting mine, her eyes glassy with tears.

Crap! I was the worst sort of brother.

I swallowed back my own emotions and cleared my throat. "I truly am sorry, sweetheart." I wrapped my arm around her shoulders. "I've screwed this up with you, with Mom, with the whole damn family."

She slid an arm around my waist and smiled up at me. "It's okay." In typical Victoria fashion, she tried to console me. "I'm just glad you're here now, big brother."

I leaned in and kissed her head, squeezing her tight.

She returned the embrace then leaned back, smiling. All was forgiven. And with Victoria, it was just that easy.

"So, what's going on between you and this girl?" she asked, her brows waggling.

I gave a breathy laugh and shook my head.

"What's wrong?" she asked. "Have you screwed it up already?"

"Shouldn't we go check on Mom?" I asked, releasing Victoria and scooting my chair away from the table.

"Oh, no you don't." AJ laughed. "Tori threw me under the bus, now it's your turn."

"I'll tell you, but if it's all the same to you guys, I'd rather do it just once. Let's go up to Mom's room so I can figure out where my phone is, and then I'll explain everything."

"Good aversion tactic." AJ slapped me on the back.

"Maybe you can give me some advice. Obviously, whatever

you're doing seems to be working since my mother appears happier than I've ever seen her."

"And quite satisfied." Victoria threw back her head and laughed. The carefree sound echoed through the cafeteria, reminding me of another woman I loved.

Dana.

If I ever stood a chance at a future with her, I needed to contact her. The sooner the better.

CHAPTER 3

PETER

"So, let me see if I have this right, Peter Joseph Fontenot," my mother said in her most intimidating voice.

She'd pulled out my middle name. This couldn't be good.

"This woman—"

"Dana," Victoria added.

"Yes. Dana." My mother nodded. "Dana tells you her deepest, innermost secrets—that she's had cancer, that she almost died, that she loves you—and you left her without saying anything? Do I have that correct?"

"It wasn't like that, Mom." I tried to explain. I *tried*, but it was pointless. My mother was right.

Dana had confessed her biggest fears to me, and what had I done? I'd left her before making things right, without assuring her I was completely okay with her revelation that she couldn't have children. Without telling her that I loved her beyond measure no matter what she'd been through. What had I been thinking?

"But she did tell you she loves you?" my mother asked. "Before you left? Right?"

I nodded, fearing where my mother was taking this line of questioning.

"What did you say?"

"Well, I love her."

"You told her that, right?" My mother's brows lifted in question. "Before you left, I mean?"

I pressed my lips together and shook my head.

"You didn't tell her, Peter?" Her shrill voice cut through my soul.

I jerked my head up. "Look, Mom, I love Dana, no matter what. No, I didn't say the words before I left. But she knows."

My mother rolled her eyes.

"Just because I didn't say it doesn't mean I don't love her," I went on. "I do. I do love her. I was just overwhelmed about her revelation that she'd had cancer. My brain kind of went berserk, thinking about her not being here with me, thinking of the cancer coming back, of facing a life without her." Hot tears burned my eyes and I pushed my thumbs deep into the sockets, trying to keep them at bay.

"Oh, Peter," Victoria soothed, coming to sit on the arm of my chair, rubbing my back.

"Did you at least tell her you were concerned about her health and safety?" my mother asked.

"I think I did." I shook my head. "I actually don't know, Mom. She told me about the cancer, and then Victoria called and then...." And then I'd walked out on her.

"But you didn't say anything to her about it being all right that she couldn't have children, I mean, physically carry them?" My mother was not going to let this go.

"I don't think so," I said quietly, my tone as defeated as I felt.

It wasn't like Dana's inability to carry a child changed how I felt. But somewhere in my haste to get to my mother, I hadn't expressed that, not in a way that would put Dana's fears at ease and reassure her that I still wanted to be with her. Forever. No matter what.

"That's why I've got to find my phone," I said.

"We've torn up this entire room," AJ said.

I glanced around the area. Random items were strewn about the floor and windowsill. "It's not here. I may have left my phone on the plane, or anywhere really." I dragged a hand through my hair, trying to ease the pounding in my head. I had to talk to Dana, tell her that I loved her. "Call my phone again," I demanded to no one in particular.

"Just use my phone." Victoria held out her phone toward me.

I laughed at the absurdity of my situation.

"What?" she asked.

"I don't know her number. It's in my phone." I barked a humorless laugh. What the hell was I going to do?

"What do you mean you don't know her number?" my mother asked. It was obvious she was still extremely perturbed with me for not settling things with Dana before I left Austin.

"Look, Mom, I already feel like crap, and you going off on me isn't helping, okay. I just need to call her, talk to her and settle this."

"Are you sure she'll even talk to you?" she asked.

My gaze snapped to hers. I wasn't surprised to find one well-manicured brow arched in question.

Suddenly I was transported back to the third grade, remembering when I'd cut off half of Brenda Randall's pigtails. Back then, the displeasure in my mother's expression had been the worst form of punishment. Now her disappointment felt infinitely worse.

"I don't know," I admitted, "but I have to try. If I can just talk to her—" I swallowed back the emotions threatening to choke me. Just thinking of Dana refusing to accept my apology, of her never forgiving me, made me want to vomit.

My mother reached out and grasped my hand. "We'll find the phone, Peter."

"What about her work?" Victoria asked. "Wouldn't they know how to reach her?"

"Her dealership is closed now."

Victoria's expression fell, but suddenly lifted again. "I know!"

She held up one slender finger. "I'll look up your cell phone bill online." She pulled her own phone from her back pocket. "It will have a list of all the numbers you've called since your last billing cycle."

"How can you find my phone bill online?"

"Your line is still part of the business, remember?" she said, typing away on her phone.

Why hadn't I remembered that?

"Crap," Victoria grumbled.

"What?"

"There's no Wi-Fi connection here in the room. And the data range on my cell phone sucks. It's too weak to pull up anything on the internet."

"Great," I sighed.

"I'll call my friend Jesse real quick." Victoria lifted the hospital phone as she scrolled through her list of contacts.

"What can she do?" I asked, feeling somewhat relieved.

"*He*," Victoria corrected with a wink.

I felt sick to my stomach when I registered what the twinkle in her eyes really meant. First my mom, now my baby sister? "Please," I said, holding up a hand, "say no more."

"He works at a cell phone kiosk in the mall," she continued, despite my pleas. "He'll have access to your cell phone records in no time. Besides, he owes me a favor." She waggled her brows.

"For heaven's sake, Victoria," my mother fussed, "I'm hooked up to a heart monitor. Are you trying to give me a heart attack?"

The air was sucked from the room as everyone stopped and stared at the monitor next to my mother's bed.

"I'm kidding." She laughed, her face alight with amusement.

We all released a collective sigh of relief at her admission.

"But really, Victoria. No more talk of favors, hmm."

Victoria giggled but nodded.

"Isn't the mall closed now?" I asked. She shrugged one shoulder and smirked, giving me her silent answer. "Is that even legal?"

"Does it matter?" she asked, not waiting for my response before dialing her friend. When had my kid sister turned into such a cunning predator?

"Hey, Jesse," she spoke softly into the receiver, her voice laced with seduction. "I need your help. I need a copy of my brother's cell phone bill." There was a slight pause and I feared he might deny our request. "Yes, I have a brother." She smirked, cutting her eyes up at me. "Whatever, look my mom's in the hospital, I need it ASAP, okay?" There was another pause in her conversation and my stomach cramped in fear. "No, she's fine. Her boyfriend just rode her too hard in the sack and she had a heart attack." She laughed hysterically.

My mother's face flushed bright red.

My mouth fell open.

And AJ smirked in the corner.

I yanked the trashcan closer to me for fear of vomiting at Victoria's suggestion. Feeling the room begin to spin, I plopped down in the chair next to my mother's bed, burying my head in my hands and shaking it aggressively in an effort to rid myself of all the awful images flying through my mind.

"Peter, what's your number?" Victoria asked. Thankful to have something else to concentrate on instead of my mother and sister's love lives, I rattled off my phone number.

I listened intently while she repeated it to her *friend*, thankful that perhaps we'd found someone to help.

"Do you think she'll forgive me?" I asked, looking up to my mom for motherly, female advice.

She peered down at me with anticipation. "Do you love her?"

"With my whole heart, Mom. I've never felt like this with anyone. Ever," I added.

"She'll forgive you, Peter," Victoria answered.

I turned and stared at my sister. "How do you know?"

"I just do." She smiled with all the confidence I wished I had.

"What makes you so sure? I mean, she told me her deepest fears and I just…walked away. I didn't even tell her I loved her before I left. I'm an idiot. She'll never forgive me."

"I'm not saying there won't be groveling on your part," Victoria said.

"With lots of flowers," my mother teased.

"And candy," Victoria added.

"And a ton of 'I'm sorrys,'" AJ said.

I stared at him.

"A ton," he repeated as if he had firsthand knowledge.

"I'll do it, whatever she wants," I said, meaning every word.

"And that, my dear, is how I know she'll forgive you," my mother said with a small smile.

"How?"

"You're willing to do anything, including groveling, at the expense of your own dignity. Am I correct?"

I nodded. I truly would do anything for Dana's forgiveness.

"Are you sure you're all right with what she's revealed to you, Peter?" she asked.

"What do you mean?"

"Her not being able to carry your children?"

"Mom, there are so many other options for us. And if she doesn't want that then, I don't know, we'll figure something out. All I know for sure is, I have to hear her voice or I'm going to die." And I meant it. Dana was my lifeline and I felt dead inside.

"Wow!" AJ exclaimed.

"What?" I stared at him.

"Sounds like you've got it just as bad as I do." He smirked, looking over my head at my mother, giving her an all-knowing wink.

I waited for the nausea to overtake me but it never came. The truth was, I was actually happy for my mother and AJ. If there was anyone I'd ever want my mother to be with, it was AJ Rhyne. They both deserved to be happy, and I knew they would be, with one another.

"I'm sorry, Mom," I said, turning to face her.

She tilted her head and stared at me. "Why?"

"For leaving you. For putting the sole responsibility of the company on you. I can't help but feel somewhat responsible for this," I said, motioning toward the monitor now beeping with lines and blips.

"Peter, I'll never fault you for living your life the way you wanted to." She cupped my face. "I won't lie, having you here helping me probably would have been easier. But AJ was here." Her hand fell away as her gaze moved behind me.

I turned and saw AJ staring at my mother, a loving smile spread across his face.

"Truth be told," she continued, "taking over the company is probably what brought us closer. Maybe I should thank you."

I glanced back at my mother.

She was smiling, that same loving expression, her hand outstretched toward AJ.

He pushed off the wall and strode to her bedside. The guy was hopelessly in love. I recognized the signs because I wore them myself.

"Well, still," I said, staring between the two, "I should have at least called."

"Yeah, you should have," my mother said. "But the phone works both ways so I was just as guilty as you were."

I drew in a deep breath and closed my eyes, trying to exhale the guilt threatening to suffocate me.

"Peter," she said, hesitating.

I opened my eyes and watched as she released AJ and reached for me.

I slid my hand into hers, gazing down and admiring how similar we were.

"It doesn't really matter what happened in the past," she said, squeezing my hand.

I lifted my head and stared into her eyes.

"I'm just very glad you're here now."

My chest tightened with emotion, an overwhelming feeling of love I hadn't received from my family in a long time. I was sure the sentiment had been there all along, I'd just never realized it, or maybe I'd never allowed myself to feel the love.

"Hey," she said, shaking my hand, "it doesn't really matter now. Neither one of us will have to worry about it for much longer."

I cocked my head and stared at her. "Why?"

"We're going to sell the company."

My brows rose to my hairline. "What?"

"I know half of Salt Lake City will probably rumble with an earthquake from your father rolling over in his grave," she laughed, "but it's time I started living *my* life." She lifted her hand to stroke AJ's face and the light in her eyes brightened the entire room.

For my mom it was clear, AJ would be a part of her life. Just like mine would include Dana. I missed her more than I thought possible. My hands itched with a deep need to find her, to talk to her and make things right. She had to understand that whatever had happened to her in the past wouldn't change my love for her.

Victoria's words cut through my thoughts. "He's downloading your records." She smiled in triumph. "He's gonna call me back in just a minute. He said there are several numbers on your records from an Austin area code."

"Can't he just read it to you?" I asked impatiently.

Her eyes narrowed and I knew I'd crossed a line. I'd already asked her to sacrifice too much as it was. I shut my mouth and smiled.

She nodded in silent acknowledgment of my apology before turning her attention back to the phone call. "Thanks, Jesse." There was a pause and she rolled her eyes. "I know you do, but not tonight."

My stomach cramped and I suddenly felt nauseous. I didn't even want to think about what Victoria's comment alluded to.

"Yeah, okay." She stared at me and winked. "I'll call you later."

She hung up the phone with self-satisfaction and chuckled. "Yeah, like that's gonna happen."

"Well," AJ said, "it looks like you'll be reunited with your lovely lady soon. And if you sign the papers, you'll be able to provide for her, regardless of what happens with your motocross career."

"What do you mean?" I asked, staring at him blankly.

"Oh, I keep forgetting," he said. "You didn't stick around for the reading of your father's will."

"What did the will say?"

AJ remained silent.

I turned my attention to my mother. "What did the will say?"

"You own forty percent of the company," she said.

I shook my head and reared back, not understanding. "What do you mean, I own forty percent?"

"Your father left you forty percent of the company."

"Why didn't you ever tell me?" My words were sterner than I intended, but the revelation shocked me.

"We didn't know until after we buried your father. You left immediately after the funeral."

My mind raced. How could my father have left almost half of his company to me when he'd basically cut me off? I stared from my mother to AJ and back. "Did you know this was in his will the whole time?"

They both shook their heads.

"Not until the attorneys read the will," my mother said.

I grasped my head with one hand, my fingers pressing into my temples. "I don't understand," I said to no one in particular.

"I think deep down your father really thought you'd come back to run the company," she said. "He wanted to make sure you held controlling stock."

I raised my head and stared at her. "It's only forty percent."

"Forty to you," AJ said, "thirty to your mother, and thirty divided equally between your brothers and Victoria."

This couldn't be right. I had more of a stake in my father's company than my mother did? Than my siblings. "Why?"

My mother reached out and took my hand. "Because he trusted you."

I bit back a sarcastic laugh.

"It's really up to you, Peter," she said.

"What is?"

"Selling the company," she answered softly. "I want to, the boys and Victoria want to."

I turned to see Victoria smiling and nodding her head.

My mother squeezed my hand. "But we need your approval."

I stared down, marveling at our hands. My mother hadn't held me like this in a long time.

"We need you to oversee the sale and sign the papers," she said. "Ultimately the decision comes down to you. I think your father wanted it that way."

I jerked up, my gaze meeting hers. "How in the world could you think my father wanted me to have anything? Least of all controlling stock in his company?" My words were clipped, my breathing labored from the anger bubbling up inside me.

She smiled, the kind expression that she offered when trying to reassure us that everything would be all right, even when she knew it wouldn't.

"Your father always said you were the smartest child with more intelligence than a young boy should have." She chuckled, but I didn't see any humor. She released my hand.

I sank back into my seat, rubbing the back of my neck. This was surreal.

"He trusted your judgment over all of ours," my mother said. "He knew you'd make the best decision for this family, if anything happened to him. And he was right," she said with genuine admiration in her voice, her eyes alight with motherly affection.

"So, what's next?" I asked, staring around the room.

"Well, you have to sign off on the contract to negotiate an initiation for sale," AJ said. "Putting the company out on the market, so to speak."

"Then what?"

"Then we select the best offer," he said, as if the sale of a multi-million-dollar company were that easy.

"Best offer?" I laughed at the absurdity.

AJ remained silent.

"Wait, you mean you already have potential buyers?"

"Companies have been knocking on your father's door for years wanting to buy the business."

"Why haven't you contacted me before now?"

"Coming home was your choice, Peter," my mother said.

I turned at her words. "So, what? You faked a heart attack to get me here," I teased.

My mother's smile fell and instantly I knew my attempt at a joke at her expense was inappropriate and hurtful.

I grabbed her hand, holding it tight in both of mine. "I'm sorry, Mom. That wasn't funny, and I didn't mean it."

She brushed a stray hair back from my forehead. "I think everything happens for a reason, Peter. You being here is an indicator that it's time for all of us to move on, don't you think?"

"I'll sell anything you want if it means you can live your dreams." I scooted closer to her bed. "I'm sorry for the way I've treated you."

"You're here now." She smiled. "That's all that matters, sweetie."

I smiled, warmed by my mother's admission.

"And we're glad to have you back," AJ said.

I turned to face him. "What did you mean earlier when you said that I would be able to provide for Dana no matter what happens to my career?" I asked.

"You really have no idea how much the company is worth?" AJ asked.

I shook my head. I knew my father had built up a solid company during his years in business, but since I'd left for college, I'd never really kept up with his net worth.

AJ glanced at my mother then Victoria before returning his attention to me. "Let's just say with your forty percent, you won't have to worry about anything for the rest of your life."

I sat stock-still, dumbfounded by his words. No worries for the rest of my life? Was he serious? "Financially?" I asked.

"Nope. Definitely no worries financially."

He couldn't be serious. Was it possible that I could make my dreams come true—my *real* dreams—with Dana? That I could truly offer her the life and security she deserved?

"Oh, God," I said, suddenly feeling panicked. "My dreams include Dana." My gaze darted around the room. "What if she really doesn't forgive me? The rest of my life won't mean anything without her."

"She'll forgive you," my mother said.

"I still haven't heard from Jesse with your phone records yet," Victoria said. "Your phone has to be here somewhere. Have you looked in your bag?"

"My bag!" I yelled, jumping to my feet. "I completely forgot. I left it at the nurses' station. I'll be right back, Mom." I kissed her lightly on the cheek and headed for the door. Pulling it hard, the door swung open and I skidded to a stop, staring at the sight before me. Or rather, the person in front of me.

My wife.

My *ex*-wife.

"Looking for this?" an all too familiar voice asked as she held my cell phone in front of me. Jillian's green eyes held my gaze, her lips curling into a diabolical smirk I was well familiar with.

What had she done?

"What the fuck is she doing here?" Victoria said, pushing past me and making her way into the hallway.

Jillian remained quiet, staring between the two of us as if we were missing out on some important fact. Which we probably were.

I posed the question again. "What are you doing here, Jillian?" I worked to hold back the anxiety in my voice.

"What?" she asked, her smile widening. "You're not even going to offer your wife an 'I've missed you, sweetie?'"

My body burned as if I were being stung by a thousand scorpions. The air in the hallway turned to ice and I had a hard time drawing in a breath.

I thought I'd escaped Jillian years ago, along with all the hypocrisy that she represented. In my mind, my relationship to Jillian Vanguard had been a huge nightmare that I'd worked hard to forget. But now, here she was, standing before me, her mere presence threatening to cost me every good thing in my life.

Dana.

My legs felt weak and I clutched the door handle for balance. I'd never told Dana that I'd been married before.

No matter how much I loved her, no matter how much she cared for me, I knew enough about Dana Di Grazio to realize one thing. She would see this as betrayal of the worst kind. And my heart told me she would never forgive me for it.

CHAPTER 4

DANA

I sat on the sofa, legs tucked underneath me as I stared down at my phone, willing it to ring for the hundredth time. I'd made countless phone calls to Peter, left a dozen messages, and still, I hadn't heard anything from him.

"What the hell is wrong with me?" I yelled to no one in particular, jumping to my feet.

I was a strong, confident woman, yet in the span of a few weeks, Peter Fontenot had turned me into a simpering, whimpering fool.

I paced around my large living room, stopping in front of the mantel. Reaching up, I pulled down the framed picture and stared at the photograph. I'd snapped the picture just before he'd left.

The shot was a candid photo of me and Peter sitting on the sofa one evening.

His long, lean body was sprawled out, one hand tucked casually behind his head. I was nestled next to him, my arm wrapped around his waist, face pressed against his chest. He was staring at the camera, smiling. But my eyes were focused on him. I was staring at him as if he was my saving grace.

Peter had loved the image so much, he'd had the picture enlarged, saying I was the first person who saw him, truly saw, flaws and all, and still cared about him. I hadn't the courage to tell him that I felt the same way.

I snorted. Cared about him wasn't even the word. I loved Peter. I thought he'd loved me too. But his silence spoke louder than any words of love could.

I held the frame high above my head, preparing to smash it into the fireplace when my phone rang. I raced toward the couch, picture in hand, and scooped up my phone, not even bothering to check the caller ID before answering.

"Hello?" I asked, out of breath. "Peter?"

"No, honey, I'm sorry. It's Geneva."

I collapsed into the sofa with a heavy sigh, tossing the photo to the side.

"Still no word?" she asked.

"Nope."

"Oh, Dana, I'm so—"

"Don't say it," I said, holding up my finger as if she were here with me.

"Okay, I won't." There was a long pause. "But I am. And I'm here for you."

"I know." And I did. It was the biggest shock to all of us that Geneva had become such a trusted friend to me.

"Have you tried calling him again?"

I laughed. "I've called him so many times I've qualified for psycho ex-girlfriend at this point. I even called the airlines and the hospitals in Salt Lake City."

"And?"

"Nothing. I couldn't find out anything."

"I just don't understand."

"Yeah," I nodded, "neither do I."

"This is so unlike Peter. I mean, he loves you. Why would he do this?"

"He doesn't love me, Gen."

"Just because he hasn't said it doesn't mean he doesn't."

I wanted to argue with her but at this point I was too worn out.

"You'd just disclosed a huge bit of news to him, Dana. He was probably freaking out."

"Exactly. And wouldn't someone who loved you stay and talk about it?"

Geneva remained silent.

"That could only mean one thing," I continued. "Peter isn't okay with the fact that I'm not a real woman."

"Dana." Geneva drew out my name in a scolding tone.

"What? I'm not."

"Of course, you're a woman. There's more to being a woman than bearing children."

"Obviously, not to Peter."

"Stop! You're being irrational."

"Irrational?" I laughed, no humor in my tone. "I'm being irrational?"

"Yes."

"Look, Geneva, I need to face the facts. Peter hasn't returned any of my phone calls. I expressed everything to him, more than I've told almost anyone. I even declared my love for him and he gave me nothing." Tears burned my eyes and my throat began to constrict as I swallowed back my emotions. "Because I can give him nothing. I can't give him what he wants."

"And what's that?" she asked.

"A family," I whispered.

"Oh, Dana," she said. "That's it, I'm coming over."

I wiped away the tears now sliding down my face. What the fuck was wrong with me? I had no desire for Geneva to see me like this—battered, broken...vulnerable. This was exactly why I never let my guard down, why I never let anyone get close.

I shook my head. "No, don't."

"Dana," she pleaded.

I remained silent, trying to reel in my emotions.

"Well, at least come out with me tonight," she said.

Normally, a good night out drinking, dancing and fucking could get a man out of my mind. But I knew that would never work, not with Peter Fontenot floating through my thoughts.

"No thanks," I said.

"Are you sure I can't come over? We could have a girls' night, get a good movie, pop popcorn, swig vodka from the bottle."

I laughed, which was a shock to me at this point. "No, no vodka."

"Well, will you do something for me?"

"Probably not."

She snorted.

"What?" I asked.

"Call him. One more time."

"I can't." I had my pride for God's sake.

"One more," she pleaded. "And then I'll throw you the biggest pity-party you've ever seen."

I thought about it for a second. What did I have to lose at this point? My dignity was already shot. "Fine, one more time."

"Oh, bless," she said. I could picture her hands raised to the heavens in thanksgiving.

"But that's it."

"Totally."

"And I want a big pity-party, balloons and all." I laughed.

"You got it. But I don't think that's going to happen."

I sighed, wishing I had as much optimism as Geneva. If Peter didn't answer, if he didn't call me back, could I really let him go?

"Call me as soon as you're done," Geneva said. "Or actually, call me tomorrow because I'm sure you're going to reach him tonight and you'll have some great make-up phone sex."

I laughed. "Yeah, right."

"Love you," she said.

"Love you too." And I did, heaven help me but I did.

I clicked off the call and stared down at the blank screen. "One more time," I whispered, pulling up Peter's phone number and pressing the call button. "One more time."

I sat stock still, listening to the incessant ringing as I had a hundred times before. After the fourth chime, I prepared to deliver one final voicemail. Drawing in a breath, I mentally prepared what to say, how to break this off, how to let him know that I wouldn't call again. How to say goodbye.

"Hello?" a voice said.

Oh, shit. Someone actually answered. But it was a woman. I pulled the phone from my face and stared down at the screen. It was Peter's phone number.

"Hello?" she repeated.

"Oh, yes, sorry. May I speak to Peter?"

"Who's calling?"

Who's calling? I wanted to say it was none of her damned business but I realized this might be his sister, or his mother.

"This is Dana."

"Dana who?"

Okay, I couldn't get upset. Peter probably hadn't told his family about me.

"Dana Di Grazio."

"Oh, yes. Dana." She laughed, saying my name with an air of condescension that prickled my skin.

"Is Peter there?" I asked again.

"Oh, I'm sorry. He's in the shower right now."

Shower? This fucker had time to bathe but didn't have time to call me?

"Would you like me to tell him you called?"

Did I?

"Um, sure, yeah. I guess. Thanks."

"By the way," she continued, "his family and I would like to offer our deepest thanks for tending to Peter while he was injured."

I nodded as if she could see me.

"Peter will be staying here in Salt Lake for the duration of his recovery though. He won't be returning to Austin. It's best for him to be with family. We can give him," she paused, "better care than you, I should think."

What the fuck? Family or not, I'd had it with this pretentious bitch.

"And you are?" I asked, placing my hand on my hip.

"Oh, I'm sorry, I'm Jillian. Jillian Fontenot."

Jillian? I didn't remember Peter telling me he had any family members named Jillian.

"Are you his sister?"

She chuckled. Her laughter sounded wicked, almost evil. "Oh, heavens no, sweetheart."

I blew out a sigh of relief. "So, you're his mother? You've recovered from your heart attack?"

"God, no," she said as if I'd gravely offended her.

I wanted to reach through the phone and punch this bitch in the face.

"Then who exactly are you?" I waited, holding my breath, instinctively preparing for something bad.

"He hasn't told you?"

I shook my head. "Told me what?"

"I'm Peter's wife."

Wife? I sucked in a breath, my hands trembling. This couldn't be right. She was lying.

"Hello?" she said. "Dana? Are you still there?"

I pulled the phone away from my face and stared at the screen. His wife? His wife?

His fucking wife.

With one loud roar I reared back and threw the phone at the fireplace.

Peter Fontenot was married. And I was a fool for falling in love with him.

I fell onto my couch, dragging my hands through my hair. What the fuck was happening? And how would I ever survive this kind of betrayal? One thought came to mind.

I jumped to my feet and walked to the fireplace, reaching down for my phone. Thankfully, Peter had talked me into buying a shatterproof case so my phone was still intact. I pressed the button and the screen lit up. The phone was still working, and thankfully, the call had disconnected.

I pressed Geneva's number and walked back toward the couch.

"Hello?" she said.

"Still want to go out?"

"Oh, Dana. No. He didn't answer?"

"He didn't answer. But someone did."

"Who?"

I paused, staring down at the photo of Peter and me. How had I ever thought he could make me happy? "His wife," I finally said.

"His wife?" she shrieked.

"How long will it take for you to get here? I want to go out."

"Are you sure that's a good—"

"I want to go out," I repeated through gritted teeth.

"Okay, I'll be there in thirty minutes."

I hung up the phone and turned toward my bedroom before I saw the picture laying on the sofa. I reached down and grabbed the photo. I wanted to throw it into the fireplace like I had my phone, but something stopped me. Instead, I undid the frame and pulled the photo out.

Staring at the picture, I ran my thumb over Peter's beautiful face. "Wife," I whispered. He had a fucking wife.

I dropped the photo as if it were on fire and turned to make my way to my bedroom. Like I always said, there was only one way to get over a man. And that was to get under another one.

CHAPTER 5

DANA

THE POOL HALL was crowded for a weeknight. The air was thick with cigarette smoke, and the jukebox in the corner blasted some 1970's country ballad. Not exactly the night out I'd wanted.

Geneva had thought it best to stay away from the dance clubs downtown, and she was probably right. Instead, we'd met up with the guys from the dealership for their weekly pool night tournament.

I had yet to pick up a cue stick, instead opting for shots of whiskey. After several hours of drinking with the guys, I was well on my way to oblivion.

"So, tell me again why you're here with us tonight, Dana?" Dillon asked. He was the head of our service department and had been part of our company's family for almost ten years. He was hot as fuck too. The only problem was, he was married, hopelessly in love with his high school sweetheart, and committed to her and their three rug rats. And he was like a brother to me.

I glanced across the pool table at his equally hot, runway-worthy wife who was staring back at him adoringly. Her brows rose and fell and she shrugged one shoulder with a coy smile. Dillon's eyes roamed her body as if surveying her for dinner.

God, they made me sick as fuck.

"Your turn," someone called out, poking a stick in my back.

I turned to see who was assaulting me but thanks to the effects of the lethal amount of alcohol I'd already consumed, my eyes crossed. I shook my head to straighten my gaze but it only made me dizzier.

"Are you okay?" he asked.

I leaned forward and he caught my arm. "Chase? What are you doing here?" My words sounded slurred even to me. "This is usually an event for the garage gorillas, not stuffy admin dudes."

"Chase has been coming out with us for months," Dillon said from across the table. "He's in on our Ponzi scheme."

"Ponzi scheme?" I asked, looking from Chase to Dillon.

"Yeah," Dillon continued, "he's a fucking pool shark. He scams unsuspecting saps out of their money every week." Dillon chuckled as if that was a good thing.

"That's not true." Chase shook his head, his lips spreading wide to reveal white teeth. Unable to focus on his face, I was drawn to his mouth. His lips were full and plump and curled into an innocent grin.

"You have really nice lips, Chase," I mumbled, sticking my finger out to touch them. Instead, I stumbled over my feet.

He caught my arm and moved it away from his mouth, steadying me on my feet. "Uh, thanks." He smiled again, his delicious lips curling up in a sideways smirk that had my head spinning. Why was I so mesmerized by his lips?

Because you miss the shit out of someone else's lips.

"Yeah, well, fuck him!" I shouted, answering my own silent thoughts.

"Excuse me?" Chase stared at me.

Dillon laughed. "Turns out her sexy, motocross lover is married."

"Fuck you, Dillon," I spat out, along with half the contents in my mouth. I rubbed the back of my hand across my chin, trying to wipe away the spittle and whiskey covering my face. It was official. I was a drunken mess.

"Dillon, stop." His wife jabbed him with her pool stick.

"Is that true?" Chase asked, coming to stand directly across from me.

I closed my eyes and swayed, willing away my tears. My chin quivered and I cursed myself for being so emotional.

"It's okay, Dana," Chase said softly as he slid an arm around my shoulders and led me to a stool. "Hop on."

I put one foot on the wrung but missed and slipped, grasping the stool before I fell.

"Whoa," Chase said, grabbing my waist. "Let me help." He lifted me easily onto the stool.

I held on to the table, my gaze lifting to meet his. Something in my gut twisted when I saw his hazel green eyes searching mine. Without warning, the soft sting of tears rolled down my cheeks. "Why?" I whispered.

Chase gave me a sad smile and shrugged. "I don't know." He took a napkin and wiped my tear-stained cheeks. "It will be all right though. I promise."

How could he possibly know that?

Unable to hold myself up, I fell forward, resting my forehead on his shoulder.

I felt his warm hand rub my back, soothing me. It felt so good. All I could think of was Peter, how he always comforted me. I inhaled deeply, surprised by the unfamiliar scent. This wasn't Peter. He was gone. And I had no idea when, if ever, he'd be back.

Choking on Chase's cologne I pushed back and wrapped one arm around my stomach.

"Are you all right?"

I covered my mouth and shook my head, which only made me more nauseous. "I think I'm gonna be sick." I tried to stand but swayed again.

"Dana, are you okay?" I heard Geneva ask beside me.

Chase held me around the waist. "I'll take her outside." He walked me through the pool hall and through the front doors until we were standing in the parking lot.

The cool night air hit my face and I felt my nausea subside. Suddenly, memories of Peter and me sitting on the rooftop of my building, gazing up at the stars flashed in my memory. The painful reality that we'd never be together had me doubled over in pain.

My body lurched forward and I vomited everything inside me. Short sobs mixed with the convulsing wretches continued for what seemed like forever. Someone from behind pulled my hair back from my face with one hand while the other held me upright, keeping me from falling over into my own vomit.

When I finally stopped, someone led me to a bench nearby. Sitting slowly, I lifted my head and blinked several times, bringing his face into focus.

"Chase," I whispered. Had I really been hoping for Peter?

He sat down beside me. "Is he really married?"

I nodded once, my head falling to my chest in a gesture of defeat. The warm sting of tears pressed against my closed lids and I willed them away. The last thing I needed was to break down in front of my chief financial officer.

"I'm so sorry, Dana," he whispered, wrapping an arm around my shoulders and tugging me into his chest.

I sank into his embrace, surprised and a little thankful when he pressed a soft kiss to the top of my head. Wrapping my arms around his waist, I squeezed tight, surprised by the strength I felt. "You work out," I said.

"Sometimes." He chuckled.

I lifted my head and stared up at him, not surprised to find his eyes locked on mine. "What?" I asked.

"I think we should probably get you home, sweetie."

Sweetie? Had anyone ever called me sweetie before? Had Peter? No. He'd only called me Dolly.

Dolly.

I swallowed down tears and stifled a sob but to no avail. Tears came unbidden and spilled down my cheeks as I thought of the man I loved, the man who had left me. The man who was fucking married.

"Fuck that!" I shouted, jumping to my feet. I wobbled a bit and Chase caught my arm to steady me.

He stood and stared down at me. "What do you mean? You don't want to go home?"

I shook my head.

"Where do you want to go?"

His voice was low and raspy and my stomach roiled. I waited for another wave of nausea to come but thankfully it never did.

"Dana," Chase said.

I wrapped my arms around him, my cheek pressing against his chest and inhaled deeply. He smelled so good. Why hadn't I ever noticed that about Chase before? He wasn't Peter, but he was enough.

"Let's go home," I finally said on a breathy sigh.

"Okay."

"Your home," I added.

"Dana, are you sure?" Chase squeezed my shoulders and pushed me back. His brows were furrowed as his green eyes searched mine.

"Yes," I whispered, "I'm sure." But I wasn't.

I was drunk and sad and completely fucked up thanks to Peter Fontenot. He'd forgotten about me. The only thing I was absolutely sure of was that he wasn't coming back. And I didn't want to be alone tonight.

I scooted closer and pressed my body into Chase's. "Take me home."

Forgetting about Peter wouldn't be easy but tonight I sure as shit was going to try.

CHAPTER 6

DANA

"Hey, babe," someone whispered in my ear as they gently brushed away a piece of hair from my forehead. "Babe," he said again, his hand skimming down my neck and over my shoulder.

"Peter?" I asked, choking on my dry mouth.

He chuckled but it didn't sound like Peter's. "No, not Peter."

Oh, shit! Oh, shit! What had I done?

I bolted straight up but fell back again as the room spun around me. My pounding head beat like a tribal drum. Oh, God, what the fuck had I done? Or more to the point, *who* had I done?

"Dana, are you all right?" a man next to me asked.

I turned and blinked several times, trying to bring the man into focus. "Chase?" I asked, pushing up on one elbow.

"Yes," he laughed, "it's Chase." He held out his hand. "Here, take these."

I glanced at his palm and saw three orange pills. "Are those—"

"Ibuprofen." He smiled. "Why? Did you think I would try to kill my boss after such a great night together?"

Bile rose in my throat. What was I going to do if I fucked Chase last night?

I grabbed the pills and threw them into my mouth, washing

them down with the drink he thankfully held in front of me. "Thanks," I said, handing him back the bottle. "Oh, God," I groaned, "I hurt everywhere." Especially my heart.

Chase chuckled, placing the bottle on the bedside table.

I blinked and studied my surroundings, not recognizing anything. I sat straight up. "Oh, shit. Where am I?"

"You're at my place."

"Oh my God," I groaned, covering my eyes. "We didn't, um," I pointed from me to him and back again, "you know?"

When he didn't answer, I uncovered one eye.

"Do what?" he asked teasingly, sitting down next to me with a shit-eating grin.

Fuck. I recognized that look.

We had. I'd had sex with Chase and didn't even remember it. Tears burned my eyes and I yanked the covers over my head so he couldn't see how upset I was.

"Dana," he said, pulling the covers back down. "Look at me."

My eyes were squeezed shut and I shook my head. That was a big mistake as I felt the pills from earlier working their way up my throat.

"Dana," he said again, sounding like a cautionary parent. "Look at me."

I slowly pulled the covers down and stared at him. He was still wearing that fucking grin.

"If you are asking if we had sex last night, the answer is no."

"Seriously? We didn't?" I fell back with an audible sigh.

"Wow, would it be that bad to sleep with me?"

"No, I didn't mean it like that." I raised up.

"I'm joking, Dana."

I gripped the sheets, my eyes widening. "Joking about what? About us not having sex?"

"No, not that." He shook his head. "We didn't have sex."

"Oh, thank God," I said without thinking.

"Boy, you sure know how to make a guy feel special." He

laughed. I opened my mouth to explain but he held up a hand. "Just kidding, babe."

Words couldn't express how thankful I was that I hadn't let my jealousy lead me into another man's bed. I pushed the hair from my face, knowing I had to look like a hot mess. "What time is it?"

"It's a little after twelve."

"Twelve!" I shrieked, sitting up. "Aren't you supposed to be at work?"

"I called in sick. Told them I had to take care of the owner." He laughed.

"No, you didn't." I swatted his leg.

"Calm down, babe."

"Why do you keep calling me babe?" I asked, somewhat irritated by his term of unwanted endearment.

Shortly after Chase had begun working for our dealership it had been evident to most that Chase desired something more between us. I'd quickly nipped his advances in the bud and we'd reached an understanding. Our relationship was platonic and professional. Until now, it had been.

I silently scolded myself. Some professional I was last night.

Chase stood and stepped back, his once easy-going smile now gone. "I'm sorry. You didn't say anything about me calling you 'babe' last night so I just assumed. . ." He paused and suddenly I felt like the biggest bitch alive. He'd taken care of me last night, and now here I was, chastising him just for referring to me affectionately.

"No, I'm sorry." I reached out for his hand. "I guess it's just—" I swallowed the words that threatened to destroy me. How could I articulate what I felt when I didn't even know myself?

Chase squeezed my hand lightly and released it. "Peter's abandonment is still fresh," he said. "You're in defense mode. Only your closest friends are allowed inside your heart right now."

I nodded, surprised that he was able to put into words something I couldn't.

"I won't cross that line again, Dana. Here." He held out a glass filled with something that looked like it had come from the sewer.

"What's that?"

"It's tomato juice mixed with kombucha, cayenne pepper and Pedialyte."

I took the glass and stared at it as if it were a science project gone horribly wrong. "I'm afraid I'll puke it up if I drink it."

"I think you puked enough last night to last a lifetime." He snorted.

"Oh my God, Chase, did I puke on you?"

"No," he laughed.

"So, why did you bring me to your house?" I asked.

"You were sick as a dog and didn't have your keys. I actually have no idea where you live so I decided to bring you back here. I slept on the floor." He pointed to a makeshift pallet by his feet.

My face blazed with embarrassment.

"I didn't want you to get sick during the night and choke, so I stayed close to you."

"You slept on the floor? In your own house?" I asked, surprised by his chivalry.

"It's no big deal, Dana." He grinned and something in my chest tightened. "I'd do anything to keep you safe." His eyes searched mine and I knew he was completely serious.

I slipped my hand over his and squeezed. "Thank you, Chase."

He brushed away a piece of hair from my forehead. "Anytime." His fingers lingered on my face for the briefest of moments before pulling away. "Oh, here." He reached toward the side table and picked something up. "It's your phone." He held it out to me. "It's been blowing up all night."

"I thought I turned it off yesterday," I whispered to myself, trying to forget the memory of talking to Peter's wife.

"Yeah, you did, but when we got back home, you insisted on turning it back on. I knew you'd try to drunk-dial Peter, so I took it away from you and put it in the kitchen." He held it closer to me. "Interesting case."

I took the phone, my heart aching as I remembered Peter trying to fit that damn cover onto my phone, but failing miserably.

Yeah, well, fuck him! Who was careless and haphazard now? At least I wasn't fucking married.

No, but you can't have kids, a little fact you decided to keep secret from him.

I wanted to tell myself to fuck off, but I was right. Maybe Peter's absence was my penance.

I stared down at the screen—thirty-four missed calls and enough texts and voicemails to have locked up my inbox.

"It appears your *married* boyfriend wants to talk to you," Chase said with equal parts sarcasm, playfulness and disgust, none of which sat well with me.

"Did you answer my phone?" I asked. Part of me wished he had, just to make Peter's heart shatter into a million pieces like mine had.

"No." He grinned, his eyes alight with amusement. "I mean, I wanted to."

"Why?"

"He obviously hurt you, Dana. Completely devastated you from what I could make out of your drunken words last night. My natural instinct was to protect you."

"Why?"

"Because you're my friend."

"What did I say last night? About Peter, I mean?"

"You just said you couldn't believe he'd screwed you over, that he was married."

"That's it?"

"Your words were a little more colorful last night."

I laughed, imagining the language I'd used to describe Peter's betrayal. "I appreciate you taking care of me last night, Chase, I really do. And I'm especially grateful that you didn't take advantage of me."

He recoiled as if I'd slapped him. "Dana, I would never take advantage of you."

He moved to stand but I caught his arm and brought him back down. "I'm sorry," I said.

He stared down at the comforter.

"Chase, would you look at me?"

Finally, he lifted his head, his vivid green eyes staring back at me.

"I'm sorry," I said. "Truly. I know you would never hurt me."

He nodded and smiled. "I wouldn't." He paused then patted my leg. "I'll just give you some privacy so you can return your calls. Several are from a doctor's office." He nodded to the phone in my hand.

Doctor?

He stood and walked toward the door. "Oh, and I washed your clothes. They're hanging in the closet in the corner."

"You washed my clothes?" I said. Then what the hell was I wearing now? I lifted the covers and peered down at my body. I blew out a sigh of relief when I saw I was wearing a white T-shirt and baggy cotton shorts.

"Don't worry," he said, smiling, "I didn't see anything."

"Oh, thank God."

He laughed. "You changed yourself last night. I didn't think it would be a good idea for you to go to bed in clothes covered in vomit, so I put out a shirt and shorts when we got home."

"Thank you," I said quietly, completely embarrassed by my drunkenness.

"I did help you brush your teeth and go to the bathroom once, but I promise I didn't see any of the good parts." He smiled.

I laughed. "I don't deserve you, Chase."

He stared at me for a long moment before speaking. "You do deserve me, Dana." His expression was serious now. "You deserve a good guy. Someone who won't lie to you. You deserve so much more than Peter."

Before I could defend Peter, the door gently closed and I was left with Chase's words. He thought I deserved a man like him, someone chivalrous and caring. And not a liar. I realized I did deserve a man like Chase, not one who manipulated me and lied to me like Peter had for weeks.

Trying to put the thoughts behind me, I stared down at my phone and saw my gynecologist's office had called several times. I pushed back my fears, reminding myself of what Dr. Stedmond always said to me—*We don't worry until there's something to worry about.*

I'd completely forgotten about my appointment a few days earlier. I hadn't felt right for several weeks, moody with headaches that wouldn't go away. Her nurse had told me to stop by for blood work. That had been almost a week ago. I figured no news was good news. But now, lying here in Chase's bed trying to chug down this hangover concoction from hell, I wasn't so sure, about anything.

I dialed the number and waited, biting my thumbnail. I swore to myself for worrying and removed my thumb from my mouth, replacing it with Chase's hangover concoction. Taking one sip, I nearly gagged.

"Dr. Stedmond's office," the receptionist answered.

"Hey, Frances, it's Dana Di Grazio—"

"Oh, Dana, thank goodness," she cut me off, the relief in her voice palpable. "The doctor's been trying to reach you all morning."

Wait, the doctor was trying to reach me? This wasn't good. In the past it had always been her nurse or physician's assistant who called with results. I knew from past experience that when doctors called you directly, the news was never good.

"Let me get Dr. Stedmond on the line. Can ya hold on, dear?" Her deep Texas drawl normally made me laugh but today it just made my stomach burn. I seriously thought Chase's concoction was going to find its way out of my stomach and onto his pallet on the floor.

"Sure," I said, my head pounding in anticipation. I listened to the God-awful music play while I waited, trying to rid my mind of every worst-case scenario I could think of. I chugged another gulp of Chase's concoction, which seemed to help me forget.

"Hey, Dana." Dr. Stedmond's familiar voice rang through the line.

"Hey, Doc, what's up?" Normally my sarcastic greeting had us both snorting, but her silence scared the living shit out of me.

"I'm glad you called. I've been trying to reach you."

"I know, I'm sorry," I said. "My phone was turned off. Is everything all right, with my blood work I mean?"

"I know you originally came in because you thought your hormone levels were off, but I went ahead and ordered a complete blood count and other tests for markers of recurring cancer just to be safe."

Recurring cancer?

Oh, shit! I mean, it wasn't like I didn't know recurring cancer was a possibility, but the thought that my symptoms had anything to do with a recurrence had never entered my mind. Especially given the fact that I'd just gone in for my yearly checkup only a few months before. My chest burned and I slumped down in the bed, the ache in my gut curling me into a tight ball.

Recurring cancer, I repeated to myself.

"Don't freak out, Dana," she interrupted. "It's just precautionary, I do it with all my patients, you know that. I don't want anything to slip by me."

I drew in several deep breaths to calm my racing heart. Over the nine years since I'd been treated by Dr. Stedmond after my initial cancer diagnosis and surgery, she had always been thorough—to the point of obsession—with everything. Today, though, I wasn't so sure I was happy about it. I was certain my silence was enough of an indicator that her warning came too late.

"I also ordered a urinalysis too, as a precaution," she added.

My head spun and I thought I might be sick again.

Even after uterine cancer was treated, the disease could reoccur in several organs. I'd always assumed I was in the clear, especially since my tumor had been contained and removed, and had never spread anywhere else after the first five years.

Now that I was eight years past my final treatment, I naively thought I was cancer free. How could I have been so stupid?

Recurring cancer.

My hands shook uncontrollably, and I fought for every breath. Shaking out my arms, I willed myself to calm down. "Why are you worried?" I asked. "What do you think is going on?"

"Probably nothing, but I don't want to take that chance. Not with you."

Not with you.

I understood what she meant. My diagnosis of uterine cancer at such a young age was rare. Because of that, Dr. Stedmond monitored me more closely than most survivors. I tried to let the thought soothe me—knowing I was under her watchful care—but today, as I nursed a mammoth hangover, I found no peace in her thoroughness.

"I can hear the 'but' in your voice," I said.

There was a slight pause and I sat up straighter, my gut clenching.

"The tests I ran indicated a high level of white blood cells in your urine."

I felt light-headed as the room started to spin. Bladder cancer was a secondary diagnosis for uterine cancer. This wasn't good.

"As you know," she said, "it could mean any number of things."

Yeah, like fucking bladder cancer, I wanted to scream.

"Don't go there, Dana. I'm not saying it's cancer, but I have to monitor you closely, you know that. This is just precautionary. If these results had come back with anyone else it wouldn't alarm me."

"So, you're alarmed?"

"I'm cautious."

"What could the high white blood cell count mean?" I bit my lip and willed away my tears.

"It probably just means that you have some type of infection. Have you felt feverish or sick lately?" she asked.

Only if alcohol poisoning counted, I laughed to myself.

I shook my head. "No. So what does that mean?"

"Let's take this one step at a time. You know how I operate. We'll rule out things as we go, and we won't think anything about what this could be until we've ruled out everything else."

I knew what she was doing, and part of me was grateful. Dr. Stedmond was a strong proponent in the power of positive thinking. That was one of the many reasons I trusted her.

She'd told me time and time again—the people who focused on the negative, focused on the cancer cells destroying their body, always seemed to fare poorly. She wasn't going to let me worry until there was actually something to worry about. But it was too late. My mind was already there, knee deep in full-on freak out mode.

"I'm going to start you on a round of antibiotics for ten days," she said. "Then I want you to come back for another set of labs, blood work and urinalysis. In the meantime, I don't want you to think about this. Is there something you can do this weekend? Something to get your mind off of this? I know how your brain operates."

Our girls' trip to California came to mind, but I wasn't sure I could go now. Hindley would see right through me. She'd know I was worried about something, and then when I wouldn't tell her, she'd worry too. According to Dr. Stedmond though, I needed to do something besides sit around and freak the fuck out.

"Actually," I said, "I made plans to visit my friend in California for a few days."

"That sounds perfect, Dana. Just remember, there's absolutely no drinking while you're on these antibiotics."

Even though I was nursing the hangover-from-hell right now, it didn't mean I wanted to forego all alcohol this weekend with Hindley and Geneva. Especially with the way my mind was racing right now with thoughts of cancer.

"Are you serious?" I asked. "Ten days?"

"Yes, I'm serious, Dana. Absolutely no drinking. We need to rule out everything one step at a time. If you drink, then the antibiotic won't work, which means we won't be able to tell if these white blood cells are coming from some type of bacterial or viral infection or something else."

It was the 'something else' that brought stinging tears to my eyes. I bit my thumb to silence the sobs bubbling just under the surface.

"Dana, this is probably nothing."

"But it could be something," I stuttered through my tears. "It could be cancer, couldn't it?"

"Is someone there with you?" she asked.

Even though I knew Chase was waiting just outside the door, I had no desire to share this news with him. I didn't want anyone to see me in such a state. Once again, I was all alone.

"Let me call someone for you, Dana, someone who can support you right now."

"No," I choked out on a sob. "Please don't." Tears streamed down my cheeks and dripped onto my lap.

"Dana, you can't do this alone again. You know that."

"There's nothing to worry about right now, isn't that what you said?" I threw her own words back at her.

"Yes. You're absolutely right."

I sat up straight, trying to even out my breathing. Grasping the collar of Chase's T-shirt, I bent and wiped my eyes and nose.

"I've already called in the prescription to your pharmacy. Pick it up and start on the meds right away. Once you're finished, I'll have Debbie call you and set up an appointment for lab work."

I sat stock-still, staring at the wall in front of me, dazed by news that my cancer may be back. What the fuck was I going to do now?

"Dana?" she said.

"Yes," I whispered.

"Please, don't do this alone. Not again."

Dr. Stedmond knew me so well. When I'd first been diagnosed with cancer, my parents had just died and my boyfriend had left me thinking I was pregnant. At the time, I felt like I shouldn't burden anyone else with my problems, so I pushed them all away. Even Hindley.

But Dr. Stedmond had gradually convinced me I needed to be supported by family and friends if I were going to get better. Especially as I went through my chemotherapy and radiation therapy.

"I'll be fine, Doctor," I said flatly. "Thanks for calling." I hit the end button and let the phone slip out of my hand.

Deep inside I knew this was no infection. Peter was gone and my cancer was back, history repeating itself. What a cruel joke. There was no way I was going to burden anyone else with this, not again, not until I absolutely had to.

I fell back onto the bed and curled into a tight ball, whimpering like an injured animal as the darkness overtook me.

"Dana," Chase called, knocking on the door. "Are you all right?"

I couldn't answer, too overcome with grief.

I felt a cool breeze on my back as Chase lifted the comforter and slid in behind me. His strong arms wrapped around my waist as my body shook uncontrollably. I turned in his arms, my face pressed against his chest. He tightened his hold and cradled me as I broke down and bawled.

Everything inside me said to push him away, but as he brought me in flush to his hard chest, I realized I was defeated, unable to fight anything or anyone. I needed the comfort Chase was freely offering.

My tears came unchecked as I thought about the cancer, and the one man I really wanted here with me. Peter was gone though, married to some bitch, and would never be back in my life. Of that I was certain.

I pulled my head back and stared into Chase's green eyes. "Guess this isn't very professional, huh?"

He smiled a lopsided grin that did strange things to my insides. "Being professional is overrated. Boss."

I laughed and shook my head. "Thanks."

"Want to talk about it?"

Recurring cancer.

Tears began to fall again, and I burrowed in deeper, shaking my head.

"Okay," he said, pressing a kiss to the top of my head. "But I'm always here if you need me."

And wasn't that just the kicker. Chase would always be here, of that I had no doubt. But the one man I really wanted was nowhere to be found.

I wrapped my arms around Chase's lean torso and snuggled in close. I needed someone, and today, Chase would do.

CHAPTER 7

DANA

"GOD, THIS PLACE IS AMAZING, HINDLEY!" Geneva shouted over the blaring music. We sat in a posh velvet-covered booth inside an upscale nightclub in California that Hindley had brought us to after dinner.

Geneva and I had arrived at Hindley and Rory's home yesterday. I'd left Chase's house shortly after my mental breakdown with the doctor. Geneva and I had boarded a plane bound for California shortly thereafter. Thankfully, Chase hadn't asked for details of what had upset me. I figured he must have assumed it was Peter, which was partially true, so I didn't offer him anymore information. No one needed to know about the cancer scare.

The club we were sitting in was stop number four on a long list of outings planned by Hindley. She'd referred to our night as "Girls Gone Wild Tour." No matter how many places she took us, it still couldn't erase the one word festering in my mind like the toxin it was.

Cancer.

The word was like a living, breathing presence. I knew no matter how much I had to drink this weekend, the thought of my possible recurring cancer would never be far from my thoughts.

The club was packed, and judging from the glacial stares we were getting from the trampy women in sky-high heels, it was evident that our seats were coveted. Normally, I would have told the bitches to fuck off but tonight I just didn't have the fight in me.

Hindley leaned in close and cupped her mouth. "One of the marketing directors for Rory's sponsor has a brother who owns the place," she explained. She glanced over my shoulder and smiled so wide I thought Rory might have shown up. But that was impossible. He'd left earlier this morning for a charity event in Seattle. "Matt!" Hindley yelled, waving her hand.

I glanced over my shoulder, following her gaze.

A gorgeous man with dark hair and a lean torso turned to face us, returning Hindley's smile with one just as broad.

Holy hell. If Hindley was trying to distract me, this man was doing it.

His hair was brushed back from his chiseled face, showcasing his strong jaw and plump, firm lips. His suit fit him like a glove and was obviously tailor-made, and looked expensive as shit. He wore a lavender shirt, unbuttoned just enough to showcase a muscular chest with a smattering of hair that would make any sane woman want to drop her panties.

The man knew how to dress, and he probably smelled just as rich and masculine as he looked. He looked like a fucking Calvin Klein model. Oddly enough though, he held no appeal to me, and I knew why.

Damn you, Peter Fontenot!

Geneva bumped my arm, nodding toward the man walking toward us.

"What?" I shouted.

"Check him out."

I stared at the man. Again. Still nothing. The only thing I felt was light-headed, and dizzy, and not from the hottie sauntering toward us.

Thanks to the antibiotics, I hadn't been drinking, and yet I still felt like shit. I mean, yeah, the guy was hot, *really* hot, but my heart still belonged to one man. A man who'd crushed it and left me for dead. I wanted to hate Peter, I really did, but I just didn't have it in me. Not tonight.

"Hindley." The Calvin Klein model grinned, making his way over to our booth and sliding in next to her.

Oh, damn, even his voice was sexy.

Hindley tossed her arms around the man's neck, dragging him in to an embrace that seemed much more familiar than I thought was necessary.

"She's drunk," I muttered to Geneva. Drunk Hindley was flirty, and flirty Hindley could get into trouble. I was grateful her husband wasn't here to witness her behavior. I realized I needed to keep an eye on her for the rest of the night.

"Guys!" she shouted, twisting around to face us, taking Mr. CK model's hand in hers. "This is Matt Davis. He represents Sonora Water, one of Rory's sponsors," she added. "You remember Matt, right, Dana?" She asked as if there was a reason I should.

I sat silent, studying the guy. Then it hit me. Matt, the douche bag from Sonora Water. The guy had practically thrown himself on Hindley after a drunken afternoon of lethal margaritas at a local restaurant in Austin. Thankfully, Rory had put him in his place. I bit my cheek to stifle a laugh.

Hindley had mentioned Matt a few times but I'd never officially met him. Now I wish I had. Maybe it would have spared me the heartache I was in now.

"Matt, this is my sister, Geneva." Hindley pointed toward Geneva.

Sometimes it still floored me when Hindley referred to Geneva as her actual sister rather than her stepsister. There was a time, not too long ago, when neither girl would have claimed the other as family, let alone sisters.

"Hello, Geneva," Matt spoke softly but loud enough for us to hear his raspy tone.

Geneva's eyes went wide and she blushed. Actually blushed. What the fuck?

He grasped her hand, stroking it gently before lifting it to his lips for a light kiss.

Geneva whimpered.

Oh, Lord. What the hell was wrong with this girl? She never showed all her cards this early in the night. I rolled my eyes, unable to hide my disappointment. She was as good as gone for the rest of the night.

"And this is Dana," Hindley said, smiling and pointing to me. "My best friend. You remember her, right?"

"Ah, yes, Dana," he said, releasing Geneva's hand, reaching for mine. "I've heard so much about you, I feel like I already know you." The way he said the statement made me uneasy and I pulled my hand away before he could lip it to death like he had Geneva's.

Hindley glared at me, as if I'd insulted her.

"What?" I asked, shrugging my shoulders.

She shook her head and spun back toward Matt. "You'll have to forgive her, Matt. She's nursing a broken heart tonight."

"What the fuck, Hindley?" I shouted. Why was she sharing my business with a known douche bag? My broken heart wasn't the only thing consuming me. The threat of recurring cancer was in the forefront of everything I did, but I couldn't share that bit of information with them. Hindley and Geneva would completely flip their shit.

"It's all right," Matt assured her. "I just recently broke up with a long-time girlfriend. I'm pretty crushed about it."

Geneva grasped his hand in hers. "Oh, Matt, I'm so sorry."

Was she gushing? Good God, the woman was actually gushing. Yeah, she was toast too. It was a good thing I was sober tonight.

"Thanks." He smiled at Geneva. "My brother Mase thought coming out tonight would help."

I shrugged. If his heart was as broken as mine nothing would help—except a gallon of tequila.

"Speak of the devil," Matt said, cutting his eyes toward the dance floor. The three of us followed his gaze and I thought I was gonna pass out. From the movement, and the sight before us.

The dude walking toward our table made Matt look like chopped liver. This guy was tall, really tall, with shaggy black hair you just wanted to yank on during sex. He strutted with all the confidence of a true player—someone who didn't even have to try—and I was instantly turned off. Any other time I might have taken the bait. Tonight, I felt like shit and my head was killing me—and so was my heart.

"Hey, Matt," the man said, his voice higher than I expected for a guy so well-built.

"Ladies," Matt said, holding his arm out, "this is my brother, Mason Davis."

His eyes locked on mine. "But you can call me Mase." A cocky smirk spread across his face.

I wasn't in the mood for fucking a virtual stranger. I gave him my best "fuck off asshole" face but apparently it wasn't working.

One corner of his mouth curled up and he winked.

Oh, fuck me. I opened my mouth to say something but his gaze left mine as he surveyed everyone at the table.

I didn't want to be attracted to him, but any breathing, sane, red-blooded girl would be. The dude was hot as shit. Still, I didn't feel that pull in my belly, the one that had drawn me to Peter. One look from Peter would have me giddy as a schoolgirl, and my stomach twisted with butterflies.

But he wasn't here, and Mason Davis was.

"Cool eyes," he said.

I blinked several times, not realizing he was talking to me. I grabbed my water and took a sip, feigning disinterest.

Mason slipped in beside me in the booth, forcing me to move to make room. His elbow bumped my arm and my water sloshed out of the glass.

"Dammit!" I yelled.

"Oh, gosh, I'm so sorry." He pulled several napkins from his suit jacket and dabbed at my hand before wiping the table. He leaned in close.

I drew in a breath and caught the scent of his cologne. I silently cursed myself for being slightly aroused. When I turned, our faces were inches apart. The light from the candle on the table cast his face in a warm glow. He smiled and I noticed tiny crinkles appear at the edges of his honey-brown eyes.

Okay, so maybe one good shag wasn't out of the question, right?

"Can I get you something else to drink, Dana?" His voice was smooth like velvet.

I drew back and stared at him. Was he trying to put the moves on me? I mean, he was good-looking, definitely hot, but I was here with friends. We were grown women for God's sake.

I glared at Hindley across the table but noticed her attention was elsewhere. She and Matt were hunkered low, giving each other a conspiratorial smile. Then it dawned on me. This was a fucking set-up.

For years, I'd told Hindley the best way to get over a guy was to get under a new one. The only thing I wanted to get under now was a huge blanket so I could burrow myself in deep and forget I'd ever met Peter Fontenot.

I turned my cool gaze back on Mason. "No thanks, I'm good."

He recoiled as if I'd surprised him. Seeing how hot he was, I was sure he wasn't used to being turned down for anything.

"I'm going to the bathroom." I pushed on his hip and thankfully he scooted out of the booth and let me leave. As I walked away, a hand caught my wrist. I turned and found Mason smiling.

He tugged me close and I fell against him. "Dance with me," he whispered in my ear.

I closed my eyes, my thoughts going to Peter and the hundreds of times he'd done the exact same thing—pulled me in close and whispered against my skin. I missed him so much. Tears burned my eyes and I pulled away from Mason, trying to make my escape before I became a blubbering mess in the middle of this nightclub.

"One dance," Mason said, still holding me.

I glanced down at where his hand was wrapped around my wrist. Peter wasn't coming back. He was married, I reminded myself. Would it be so bad to let another man care for me tonight?

My gaze roamed over his body, tall and muscular. The man was gorgeous no doubt. I could do worse, a lot worse.

"Okay," I finally said.

He smiled and for a brief moment I forgot about Peter, about recurring cancer, about anything that troubled me. "Let's go then," he said, pulling my hand.

I let him lead me toward the dance floor, a small smile tugging at my mouth. Maybe I could get over Peter by getting under Mason.

"This is a great song!" Mason yelled above the obnoxious rap song.

I hated the song. "Yeah, sure," I said, nodding. Suddenly the room started spinning and my head throbbed with every beat of the song.

"Do you live in California?" Mason asked, yelling above the beating rhythm of the God-awful music.

"You should know."

"How should I know that?" He stared at me, brows raised. God, he was so bad at this game.

"Yeah. Like Matt and Hindley didn't put you up to this shit," I groaned.

"Put me up to what?"

"What did Hindley tell you about me before you came up to our table?" I yelled above the noise and chaos. My head felt like someone had it in an iron vise.

"Who?"

"Come on, Mason, you're not an idiot and neither am I."

He shrugged and had the good sense to look sheepish at least.

"Well?" I asked.

"They told me about your breakup."

I wobbled on my feet and Mason reached out an arm to catch me. He was solid and muscular underneath that gorgeous suit.

"Dana, are you all right?"

I clutched his shoulders, trying to steady myself. "I don't know," I said more to myself as I closed my eyes. I couldn't picture myself with Mason anymore than I could have Chase.

Fucking Peter Fontenot, I wanted to scream.

I opened my eyes and steadied myself, staring up into his gorgeous face "Thanks for the dance, Mason, but I really do need to go to the bathroom."

"I'll come with you," he said.

"No," I patted his chest, "I'll be fine." I took a step back and bumped into a solid wall of muscle. A familiar tingle started at the base of my skull and traveled down my spine. Only one person had ever made me feel this way, but he was gone and I was alone.

I closed my eyes, willing the image away. I felt myself wobble and reached out a hand.

"What are you doing, Dolly?" a deep voice growled in my ear as strong arms wrapped around my waist.

I drew in a deep, steadying breath and was overwhelmed by his familiar scent. This couldn't be Peter though. He'd left me. He was married. Besides, we were at an obscure club in Laguna Beach. He could never find me. The only place I saw his face now was in my dreams. Maybe that was it. Maybe I'd passed out on the dance floor and was dreaming.

Soft lips brushed along my neck and my body melted into his. He was so strong and solid, just like I remembered. I had to be dreaming, hallucinating even, but it felt so real. There was only one way to know for sure.

I turned in his arms, lifting my lids slowly. My eyes found mismatched ones staring back at me. His face awash with the colorful lights overhead. My heart seized in pain as if someone were reaching through my chest and crushing it.

His mouth slowly lifted into a beautiful smile. All I wanted to do in that moment was kiss him. But something niggled in the back of my mind.

He's married!

He's married!

Shit, how could I have forgotten? He wasn't mine. He'd lied to me. He'd left me when I told him I couldn't have children. I gathered all my strength and shoved at his chest. "Let me go!" I yelled above the music.

"Stop, Dana! You're not running away from me again," he said.

"It worked for you!" I screamed as tears rolled down my cheeks. "For fuck's sake, you're married, Peter!"

He stared at me as if I had three heads.

"Yeah," I said, "I know you're married."

His eyes went wide and his mouth slack.

"Fuck off." I turned, about to make a grand exit when suddenly the room began to spin.

"I'm not married, Dolly." It sounded like that was what he said but I couldn't be sure. Everything sounded like I was under water and my legs felt like jelly. What the hell was going on with me?

"She told me she was your wife, Peter," I said as I walked away.

He moved quickly to stand in front of me, his arms gripping my shoulders to stop me. "She lied, Dana."

I shook my head, not understanding. Sweat was beading on my forehead and my hands grew clammy and cold. "But," I paused, trying to make sense of it all. "But I saw pictures. On the internet. Pictures of you and her, wedding photos." I swallowed down the sobs, trying to wiggle my way free from his hold.

"I *was* married, Dana," Peter confessed, "but I'm not anymore."

I shoved at him, to no avail. My strength was failing me. "You lied to me!" I yelled, but my voice was barely above a whisper, broken and defeated. "You lied," I repeated.

"I didn't lie. I just didn't tell you."

"It's the same thing. How did you even find me?"

"Geneva."

Fucking Geneva. I wasn't surprised she'd betrayed me. That bitch! I was going to kill her, but first I had to get out of this man's death grip. Peter tightened his hold, refusing to release me. Unable to struggle any longer, I surrendered to his strength, my head falling against his chest.

"God, Dana, you're burning up." He sounded panicked, his voice laced with fear.

"I don't feel right. I think I'm going to be sick." My legs buckled and my body collapsed.

"No!" he yelled, sweeping me off my feet before I hit the floor. "Hold on, Dolly. I've got you." He rushed us off the dance floor and I closed my eyes, burrowing myself into his arms.

"Hindley!" Peter's voice echoed in my ear, the vibration pulsing against my cheek. My body began to shake uncontrollably and I had to fight back the urge to vomit. "Hindley!" Peter shouted again.

I opened my eyes to find him staring down at me, his eyes wide, his face shadowed with an expression of fear that I didn't understand.

"What's happening to me?" I mumbled, mostly to myself.

Only one word came to mind.

Cancer.

"I've got you, baby," Peter whispered in my ear, tucking me closer into his chest.

I snuggled into him, closing my eyes, dreaming of a time when it was just me and Peter, lying in the bathtub, surrounded by warm water, and each other.

"Dana," Peter said, jostling me.

I tried to answer but no words came out.

"Dana!" he shouted. "Oh, God, I love you so much, Dolly. Just tell me what's wrong, tell me what to do. Talk to me!"

Wait, did he just say he loved me?

Yeah, this was definitely a dream. A beautiful hallucination that I never wanted to wake up from.

"Oh, God, Hindley," Peter cried out. "What's wrong with her? She won't answer me!"

I snuggled in tighter to his chest, feeling so cold, aching in every part of my body, deep down to my bones. Was this the end for me? It had to be.

At least I was safe, in the arms of the man I loved, and I'd been able to see his beautiful face one last time. He'd given me the hope I'd clung to for several days, declaring he *wasn't* married. And he had professed his love for me. At least I think that was what he said. My brain was so fuzzy I couldn't concentrate on anything except Peter's face.

"Oh my God!" Hindley yelled, grabbing my arm. "Dana!" She shook me hard but I couldn't open my eyes. "Dana!" she shouted again.

Her voice drifted away like an afternoon cloud. Then I realized it wasn't Hindley, it was me who was drifting away, high above my friends, above the club and up into the dark night sky. Beyond the reach of anyone or anything. For the first time in years, I felt at peace.

CHAPTER 8

PETER

I SAT NEXT to Dana on the queen-sized bed in Hindley's guest room and pulled the covers up higher over her feverish body.

God, please let her be all right.

Against my better judgment, I'd let Hindley talk me out of taking Dana straight to the hospital. She'd been burning up with a fever, but Hindley insisted we'd only end up waiting hours in the emergency room if she didn't have any other symptoms. Instead, we brought Dana to Hindley's home where we could monitor her temperature and administer medicine.

I watched anxiously as Hindley rubbed Dana's forehead with a thermometer. I questioned the awkward contraption but Hindley said she used it on her own daughter and assured me it was accurate.

Geneva sat across from me in the bedroom, her hands clasped around each other so tight, her knuckles were white. The thermometer beeped and she jumped.

Hindley stepped back and glanced at the readout.

I leaned forward. "Well?" I asked.

"One-oh-three point four," she whispered.

"That's it!" I yelled, jumping to my feet. I threw back the covers and scooped Dana's small body into my arms. "We're going to the hospital. Now."

"Don't go, Peter," Hindley pleaded. "I only gave her the ibuprofen twenty minutes ago. Let's give the medicine another twenty and then if it doesn't come down, we'll call her doctor."

"You can call a doctor," I said, gripping Dana tighter, "but I'm taking her to a hospital."

"Peter, trust me." She placed a hand on my arm to stop me. "We've been to the hospital emergency room several times with Abbi. All you'll do is wait. It could take hours for them to see her."

"Not with a fever like this."

Hindley stared at Dana, biting her lip.

"Look at her," I said. "She's limp and lifeless, whiter than this blanket."

She lifted her gaze from Dana and stared at me, her eyes red-rimmed and filled with as much apprehension as my own. "I'm worried too, Peter, but I'm also a mom. All the doctor is going to say is give her medicine and wait to see if the fever comes down."

I stared down at Dana. Her usually tanned face was flushed with fever but I noticed that she was curling into me. "Ten minutes," I said, my eyes never leaving Dana's frail form.

"Ten minutes," Hindley repeated.

I collapsed back onto the bed, holding Dana close. I reached out a finger and traced her brows. "Please wake up," I whispered, kissing her forehead. She remained still in my arms but I noticed she felt cooler. "God, I've screwed this up bad, haven't I, Dolly?"

"Yeah, you have," Geneva said.

I lifted my head and stared at her. She still sat in the corner, glaring at me.

"What were you thinking, Peter?" she asked, pushing herself out of the chair. "I mean honestly? Married?"

I closed my eyes and took in a deep breath, falling back onto the headboard. I wanted to argue with Geneva, wanted to plead my case, but she was right. I hadn't been honest with Dana.

"She tells you she can't have children, and what do you do?" she asks, stomping toward me. "You up and leave her with no words of acknowledgment or understanding, no acts of comfort or support. You even promised to call her, but never did?"

I flinched at the reminder. All of this was true.

"Did you know that she called you all frigging day and night, Peter? You never answered. Then, when someone finally does pick up your phone, it's some stupid bitch claiming to be your wife. And what does she tell Dana? She thanked her for looking out for you but said you're never coming back to Austin."

I opened my mouth to explain but Geneva came at me, finger pointed like a pistol. She wasn't done, not by a long shot.

"Oh, yeah, and what else does that bitch wife of yours say?"

I knew better than to ask what.

"She tells Dana you're in the shower. Then the bitch actually laughed at Dana, as if she were so gullible. And I guess she really was to believe you."

"Geneva," I said, "it wasn't—"

"How the hell did you think that was going to make her feel, Peter?" I opened my mouth to answer but she cut me off. "Like shit! That's how it made her feel, Peter. Like shit! She was devastated."

I drew in a deep breath, and closed my eyes, willing away the tears. I never wanted to hurt Dana. Ever. And yet, somehow I'd managed to destroy her if what Geneva was saying was true.

"You're lucky as shit that Dana loves you so damned much," Geneva continued. "Otherwise, she might have fallen into her usual MO and found some random guy to screw."

My body stiffened and I sucked in a breath, holding it for several heartbeats. The thought of Dana being intimate with another man—someone else touching her silky skin, stroking her curly black hair—made me physically ill.

Geneva moved closer, eyes narrowed. "And you're lucky as shit that your sister found me and told me the truth. Although honestly, I still have no idea how she did."

I pulled Dana tight against me as if she might blow away.

"Why did you leave without at least talking to her, Peter?" she asked.

Why hadn't I stayed? It was a question I didn't have the answer to. Instead, I shrugged and buried my face in Dana's hair as hot tears burned my eyes. I'd done this to her—broken her spirit—and if anything happened to her...I would never forgive myself, and neither would her friends.

A warm hand gripped my shoulder. Pulling back from Dana, I glanced up and saw Hindley standing beside me, her face forlorn but offering an understanding smile.

"She'll be all right, Peter," she assured me.

"What if she's not?" I stared down at the woman I loved, lying listless in my arms. "She has to wake up, Hindley," I whispered. "I have to tell her." My voice cracked.

"Tell her what?" she asked, her hand still on my shoulder.

"That I love her. That I want to be with her. That I want to have a family with her, no matter how we go about it. Adoption, surrogate, whatever she wants, I want it too."

Hindley pulled her hand away and stepped back. "Peter, you're still married."

"No, I'm not, Hindley," I said. "She was lying. Jillian was lying, I swear. She's known for it."

"What do you mean? Who's Jillian?"

"His wife," Geneva said before I could.

"*Ex*-wife," I said with emphasis on the ex. "Jillian is my ex-wife. She was trying to scare me into helping her and her father. Their family's company is in trouble, financially, and he may actually end up going to prison."

Hindley stared at me, eyes narrowed as if trying to decide whether or not to believe me. "You're serious?"

"Yes. I was married. Once. But not anymore. The marriage was annulled. According to the state of Utah, it never happened."

"Why didn't you tell Dana?" Geneva asked.

"Honestly, it doesn't even feel like I was ever married. It was just a horrible mistake on my part, and most days I try to forget it ever happened. It didn't feel like a marriage to me, because it wasn't."

"What do you mean? What was wrong?" Hindley asked.

Where did I begin? I knew this was a story best kept for Dana.

"The most important thing is, I didn't leave Dana because she couldn't have children. Or because she's had cancer. Although that did scare me." I pressed a kiss to her temple. "It still does."

"We don't think about that," Hindley said.

I stared at her in confusion.

"So why didn't you at least talk to her? Or call her once you got to Salt Lake City?"

"When my sister called, I was in shock about my mom's supposed heart attack. All I could think of was getting back to her. Victoria was crying and begging me to come home. I hadn't seen them in awhile so I was freaked out about what I'd find when I returned."

"How is your mom?" Hindley asked.

"She's better now, thanks. When I got to my mom's hospital room, I couldn't find my phone, and Dana's number was stored in my contacts. I never memorized it. I couldn't call her."

Hindley and Geneva stood still, faces expressionless. They weren't buying it. And to be honest, I wasn't believing it all myself.

"God, I'm such an idiot. I swear I tried to get her phone number, I really did. My entire family was trying to help."

"And?" Geneva asked, crossing her arms over her chest.

"And...my ex-wife showed up before I could call Dana."

"So how the hell did your ex-wife get ahold of your phone?" Geneva asked, one brow lifted with skepticism.

"Jillian said she found my phone at the nurses' station, inside my bag, when she came to visit my mom."

"Yeah, right," Geneva scoffed. "How the hell did she know it was your bag? And how the hell did she even know your mom was in the hospital?" I opened my mouth to answer in defense, but she continued, cutting me off. "Someone had to have told her, Peter. Your story is lame as shit and totally unbelievable, you know that, right?"

I nodded. It did sound lame as shit, but I had no excuses to offer her. "I don't know, Geneva," I said. "Jillian probably recognized my bag at the hospital. I've had it since I was in middle school. I'm guessing that's where she found my phone and maybe answered Dana's call. She's a very conniving and vindictive person. I certainly wouldn't put anything past her."

"What does that mean?" Hindley asked, studying me.

"It means I need to protect Dana now more than ever."

Geneva stepped forward. "You think Jillian will hurt her?" Her once angered expression was now replaced with fear.

"I don't think so. Jillian has never physically hurt anyone, that I know of." Images of her betrayal flashed through my mind. "She can be vindictive though. Especially if she wants something bad enough."

"So, you're not married?" Geneva asked.

"No," I said with more anger in my voice than I meant. I was frustrated, having already explained everything. "Look, my attorney has the paperwork to prove our annulment. As far as the state of Utah is concerned, I was *never* legally married."

"Annulled?" Geneva asked.

"Yes, annulled. We aren't divorced. She's not my ex-wife. Well, legally anyway. To me, she's nothing."

"Wow." Geneva shook her head.

"And you're all right with the fact that Dana can't have children?" Hindley asked.

"I'm not going to lie, that was a shock. But honestly, I was more concerned about the cancer than the children. That's the reason I froze."

"And now?"

"Is she really okay, I mean with the cancer?"

"She's been cancer free for eight years, Peter," Hindley said matter-of-factly. "The doctor said her chance for recurrence dropped dramatically at the five-year mark."

"It could come back though?" I asked, my voice shaking.

"It could."

What was I saying, of course, it could come back. At any time. Maybe that was why she was sick now. Was Dana's fever and lethargy due to recurring cancer? My pulse beat wildly in my chest and my stomach clenched. I pressed a hand to my mouth to keep from screaming out—or puking. I couldn't lose her now that I'd come home.

Home. That was what Dana was to me. Home.

"You're damn lucky your sister called me," Geneva said. "How did she even get my number anyway?"

"Sometimes I find it best not to ask Victoria how she acquires information."

Geneva laughed.

Hindley stared between the two of us. "Your sister called Geneva?"

"Yeah," Geneva finally answered.

Hindley stared at Geneva in confusion. "Why didn't you tell me?"

Geneva shrugged. "I wasn't purposely trying to keep it from you."

Dana had told me a little of Hindley and Geneva's history. They'd hated one another for years and I assumed that sometimes even now they had doubts about one another's loyalty. Just like I did about my family.

"Does it really matter?" Geneva asked. "Peter's her true love."

Hindley smiled as if understanding an inside joke.

Geneva sat down opposite of me. "I tell you, that sister of yours is one smart cookie. She must really love you to get in the middle of all this." She reached out and brushed a lock of Dana's hair off her forehead.

I nodded and closed my eyes. I would never be able to pay Victoria back for her help. "What made you decide to answer my call and tell me where you guys were?"

Geneva picked up one of Dana's small hands and stroked her fingers gently before raising her head to answer. "We all deserve a second chance."

I thought of my family and what we'd been through together. Were any of us ready for a second chance?

Geneva released Dana's hand and patted it gently. "Please don't screw this up, Peter." She paused and didn't meet my gaze. "You really did a number on her. I've never seen Dana like this before." Finally, she glanced up and I saw the same anguished look on her face that I'd seen in Dana's when I left.

"I'm so sorry," I said. "I never meant for any of this to happen." I closed my eyes and burrowed in even closer to Dana. Fear gripped me hard as I felt her heated face. The fever wasn't coming down despite our best efforts.

"What's this?" Geneva asked.

I opened my eyes and saw her standing by the nightstand, holding an orange plastic bottle in her hand.

"It's a prescription," Hindley said, walking around the bed to join Geneva. "Is it Dana's?"

Geneva studied the bottle. "Yeah, it's got her name on it."

"What's it for, what's the drug?"

"It says amoxicillin."

"That's an antibiotic," Hindley said.

"Maybe she just has an infection."

"If she has an infection and she's burning up with a fever, this isn't good," Hindley said. Her forehead creased as if she were trying to solve a difficult equation.

"What does that mean?" I asked, sitting up straighter.

"Let me see the bottle, Gen," Hindley said. Geneva passed the container to her and I waited, holding my breath as Hindley studied the label.

Her silence was deafening.

"What's wrong?" I asked. "What are you not telling me?"

Without answering me, Hindley pulled her phone from her pocket and pulled up her contact list.

"Who are you calling?" I asked, sounding just as desperate as I felt.

"I'm calling her oncologist." Her words were as flat and lifeless as Dana's body.

Oncology? Oh my God. "Cancer," I whispered. I drew Dana tighter into my chest as if she would float if left untethered. Dark thoughts raced through my mind and I willed them away.

Hindley paced nervously, biting her thumbnail.

"Hindley, what's going on?" I asked.

She held up a hand to silence me.

"Hindley, please," I begged.

"Just hold on, Peter," she snapped. "Um, yes," she spoke into the phone, "I'm trying to reach Dr. Gail Stedmond, please."

There was a pause and I wanted to rip the phone from her hand.

"Yes, the nurse would be fine." She turned her back on me, continuing to stalk around the room.

I slowly lowered Dana to the bed and stood, making my way to Hindley. I would make her talk to me one way or another.

"Hi, I'm Hindley Gregor. I'm calling for Dana Di Grazio. D-I capital G-R-A-Z-I-O." She shook her head. "No, I'm a friend, but I'm on her medical release form. Oh, yes, I'm sorry, it was Hindley Hagen, I'm married now."

I swallowed hard, praying Hindley would find the answers we needed.

"Yes, Dr. Stedmond will know who I am."

There was another interminable pause and I feared I might actually pass out from the wait.

"Well, she's running a very high fever. It was over one hundred and three just a few moments ago." She paused and nodded. "Yes, we've given her ibuprofen."

My hands trembled and I shoved them in my pockets so Hindley and Geneva wouldn't see. The thought of Dana having cancer again was unfathomable to me, my worst nightmare come true. I couldn't exist without her. I wouldn't.

Hindley's words from earlier echoed in my mind.

Dana had been cancer free for eight years. After five, her chances for recurrence went down dramatically.

That was what she'd said, and that was what I was going to concentrate on.

"All right, thank you," Hindley said. "I'll call you back if I don't hear from her in ten minutes." She nodded. "Yes, thank you."

Her tone was calm and cool, unlike the fear coursing through me. I reminded myself that Hindley was a mom, she'd dealt with illness more.

She turned and stared at Geneva. The anxiety in her eyes was undeniable. "Did you know anything about this?" Her voice was sterner than I'd ever heard.

"No," Geneva shook her head, "I swear. She said she thought her hormone levels were off and she was going to get them checked out. But that's all I knew."

"She didn't say anything about a doctor's appointment or new meds?"

"No." Geneva shook her head. "Not to me."

Hindley's eyes narrowed as she stared down at Dana's limp body. "That's *just* like this little shit," she growled through gritted teeth.

"What is?" I asked, completely confused by her set-down.

Hindley raked a hand through her long hair, grabbing it to the nape of her neck. "Dana thinks she has to go through everything by herself. Like she's protecting all of us by not telling us as soon as she knows something's wrong with her—physically or emotionally." Hindley closed her eyes and drew in a deep breath.

I watched, wordlessly as Hindley grappled with some type of emotion I didn't understand. Wasn't she Dana's best friend?

"Dammit, Dana!" she shouted, her hands fisted. "Get up, Peter!" Hindley ordered.

Without a thought, I jumped to my feet.

She grasped the bedspread and yanked it off Dana with such force, she nearly fell over. This was Hindley pissed, *really* pissed, and I felt sorry for Rory or anyone else who crossed her.

"Hindley, what are you doing?" I asked, grabbing the blanket back. Dana's body shivered, and her arms quickly dimpled with goose bumps.

My stomach clenched when I saw tears well in Hindley's eyes. Whatever was going on with Dana, it was obvious she was worried, almost petrified. The thought had my heart racing with fear.

"She needs to stay uncovered, Peter, to bring down her fever."

"But she's freezing."

She glanced up at me. "Trust me. I know what I'm doing. The blanket is only making her temperature increase."

Unable to help myself, I laid back down, wrapping my body around Dana's to ease her shivering.

"Don't!" Hindley shouted.

I sat straight up, fearing I may have hurt Dana. "What?"

"Don't cover her. She doesn't need anything keeping the heat in."

"You must be out of your mind if you think I'm going to lie here and just watch her suffer without doing *something*."

Hindley's eyes darted from Dana's small form to me, then back again. Her face was sheet white, her eyes red-rimmed. She was terrified, and now, so was I.

"Let's take her temperature again," I offered, thinking that maybe giving Hindley something to do would get her mind off the fear of Dana's prognosis. Maybe that one small act could help all of us forget the very real fact that Dana might have cancer again.

Hindley nodded in agreement.

Geneva reached for the thermometer and carefully handed it to Hindley.

"How long has it been?" I asked. Time was standing still for me —I had no concept of beginning or end, start or finish. The thought of my life without Dana was unbearable.

"Almost ten minutes," Geneva answered.

"That hasn't been enough time for the medicine to work yet," Hindley said.

"I don't care," I said. "Take it anyway." Hindley needed to do something or she was going to break.

I held my breath, waiting for Hindley. If Dana's fever hadn't broken yet, I was going to throw her in the car and take her to the nearest emergency room and demand a doctor examine her immediately. And I couldn't care less what Hindley had to say about it.

Her eyes found mine and I nodded, trying to reassure her, not all together convinced I could.

She gently rubbed the ball of the thermometer across Dana's forehead.

Dana stirred from the touch but didn't make a sound.

We all leaned closer, holding our breaths, the seconds seemingly turning into hours as we stared helplessly at the thermometer's readout.

Hindley sighed with relief. "One-oh-two point two. It's coming down. Thank God." A small smile broke through her misery. "But we have to leave her uncovered, Peter. I'm sorry. I know it sucks, I've had to do it with Abbi before and it breaks your heart. But trust me, it helps." Her eyes met mine and I couldn't help but nod. Hindley had wisdom beyond me.

I released Dana and rolled onto my back, my hands scrubbing my face as if I could wash this nightmare away. *This cannot be happening, this cannot be happening*, I repeated to myself. *Dana is fine, she's healthy, she's just got a nasty bug, maybe even the flu.*

The piercing ring of the phone interrupted my thoughts and I bolted straight up. Before it could ring a second time, Hindley grabbed the receiver.

"Hello?" she answered.

I drew in a deep breath as if it were my last. If Dana was sick, really sick, I knew it just might be.

"Hi, Dr. Stedmond," Hindley spoke softly into the phone. "Yes, I'm calling about Dana Di Grazio." She paused. "I'm sorry, I thought I explained it to the nurse earlier. It's Gregor now, I'm married. Yes, Hindley Hagen Gregor." There was another pause and I feared perhaps the doctor wouldn't divulge any of Dana's information. "Oh, thank you. Well, we were out tonight and she basically passed out, burning up with fever. She'd been complaining of a bad headache and feeling achy most of the day."

She had? That was news to me. Why hadn't Hindley explained any of that before now? *Focus, don't get angry. Focus.*

"Yes, I gave her ibuprofen." She bit her lip and waited. Geneva and I leaned closer. "It was one-oh-three point four when we got home but it's come down to one-oh-two point two now."

There was another longer pause and I could literally hear my heart beating in my ears.

"Okay, yes." She nodded.

I tried to find Hindley's gaze, to gain her reassurance, but she kept her eyes down, staring at the floor. For some reason, that worried me most of all.

"Well, we found a prescription for amoxicillin next to her bed tonight," she continued. Another awkward pause. "No, she's visiting me in California right now. I didn't know she'd been to see you." God, another gut-wrenching pause. "I'm on the medical release, yes." Hindley's back straightened like she'd been hit with a steel rod as she drew sharp breath. "How long ago?" Another wretched pause lingered on. "What could that mean?" Her voice broke and she walked from the room, her words trailing off.

Crap! I was torn—follow Hindley and find out what was really going on or stay here with Dana.

I stared down at Dana. Her long dark lashes fanned over her flushed cheeks and her curly black hair stuck to her damp forehead. I gently brushed it back from her face so I could revel in her beauty. I would *never* leave her again. There was no question about that.

Despite Hindley's instructions, I curled up next to Dana, my face mere inches from hers. I wanted to be the first thing she saw when she woke. I didn't care if Dana hit me, spat on me, or cursed me, I wasn't going to leave until I made her understand why I hadn't talked to her before I left for Utah. Why I hadn't called her once I was there.

Seeing Dana lying there, so still and lifeless, knowing I'd never reassured her of my affections before I left, I panicked, realizing it might end up costing me the love of my life. Dana very well may reject me now, and I couldn't say I blamed her. I slammed my eyes shut, trying to will away the tears threatening.

"Okay, I will." Hindley's voice came closer as she reentered the room. "Thank you, you too." She clicked the phone off and that was when I noticed her cheeks were stained with tears.

I bolted upright. "What is it?"

She stared at me for a long moment.

"Please don't lie to me. I'm here for the long haul. I'm not leaving Dana," I said, shaking my head. "Ever."

She stood still, staring at me, as if trying to decide if my words were true.

"Please," I begged, my own voice hoarse with emotion. "Just tell me."

Hindley walked closer to the bed, rubbing Dana's bare arm. Worry lined her face, her grief-ridden expression causing my heart to ache. I didn't think it was possible for anyone to love Dana as much as I did, but in that moment, I realized just how close the two of them really were. Hindley had cared for her best friend for years. Whatever the doctor told her had affected Hindley deeply, and instinctively I knew it would me as well.

"Let's go outside," she whispered, finally lifting her gaze to mine.

I swallowed back tears.

Cancer.

It was the only word my mind could think of.

"I don't want to leave her," I choked out, staring down at Dana's pale face. "Ever," I added.

"We need to talk, Peter, but we can't do it here."

I glanced up and saw her nod toward Dana.

"I'll stay," Geneva said. "I'll come get you if she wakes up."

I stared between the two of them. Really, what choice did I have?

Leaning down, I gently kissed Dana on the forehead. She wasn't as hot as she'd been at the club but she was still too warm for my liking. "Sleep, Dolly," I murmured against her skin. "I'll be back in a bit."

Her body shifted and she moaned.

I tricked myself into believing she'd heard me. Hopefully, it would give me the strength I needed to hear what Hindley had to say.

Hindley led us out of the room and I followed, glancing over my shoulder one last time.

"She'll be all right," Geneva said, trying to reassure me.

Hindley led us into a larger room down the hall. "Sit," she said, pointing to the sofa.

I obeyed, not knowing how I'd made it this far.

"How much of Dana's cancer situation do you know about?" she asked flatly.

My heart hammered and I fought the urge to vomit. Dana had only shared a little of her story with me before I'd abruptly left her.

Hindley nodded. "That's what I thought." My answer had obviously been written on my face. "Look, Peter, I'm not going to lie to you or sugarcoat this."

"Okay."

She stopped before me, hands on her hips. "I need to ask you one question, and you need to tell me the truth, not what you think I want to hear. And not what you think Dana would want you to say."

"All right," I said, intimidated by this powerhouse of a woman lurking over me. She would obviously protect Dana at all costs. Even if I was the obstacle.

"What are your intentions with Dana?" she asked.

"What do you mean, intentions?"

"You know exactly what I mean, Peter. Don't screw around with me."

"I love her, Hindley."

"Enough to go through this with her?"

"Go through what?"

She raised a brow.

Cancer.

I knew the answer, I just didn't want to say it out loud.

"She can't have kids, Peter. She's had cancer. It could come back. It may already be back." Her voice cracked. Hindley may be strong, but she was only human.

"I don't care about any of that, Hindley. I love her and I want to be with her for as long as I possibly can."

"Then why did you leave her without reassuring her? Without telling her you loved her first? Why did you leave when she opened up to you and told you everything about herself? You didn't even respond to anything she said before your ass took off."

I'd messed up, irrevocably perhaps. Gaining Dana's forgiveness would mean securing her best friend's understanding first.

"I messed up," I said quietly, staring down at my twisted hands. There was no other way to describe my actions, and no excuse I could offer Dana's best friend would pacify her.

"She's never opened up to anyone before. *Anyone,* Peter!" she practically shouted

Suddenly it dawned on me. Hindley thought I'd left Dana because she couldn't have children, because she'd had cancer. Before I could explain, Hindley continued.

"God, Peter, she's been heartbroken. Destroyed. You destroyed her." She shoved an accusatory finger at me. "I've never seen her like this before." Tears welled in her eyes.

I winced, gritting my teeth for fear I might vomit. I had no idea my departure would have caused Dana such agony. I opened my mouth to speak but Hindley once again cut me off, holding her hand up to silence me.

"Seeing her like this, so devastated, it killed me, Peter." She pounded her chest.

I stared at her, watching in agony as tears rolled down her face.

"You can't do this to her," she stuttered through her pain. "If you don't love her, if you're really married to someone else, then you need to leave. If you can't handle the fact that Dana will never be able to carry your children, that she may have cancer coursing through her body at this very minute, then you need to go. Now!" she shouted, pointing at the stairway.

I moved to stand but she continued.

"Cancer is serious, and dealing with it is gut-wrenching. If you're not willing to love her in spite of it all, then you need to leave. I will *not* let you break her again. You need to get the fuck out of my house and out of Dana's life. For good."

I jumped to my feet, completely shocked by her outburst. "Hindley, I'm not going anywhere!" I yelled, matching her indignation. "You must be out of your ever-loving mind if you think I'm going to leave Dana again." Tears threatened but I held them back.

She studied me, her gaze locking on mine.

I held up my hands in surrender. "I swear," I whispered. The tears I'd tried to hide broke free and rolled down my face. I fell onto the sofa, burying my face in my hands, unwilling to let her see me totally break down.

"I'm sorry," I said, gripping my hair and tugging. After several beats of silence, I lifted my head.

Hindley stood where she'd been earlier but some of her fury had dissipated, thank goodness.

"I didn't leave because she can't have children," I said. "I didn't leave because she had cancer. You have to believe me."

She stood still, staring at me without a word.

"Dana had just told me about the cancer, about everything, right before my sister called to tell me my mom had had a heart attack. I was in shock. I was scared to death thinking about losing Dana."

Hindley took a step closer, her hands unclenched. She sat beside me, a hand on my leg.

"Then I lost my phone and I couldn't call Dana because I only had her number in my cell phone. I swear, Hindley, my family tore up half the hospital looking for it. And then my bitch of an ex-wife showed up, trying to make me believe we were still married, acting like she had some kind of a claim on my family's company. I swear, I had no idea she'd talked to Dana, Hindley. I swear it."

"What are you talking about, claim on your family's company?" she asked. "What is your ex-wife trying to do?"

"It's a long story. But I promise you that I had no idea Jillian had spoken to Dana until Geneva told my sister. I know I screwed up. Bad. I should have told Dana I'd been married before but I panicked. I know I completely screwed up by not telling Dana how I really felt before I left. I was just in shock, from everything."

"Why didn't you call Dana once you got your phone back?"

I jerked my head back in surprise. Was she serious?

"What are you talking about?" I asked, annoyed by her accusation. "I called her probably over a thousand times since then."

Her brows furrowed. "You did?"

"Hell, yes I did. I blew up her mailbox, completely filled it to the point I couldn't leave anymore messages. She never returned any of my calls. She never once picked up the phone."

Hindley fell back onto the sofa, her hands on top of her head.

I realized that was part of our story that Dana had conveniently left out. No wonder Hindley and Geneva were so pissed at me. Part of me was pissed at Dana, but not enough to worry any less about her.

"Please tell me what the doctor said," I begged. "I'm not going anywhere. It doesn't matter to me. I'm not married. I was, but my annulment is real."

She turned her head and stared at me. "Are you in trouble, Peter?"

"I still have some things to work through, with my family and our company," I said, "but trust me. I'll do it all with Dana by my side. I'm not leaving her again."

Hindley tilted her head and frowned.

I wanted to reassure her but part of me was scared to death. What if Dana's cancer had come back? There was no way I'd ever be able to protect her, or to exist without her.

"I swear, Hindley, I'll be here, for the duration, no matter what Dana's future holds."

Hindley's face transformed with a small smile as she nodded.

I released a heavy sigh, as if I'd been pardoned. And really, I had.

"The doctor's not completely sure what's wrong with Dana," Hindley said. She drew in a deep breath, holding it for what seemed a lifetime.

I remained quiet, trying to show that I would take whatever she was willing to give me.

Slowly, she started again. "When Dana was first diagnosed with cancer, her surgery and treatments were excruciating, physically and mentally," she said. "There's something about being told you'll never be able to bear children that fucks with a girl's mind, ya know?" She turned her head and stared at me, tears in her eyes.

I couldn't imagine the agony Dana had endured being given that kind of news with no mother or father to comfort her. And then what had I done? I'd left her. I nodded, unable to speak.

"She learned to deal with it," Hindley went on. "Built up her walls and engaged in meaningless relationships with men she knew she'd never create anything lasting with," she added. "When she met Leif, I really thought that would be it, her turning point, perhaps her soul mate." She rolled her eyes up to the ceiling again and let out a small laugh. "Too bad he turned out to be gay."

"She told you?" I asked, surprised.

"No one had to tell me, Peter." She smiled, turning to face me again. "Dana's beautiful, with a heart bigger than her mouth. When a good guy doesn't fall for her, he has to be gay. Actually," she confessed, "Dana said it from the beginning, but I really wanted her to find a decent guy so I didn't believe her." I totally understood her assessment but chuckled anyway.

"And now?" I asked. "Has Dana ever told you about Leif?"

She shook her head. "You?" she asked.

I answered with a silent nod of confirmation.

"See, Peter, that's what I mean. Dana's told you things that she's never told anyone else before, including me."

I knew Dana confided some things to me but the revelation that Hindley had just hit me with brought me to my knees.

"Do you see the power you have over her now? The power she's given you?"

"Hindley, she has the same power over me. I want to give her everything. That's what all of this has been about."

She stared at me in confusion. "What do you mean?"

"Just know that I love her and I'll never leave her again. I swear." I didn't want to get into the particulars of all my financial woes. I just needed to convince Hindley of my love and devotion.

Hindley smiled. "I know."

My heart tripped in my chest. Hindley was letting me in, and it was a fact I would never take for granted.

"Dr. Stedmond said that Dana came in last week to check her hormone levels. She'd felt like they'd been off for a while. Even though Dana just had her yearly checkup a few months ago, Dr. Stedmond decided to run all her labs again, including blood and urine."

"Is that normal for the doctor to do?"

"Not necessarily," she said, "but Dr. Stedmond is very thorough.

That's why we love her. She won't let anything slip through the cracks."

"That's good. So, what did the doctor find?" I held my breath, waiting for the inevitable news that I knew could change my life forever. I loved Dana with all my heart, like I'd never loved anyone before. The thought of losing her was horrific. I'd never recover, but if that was my destiny, I knew I'd stand by her, take care of her until the end. I'd never let Dana be alone again.

"The doctor said Dana had a high level of white blood cells in her urine."

"And?" I asked.

"And..." She stumbled over her words. "It could be nothing, just an indicator of a bacterial infection, maybe even a urinary tract infection."

"Or?" I leaned closer.

"We don't go there, Peter."

"Just tell me, Hindley. I deserve to know. I want to know." I scooted closer, reaching out to touch her, to reassure her I was in this for the long haul, no matter what my prior actions might have indicated.

"Dana had uterine cancer at such a young age that her chances of developing a secondary cancer were very high," Hindley explained. "After five years of being cancer free, her odds were better, the chance of recurrence went down exponentially. I won't say we didn't *think* about cancer, but Dana was finally able to breathe again."

Hindley paused, and I thought I might die from the anxiety of it all.

"Now though," she finally started again, "the high white blood cell count could also be an indicator of another type of cancer, bladder cancer to be specific. It's the type of cancer that goes hand-in-hand with uterine cancer. If Dana's cancer were to spread, the bladder would probably be the first place it would reoccur."

The blood drained from my face and my body went numb. This

was real. The chance that I could lose Dana was staring me in the face, and I was scared beyond belief.

"Bladder cancer can be a secondary byproduct of uterine cancer," she said, "but it's usually diagnosed at the onset of the original cancer diagnosis, as an increased staging. Does that make sense?"

I nodded my head, even though I didn't really understand what the hell she was talking about. The only thing echoing through my head was *cancer, cancer, cancer.*

Hindley continued, her voice strong and without emotion. "Thankfully, Dana's cancer was detected early and never spread. With the aggressive chemo and radiation she underwent, the cancer has never come back."

"Until now?" I whispered.

"It hasn't come back, Peter," she stated flatly.

I forced myself to stare at Hindley's blue eyes as if they were the tether holding me to this moment. She'd been through this before and I had to trust her.

"Dr. Stedmond feels certain that it's just some type of bacterial infection and that's why she prescribed the antibiotic. She says a fever won't spike like this with cancer and that actually everything Dana is going through right now is a good sign."

"But?" I held my breath.

"No buts, Peter. This is how we operate. Get used to it."

I squeezed my eyes shut, reflecting on her take-charge attitude. I envied Hindley for being brave during this anxious time.

"We don't worry until we have to. It's not worth it, and it only makes things worse in the long run. For Dana," she added.

"But how can you do that, Hindley? Aren't you scared? What if it's something more?"

"You can't go there, Peter," she repeated, chastising me with her words. "And more importantly, you can't let Dana go there. It's not healthy for her. For anyone."

"How do I stop it? How do I stop myself from worrying about her, about her future?" My words sounded as desperate as I felt.

"You can't do that. All of us worry, but it can't consume you. And you can't let Dana see your fear. She hates that most of all."

"Okay," I said quietly, not sure if I was up to the task.

"The doctor said to just monitor her, make sure her fever continues to come down. As long as that happens, everything should be fine."

I drew in a deep breath and sighed. This was good news.

"The doctor said Dana probably passed out from dehydration so we need to load her up with liquids when she wakes up. I've got some great water that's infused with electrolytes and nutrients that we can give her. Dana has an appointment next week to recheck her blood work and urine. Dr. Stedmond seemed certain Dana would be fine."

"That's great news."

Hindley sunk back, her hands wrapping around the nape of her neck. "It's very good news."

"Peter?" Geneva called from the hallway.

I jumped to my feet. "Is she all right?"

Geneva smiled and nodded. "She's asking for you."

I took one step but Hindley caught my hand, gently pulling me back.

"This is all Dana's story to tell, okay?" she asked.

"Okay." I knew what she meant and I wouldn't break Hindley's trust.

"She doesn't want your worry or your pity, Peter. She just wants your love."

"She's had that from the beginning. Ever since she spilled that damn beer all over my shirt." I laughed. "Dana looked up at me with a sheepish grin and suddenly, I knew. I saw my future in those bright blue eyes. In that moment, I knew she belonged to me. She'll always belong to me." That was the truest thing I'd ever said in my life. With Dana, I knew she was it for me.

"Oh my God," Geneva whispered.

"What?" I asked, my body tense with fear as I turned to face her.

Her hand was pressed to her heart. "That has to be one of the most amazing declarations of love I've ever heard in my life."

"It's true," I said, walking toward the bedroom. "I just hope Dana will forgive me for leaving without explaining everything."

"Tell her what you just told us and I'm pretty sure she'd forgive you for anything," Hindley said. Her words filled me with hope.

Maybe, just maybe, Dana would give me a second chance.

CHAPTER 9

PETER

"More?" I asked, holding the spoon to Dana's mouth.

"Peter, I can feed myself." She laughed.

I moved the spoon closer. "I'm well aware of all the amazing things you can do, Dolly."

Her eyes narrowed but she opened her mouth.

"Good girl." I smiled as she took in another spoonful of soup. "I'm only following doctor's orders."

"What?" she asked, wiping her chin with the napkin I handed her. "'Feeding me' is doctor's orders?" She smiled. The deep dimples in each cheek made my knees weak.

"She said keep an eye on you, and that's what I intend to do."

"In your bed, no less." She laughed.

Thankfully, my house was just a few miles away from Rory and Hindley's. I'd decided that Dana would stay with me while she recovered, much against the wishes of Hindley, but I didn't care.

I convinced Hindley by reminding her of what the doctor had told her. Dana's illness was likely a virus, and certainly Hindley didn't want to expose Abbi.

Even though it pained Hindley, she allowed me to take Dana home with me so I could care for her and nurse her back to health.

In true motherly concern for her life-long friend though, Hindley insisted on stopping by at least three times a day to check on Dana.

"I don't think the doctor meant you had to feed me," Dana said.

I held up another spoonful but she shook her head.

"She told me to take care of you, Dana. And that's exactly what I intend to do." I set the bowl on the tray next to my bed. "Are you full or did you just not like my chicken noodle soup?"

"I know a better way to take care of me." She laughed, waggling her brows.

I shook my head in answer but reveled in the glorious sound of her laughter.

"Your soup was amazing, by the way," she said. "Everything you make is amazing."

"How does your head feel?" I asked, placing the back of my hand on her forehead. "It feels like your fever's gone."

"It still hurts some, and I'm achy, but I feel better than I did." She reclined on the pillows with a satisfied sigh. "Tell me something."

Oh, no, this was it. We'd steered clear of deep conversations for the last few days while I waited for the fever to break. Now she seemed to be feeling better. I prayed to God it had been the flu or a cold or some other type of recoverable illness that had been affecting her. I couldn't let myself think about cancer.

"What do you want me to tell you?" I asked, scooting closer to her, not really sure I wanted to know the answer.

"Why is your mattress laying on the floor with no headboard or box spring?" She peered around the room. "And why aren't there any pictures or furniture in here? It looks like a frat house."

"I'm actually in the process of selling my house."

She sat up, her back straight as an arrow. "Are you buying another house?"

"Yes," I said, revealing nothing else.

She stared at me, raising one perfectly arched brow but remained silent.

I had plans, but she didn't need to know about them, not yet. Not until they were finalized.

"Here," I said, picking up a glass of orange juice and holding it out to her. "Drink this."

"I'm not thirsty."

"Drink, Dana. You've been dehydrated. That's why you passed out in my arms."

"I'm glad you were there to catch me." She bit back a smile, her lips curling around the straw as she sucked. Her eyes never left mine as her cheeks hollowed.

Holy hell. I swallowed nervously. Even sick with a fever this girl could still stir desire and longing inside me.

"How did you know where I was that night?" she asked.

"You don't remember?"

"Remember what?" she asked.

"I told you on the dance floor."

"The last thing I remember was getting up from the booth to go dance."

Fury raced through me as I remembered the stranger's hands roaming all over Dana's body while she gyrated on the dance floor with him.

"Hey," she said, stroking my face, "what's wrong?"

"Nothing." I shrugged off. She didn't need to know how jealous I'd been. Not now. "It was Geneva," I finally answered. "But it wasn't her fault. It was my sister's." I had no idea why I felt the need to come to Geneva's defense.

"Your sister's? How?" Her nose wrinkled with the cutest little confused look on her face.

"My sister knows how much I love you."

She pushed back in the bed and sat straight up. "You love me?"

"Of course, I do, Dolly. I've told you like a million times already."

Her eyes searched mine as if trying to comprehend my statement.

"I guess you've really been out of it, huh?"

"You love me," she whispered. It was a statement rather than a question, as if she were reassuring herself.

"Yes." I smiled, scooting closer. "I love you, with everything in me, Dana Di Grazio."

Tears welled in her eyes as she wrapped her hands around my neck, dragging me down for a hug.

"I love you too," she whispered in my ear. Her body melted into mine, her relief palpable. "Wait," she said, pushing me back. "How does your sister know?"

"I told her. After I found my phone, I tried calling you so many times but you never answered. Why was that?"

Her eyes narrowed and she glared at me.

I knew better than to chastise her anymore for her stubbornness.

"Go on," she said.

"Geneva explained to my sister what Jillian had said to you. I knew you'd probably never talk to me again, so Victoria intervened."

"Victoria? Your sister?"

"Yes. Most of our family calls her Tori."

"So, you called Geneva?"

"No. Victoria did." I laughed at the memory.

"For real?"

"For real."

She scooted closer. "How's your mom today?"

"She's doing well. The stent they put in to open up her clogged artery is doing well the doctor said."

"Oh, Peter," she sighed, placing her petite hand on my chest. "Thank goodness, I was so worried about her."

"I know, Dolly, and I'm so sorry I didn't call. And I'm sorry for the way I left. I was just in shock, I swear. It had nothing to do with the fact that you can't have children. I was just so afraid of losing you, thinking of you—"

"Enough," she interrupted. Sliding her arms around my waist, she drew me into an embrace that felt like home. We held each other in silence for a long while before she spoke again. "How did you leave things with your mom?"

"It actually went really well. She's in love."

Dana pulled back. "Really?"

I nodded. "Yeah, really."

"With who?"

"My father's best friend, if you can believe it."

"Well, that's not weird," she teased.

"Actually, it's not. I've loved AJ like a father my whole life." Memories of AJ filled my mind as I remembered all the amazing things he'd done for me over the years.

"So, you're happy, for your mom I mean?"

"Yeah," I smiled, "I think I am. It turns out my mom pretty much had her life planned out for her like I did. Now that my father is gone, she's finally free to live her own dreams."

"That's wonderful. Isn't it?"

I grinned, thinking of how happy my mom had been with AJ. "It's amazing. My mom and I have both made mistakes."

"Have you forgiven one another?"

"Let's just say we're trying to make amends."

Dana sat back in the bed. "I'm glad."

"Why?"

"Because everyone needs the love of their mother." She released a heavy sigh.

"You miss your mom, don't you, Dolly?" I asked, lightly caressing her cheek with my knuckles.

"Every day," she whispered. Her eyes fluttered closed and a broad smile spread over her face.

I assumed she was cycling through a lifetime of memories in her mind. I felt like an outsider, an intruder interrupting a special moment.

Her eyes finally opened and she stared at me. "Why didn't you tell me you were married before?"

And there it was. The question I'd tried to avoid for as long as possible. Dana was obviously feeling better, and I couldn't hide anymore.

"I guess because, technically, I never had been."

She cocked her head and scowled. "Technically?"

I heaved out a deep breath I'd been holding. "I know, I know. I should have told you from the beginning. I mean, I stood before God, our pastor and members of our church, and dedicated my life to another human being. Whether or not it was absolved six months after the ceremony isn't the point."

She reached out and touched my hand.

I stared down at her dark skin and intertwined our fingers before finally looking up and staring into her beautiful eyes. "I was married. I had a wife."

There, I'd said it. She remained silent, just staring at me, and I feared what was going through her mind. Would she forgive me? Would she leave me?

"You could have told me."

"I was embarrassed, Dana."

"Why?"

"Because I was a failure—as a husband—and I don't like to fail. At anything." I paused before telling her the real reason I'd never disclosed my marriage. "I was afraid you'd leave me."

She remained quiet and I had to convince myself that she loved me and would never leave me. At least, I prayed she wouldn't.

"So, what happened?" she asked, completely oblivious to my fears. "Why did she file for an annulment? And why does she think you're still married?"

I drew in a deep breath, unsure of how to explain it all. Reliving this part of my life was hard.

Dana squeezed my hand and somehow her assurance gave me the strength I needed.

"Jillian and I grew up with one another," I said, "almost like brother and sister. Somewhere along the way, people just assumed we'd fallen in love."

Dana remained quiet, something unusual for her. I prayed it was a good sign, so I went on.

"She was the only girl I was close to so I thought I was in love with her. When I graduated high school, I really just wanted to go to college straight away. My faith encourages young men to start missionary service first though. My father wanted me to be the head of his company someday, so he favored the idea of me completing school first. Marrying Jillian was his way of pacifying the Mormon Church. He convinced the elders that Jillian and I could do our mission trip together, after we married and graduated college."

I paused, remembering the pressure my father had put on me to marry Jillian. I knew, even back then, he couldn't care less if I loved her or not. It was his way of keeping his prominent position in the church. Despite his son breaking tradition and taking his spiritual pilgrimage when most boys in the Mormon faith were expected to.

"My father convinced me that marrying Jillian would be the right thing to do if I wanted to go directly to college. So, I asked her. She'd been pressured by her parents as well, so certainly she agreed. Plus, I think she wanted to get out of Utah."

I stared out the window, not wanting to relieve these memories, but knowing I had to in order to win back Dana's trust.

"And?" she asked.

My gaze returned to her blue eyes. "I told my father the only way I'd marry Jillian before college was if he let me attend UCLA as I'd planned. He'd wanted me to attend Brigham Young, a university predominantly filled with students of the Mormon faith. Eventually he conceded. Three months later, Jillian and I married and shortly after, moved to California to start college and our new life together."

I watched as Dana sat upright in the bed, her hand still in mine as she stared at me. I saw no judgment so I continued.

"Jillian was young and impressionable. We both were. I think that's why our fathers pushed us so hard to marry young. They believed our marriage would be the merging of two powerful companies, potentially earning them both a lot of money. Forget if we were in love or not."

"That sucks," Dana said. "But I know from experience that having a lot of money changes people."

I nodded, happy she understood. "I really believed I loved Jillian, and I tried to convince myself that she loved me too." I paused, pushing down the anxiety pounding in my chest as I thought about our time together. "Looking back now, after experiencing what I have with you, I realize what Jillian and I had was nothing more than teenage infatuation, if even that. We were using each other."

"So, what happened?"

"We were both in school in California and spending a lot of time studying. We really didn't see each other much. When I fell in love with motocross riding and wanted to pursue my dream, I told Jillian and she went ballistic. She insisted that I stick to the plan of returning to Salt Lake to take over my father's company once we graduated. She had plans herself and they didn't include motocross.

"I probably would have gone back to Utah, but it seemed Jillian was more in love with my family's money—and other men—than she was with me."

Dana gasped.

"Something in my gut told me she was cheating on me, but I didn't want to admit it, to myself, or to anyone."

"Oh, Peter," Dana reached out to stroke my face, "that's awful."

"One evening I came home early from class and actually caught her having sex with another man. On our couch." I shuddered at the memory.

Dana rose up on her knees and encircled her arms around me. "Peter, I'm so sorry."

My ex-wife's words echoed through my head.

You just didn't satisfy me, Peter. I needed someone else.

I shook my head to rid myself of her words.

"What is it?" Dana asked.

I didn't want to tell her that the man Jillian had been screwing on our couch was actually my own brother. It was still unbelievable to me all these years later. Dana didn't need to know all the details. It would only taint her image of my family more.

"It's okay," Dana said, squeezing my waist. "I'm here."

I stared down at her face, still flushed with the aftermath of her fever. "You need to lay down, sweetheart."

"I feel good right here in your arms."

Scooping her into my lap, I scooted back and leaned against the wall, draping us with the covers and settling in. Dana was my balm, soothing all my old wounds.

"What happened after that?" she asked.

"Jillian totally crushed my spirit. It was the last straw for me," I said. "And that's when *she* asked for the annulment. I should have seen it coming. I mean, in the Mormon faith you don't get divorced. Ever. She would have been a tainted woman."

Dana squeezed me tighter.

I worked to contain my fury with my ex-wife. "Actually," I continued, "she was already a tainted woman the minute she slept with someone else and broke our marriage vows. I'm not even sure if she was a virgin when we married." My head fell back against the wall and I stared up at the ceiling. Talking about this time in my life was harder than I thought it would be.

"It's okay, Peter, you don't have to say anymore," she whispered.

"No, I want to. I want you to know everything. I should have told you sooner. I'm sorry."

She lifted the covers higher around us and burrowed in deeper. "So, what happened next?"

"After I discovered her on the couch, I contacted AJ. He's also on the board of my father's company and an attorney. And apparently dating my mother now." I chuckled at the thought.

"That's so cute." Dana smiled, a small giggle escaping her lips.

"God, I love that sound."

"What sound?"

"Your laugh."

Dana's dimples appeared as her smile broadened. I stared down at her, mesmerized. She literally took my breath away.

"So, what happened then?" she asked. "With you and Jillian, I mean."

"My father was furious when I told him about the annulment."

"Did you tell him about the cheating?"

I shook my head. "I wanted to. I should have. But something inside me still wanted to protect Jillian. Is that weird?"

She shook her head. "No, that's not weird, Peter, that's just who you are. You care about people. You're an amazing man." She reached up and brushed her lips against my neck.

I lifted her hand and pressed a kiss over her knuckles. Dana was everything I always wanted in a woman but had never found.

"So, then your dad cut you off, after the annulment?"

"He threatened to, but he still needed me to run his company, so he continued to pay my tuition. Until my senior year. By then, the annulment was finalized and I was riding motorcycles full-time. I'd fallen completely and totally in love with motocross."

I smiled as I thought back to how much motocross had healed my broken heart.

"I'm glad," Dana said.

"Why?"

"We all need to fall in love with something." Her eyes met mine. "Or someone."

I leaned down and pressed a soft kiss onto her head, her wild curls tickling my face. She was my "someone" and she knew it.

"What happened after you discovered your love affair with motorcycles?" She laughed.

I was so happy she understood my heart.

"Well, my friends convinced me that I could make a living

competing in motocross, so my father's threats didn't bother me anymore. I finished my last semester of college on my own, without the help of my family. Then I joined the ranks of pro motocross, and never looked back."

"Until?"

"Until my father died last year. I went back, but it was only for the funeral. My mother begged me to stay in Utah to run the business, but I refused. I was pretty rude to her, to my entire family. It just hurt too much, being there, knowing how much I'd disappointed all of them."

"How did you disappoint them?" she asked, snuggling in closer.

"Everyone in my family expected *something* out of me. My father and brothers expected me to run the business. My mother expected me to marry Jillian and give her a ton of grandchildren."

Dana tried to pull away, but I drew her in tight, trying to reassure her. We sat in silence for a long moment before she finally spoke again.

"And your sister? What did she expect from you?"

I thought about the question. What had Victoria expected of me? "Nothing," I finally said. "She's the only person who's never expected anything from me. And I love her so much for that."

"What's she like?" Dana asked, giddy with anticipation.

"Well, she's beautiful."

"I'm sure." She winked. "Her brother is extremely handsome after all."

I rolled my eyes and laughed. "Whatever."

"What? You are." She pressed a kiss to my throat again and I felt my pulse racing. Not now, I reminded myself.

"Victoria is smart as a whip. She's studying environmental sciences at UCLA. She wants to work with natural resources to build sustainable ecosystems that protect the environment, or something like that. She can explain it a lot better than me."

"I'd like to meet her," Dana said quietly. "I mean, someday. If that's okay with you."

"Are you kidding?" I laughed. "Victoria will kill me if I don't introduce you two soon."

"How old is she?"

"Twenty-one, but she's very mature and focused for her age. My mom always said Victoria had an old soul. She's also got a smart mouth like someone else I know."

Dana smiled, her dimples on full display. I couldn't help myself. I leaned down and kissed her, pulling away quickly before I took more than she could give right now.

"Victoria," Dana said softly as I pulled away. "That's a beautiful name."

I laughed at the memory of Victoria's name.

"What's so funny?" she asked.

"Being the dutiful Christian that my father was, he decided to name his children after 'Strong men of the Bible'," I said sarcastically. "It started out with Matthew, then James, Phillip, me—Peter, and Thomas." I paused, remembering my baby brother's betrayal. "And finally, John," I added, trying to hide the disdain for my brother. After all, he had slept with my wife. Thankfully Dana didn't notice my contempt.

"So where did Victoria come from?" she asked. "It's not very biblical, is it?"

"No." I laughed. "My father had a slew of biblical female names ready when my sister was born, but my mother shot them all down. She told my father she'd waited nearly fourteen years to have a girl and she wasn't about to waste it on something common."

Dana threw back her head and howled with laughter. "I think I love your mother. That's hysterical. I don't blame her one bit. So where did Victoria come from?"

"It was my grandmother's name, my mother's mother. Her name was Alberta Victoria."

"You mean the one who taught you so much about cooking?"

"Yes," I answered softly, trying to hold back my emotions as I thought about how much my grandmother had taught me. She was tough and fierce, all the things I aspired to be. All the things that Dana was.

"Well, it's a beautiful name and I can't wait to meet your sister."

I studied Dana's face. Dark smudges were forming underneath her eyes and her lids were drooping. She was getting tired.

"You need to get some sleep, Dolly."

She shook her head. "I like being here." She nestled closer to me, wiggling her hips.

"Dana," I admonished.

Suddenly her smile faded and she sat straight up in my lap. "I need to talk to you about something first."

My eyes scanned hers. I was almost sure of what she wanted to talk about and I wasn't sure I wanted to have this conversation. Not now. Not when she wasn't fully recovered.

"Dana, I know you can't have children," I said, beating her to the punch. "I know you've had cancer. I know you will always live with a certain amount of fear and doubt. I don't care about any of that. I love you and I want to be with you."

"But, Peter—"

I pressed a finger against her soft lips. "There are no 'buts.' We'll talk about everything when you feel better, not tonight. You need your rest."

Her shoulders sagged and I was surprised she was giving up the fight so easily.

"Just go to sleep and dream of me," I said, "and know that I'm not going anywhere, Dolly. I'm sorry I ever left you, especially the way I did. Trust me, I would have come back."

"Was it because of the whole annulment thing?"

"That was part of it, I guess. I promise I didn't want to leave you but I had to. For my mother. And it wasn't because you told me you couldn't have children."

She nodded but I wasn't sure she was convinced.

"Victoria was scared," I said, "worried about my mother's condition. She begged me to come, so I did. I needed to be there, for her, and for my mother. My family has a history that is too long to discuss right now. Go to sleep, and we can talk about it when you wake up, okay?"

She nodded and smiled. "Okay. But will you do me a favor?"

"Anything." And I meant it.

"Will you lie down with me?"

I laughed at the absurdity of her question. Without saying a word, I took off my shirt and jeans, kicking them to the side as I nudged her over.

As she slid over, the large T-shirt of mine she was wearing rode up her legs, exposing simple yet sexy underwear. God, she was beautiful.

"I missed you," she whispered in a sultry voice, her eyes gazing up to meet mine. Her lashes fanned out like a raven's wings and my breath caught in my throat at the sight of her.

"Not tonight, Dolly," I growled.

"But, Peter," she begged.

"You're just starting to feel better, Dana. I don't want a relapse."

She pouted and I bit back a laugh.

"We'll have plenty of time to catch up, later," I assured her. "Until then, just let me hold you and take care of you."

She scooted closer and settled against my chest.

I wrapped my arms around her and buried my face into her hair, drawing in a deep breath. The scent made me think of home.

Her small hand pressed against my chest but began to move lower.

I grabbed her wrist. "Dolly," I scolded.

"What?" Her voice was higher, feigning innocence.

"Just sleep," I said softly against her hair, gliding my arm around her waist and tugging her into my chest.

"I'm sorry, Peter," she said, her voice just above a whisper.

Her comment shocked me. "For what?"

"For everything. For not telling you about my cancer sooner. For not telling you I couldn't have children."

"Shhh," I hushed her. "We both messed up, okay?"

She nodded against me. "Okay."

"All that matters now is you're back in my arms." I pulled her tight against me.

Her hand found mine and we intertwined our fingers.

"I always want you to trust me, to be honest with me, and I will be too. Okay?" I said.

"Please, don't ever leave me again," she whispered, her fingers tightening around mine.

I rolled her over so I could look at her face. Her eyes were brimming with tears and my heart nearly broke in two. "I'm so sorry. I didn't mean to leave you, I swear. I was coming back. I just...." What could I say to make her believe me? "You're mine."

"Okay." She nodded. "Just don't ever walk out on me again. Not like that, not without telling me why first."

I remained mute, paralyzed with guilt for what my actions had done to her. I'd made her doubt me, and that was something I never wanted to do again. "I love you, Dana," I said, placing a kiss on her lips. "I'll never leave you again. I swear."

She reached up and stroked my cheek, her dimples reappearing. "I love you, Peter. I always have." She leaned up and kissed me. "And I always will."

Her words sounded like a benediction, a closing prayer for my broken spirit. Her soft lips pressed against mine but before I could return her passion, she rolled away from me and pressed her back against my body. "Hold me," she said softly.

Sliding my arm around her I realized, this was it. The moment I'd dreamt of my entire adult life. I was happy, at peace, holding the woman I loved in my arms. I truly was complete.

Tugging her in tighter against me, I knew I wasn't entirely sure how our future would unfold, but as I drifted off to sleep holding her in my arms, I knew one thing for sure. Dana Di Grazio would always be in it.

CHAPTER 10

DANA

"WELL, DANA," Dr. Stedmond said as I sat on the examining table in a paper gown that was less than flattering. "I think you just had some type of bacterial infection that caused your white blood cells to increase. I checked all your blood counts, and your urine, and everything is back to normal."

I smiled at Peter, who was sitting across from me, and tried to hide my relief. No matter how many times a doctor told you that you were cancer free, you always lived with the anxiety that it might return.

Dr. Stedmond stared at the computer screen then glanced at me. "You finished your antibiotics completely, right?"

"Yes," Peter answered before I could. "I made sure of it." He smiled at me and something inside me melted. Knowing that Peter was in my life, that he would always be there to care for me, relieved some of the anxiety I'd lived with since my parents died.

"Well, as a precaution," Dr. Stedmond said, "I'd like to see you in another two weeks just to repeat the labs and see how you're doing."

Peter stood and grasped my hand. "We'll make the appointment as soon as we check out." I knew he cared about my well-being, but his growing anxiety about my health concerned me. I didn't want him to take on the burden of worrying about me too.

"Good," Dr. Stedmond replied, giving me a wink and a small nod. She was obviously happy with Peter's protectiveness too. "It was very nice to meet you, Peter." She stuck out her hand. "I hope your elbow continues to heal nicely."

I gazed down at Peter's arm. His doctor had removed the brace and cleared him to resume normal activities, just no sports. And definitely no motorcycle riding. Thankfully, sex was considered a "normal activity." Although Peter had so far refused to give in to my desires until after this appointment.

"The doctor said it's healing better than expected," Peter said.

Part of me withered inside, knowing soon he'd be going back out on the extreme sport tours.

As if sensing my fear, he amended his comment. "But it will probably be a while until I can compete again."

"Keep an eye on this one." Dr. Stedmond nodded toward me.

"I'll try." Peter laughed.

I hit his stomach. "Hey, I'm right here in the room."

"Stay well, you two," she said then left the room.

I jumped down from the table and dressed quickly. "Let's go," I said, yanking on his hand.

"I know I said no sex until after this appointment, but this is crazy, Dolly."

I smiled and waggled my brows. "Later. First, I have something I want to show you."

"Not much later, I hope." Peter grinned and I nearly came in my jeans. Those mismatched eyes were filled with desire, all for me.

"There's always the car," I said.

He yanked on my hand, pulling me behind him. "Let's go," he growled.

≈

We found my car in the parking garage and Peter helped me in before sliding into the driver's seat.

He stared at me then down at the console between us. "Didn't you say something about the car?"

I laughed, amazed by Peter's new-found brazenness. "We have a meeting at the dealership."

He groaned and put the car in gear, driving out of the garage.

"Soon," I said.

He glanced at me and winked. "Very soon."

I leaned back in the seat and stared out the window, happy just to be out of the house.

"I'm glad you're getting better," he said.

"Me too." We sat in comfortable silence, the miles ticking by. As we got closer to the dealership, I fiddled with my seat belt, unsure of how to ask my question.

"Just ask, Dolly."

He knew me so well.

"Well, I was just wondering. Why does your ex-wife want money from you and your family? Why is she back now?"

Peter turned into the dealership and I directed him to the back lot. "You can park there," I said, pointing to my usual spot by the garage.

He pushed the gear shift into park before turning to face me. "Her father's in trouble."

"What kind of trouble?"

"He owns an accounting firm in Salt Lake, and according to AJ, he's been taking a little off the top from some of his biggest clients."

"Seriously?"

He nodded.

"Could he go to jail?"

"He could. Not only that though, apparently some of the 'companies,'" he said, using air quotes, "aren't the most legitimate businesses, if you know what I mean."

"No way." I covered my gaping mouth. "Like the mob?"

"I don't know if you'd call them the mob, per se. Let's just say they have their own method of dealing with someone who steals from them."

"Wow," I breathed out, falling back into my seat. "Who knew Salt Lake City, home of the Mormon Tabernacle Choir, was a mecca for the mob." I laughed.

"Yeah, who knew."

I sat straight up, staring at Peter. "Oh my God. You and your family aren't involved, are you?" If this skank bitch was threatening Peter or his family in any way, she was going to deal with her own mafia smack down called Dana Di Grazio.

"No," he smiled, patting my leg, "she was just looking for money to save her dad, I think. She actually came to the hospital to see my mom, trying to act like she was concerned for her health. In reality all she really cared about was money. Me being there was a complete shock to her."

"Really?"

"Really." He nodded. "But I think when she saw me, it set her conniving wheels in motion. Seeing me maybe made her think that she might be able to convince me we were still married and she might be entitled to some of my family's money."

"But you're not still married, are you?"

"No. When AJ confirmed that he'd filed the annulment papers himself, and explained that she wouldn't get anything from me or my family's business, Jillian left."

I stared out in front of me at the busy dealership. It was hard to believe what all had happened to me in the last few weeks.

"Dana," he said, leaning in closer, "I can't tell you how sorry I am that I put you through all of this."

I turned and stared at him. I really didn't want him to feel guilty anymore.

"I'm sorry that I even made you think for one minute that you not being able to have children was an issue for me. I never thought that. I was just so worried about you. As soon as you said you had cancer, my whole future flashed before my eyes. I'd always pictured you in it. And then my sister called and—"

I pressed my fingers to his lips to stop his words. "I know, Peter. I know." I removed my hand. "Kiss me," I whispered.

He stared at my lips, his eyes wide with anticipation. Slowly he leaned over, one hand braced on the console as the other wrapped around my neck. He pulled me closer, his lips only inches away from mine. "I love you so much, Dana. I'll never leave you again."

Before I could respond, his lips touched mine, gentle at first then firmer, his tongue sliding across mine. "Oh, God," he moaned, yanking me across the console until I was fully in his lap.

"Peter," I squeaked.

His mouth found mine again and my hands wound through his thick hair. My body hummed with anticipation as his mouth consumed me. I worked my hands down his body, sliding over his broad chest and across his taut abdomen. He felt amazing, so toned and muscled.

"Oh, God," Peter repeated.

Straddling his lap, I ground myself against his erection, mewling with the need to get closer.

His mouth moved against mine as his hands cupped the underside of my ass, guiding me against him. We rocked into each other and I felt heat prickle my core.

"Oh, Peter," I sighed, needing more of him.

Suddenly, a banging sounded from the passenger side window, jarring the car.

I sat up, disoriented. "What the fuck?"

"Nice show, Di Grazio!" someone yelled from outside.

I slid back to my seat, still dazed. Rolling down the window, I wasn't surprised to find Rico and Damion from the garage, standing next to my car.

Rico had a dirty rag in his hand, circling it high above his head as he whistled catcalls that had me beet red. "Guess you and lover boy made up." He snorted.

"Fuck you, Rico," I said, opening the car door and punching him in the chest.

"Fuck, Di Grazio," he rubbed the spot I'd just hit, "that hurt like shit."

I waggled my finger in his face. "There's more where that came from if you ever fuck up another make-out session of mine."

Damion roared with laughter, the sound echoing in the parking lot. "That was funny as shit."

"What part?" I asked.

"All of it." He grinned. "Pool this Thursday if you feel like losing more money."

"Lose?" I scoffed. "Please."

Peter stepped out of the car and stood beside me.

"Maybe this time you can hold your liquor better," Rico said.

I cringed at the memory of pool night, or lack thereof.

"What are they talking about?" Peter asked.

Rico turned and walked toward the garage. "Later, *chica*," he called over his shoulder. "And leave the whiskey at home."

"Nothing," I moaned, trying to hide my embarrassment. The last thing I wanted to admit to Peter was how trashed I'd gotten after finding out he was married. And I certainly didn't want him to find out I'd spent the night at Chase's house.

"Are you sure you don't mind doing this?" I asked, trying to change the subject. Uncle Nic asked if I could bring Peter in to do a quick audit of our accounting system and he had willingly agreed.

"Dana, I've already told you. I'll do anything for you." He was right, he had told me, many times. I just didn't believe him. "I meant it."

"Promise me one thing, though," I said.

"What's that, Dolly?" He smiled, placing his large hand in mine as we walked across the parking lot. His touch sent a buzz of excitement through my body, knowing what the night held for us.

"If you can't do this," I said, "or even if you don't *want* to do this, just tell me, okay? Don't feel obligated."

He shook his head in obvious impatience. "Let's go, Dolly." He tugged on my hand, and just like that, I knew it was over. Peter was not going to leave the dealership until he'd figured out exactly what was going on with our finances. And strangely, I was all right with that.

CHAPTER 11

DANA

As we walked toward the main offices of the dealership, I thought about how much Peter meant to me. About how much his leaving had completely destroyed me. He smiled down at me, lifting our hands to press a kiss on my knuckles.

I squeezed him tight, adding my own vow. I would trust him, with my dealership, and my heart.

"Enjoy your vacation?" Andre's snarky voice broke through my thoughts.

I turned to face him, trying hard to mask my annoyance. Peter and I were here to help Uncle Nic today. I couldn't let my personal distaste for Andre distract me.

"Actually, no. It wasn't a vacation," I said. "I was sick."

"Oh," he said, sounding surprised, and maybe a little sympathetic. "Well, Dad and Chase are in the conference room. I'm just going over to the service department to pick up some papers, then I'll head over for the meeting."

"That won't be necessary," Peter said in a deep voice.

"Ah," Andre smirked, "so, I guess your boyfriend's back, swooping in to save our little dealership, huh?"

I wanted to reach out and slap that smug look off his face, but Peter pulled me back.

"Something like that," Peter said. "This meeting is for the principles."

Andre stared Peter up and down. "Then why are you going to be there?"

"I've been called in as a consultant."

"Consultant?" Andre laughed. "Is that code for Dana's Fuck Buddy?"

Now it was my turn to pull Peter back.

"Ignore him," I said. "Most people do."

"As I said," Peter said, "your presence won't be needed today."

Andre pointed a skinny finger at Peter. "This ain't your fucking dealership, dude! You're not the one who's been here day in and day out, busting his ass to make this business work."

"Well, according to Dana and your own father, neither have you." Peter's words were like gas on a flame.

"Who the fuck do you think you are, asshole?" Andre puffed out his chest and moved toward us.

Peter released my hand and stepped forward. "I'm the asshole who was hired by the CEO of this company to straighten out this God-awful mess of an accounting system you seem to have weaseled your way into. Now, if you'll excuse me, *your* boss and I have a meeting to attend."

Oh, shit! I'd never seen this side of him before—and I loved it.

Andre's eyes narrowed and his jaw clenched as he studied Peter. I knew he wanted to fight but he wasn't a complete idiot. "Whatever, man." He turned and stomped off toward the garage bays.

"Damn, Peter, that was hot." I grabbed his neck and pulled him down, pressing a kiss to his lips.

He drew back, a frown on his face. "I'm sorry, Dana. I don't know where that came from."

"What the fuck are you talking about? That was like one of the hottest things I've ever seen." My entire body shivered and I seriously thought of cancelling the meeting and going back to the car to finish what we'd started.

He studied me, eyes narrowed. "What are you talking about? I was rude, to your family."

"You rescued your damsel in distress. And you shoved the villain's dick in the dirt in the process. It was awesome."

"Well, it didn't feel awesome." I could see the self-loathing in his eyes.

"Trust me. Give it a few more tries and soon it will be the best feeling in the world," I teased.

"That's not true." He grabbed me around the waist, pressing me against his body. Desire burned through my clothes. "This right here," he said, his hands lowering to my ass, "this is the best feeling in the world, having you by my side."

"You can't keep doing this to me, Peter," I moaned.

"What?" He moved to push me away but I held him tight.

"You haven't made love to me in forever. I'm literally aching for you."

He grinned, as if he'd done something wicked. "Well, Miss Di Grazio, let's fix your accounting system." Leaning closer, he whispered in my ear. "Then we'll see if I can fix that other problem for you." His hands brought my hips between his legs.

The bulge in his pants pressed against my belly. "Oh, shit," I whimpered.

"You see, you're not the only one who's aching, Dolly."

My mind whirled with the promises of things to come. "Fuck, Peter," I growled, grinding my hips into his.

His deep laughter had my legs trembling. If I didn't break our embrace soon, we were going to commit a felony right here in the parking lot of my own dealership.

With great reluctance I pulled away before someone called the cops. "Come on," I said. "Let's go fix this accounting system. Then we're going home and I'm going to fuck you so hard you won't walk straight for a solid week. Maybe two."

His head fell back and he barked with laughter. The sound soothed me. "I love you, Dana De Grazio," he said.

I realized, not for the first time, that he truly did love me. It was this kind of love I'd longed for since my parents died. For the first time since my cancer diagnosis, I had real hope for my future.

CHAPTER 12

DANA

PETER and I entered the large conference room and immediately and Chase stood.

"Hey, Dana." He walked around the table and took me into an embrace that felt too intimate for work—or any setting.

"Hey, Chase," I said. I patted his back with one hand then quickly stepped away.

He gazed down at me, studying me from head to toe. "I see you survived your hangover." He laughed.

Ah, shit. I really didn't want to discuss my drunken night with him right now, not here in front of Peter. It wasn't like Peter was the jealous type but I knew he would have a shit fit if he found out I'd spent the night with Chase.

"Yes, thanks," I said quietly, trying to end the conversation.

He nodded but thankfully said no more. I would tell Peter, eventually, but now wasn't the time.

"So, you must be the infamous Peter Fontenot," Chase said, holding out his hand.

Infamous? Where was Chase going with this? I thought he understood my silent wishes.

"Not so married after all, eh?" Chase said with a grin.

Peter's gaze cut to mine then back to Chase, his brows furrowed.

Fuck! I had to nip this in the bud.

I cleared my throat and squared my shoulders, trying to appear in control. "Peter this is Chase Carlson, our CFO."

"Nice to meet you, Chase," Peter said, displaying no emotion. "And to answer your question, no, I'm not married. I never was."

Chase cocked his head and stared at me in confusion before turning back to Peter. "Never? Hmm. I must have been mistaken."

Peter shrugged. "Yeah, must have been." The two stared at each other, and somehow I couldn't help feel there was a silent battle being waged between them.

Thankfully Uncle Nic interrupted. "We've pulled up the accounting system for you, Peter." He pointed to two laptops on the table.

I'd never been more thankful for my uncle in all my life. I knew after this meeting I had a lot of explaining to do.

Peter sat down and I followed, sitting next to him. He studied the screens on both computers. "The first thing we need to do is revoke everyone's access to the system."

Chase sat across from me and stared at Peter. "How will we get the day-to-day accounting done?"

"Instead of giving a few people access to everything, you'll give each person access to only a few things. That will help us determine where in the process there's a weak link. And it will give me time to assess this entire system."

"I just don't understand," Uncle Nic said, falling into one of the chairs. "How is this happening?"

I felt a wave of guilt wash over me, knowing my uncle had been dealing with this so long on his own.

Peter typed on the keyboard, his eyes scanning the screens. He was brilliant, and he was all mine. If anyone could figure this out, I knew Peter could.

"Who did you say designed the system?" he asked.

"I have no idea," Chase said. "It was in place when I got here."

Peter stared up at Chase in disbelief. "It's possible these losses could be coming from within the company."

"There's no way." Uncle Nic shook his head. "These people are like family. They would never do this to us."

Peter glanced up. "I hate to tell you this, but when people are desperate, they'll do desperate things, no matter how familiar they are."

"I guess a large part of this is my fault," Chase said. "I should have been looking at everything, and everybody." He exhaled deeply and I could see the guilt in his expression. "I just never even thought about it being an employee inside the company."

"Chase," I reached across the table and touched his hand. "Everyone here knows how dedicated you are to this dealership. Especially me."

Even though Chase and I had never been involved romantically, everything he did at the dealership had been done specifically to protect me, and I knew it, even if I never voiced it.

I gave his hand a gentle squeeze.

His warm hazel eyes remained fixed on mine. He needed reassurance from me, acknowledgment that I trusted him. And I did. That was what I wanted to give him. Especially after he'd cared for me so well when I'd been totally plastered.

Suddenly, I realized I'd been staring at him way too long. There were two other people in this room, and I had no explanation for my extremely unprofessional display of affection. I didn't care though. Chase was first and foremost a friend, and I didn't want him to feel guilty about a situation he had no control over.

Chase carefully pulled his hand away from mine, sensing the same type of awkwardness.

I stared down out the window, afraid to look at Peter for fear he may see the guilt on my face. After taking a few deep breaths, I finally glanced at Peter from the corner of my eye.

He was staring at Chase, almost glaring. Peter was an intelligent man. I could see in his expression that he knew more was going on between me and Chase. I needed to tell him the truth. It was what we had both committed to.

"I just hate to think of someone here working against us," Uncle Nic said. "I can't imagine anyone in our own company doing this to us."

"I know." Peter tried to console him. "We saw it in my father's company, as well. Some people are ruthless." He turned his attention back to the computer, never once looking at me. Something deep in the pit of my stomach burned. He was upset, and he had every right to be.

"What we need to do after revoking everyone's access," he said, "is reassign them their jobs and only allow them access to very specific parts of the system. We will set their passwords, not them. That's very important."

"Why?" Chase asked.

"If we need to revoke their access then we'll have control. In addition, we'll be changing their passwords once a week."

Chase shook his head. "But how will they keep up with that?"

"They'll just have to figure out a way if they want to keep their job," Peter said flatly, no empathy or emotion in his voice. This was the financial-techy part of him speaking. It was surprising to see Peter in this dominant role. But if it meant my dealership would stay afloat and our employees wouldn't lose their jobs or their benefits, then I was okay with his new persona.

Plus, his dominance was way sexy.

"I'll call my family's company this afternoon and try to get a few of the programmers to help revamp this system," he said. "It's pretty lax."

"I'm not sure BMW Group International will approve that," Uncle Nic said. "They have very strict guidelines for BMW dealerships worldwide."

"Well, your job is to make them understand the severity of this situation," Peter said, pointing at the laptop. "This is a horrible computer system. If they created it, then they need to understand that it's not just your dealership that's at risk."

"I think this program is specific to our dealership, isn't it, Uncle Nic?" I asked.

"Well, there's a way to find out," Peter explained.

"How?" Nic asked.

"I'll have the programmers go in and look at the electronic copyright to see who developed it."

"What does that mean?" Chase asked.

"Most software companies will attach special coding within their program marking it as their own, listing who developed it. It will also include a special line similar to a serial number or signature that guarantees the authenticity of the program, claiming it under any applicable copyright laws. Once we find that out, we'll be able to definitely say who created it and go directly to the source."

God, this guy was a fucking genius. And all his computer talk was turning me on, big time.

I'd never gone for computer geeks before, but Peter was built like a Greek god, lean and hard, not your typical nerd. Plus, he always satisfied me, bringing me to an orgasm quicker than any man I'd ever met.

Peter Fontenot was single-handedly saving my company, and that made him completely irresistible, nerdy geek that he was.

He turned toward me, his gaze holding mine.

I smiled, praying he understood my vow. I was his—body and soul.

He smirked and shook his head. I heard his silent words. *Not now, Dolly.* I couldn't help but laugh.

He turned his attention back to the room. "What we need to start working on is developing a new system. My family's company can do that for you."

"Why are you doing this?" Chase asked skeptically. "I mean, I'm very appreciative that you are, don't get me wrong, but why?"

I held my breath, wondering what he would say.

He gently closed the laptop and took my hand in his. "Because I love Dana with all my heart. Her future is my future. I'll do whatever I have to in order to make sure she's safe, even if it means protecting her life with my own."

Holy fucking shit! Had he just said that, in front of these men who meant the world to me?

His declaration was one of the most loving things anyone had ever said about me. I mean, I knew he loved me, but he'd basically just announced that for better or for worse, he was going to be with me. Not only that, but he was going to protect me, from anyone or anything that threatened me.

For a girl, it just didn't get any sexier than that.

Peter stared at Chase, holding his gaze for a bit longer than necessary. I knew what he was doing. He was marking his territory, pissing around me, and I was surprisingly okay with that. Hell, I was so turned on I nearly jumped in his lap and started dry humping him.

Peter cherished me. He was making that fact known to these men. I couldn't even begin to describe how incredible his words made me feel. Especially after everything we'd been through.

Chase smiled and I hoped he was happy for me. But I couldn't shake the feeling that deep down he wasn't, that he thought I'd rejected him in some way. Or maybe Chase was still feeling protective over me as well, like he'd always been. After all, he had taken good care of me after my night of drunken debauchery.

"I understand completely," Chase finally said, his smile flat. He pushed out of his chair and extended his hand across the table toward Peter. "Thank you. Nic and I really appreciate your help." He sounded sincere, and for all of our sakes, I hoped he was.

Peter took his hand and the two shook.

I breathed a sigh of relief, knowing Chase and Peter would work together despite their personal feelings for me. Or maybe because of them.

"And, Dana," Chase said, still holding Peter's hand, "if you ever find yourself on the short end of a shot glass again, you know you can always call me and I'll be there to take care of you all night, just like I did when Peter left you." Without another word, Chase dropped Peter's hand and walked from the room.

Fuck!

Peter stared at the closed door for a long moment before turning to face me. His mismatched eyes narrowed, his lips pressed into a flat line as he gripped the conference table.

If looks could have killed, I would be six-feet under for sure. How the hell was I going to get out of this one?

CHAPTER 13

DANA

"So, you're not going to say anything about what Chase just said?" I asked Peter as I tried to keep up with his strides.

He stared down at me, his expression hard to read.

After saying our goodbyes to Uncle Nic earlier, Peter hadn't spoken a word to me. He'd only taken my hand and led me out of the offices.

I tugged on him, pulling him to a stop in the middle of the parking lot. "Peter. Talk to me."

He gazed up at the sky and drew in a deep breath before glancing down at me, sighing. "There's nothing to talk about. Leaving you the way I did, with no explanation, putting you through so much grief, was unforgivable. And yet, somehow you understood Anything you did after I left is on me. I don't have the right to question what you did while I was gone. Or who you did it with."

God, this was going to be worse than I thought. I knew he wanted to believe his words, but there was no way he could. How could he believe I'd slept with someone else?

"Well, I want to tell you."

"Okay," he said quietly.

Holding his hand, I led us to the side of a warehouse where no one was milling about. I turned to face him. Those beautiful eyes stared down at me, and a whirlwind of emotions danced inside me. Where could I start?

"When you left for Utah and never called me," I said, "I was really upset." That was an understatement. "I tried to call you for hours."

His arm tensed and his hold on my hand tightened.

"When your ex-wife answered your phone, I pretty much freaked out." He grimaced but I went on. "She said you were in the shower and insinuated you two had just been fucking your brains out."

"Dana—"

I held up my hand. "Let me finish."

He nodded.

"She told me you weren't coming back to Austin at all. The stupid bitch even thanked me for all that I'd done for you, taking care of you and nursing you back to health."

Peter clenched his jaw and I knew he was trying to hold back his fury.

"So, I said, fuck it. If you were screwing your wife and were never coming back to me, then I was gonna drown my sorrows. I met up with the guys from the shop and that's exactly what I did."

Peter remained silent, but released my hand, balling both of his into fists.

"Anyway," I continued, "I proceeded to get pretty fucked up, as you can imagine. Chase was there and he took care of me. I threw up several times, and basically passed out on him, so he brought me to his house."

Peter's nostrils flared as his hands flexed open and closed.

Shit! I hadn't meant to upset him. I was just trying to be honest, like we agreed to be.

I stepped closer, taking his hands in mine. "Nothing happened, Peter, I swear."

"Not because he didn't want it to happen," he said through gritted teeth.

I didn't answer because on some level, Peter was probably right. My stomach clenched as I went on with the story, knowing this would be the whopper.

"I woke up in his bed but he'd spent the night on the floor. He wanted to stay in the same room with me because he was afraid I would choke on my own vomit."

Peter laughed but there was no humor. "Is that what he actually told you?"

"It's the truth, Peter." God, I hoped it was. "I left the next day shortly after I woke up. Chase called me a cab. I didn't even shower there or anything."

He lifted his head high and squared his shoulders like a soldier. "It's none of my business, Dana." He turned and walked toward my car.

"Stop, Peter!" I yelled.

Thankfully he did.

I walked around until I was standing in front of him. "This is your business. *I'm* your business." I pounded my chest. "At least, that's what you said inside. That's what you told Chase and Uncle Nic in the conference room, isn't it?"

His large hands framed my face as he bent down, our eyes almost level.

Oh, God, this was it. He hadn't meant his earlier words. They'd only been a show for Chase's sake. Peter was going to leave me. My heart pounded in my chest and I felt light-headed.

"You will always be my business, Dana," he growled, his voice almost predatory. "What happened in the past while I was gone doesn't concern me. All I want to know is if you see me in your future?"

I stared at him through pooling tears. His mismatched eyes held my gaze, one dark blue, one hazel green. "Peter," I whispered as I drew his face close to mine, our lips almost touching, "you're not just in my future, you *are* my future."

His sullen expression vanished as a smile spread across his gorgeous face. He pulled me in the rest of the way for a heated kiss, part desperate, part desirable.

I sighed in relief, knowing we would be okay. We had weathered our first of many storms.

Peter pulled away before I was ready. "We're in public," he whispered against my lips.

"I don't care." I lifted up on my tiptoes to steal one more kiss.

He laughed. "Later, Dolly."

I smiled. "You've said that several times."

"And I mean it."

"Does your arm feel better?" I asked, leading us a different direction than my car.

"Where are we going?"

"Does your arm feel better?" I repeated.

"Yes. Why?"

As we rounded the corner to the motorcycle showroom, Peter's face lit up.

I gestured toward the showroom that was built of glass and housed most models of the BMW line. "That's why."

"This is the motorcycle showroom?"

I knew it had been several months since he'd been on the back of a bike. The doctor had given him the all-clear to ride again. Maybe not jump, yet, but I knew he could at least ride one.

"It is." I smirked, leading him inside.

"What does that look mean, Dolly?"

"What look?" I shrugged my shoulders and smiled.

His eyes narrowed. "You're up to something."

"Oh, trust me, Mr. Fontenot, I want to be up to something." I moved closer and whispered. "Or rather on top of something."

He laughed, the sound glorious to my ears as it echoed through the vast showroom.

"Pick one," I said, waving my arm out toward the showroom floor.

"What are you talking about?" He glanced back at me as he walked through the motorcycles.

"Pick one," I repeated. "Any bike. And we'll take it for a ride."

He jerked to a stop and stared at me, eyes wide. "Are you serious?"

"Very."

He smiled, but his expression still showed reluctance.

"The doctor said you're good to go, to ride I mean, right?"

"Yeah," he said cautiously, "but…"

"Just no jumping today, though. Okay?"

"Are you sure? I don't want to worry you."

I grinned, knowing how much he was willing to sacrifice for me. "I'm sure."

"I can really pick any bike I want?" He looked like a kid let loose in a candy store.

"Yep." I nodded.

"Hey, Dana," a deep voice called from behind me.

I turned and saw Emo Alcott, the manager of our motorcycle division standing close.

The man was tatted up from head to toe with more piercings than a pincushion. At first, Uncle Nic had been reluctant to hire him, fearing the elitist BMW bike enthusiasts would be turned off by his dastardly appearance. Little did they know, Emo was a pussycat despite his six-foot-four, two hundred and fifty pound frame.

Emo knew his way around motorcycles, inside and out, and that was a concrete must in this industry. Plus, he knew the business side of the equation, and he had a knack for making you feel at ease. I'd witnessed him teach even the sketchiest of people how to ride a motorcycle.

"Hey, Emo, what's up?" I said.

"Trying to look like I'm working hard, now that the owner is here." He laughed. "What are you up to, little bit? Getting into trouble, no doubt," he teased with a shameless grin.

"We're just out and about. I wanted Peter to choose a motorcycle to take out for a Sunday stroll."

"I hate to break it to you, boss lady," he winked, "but it's Wednesday."

"Oh, shit. I guess we're screwed."

Emo and I both broke out into laughter.

I motioned toward Peter who was gawking at one of the BMW Sport bike models. I knew these bikes could top out at over 200 miles per hour. Maybe I shouldn't have brought him here, I thought.

"Emo, this is Peter."

Peter lifted his head.

"Ah, Dana's man toy I've heard so much about." Emo studied Peter from head to toe, chuckling under his breath.

I punched his arm, knowing it did no good.

"Watch it, Kung Fu momma," he said. "Your oriental bullshit fighting moves won't work on me."

"I bet I could take you down, asshole."

"Girl, I've seen you fight, and I have no doubt that you could."

"She is pretty feisty." Peter chuckled as he made his way toward us.

"I see you know her well," Emo said.

"Hi, I'm Peter Fontenot." Peter extended his hand, not seeming at all intimidated by Emo.

"Yes, I know who you are." Emo shook his hand. "Three-time X Games gold medalist, two-time Moto X Speed and Style World Champion and current reigning Freestyle U.S. Champion."

I stood still as Emo rattled off Peter's titles. Thanks to Luis, I'd heard them all before. I was proud for Peter, for what he'd accomplished in such a short amount of time. But how could I possibly ask him to never compete again?

"Which one do you want to take?" Emo asked.

Peter's eyes went wide. "Are you serious?"

"If little bit says so," he nodded toward me, "then I've got to follow boss's orders."

I laughed, knowing I was the last person who'd ever give Emo orders.

"I don't know," Peter sighed, perusing the vast showroom. "There are so many. Which one would you recommend?"

"Well," Emo said, "I've always been partial to the Roadster series. But considering you'll be carrying our little lady here, she'll probably be safer on something from our Touring series."

"How about the K 1600 GT?" Peter said.

"Perfect! Meet me around back and I'll have it gassed up and ready to go in about ten minutes."

Peter took my hand in his, intertwining our fingers as we strolled through the showroom. He was smirking, and my girl parts tingled in anticipation.

"What are you up to?"

"Nothing." His smile grew.

"Why don't I believe you?"

"Because you're a born skeptic."

"I am not." Well, not all the time.

He spun me around like a dancer until my chest was flush with his, then leaned his head down. "And because you love me," he whispered, brushing my ear with his lips. The heat of his breath on my skin sent shivers over my body.

"Get a room!" one of the salesmen shouted from the loft upstairs.

I draped one hand around Peter's neck and pulled him closer. "I've already got one," I murmured against his lips just before I kissed him.

Slipping both his hands around me, he returned the kiss with more fervor than I'd felt in weeks.

The catcalls and whistles from the guys in the showroom echoed throughout the large space.

Lifting my free hand in the air, I shot them all the bird, happy that they all knew I'd finally found my soul mate.

CHAPTER 14

DANA

"Turn here." I pointed to a small dirt turnoff.

Peter maneuvered the motorcycle with all the grace and style of any seasoned rider as he pulled to a stop. I gripped his waist tighter, loving the feeling of my body pressed against his.

"Where are we?"

I didn't answer, merely pointed to the keypad sitting in front of the familiar gate. "The code is one-two-one-five," I said.

Peter reached out to punch in the numbers but stopped and turned to look at me over his shoulder. "Isn't that your birthday?"

Oh, crap. I forgot he was a stickler about security. "It's Sam's birthday."

His eyes narrowed. "He's your twin."

I shrugged.

Peter shook his head and mumbled something about hard-headed Italians before punching in the code.

"Just follow the road until it ends," I said as the gate swung open.

He drove us down the long, winding path, stopping when we reached the cliff's edge. The spot overlooked the hills of central Texas with the river running below.

The property was amazing, with breathtaking views from almost every direction. Sam and I had enjoyed the land as children, but after my parents' death, I rarely visited.

After we came to a stop, Peter held my arm steady and I climbed off the bike. He exited with much more grace than I had.

He unbuckled his helmet and pulled it off, shaking his head before wiping his brow with his forearm.

His movements were slow motion, like a scene from a movie, in my mind. Good God, the man really *was* Sex-on-a-Stick, and way too hot for mere mortals like me. Desire burned low in my belly and I blew out a breath, steaming up the inside of my visor.

Peter placed his helmet on top of the seat before reaching under my chin and gently unclasping mine. He slowly tugged it off, careful not to pull my hair. The smile on his face was brighter than the midday sun overhead.

Cool wind swept across my face and I drew in a deep breath. Closing my eyes, I tilted my head back and basked in the warmth of the sun. This place, this time with Peter, was heaven to me. Anytime I came to my family's land, I always felt my parents' presence. Today was no different.

"Where are we?" Peter asked, his gentle voice breaking through my thoughts.

My lids fluttered open and my gaze fell onto his beautiful face. His eyes sparkled in the afternoon sun, the colors more intense than I'd ever seen. I could get lost in this man. Truthfully, I already had.

I stared out over the cliff, remembering all the times we'd visited the property as children.

"This was my parents'," I finally said, not wanting to reveal more. I was surprised when he remained silent.

Maybe he could feel the sacredness of this place too.

"Come on." I held out my hand, leading him to the cliff's edge. The river below was running slow.

Peter surveyed the area, seeming to take in every nuance.

"This land belonged to my parents," I said, my gaze fixed on the canyon facing us. "My mother loved the water but couldn't swim, so my father chose this piece of property. He wanted to give her the view of the lake, without the fear of falling in."

I laughed out loud at the absurdity. Her falling over the precipice of this high cliff and plunging to her death below was much more cause for alarm than being yards away from the running river. That was my father, though. He would have done anything for my mother, or for Sam. Or me.

Hot tears stung the back of my eyes and I squeezed my eyes shut to keep them at bay. This was why I rarely visited my parents' property. It brought back too many memories. This land was a reminder of what I was missing in my life.

Peter squeezed my hand, bringing me back to the present.

I gazed up at him and smiled before taking in the scenery, staring out over the sprawling Texas hills. The view was breathtaking. It was time I opened up to this man.

"My father purchased this land to build a new home for my mom," I explained, more to myself than Peter, caught up in my own memories. "They'd already started drafting the plans when my parents were killed." The lump in my throat grew larger but I pushed past the emotions that were beginning to choke me.

Peter moved closer, somehow sensing I needed his strength.

"People told me to sell the land after they died," I continued. "It's premium property and I could have made a shitload of money. I even talked to Hindley's father since he's a real estate investor."

I thought back to those dark times after my parents' deaths. It had been so long since I'd thought about this land and the house my father had dreamed of building after they retired.

I prayed for strength now, asking my parents for the wisdom and the courage I would need if I truly wanted to open up to Peter.

I'd brought him here for one reason—to meet my parents. This was where they lived now. This was where their souls rested, not in some earth-filled hole on the side of a freeway called a cemetery. Every time I came to this property, I felt my parents' presence deep within me. They'd left me physically, but never spiritually, and for that I was never more grateful than today.

"I can feel them," Peter whispered.

I turned at the sound of his voice, not surprised to see him standing a few feet away from me with his eyes closed.

There was no doubt in my mind, Peter was in the presence of my mother and father, and the idea seemed to give him peace as well.

"They live here," I said quietly. "Their spirits, I mean."

He nodded in understanding.

We stood in peaceful silence for a long moment, surrounded by my parents' love.

"I brought you here to meet them, Peter. I knew they would want to meet you."

"It's a good thing." He smiled, cutting his gaze toward me.

"Why?" His statement frightened me.

"I'm in your life now," he said, as if it were all that simple. And maybe it was. He closed his eyes again and stared up at the sky. I couldn't help but wonder if he could hear my parents speaking like I did when I came to this sacred spot.

The breeze picked up and the sounds of the rustling weeds reminded me of running through the field with Sam as a child. If I concentrated hard enough, I could almost smell my father's after-shave and my mother's floral perfume. God, I missed them, every day of my life, and suddenly, I realized why I didn't come here very often. It hurt too much to be so close to them and yet so far away.

No longer able to bear the distance between us, I walked toward Peter, pressing my chest to his back and slipping my arms around his waist.

Gradually, our breathing matched one another's. His hands slid over mine, intertwining our fingers. I knew it was crazy, but I could *feel* my parents smiling down on me, even though I couldn't see them.

The moment was perfect, something I'd dreamt about for years, bringing the man I loved here to meet my parents.

Peter had talked about forever with me, hinting that was the way he felt, but I didn't want to push him. Not after what we'd been through over the past week. We had to get this situation with the dealership under control before he and I could start planning a life together. But it was something I looked forward to with all my heart —a future with Peter. I just prayed it was what he wanted too.

We still hadn't discussed the issue of children yet, or rather my inability to give him any. Even though he'd assured me that wasn't why he'd left, I still worried. We would have to sort it all out.

Standing here holding him now, I let go of all the fears I'd carried for so long. This felt right. Peter was my destiny, he was my future, and from the depths of my soul, I begged my parents to help us work through all these issues before us.

"I think they like me," Peter whispered.

"Who?" I asked, not sure if he was fully aware of the sanctity this hallowed ground held for me.

Peter laughed and turned to face me. His hands slid up my arms to the curve of my neck before he sunk his fingers into my hair. His thumbs caressed my jaw. "Your parents, Dolly."

I smiled. "I think you have it wrong. They don't like you."

He frowned. "Why?"

"I think they love you. Just like I do."

He bent lower, pulling my face to his.

I closed my eyes in anticipation of his kiss. When one never came, I opened my eyes, surprised to find him lowering himself to the ground.

Onto one knee.

One knee?

Wait. Oh, shit.

Oh, holy fucking shit!

CHAPTER 15

DANA

I WORKED to calm my breathing. This could not be happening. Not now. Not here.

Peter reached into his pocket and my hands shook when he pulled out a small, red velvet box.

Fuck! This was it. He was proposing. And I was going to pass out.

"Dana," Peter said quietly, gazing up at me, "since I met you, I've come alive."

I forced myself to inhale deeply and exhale slowly before I passed out.

His eyes were beaming, his face filled with a kind of joy I'd never seen.

"I'll admit," he continued, "when I first met you, I wasn't impressed."

What the fuck?

I stepped back, shocked by what he'd just said. Shouldn't he be showering me with words of adoration?

I propped my hands on my hips. "Well, I wasn't really that fucking fond of you either if you want to know the truth."

Peter's head fell back and he roared with laughter, the sound echoing around us. "And that right there, Dolly," he said, staring up at me, "that's exactly the reason I love you."

I love you?

He loved me. But why?

I was crass, crude, selfish and uncouth. Why on earth would this sophisticated, refined, educated man want me?

"Your mouth." He answered my silent question as his gaze locked on my lips.

My pulse raced, heat spreading up my body.

"It's the most sinful, seductive, glorious thing I've ever seen in my life. And I know without a doubt, I can't live without it. I can't live without *you*."

Tears pricked my eyes as his words took root in my heart.

"I thought I knew what I wanted in a wife," he said. "Until I ran into you. Literally."

We both laughed at the remembrance of our first meeting in the concession line.

"You're nothing like I thought you'd be, Dana Adele Di Grazio. But now that I know you, the *real* you, I realize not only are you everything I want, you're everything I *need*."

My heart hammered in my chest. My chin quivered and I bit my lip to keep from crying. I didn't want to ruin this moment.

"Leaving the way I did," he said, "without telling you how much you meant to me, how much I love you, was unforgivable. And yet you have. My need for you, my need to protect you, consumes me."

I reached out a trembling hand and took his free one in mine.

"Even my mother saw how much you meant to me," he said. "That's why she gave me this." He released my hand and opened the velvet box. "This was my grandmother's wedding ring."

I stared down. Inside was one of the most exquisite pieces of jewelry I'd ever seen. It was indeed a ring, but not a normal engagement ring like most chicks expect. Oh, shit. Maybe this wasn't an engagement ring. Had I gotten this all wrong?

"This was my grandma Al's wedding ring," he said. "My grandpa had it designed especially for her on their twenty-fifth wedding anniversary."

The silver band was fashioned in two rows of leaves, each inlayed with diamonds and rubies that sparkled in the sun. It was the most beautiful piece of jewelry I had ever seen.

"My grandmother and I were very close," he said. "She was a rebel like you, a free spirit, ahead of her time in many ways."

I smiled, thinking of Peter's grandmother. I hoped she would have liked me.

"My grandma Al had been against my parents' marriage, but in the Mormon Church, women's opinions don't hold much value."

"That's fucked up," I said, not able to hold back.

He laughed. "Yeah, it is. I didn't realize it until I went back to Utah, but my mother had been caught in a trap, forced to marry a man she didn't love. Now that my father is gone, she's finally free to pursue her own dreams and her own love. It's the life I know Grandma Al always desired for my mother."

"Peter, this is a treasured heirloom. I can't take—"

"Let me finish, Dolly."

I bit my lips and smiled. Dominant Peter was out, and I liked him. I nodded for him to continue.

"Unlike some Mormon couples, my grandparents were actually in love when they married. They truly were my role models for how I wanted to fashion my marriage. My grandfather said the rubies in the band symbolized the blood, sweat and tears they'd put into making their marriage successful over the years. He always said, 'An easy love isn't real love. It's infatuation. Real love takes hard work and a lot of forgiveness.'"

I smiled, knowing his grandfather's words were very true.

"Shortly after their fiftieth anniversary my grandfather died."

"Oh, Peter." I cupped his cheek, kneeling in front of him. "I'm so sorry."

"My grandmother took this ring off the day he died. She said she couldn't wear it anymore. The band reminded her too much of him, too much of the love they shared and the love she lost. She kept it though. For me."

Oh, fuck. This truly was a treasured heirloom, and I knew I wasn't worthy of accepting it now that I knew the story.

"She always told me that I was destined for more in this life, more than just being a law-abiding Mormon, taking over my father's company and marrying a subservient wife. She wanted me to have the ring, to give it to the love of my life. To show her how hard I was willing to work to make our love last. Not an easy love, but a real love."

Although the sentiment was wonderful, my smile faltered. Had he given this ring to Jillian already?

"I never gave it to Jillian," Peter said. "My grandmother had been against my marriage to Jillian from the start, but I was trying to do right by my parents, going against my grandmother's advice. I never even thought to ask Grandma Al for her ring when I proposed to Jillian. Two months after Jillian and I married, Grandma Al died," he said quietly.

I nestled closer, running my hand up his arm and squeezing his shoulder. I wanted to protect him and comfort him as he always did me.

"I didn't know it at the time," he continued, "but my grand-mother gave my mother this ring on her deathbed with explicit instructions to give it to me when I finally met the love of my life. My mother, of course, was taken aback, given the fact that I'd just married Jillian. But I think somewhere deep down inside, even my mother knew Jillian wasn't my life-long love."

"Just an easy love?" I asked.

He shook his head. "Not even that I don't think. Anyway, my mom was a rebel too, she'd just gotten her spirit beaten down some-where over the years of her own marriage. My father had a way of doing that to people without them even realizing it."

Peter's story was breaking my heart and I feared I wouldn't be able to hear the rest of it. I waited patiently though, knowing he needed to finish.

"When I went back to Utah recently, my mother saw it in my eyes. In my entire being."

"Saw what?"

"That I'd finally met my soul mate."

The tears were back, pooling quickly.

"She gave me my grandmother's wedding band, no questions asked. I'd actually forgotten about the ring, assuming that perhaps they'd buried my grandmother with it."

Tears spilled down my cheeks but I willed myself to remain silent.

Peter reached out and wiped them away before handing the box to me. "This ring is for you, Dana."

I stared down at the ring again. Now that I knew the meaning behind it, I was in awe.

"And this is also for you," he said, removing an envelope from his back pocket. "From my grandmother."

A note from his grandmother? This was too much. My heart beat so fast I feared I might pass out at my own proposal.

"She wanted me to give it to the woman I chose to spend the rest of my life with. That woman is you, Dana. I want to be with you. Always."

I pressed a hand to my lips to silence the sobs threatening to burst free.

"You don't have to answer now. I want you to read Grandma Al's letter first."

"What does it say?" I stuttered through tears.

He shrugged. "I have no idea."

"Now?" I asked.

He held out the envelope. On it, in beautiful script lettering, two words were written.

The One.

"Oh, God, Peter," I said, looking up at him as I hiccupped a sob. "The One? I'm the one?"

He grinned with amusement. "You know you are, Dolly."

"I don't know." I rubbed the back of my neck, fighting off the fear of inadequacy inside me. "I don't know if I can do this."

He recoiled, his face marred with grief.

Oh, shit. I was really fucking this up.

"No, no, no," I said, clutching his shoulders. "I didn't mean it like that. I love you and I want to be with you too. I don't know. It's just that…"

I drew in a deep breath, trying to slow my racing thoughts. How could I explain these fears to the man who wanted to spend the rest of his life with me?

"Peter," I whispered, "what about children? I know they mean so much to you. How can you sit here and give this to *me* knowing what I can't give *you*?"

"Dana," he said, placing his hand on my stomach, "children aren't born here."

I stared down at his palm as it moved over my stomach and up to my chest, stopping between my breasts. "They're born here." His eyes found mine. "In your heart."

I swallowed hard, trying to hold on to the last shred of dignity I had before completely breaking down.

Heat radiated through my body as his palm pressed into me.

"Creating life starts in your heart, not in your uterus. As long as we have love between us, we'll figure out a way. You are 'The One,' Dana. My once-in-a-lifetime, real love."

He held out the envelope. My fingers trembled as I cautiously took it from his hand.

I turned the letter over and broke the seal. Inside was a neatly folded card that I carefully withdrew. The thick paper was monogramed with the initials *AVG*, his grandmother's, I assumed.

Peter remained silent but nodded for me to continue.

More tears welled in my eyes. I wiped them away with the back of my hand so that I could read the note.

My Dearest Love,

If you're reading this note, it is because my grandson has chosen to spend the remainder of his life with you. That is a high compliment, to say the least. Peter is the most amazing man I've ever known. He has a huge heart and desires true love like no one I've ever known, except my late husband. Even as a small child, while other boys dreamed of becoming famous sports figures and rock stars, the only thing Peter desired was finding his one true *love, like his grandfather and I found in each other.*

Please take this ring, my ring, and wear it, knowing it was given to you with the same adoration and devotion it was given to me. You are Peter's love of a lifetime I have no doubt, and my only regret is I was never able to meet you. I know you must be an exceptional woman to gain the love of my beautiful grandson.

Know that I will always be with you both, to watch over you and your children, to protect you and guide you, wherever life leads your family. Love Peter the way he deserves, the way I loved his grandfather. I know beyond the shadow of a doubt if Peter has given you this note and my ring, you truly are The One, *the* true *love of his lifetime. And he will love you for the rest of yours.*

All my best with love and kisses,

. . .

Grandma Alberta

I clutched the note to my chest and fell into Peter's waiting arms. My body convulsed with sobs, happy tears, that I'm sure would stain his shirt, but I didn't care. I needed this man—to support me, emotionally and figuratively. And according to his grandmother, he needed me too. What an amazing, fearless woman she must have been.

When my sobbing slowed to a few hiccups, I released Peter and leaned back. Gazing up at his beautiful eyes that were glazed with tears, I began to doubt myself.

"Are you sure?" My voice cracked. "Your grandmother says I'm the one. Your *true* love."

Peter smiled and drew me near. "Do you remember that day when we were at your condo and Hindley and Rory were leaving for their get-away weekend?"

I nodded, not sure where he was going with this question.

"The doctor wanted me to stay in Austin to do my rehab. He said it would take at least three weeks. Do you remember what you said to me when I asked if I could stay with you?"

I laughed, remembering what a shit I'd been that day—really all the days in the first few weeks Peter stayed with me. I'd been trying to protect my heart from him, but obviously I had failed.

"You told me to go where I thought I need to be," he said. "And do you remember what I said?"

I grinned at the memory, the scene forever etched in my mind. It was the first time I truly believed that Peter wanted to be with me, just for me—crassness, dirty mouth, short temper and all.

"I said I was right where I needed to be, with you, and I meant it, Dolly. From that moment on, there's never been a doubt in my mind that you are my one *true* love."

My eyes stung with tears again.

He wrapped an arm around me. "Everything I've done since

then has been to show you how much I love you. I know I've done a piss-poor job of it, but if you'll give me another chance, I promise to never let you forget how much you mean to me."

Well, fuck me. His words had to be the sweetest, most romantic thing I'd ever heard in my life.

I exhaled a heavy breath, reeling from his revelations.

He pulled the ring out of the box and held it in front of my hand. The diamonds and rubies shimmered in the late afternoon sun.

"This is for you," he said, no question or hesitation in his voice. "It represents the love my grandparents had for one another, the same love I always dreamed of having for myself and my wife one day."

My gaze moved from the ring up to Peter's eyes.

"I've found that love in you, Dana." His deep voice sounded raspy and cracked with emotion. "Will you marry me?"

"Yes," I said, throwing my arms around his neck. "Yes! I'll marry you, Peter. You're the love of my life too."

He kissed my neck, then my throat, then my cheek.

I turned and my lips found his. "Yes," I grinned, "yes. A thousand times. Yes."

He laughed and pulled away. "So, you're saying yes?"

I nodded, smiling like an idiot.

He picked up my hand and slipped his grandmother's ring on my finger.

"It's a perfect fit." He grinned, raising my hand up to his lips, gently caressing each knuckle.

"You didn't have it sized?"

He shook his head. "Nope."

I stared down at the gorgeous ring, surprised how well it suited me.

"It doesn't surprise me that it fits. You remind me of her so much, in so many different ways."

"How so?"

"You are both fearless," he said. "And you speak your own mind no matter the consequences."

"Did she curse?"

"No." He laughed. "In that you were different."

I glanced up. "Your mother gave you the ring when you were home?"

He nodded. "It seems that my mother has also fallen in love since I've been gone."

"With AJ?" I asked, remembering Peter's statement from a few days before.

"Yes. He's a widower too. Truth be told, I think he's always loved my mother from afar. I'm very happy for her. She's changed."

I studied Peter's face and could see a difference in his countenance as he talked about his mother. His expression was no longer riddled with animosity or bitterness, but admiration and empathy.

"And somehow she knew I was the one for you? That you should give your grandmother's ring to me?"

His smile broadened. "Yes."

"Will I get to meet your mother, now that you've kind of patched things up?"

"Eventually," he said, tugging me into his arms. He lowered me down to the ground, which wasn't difficult since we were both still on our knees. "Right now, I have other plans for you, Dolly."

I lay on my back and he nestled between my thighs, fitting me perfectly. I held up my left hand and gazed at the ring. The stones twinkled and I couldn't help but feel surrounded by love.

"Dolly," he whispered against my lips.

"Mmm?" I murmured, my attention focused on the exquisite piece of jewelry.

"Do you want to stare at that ring for the rest of the evening or do you want to," he paused, "hmm, how is it that you say it? Oh, yes." He laughed. "Do you want me to fuck you into tomorrow?"

I giggled at his crude words. They sounded so odd coming out of Peter's mouth.

As I gazed into his mismatched eyes, sparkling from last rays of the setting sun, I realized Peter and I were a lot like his eyes. Completely different in so many ways, but when brought together by fate, a unique fit, unlike any other two people on earth.

"Actually, it's 'fuck you halfway into next week'," I snorted, running my palms along his scruffy jaw. "But no. Not today."

He cocked his head and his brows wrinkled. "Why?"

"I think tonight I want to make love to you, Peter. Make love *with* you," I whispered, raising my head up slightly until our lips met.

Finally, I was home. And just like that I was lost in Peter Fontenot all over again.

Grandma Al was right. I was his one *true* love. And he was mine.

CHAPTER 16

PETER

DANA RUSHED AROUND THE CONDO, fluffing pillows and straightening photo frames on the walls.

The representative from the foster-to-adoption agency was due any minute and she was a nervous wreck. I couldn't help but feel sorry for her, no matter how much I'd already reassured her that our meeting would go well.

Dana accepted my grandmother's ring, but under one stipulation. She insisted we talk about children before she'd even discuss a wedding date. She knew how important children were to me and what an integral part they'd played in my dreams for the future.

The reality of it all was, the only dream I had now was being with Dana, forever. She truly was *The One,* just as my grandmother had foretold. I assured Dana that no matter what happened, whether we adopted, had a surrogate, or just chose to be a loving aunt and uncle to our future nieces and nephews, the only thing that mattered to me was being with her.

Over the next few days, we'd talked about all our options and decided adoption was best for us. But not just any type of adoption. Dana and I both agreed there were too many unwanted children in the world that needed a 'Forever Home,' as the adoption agency called it.

The paperwork had been rather painless and we'd breezed through the interviews. The agency was a little concerned that I didn't have a permanent Texas residence. We assured them of our intent to marry, even though we had yet to establish a firm date. I would have married Dana tomorrow but I knew she needed time to acclimate to the idea of vowing ourselves to one another forever. She trusted me. I knew that without a doubt, but she was wounded. And like all injured souls, she needed time.

The chime of the doorbell interrupted my thoughts. I stared over at Dana, her bright blue eyes the size of a full moon.

"Shit, Peter. What am I going to do? This place is still a mess."

I glanced around the living room, thinking I'd never seen it cleaner since I'd been living with her.

"First of all," I said, moving toward her, "you're going to calm down and be yourself." I took her small hands in mine as I led her toward the door.

"But this is a high-rise condo," she said. "I don't even have a backyard. And I'm crass and rude. I'll probably drop a shit-ton of f-bombs right in front of this chick before she even sits down. She's never going to let us have a child, and it will be all my fault."

I silently laughed at her nervousness, knowing if I did it out loud I'd probably get one of her martial art kicks to the groin. I'd never seen her like this before, so anxious and self-doubting. For some reason, the sight amused me. I couldn't stifle my emotions any longer and a small laugh escaped.

"This isn't funny, Peter." She yanked her hands from mine. "This is for real. If she hates me, if she hates us, or our home, she'll deny us on the spot."

She really was afraid we'd be denied. Suddenly I felt ashamed for laughing at her.

"That's not how it works, Dolly," I assured her, wrapping my arms around her narrow waist and drawing her in for an encouraging peck on the lips.

She pushed me away. "This isn't the time, Peter."

"Dana," I grasped both her shoulders, "stop this."

Her body stiffened and part of me worried I'd overstepped my bounds. The look of panic in her eyes reminded me that my only job now was to soothe her. I needed to help her understand that no matter what this agency and the State of Texas decided, they would all be insane not to allow her to be a child's mother. This wasn't the only way to have a family.

"You are the most loving, nurturing person I know," I said. "This isn't the only agency out there. You won't screw this up. But if they find some flaw in us, we'll just find another agency. If you want to," I added.

There was a tightness in her expression that I hadn't seen before. "Of course, I want to, Peter. I've always wanted to be a mom. And you," she smiled, "you'll be the most amazing father. Any child would be so lucky to call you Daddy."

Her words of affirmation were almost my undoing. I swallowed down my emotions. "I feel the same way about you, Dolly." I drew her tight into my chest, caressing her hair as I tried to reassure her. Reassure us both.

The doorbell chimed again and we stepped back from one another.

I gazed down at her, my heart seizing with love. "Let's do this, Dolly. Let's go get us a baby."

A small spread across her cheeks, deep dimples on display. She nodded once and turned to face the door, walking purposefully toward our future.

Dana made me a better person, a better man. My one true desire was to give her this, the opportunity to shower a child—our child—with love and affection. I wanted this representative to see that Dana and I loved one another unconditionally. All we wanted now was to share that love with another human being who needed us just as much as we needed them.

"Well, I think I've got everything I need," the representative from the agency announced, closing her folder and pulling off her glasses. "We've got the home visit knocked out so I'd say you're well on your way through this process."

Dana and I had met her once before, a few weeks ago, when we'd first filled out the adoption paperwork. Jane had been assigned as our 'adoption specialist,' as they called it at the agency. To me, she was the gatekeeper to fulfilling our dreams of becoming parents.

"I just have a few concerns," she said.

My heart skipped a beat. A few concerns? I panicked. This could mean the difference between having a child, and destroying Dana's dreams. And mine.

"What kind of concerns?" I asked, trying to hide my anxiety. I didn't want Dana to worry anymore than she already was.

"Well, first," Jane began, "Peter, you're a motocross rider, correct?"

"Yes," I answered, not fully understanding where she was going with this line of questioning.

"That means you're on the road," she said, "a lot."

Now I knew exactly what Jane was insinuating. I knew where my professional future was headed, but I had yet to share my dreams with Dana. And I certainly wasn't going to do that now. Not in front of Jane.

"He's still in rehab," Dana said.

Jane nodded and I thought we were in the clear. "What happens when your rehab is over and you begin to compete again?" she asked.

"I don't know," I said, because I really didn't at this point. "I have some plans, but Dana and I don't have any permanent ones."

Out of the corner of my eye, I saw Dana's head snap in my direction.

"That could be a problem," Jane said.

I frowned. "I don't see how. Surely your clients can't possibly know what their future holds when they choose to adopt. Our case is no different. I can make plans all day long, but in reality, nothing is a given."

Jane thumped the folder and nodded.

"I can assure you though," I continued, "if we're fortunate enough to be allowed to care for a child, his or her well-being will be our top priority as a couple, not my career."

Jane smiled, hopefully in understanding. "Okay then."

I glanced at Dana who was beaming up at me, her dimples drilled in deeper than I'd ever seen them.

"There's also one other issue," Jane said. "I know you two aren't married, yet."

"But we're planning to," I answered quickly. I didn't know what else to say. I didn't have a time frame to give her. It was really up to Dana now.

"Soon," Dana added, peering up at me with the most loving smile that instantly warmed my heart, along with other parts of my anatomy. She was free. Dana's heart was completely mine.

Unable to stop myself, I pulled her tight against my chest and kissed the top of her head. I knew the action was completely inappropriate given our setting, but I didn't care. Dana had just given me the one gift I'd ever wanted in life—confirmation that she would become my wife, sooner rather than later.

"I'm not saying they *won't* approve you just because you're not married," Jane said. "It's just that, you don't have any shared assets. Something to show your commitment to one another, financially."

I stared at her in confusion. "Lots of married couples keep their finances separate."

She held up a hand. "I know, it sounds crazy, but that's what they look for. Anything to prove you are tied to each other, for the long haul. If you're not married, then joint assets are the next best thing."

"What are you saying? We need to open a joint checking account?" I joked.

"Well, yes. That would help, believe it or not."

"Done," Dana proclaimed.

Her statement surprised me. I'd always considered Dana such an independent person, and really believed that even after our wedding she would probably want to keep her assets separate. Especially considering the huge portion of the dealership she owned.

"We'll open one up this afternoon," Dana said, staring up at me. "Won't we?"

I didn't answer, knowing her question wasn't really a question but a statement.

"Peter?" Dana nudged me.

"Oh, uh, yes. This afternoon, for sure."

"That would be really helpful." Jane smiled. "Like I said, you're engaged and that's important, but if we had a date to put on the paperwork and some financial records to show you're joined with one another, that would help as well."

My throat went dry as I cringed in fear. Pushing Dana for a date wasn't the way to go and I feared Jane's announcement might actually paralyze her and cause Dana's walls to creep back up.

"I'm not trying to rush you," Jane assured, "I'm just saying, it adds to your chances. Not being married won't keep your application from being approved. I just want to give you the best possible chance I can and speed up the process."

Dana nodded, but her twisted fingers and bouncing knee revealed just how nervous she truly was.

"I know we've talked about this before," Jane went on, "you're both open to any age child, is that correct?"

"Yes," Dana answered quickly.

"And you're all right with a special needs child?" She looked at Dana. "Your brother has special needs, right?"

Dana smiled like the proud sister she was. "Yes."

Selecting a special needs child had been an option on the application. Dana hadn't hesitated to select it. She knew how much Sam needed her. She said she didn't want to leave a child in foster care who believed they were unwanted or unloved just because they couldn't function at the same level as other kids. She always said, "Special needs means special love." And she had a lot of that to give.

"Sounds good then," Jane said, shoving the folder back into her bag before standing.

Dana and I rose from the sofa.

"The house looks great," Jane said, glancing around, "and you've got a nice size bedroom that could accommodate a child."

"Really?" Dana asked in surprise.

"Yes. Why? Did you think your home wouldn't pass?"

"Well, it's downtown, it doesn't have a yard. It's not your ideal spot for a kid, I guess."

I nudged Dana in the back, wondering why she was offering up such compromising information.

"I think the downtown area offers so many cultural opportunities for a child," Jane said. "Don't you?"

"Yes, I agree," I said, trying to dispel Dana's doubts.

"And there are plenty of parks in the city within walking distance of your house," Jane said. "I think your home is lovely and nurturing, just what a foster child needs."

Dana visibly sagged in relief. I hadn't realized how much stress she'd been holding on to until her body sank into mine.

"Don't worry, Dana," Jane assured, patting her shoulder. "This process may take a while, but I can tell you and Peter love one another immensely. That love will overflow to one lucky child very soon."

I gazed down at Dana, not surprised to see tears spilling down her face.

Jane reached out and took Dana in an embrace that spoke

volumes. She was silently giving Dana the reassurance that I couldn't.

"You'll make a wonderful mother, Dana," Jane proclaimed, gradually pulling away. "I'm sure of it."

Dana smiled through her tears and instantly, my own heart swelled at the joy radiating from deep within her.

Jane tossed her bag over her shoulder and walked toward the door. "I'll be in touch in a few days to let you know how the application is moving along. In the meantime, if you need anything, don't hesitate to call me. You've got my number, right?"

"Yes," Dana said softly.

"Good," Jane answered. "Don't worry, Dana. You're a wonderful woman and you have an exceptional home."

And just like that, Jane was gone, leaving me with a heaping, bawling mess of a woman. A woman who I knew would become my wife, and the mother of our child, hopefully very soon.

CHAPTER 17

PETER

"I LOVE YOU," Dana whispered in my ear as she sat curled in my lap.

"I love you too, sweetheart." I pushed her long hair over one shoulder and kissed her neck. "Please try not to worry. Whatever happens, happens."

"What if it doesn't happen?" she said, so softly I barely heard her. She traced an invisible pattern on my T-shirt and my heart clenched. Our pending approval had her doubting her abilities, as a wife, as a mother, as a person.

"Don't do this," I said, putting my finger under her chin and lifting her face, forcing her look at me.

"Do what?"

"Play the 'What-If' game. I hate that game. No one ever wins. We've done our best, that's all we can do."

She shrugged.

"Dana, you heard Jane. She loves us both and thinks we'll be great parents."

"Yeah," Dana sighed, staring up at me. Her blue eyes were filled with self-doubt that was so unlike her. "But she said we're not joined. Like financially, or by marriage."

"Dana, I'm not going to rush into anything with you just to help our adoption process along. When you're ready, we'll set a date. Until then, if the agency doesn't approve us solely based on that, then so be it. We'll try again later, after we're married and more vested in one another."

"I want to sell the dealership," she announced, completely changing the subject.

I jerked my head in surprise. "What are you talking about?"

"My Uncle Nic has worked so hard for so long. He deserves the profits, not me." She expelled a heavy breath, as if this were a weight she'd been holding on to for years.

I stared at her in disbelief.

"Plus," she went on, "if I sell it to him, then he can find someone to help him run it, someone who will be there on a daily basis so he can take more time off. With me having controlling interest, I know he feels like he can't do that right now. I know he feels obligated to me in some weird way, as if he still has to take care of me or something."

"Can he afford to buy you out?"

"Well, see, that's the thing," she answered sheepishly. Her finger resumed its path along my chest.

"What's the thing?"

"I kind of want to *give* it to him."

"What do you mean, 'give it to him?'" It was beyond me why she'd want to just hand over such a lucrative business. From a financial perspective, it made absolutely *no* sense.

Her hand stopped and she stared up at me. "You and I are about to start a life together. Aren't we?"

I grinned, my heart thumping hard at her announcement. I nodded, not wanting to interrupt her.

"What's mine is yours, and what's yours is mine," she said.

"Of course, but I don't understand what that has to do with selling your dealership."

"It was never *my* dealership, Peter. It was my father's. It was *his* love, *his* passion, not mine." She reached out her hand and lovingly stroked my face. "I've found my love. Now, I want to find *my* passion."

Her words humbled me. I knew even at the age of twenty-eight, Dana was still struggling to find her place in this world.

"I want to find something to do that I love," she said, "like you love freestyle motocross."

"Dana, I don't know if I'll go back to riding, especially if we adopt a child. I'll need to be here, with you and the baby."

"No," she corrected sternly, sitting up in my lap. "You're wrong. I want you to compete. I want you to pursue your passion. You have to," she said with such conviction and desperation it frightened me. "Otherwise, you'll grow to resent me, and I couldn't stand that, Peter."

"But what about you? What about our child?"

"That's just it."

I studied her, my brows furrowed, still confused.

"I've finally figured it out. Our child will be my passion. Our child already *is* my passion. That's why I'm so fucking nervous."

My breath hitched and my heart squeezed tight in my chest. I loved this woman, way more than I thought humanly possible.

She was such an amazing human being. Not only had she lost her parents as a teenager, she'd also battled cancer, cared for a special needs sibling, and tried to take on the responsibility of a major corporation. And now, she wanted to share her life and her love with a child who'd never had any. She was beyond amazing. I truly didn't deserve her.

"Those are the most beautiful words I've ever heard." I tugged her to me and squeezed her tight.

"They're true, Peter," she whispered. "Your happiness, our happiness, our child's happiness, *that* is what I want more than anything in my life." Pushing away from me, she gazed into my eyes with such sincerity.

I'd never loved anyone more in that moment than I did Dana Di Grazio.

"Sometimes, the baby and I can come on the road with you," she said. "Hindley and Rory do it just fine. Sometimes, we'll stay at home. We'll make it work, Peter. I don't want you to give up your dream. Please," she begged.

"Dolly, *you* are my dream," I said. "Creating a family with you has always been my dream, not motocross."

"Riding freestyle motocross is also your dream, Peter. Don't lie to me." Her expression dared me to deny my second love of motocross riding, and I was hard pressed not to.

Apparently, my face revealed what my words couldn't.

"See," she said, rubbing my jaw with her thumb. "This time you'll have someone who loves you *and* supports you on the sidelines. I promise. I may be scared shitless watching you compete. I may worry the entire time you're in the air. But in the end, I just want you to be happy. Riding makes you happy. The rest will work itself out."

I was about to correct her when she pressed a finger to my lips.

"That's the end of the discussion, Peter," she said, sounding like a scolding mother.

I couldn't help but smile.

Her finger slid down my lips and over my chin as she traced the line of my jaw. "I love you," she said, her face inching closer. "I want to be with you, to make you happy," she continued, "but I want *you* to be happy. Fulfilled in every way." She wiggled her hips against me.

I moaned, the aching in my mid-section almost unbearable.

"After all," she kissed me just under my chin, "isn't that my wifely duty?" She lifted herself up on the arms of the chair and twisted around until her legs were straddling my hips.

I wrapped my hands around her waist, pulling her against me so she could feel my desire.

"I love you," she whispered against my lips just before kissing me. The pressure of our contact was so tender, so loving, unlike our usual desperate exchanges. Suddenly I was lost in her kiss.

Her thighs clenched around mine as our mouths grew greedy, our tongues intertwining like our hearts and our lives. Her hands dug into my hair as they pulled my head against her mouth like she was starving for more.

I couldn't get enough of her either.

She moaned and rocked against me. Her sounds and movements were my undoing.

I cupped her bottom and lifted us from the chair, walking toward the fireplace. I slowly kneeled and lay us onto the soft rug.

"I love you," she said softly again.

Slowly undoing each button on her shirt, I smiled at the teal blue, lacy bra. "I love you too."

She laughed. "You just love my body."

I couldn't deny that her body truly was a wonderland. Her voluptuous breasts spilling over the bra had my head spinning. "I do love your body," I said, pressing a kiss against the swells of her breasts.

"Make love to me, Peter," she pleaded, her body already trembling with desire.

I stripped out of my jeans and shirt as Dana finished undressing.

I stood bare before her, physically and emotionally. For the first time in my life, I wasn't embarrassed or ashamed of my nakedness.

She gazed up at me. "God, you're beautiful," she confessed with a voice so loving it literally made my chest ache.

"So are you, Dolly." I laid on top of her and buried my face into her neck.

"Oh, Peter," she moaned.

I licked and sucked along the small divot at the base of her throat, moving along her collarbone.

"Right there," she panted. "God, right there."

I spread her legs further apart and drove my hips into hers.

"I want you so much," she said, wrapping her legs around me.

I knew she wanted me inside of her as much as I did, but she'd just declared something major to me and I wasn't going to rush us this time. I wanted to savor our lovemaking for the monumental moment that it was. We were now two people becoming one, creating a family that would last a lifetime.

I licked and sucked on the edge of her collarbone, knowing it was an erogenous spot for her.

She squirmed and begged, her cries for me nearly breaking my resolve to go slow.

Her arms slid around my shoulders, her nails gently stroking my back as they moved down toward my ass. She pulled me into her thighs, consumed with desire.

I lifted up on my hands and looked down at her lust-filled eyes. "You asked me to make love to you, Dolly, and that's what I intend to do."

"I changed my mind." She laughed, the sound vibrating against me.

"Well, change it back." I moved my mouth down to her breast. "I intend to take this slow, Dana."

She remained silent and I lifted my head, staring at her beautiful face.

She gazed up at me, reverence in her expression.

"*You* are my passion too, " I said.

Her eyes pooled with tears. The aqua-blue resembled a calm sea, but I knew we were both anxious.

I stroked her hair, pulling a stray lock from her face. "I promise to take care of you, your every need, for the rest of my life."

"Peter," she whispered, cupping the back of my neck. She tugged me down until our lips met. There was nothing slow about this kiss. It was filled with desire and need.

Dana's hands trailed over my shoulders and down my arms. "God, Peter, do you have any idea how magnificent you are?" she whispered.

I'd never had a sense of pride in my body, or in my skills as a lover, but with Dana, all that had changed. She loved me, she loved everything about me, and that made me a better person. There wasn't anything I wouldn't give to make her life complete.

I ran my hands up her thighs, my thumb tracing small circles as I moved closer to the juncture between her legs.

She trembled, tilting her hips toward my touch. "Peter," she moaned.

"Yes?"

"I think I'm going to orgasm and you haven't even touched me."

"Should I stop here, Dolly?" I asked, my fingers easing their path just inches away from where I knew she wanted.

"If you think you can stop, then yes. I'll do it myself." She smirked as she circled her nipples with her fingers, pinching at the distended nubs. "Oh," she moaned, her head tilting back.

Holy hell. My body involuntarily convulsed, and my hips pressed into hers.

"Are you about to come, Peter?" she asked in a sultry voice.

"Yes," I groaned through gritted teeth. My fingers moved to the sensitive flesh and she jolted beneath me. Batting her hand away, I sucked on one nipple.

"Oh, God," she growled, her hands roaming up and down my back. Her hips rocked against mine and I was nearly undone.

Unable to wait any longer, I slid inside her slick heat. Our hips moved in perfect rhythm, our bodies dancing to an erotic beat only we heard.

I braced myself with one hand above her, my other finding her pert nipple.

"Yes," she said, rocking against me.

I replaced my fingers with my mouth, moving from one breast to the other, and she tightened around me. Sliding one hand under her hips, I moved her to change the angle, pressing deeper.

"Oh, Peter, yes. Right there." She panted. "I'm so close."

"Come with me, Dolly," I whispered. "I love you. I need you."

"Oh, God," she cried as she drew closer. "I love you." Her legs gripped my waist tighter. "Peter!"

"Look at me, Dolly."

She opened her eyes and stared up at me.

I'd never seen anything more amazing in my life as she reached her peak. Everything I'd ever wanted was there in Dana's gaze. I couldn't wait to join myself to her in every way, for the rest of my life. Dana was my one *true* love.

Her body shuddered against me, her legs gripping me tight as she uttered intangible words.

My body shook and I threw back my head, roaring with a guttural cry as I found my own release.

After several moments, our bodies went lax. I sagged on top of her, breathing heavily, spent from our lovemaking. I was surprised that my elbow was nearly pain free.

Dana pushed back a lock of hair and smiled, her hand resting on her throat. "That was amazing."

"You're amazing." I kissed her lips, then her cheeks, but stopped when I saw my grandmother's wedding ring on Dana's finger.

She raised her hand, admiring the jewelry. "How would you like to spend forever with me?" she asked.

"That sounds fantastic."

"Fan-fucking-tastic?"

"Yeah, fan-fucking-tastic." I laughed.

She slid her hand around my neck and rubbed my jaw with her thumb. "I'm a bad influence on you."

"Probably."

"Want me to corrupt you more?" She waggled her eyes.

I couldn't imagine a life without Dana Di Grazio—foul-mouthed, ill-tempered and all. She would always be mine. Thank God.

CHAPTER 18

PETER

"So, what did you find out, Blake?" I spoke into the telephone. "Do you know who developed Dana's dealership's accounting software?"

Blake Forrester was one of the top software developers in my father's company. I'd asked him to research Dana's system as a favor to me. Thankfully, he hadn't batted an eye.

"Yeah, I do, Pete, and I don't think you're going to be happy."

"Why?"

"The coding says it was created by Vanguard and Associates."

I sucked in a breath, not really surprised by his revelation. Walter Vanguard, Jillian's father, had a very successful computer software company in Salt Lake.

"I should have known such a shoddy software program could only come from his company."

Anyone who was in the computer industry knew Jillian's father's company was flailing. What most of them didn't know was just how conniving and manipulative Walter could be, especially when he was in financial trouble. The fact that his company created Dana's software and now *her* company was experiencing losses didn't surprise me.

"AJ told me that Jillian came to visit your mom in the hospital and ran into you," Blake said.

"Yeah, she did."

"Oh, shit, man. How did that go?"

Blake was a trusted friend, one I'd missed when I'd chosen to break ties with my father's business.

"Not well I'm afraid," I said.

"AJ said Jillian told your girlfriend that you guys were still married."

I wasn't sure why AJ had shared so much information with Blake, but I trusted him, so I wasn't upset.

Blake had been with my father's company since I was in high school, seen me through all the troubles with Jillian, and never once judged me for leaving Salt Lake or my family. In my heart, I knew there was no doubt I could trust him. But my head was somewhat leery, especially now that the sale of our company was a real possibility.

I shrugged. "You know Jillian."

"She probably just wants money. As usual."

"What money?"

"From the sale of your family's company."

I held in my reaction, shocked that Blake knew so much.

"Don't worry, man. AJ already told the executive team that your mom wants to sell the company. I think it will be good for her. I know what's going on, so don't freak out."

"How could Jillian get money from me?" I asked, seriously confused.

"She's probably trying to wiggle her way back into your family. Acting like you two were still married so she could get her hands on the money you'll get from the sale of IP Software Group. Hell, I wouldn't put it past that crazy bitch to try to sleep with you just to get pregnant so she can have a little Fontenot heir."

Just the thought of touching Jillian made me sick to my stomach.

My mind raced. Why *had* Jillian showed up at my mother's hospital room? My mother said she and Jillian hadn't talked in years, and surprisingly that seemed just fine with her. I'd always assumed she liked Jillian but my mother's reaction to her presence at the hospital had been anything *but* welcoming.

"Rumor has it," Blake said, "Walter Vanguard is all kinds of bat shit crazy."

Having once had him as my father-in-law I could confirm that.

"People say he's desperate, scrambling to save his ass. He's in some kind of trouble. Some say he's even talked about buying your family's company. Isn't that a crock?"

"What?" I drew in a sharp breath. "You can't be serious."

"Totally serious. His company is in shambles right now. He's even been accused of embezzling from some pretty ruthless people, or so I've heard. And he has no money to make an official offer to buy your family's company."

I couldn't believe what Blake was telling me. I'd always known Walter Vanguard had been callous, but never criminal.

"Half of Salt Lake knows that man is a sinking ship," Blake said, "especially his business partners and family. How do you think that's going to look when stuck-up, self-righteous Mrs. Nealy Vanguard and her shithead daughter, Jillian, are cast to the curb by Salt Lake City's high society—and the Mormon Church—because their family has lost everything?"

"You really think Jillian coming to see my mom in the hospital is tied to the sale of our company?"

"Come on, Peter, I know you're naive and believe in true love and all that Cinderella shit, but you've got to see this for what it is."

"What is it?"

"Classic Jillian Vanguard manipulation."

I thought about Blake's observation for a few moments. Was I being naive?

"Don't worry, Peter. There's no way she can get her hands on your money, or her father for that matter. They probably just wanted to hit you up for a loan or something."

We both laughed. As if I'd help the Vanguards in any way.

"So, what about Dana's software?" I asked. "Walter's company being tied to it can't be a coincidence. Especially now that her dealership is missing funds."

"The software was developed years ago, back before you and Jillian were even married, so I'd say that part is a coincidence." I could hear the hesitation in his voice.

"But?"

"But…you can't ignore the facts." Blake was right. This had to be more than a coincidence. "When did Dana's CFO first start noticing the losses?"

"Just within the last quarter I think."

"You weren't even involved with Dana or her company back then."

"That's true."

"Walter's probably been skimming funds off the top for years, in small increments so the larger business owners wouldn't detect such small discrepancies. Companies like Dana's would probably just write them off. But I would think that any CFO worth his ivy league degree would have enough checks and balances in place to see this coming. Even with a corporation as large as Dana's. Who the hell is this Chase guy anyway?"

"That's a long story." I exhaled.

"Spill."

"Let's just say, I think his care and concern for the dealership runs much deeper than financially."

"Meaning?"

"Meaning, I think he has feelings for Dana."

"Ah," Blake laughed, "he wants into the boss's panties, huh?"

"Shut up!"

"Well, there's a whole other angle for us now."

"What?"

"Mr. CFO wants to screw the boss," he said, "boss gets a new boyfriend, Mr. CFO becomes disgruntled. Come on, Peter, it's classic true-crime TV material."

"True-crime TV? What does that mean?"

"You know, those television shows that investigate real murders, like *Dateline* or *Snapped* or *Killer Kids*. Usually it's the wife who poisons the husband because he's having an affair. Or it's the hubby who hacks up the wife because he wants life insurance money, *and* he's boning his assistant. Either way, it always involves sex and money. Your boy here, Mr. CFO, fits the classic tale for a true-crime television episode."

"For someone who holds a Ph.D. from Stanford, you surprise me, Blake."

"Why?"

"You watch true-crime television for starters."

"Just because I'm cerebral doesn't mean I can't watch trashy television. Come on, man, my mind needs a break from all that programming shit sometimes. You'd probably be surprised to know I watch MTV sometimes too."

I shook my head.

"Hey, I love me a good episode of *Teen Mom OG* or *Jersey Shore*. Oh, to be young and dumb again."

I laughed, not even remembering what it was like to be young.

"And who doesn't like a good cry over one of those cheesy Christmas movies on the Hallmark Channel. They even show them in July too."

"You hold a doctorate in computer science, Blake. I think that makes you a little bit smarter than a girl who purposely gets pregnant in high school just to be on television."

"Hey, don't judge my girls. They've had a hard life." He laughed.

"Whatever." I grinned. I could always count on Blake to lighten any dark mood.

"Anyone else you suspect at the dealership, besides your horny CFO?" he asked.

I rolled my eyes, fearing his description of Chase might be true. "I don't really know the employees that well. I think her uncle is a stand-up guy. He's stood by her after her parents' deaths. And she wants to sell the company to him."

"It makes sense, I guess. I mean, from what I've seen in their system, it's a pretty lucrative business. She stands to make a lot of money from the sale."

"Well—" I stifled my comment, not wanting to betray Dana's trust.

"What?"

"Dana and I are engaged now," I said, changing the subject.

"Holy shit! Are you serious?"

"Yes."

"Congrats, man." I could hear his enthusiasm through the phone. "Wait, does Jillian know?"

"I have no idea. Why?"

"Does CFO boy know?"

"Only my mom and AJ know right now. And you. But you can't tell anyone, Blake. Please, not just yet."

"You know your secret is safe with me, man."

And I did know. I could trust Blake. It was the reason I was sharing all of this information with him now.

"So why the hell did you tell me?" he asked. "I mean, I'm honored and all, but still. It sounds like it's something you're trying to keep under wraps."

"I know you. I trust you. You helped me through the whole ordeal with Jillian. I don't know, it's just, something doesn't feel right about this whole thing. I guess I wanted you to have all the facts so I could bounce ideas off of you. I can't let Dana get hurt."

"Well, you guys being engaged is definitely a deal changer."

"What do you mean?"

"Adds more motive for a true-crime television show. Now,

Jillian has some competition if she's trying to win back your affection, and your money."

"How?"

"Now there will be a new Mrs. Fontenot to get a cut in the sale of your company."

"We just got engaged. No one knows."

"Holy hell, man, Dana's not pregnant, is she?"

I stiffened at his question. There were a lot of things I would share with Blake to save Dana's company, but her medical history wasn't one of them.

"No." I swallowed back my emotions. "She's not pregnant." I purposely neglected to tell him we were looking at adoption. Maybe that could be another angle for Jillian to come from, but that was impossible. No one even knew about our decision to adopt yet, nor did they know we'd actually already met with an agency.

"Anyone else strike you as peculiar, someone with a motive?" Blake asked.

"I don't know if he would have a motive, but Dana and her cousin don't get along. It's as if he hates her or something, for no reason other than the fact that the dealership belongs to her. Dana says he's always felt a sense of entitlement even though he barely pulls in a twenty-hour work week."

"Holy hell, this is gonna be a great true-crime story now that we've got family involved. We'll keep the television viewers guessing the entire show. I should hang up and call the producers right now."

"Shut up, Blake. This isn't a *Dateline* story, or any other true-crime television show."

"How do you know?"

"For starters, there's no murder."

"True," Blake admitted, "you always have to have murder for a *Dateline* episode. So, what do you want me to do now?"

"Well, we definitely need to shut down Walter's software at the dealership."

"On it," he said. "Already got my guys nearly halfway through creating a new accounting system for them."

"We'll have to transfer her funds so Walter's company doesn't have access to any of the dealership's accounts."

"Yep, yep," he agreed.

"I'll meet with Dana and her uncle this afternoon and tell them what's going on."

"What about Mr. CFO who's hot and heavy for your fiancée?"

Fiancée.

God, it sounded amazing to hear that Dana was marked as mine.

"Peter?" Blake called out.

"Yeah, I'm here. I don't know about bringing in Chase just yet."

"Well, if you're gonna start switching around funds and changing software, you'll need to pull him in, eventually. Maybe you should bring him into this meeting, gauge his reaction."

"How?"

"Well, if he starts flipping out about the changes, that might mean he's worried because he's involved in something shady."

I sat back in my chair, trying to absorb Blake's comment.

"Or," he added.

"Or what?"

"Or, it could just mean that he's getting a woody for your girly and he has to adjust his dick." His uproarious laughter echoed through the phone.

The thought of any other man getting an erection because of illicit thoughts of Dana, especially Chase, who I knew she'd spent the night with, made me nuts. Dana was beautiful, beyond compare. Naturally, she was the source of many a man's fantasies. But she was mine now.

"Peter?" Blake said.

"I'm here."

"I'm sorry, man. That was uncool. I shouldn't have said that."

"It's all right. You're right. Dana is beautiful. Any man would have to be half dead not to notice her."

"Well, I think we're taking the right steps to ensure her company's financial well-being. Wherever this breach in her computer program is coming from, it won't continue with this new system. I guarantee it."

"Thanks, Blake. I really appreciate you working on this for me."

"No problem, man. You know I'd do anything for you or your family. Speaking of family," he added, "I heard you found out about AJ and your momma bumping uglies."

"What?"

"Bumping uglies, knockin' boots, dancing the horizontal mambo. You know, screwing each other's brains out."

"Blake!" I roared. The last thing I wanted to think about was AJ and my mother being intimate.

Blake laughed. "Ah, I'm just messing with you. I think it's great to see your momma happy. And if any man deserves joy in his life, it's AJ Rhyne, that's for sure."

"You're right, I am happy for them."

"And, I'm happy for you too, Peter," he added. "If anyone deserves true love, it's you."

I chuckled at his use of the term 'true love.' It had become a mantra for Dana and me.

"Keep an eye on Mr. CFO and cousin boy there on your end though," Blake said. "I'll watch Mr. Vanguard and his lovely viper of a daughter, Jillian, on my side."

"Thanks again, Blake, I really do appreciate it."

"No problem, man. I'll talk to ya soon."

"Okay, later," I replied as I ended the call.

I didn't want to think about anyone sabotaging Dana's company, least of all someone as close to her as her own cousin or Chase, a trusted friend. As much as I disliked Jillian and her father, it was hard for me to add them to the equation. But I was naive and always thought the best of people, until they proved me wrong and ruined my life, like Jillian Vanguard had.

CHAPTER 19

PETER

THE PHONE FELT like a fifty-pound weight in my hand. I didn't know why I thought talking to Jillian Vanguard would be a good idea. Blake had my mind reeling with ideas, and I needed answers.

Two things were certain. One, Walter Vanguard's company had created the computer accounting system for Dana's dealership—which meant he might have a hand in her business's losses. And two, Walter Vanguard had already proven himself as a cheat. Even his own business associates were on to him.

Blake's words rang through my head. He thought I was naive. Most people probably thought so. Maybe they were right. I tended to believe the good in people. Until one fateful night before my marriage ended.

It started with a cancelled college class. I would be forever grateful to the Economics professor who sent us home early that evening. Thinking back to that night, I had definitely been naive.

As I'd opened the door to Jillian's and my apartment, I smelled popcorn. For a second, I thought maybe she'd prepared us a special date night surprise, complete with a romantic movie and concessions. Then I remembered, she couldn't have because my brother

John was visiting us from Utah. Besides, she wouldn't be expecting me this early.

Entering the apartment, I stopped mid-step, paralyzed by the sight before me.

Instead of finding my brother sitting on the living room couch, I saw his bare ass pumping up and down. At first, I didn't know what to think. Maybe he was there with a girlfriend he'd brought with him. But as I walked further into the room, my heart stopped at the scene in front of me.

This was no nameless girl he was having sex with. It was my wife.

Jillian was spread eagle underneath him, her auburn hair spread across the cushions.

"More!" she shouted. "Harder. Give it to me harder, baby." Then, to my horror, she slapped him on the backside.

It took everything in my power not to become physically ill.

Everything after that was a blur. I must have shouted something because both of them jumped up from the couch and tried to cover their nakedness. I couldn't remember what I did next, I was just so overcome with grief and sorrow, to think my wife and my brother could do that to me. It was one of the lowest points of my life.

The shrill ring of my cell phone brought me back from my stroll down nightmare lane. I stared down at my phone and smiled, the memories of earlier erased. My fiancée's beautiful face lit up the screen.

God, I loved her.

Everything I had been through in my life had led me to her. As much as I wanted to hate Jillian, part of me had to be thankful that she screwed my brother. I was a weaker man back then and probably would have stayed in a loveless marriage just to save face.

"Hey, Dolly." I grinned as I answered the phone.

"Hey, hot stuff." She giggled. "What are you doing?"

"I'm at the dealership. Where are you?"

"I'm almost finished at the grocery store."

"Please tell me you're not cooking tonight."

"No, you are, sexy."

I lifted a silent thanks. Dana was many things, but a cook wasn't one of them.

"What's wrong?" she asked.

"Can you meet me at the dealership when you're done shopping? There are some things I need to share with you and Nic. Things that I just found out about."

"What things, Peter?" Her voice dropped, worry tainting her words.

"Jillian's father designed your computer software accounting system."

"Oh, shit!" she exclaimed. "Do you think he's the one who's been stealing from the dealership?"

"I'm not sure yet. We need to do some more investigating, switch software, transfer accounts."

"Oh my God, Peter," she cried, "how are we going to do all that? What if he takes all our money? What if the employees lose their jobs because we go bankrupt? What about Sam?"

"Dana," I interrupted, trying to stop her train of thought. "It's all right. We're putting steps in place to stop him. If this really is Walter, we'll put an end to it and call in the police."

"But how?" I could hear the fear in her voice.

"I already have my company working on a new accounting software program to replace Walter's. They should be done sometime within the next few days."

"*Your* company?" she asked.

Suddenly, it dawned on me. I'd never told her about my share in my father's company. Or the fact that it would soon be for sale.

"As in your *father's* company?"

"Yes, that company. It's a long story, Dolly. Why don't you meet me at the dealership? We'll go over all the changes with Nic, then I'll explain my family's business situation."

"Good or bad?" she asked.

"It's good, Dolly," I confessed with a smile. "All good."

"Good," she sighed.

"There is something I need to tell you though."

"Good or bad?"

"In between."

"Oh, shit." She paused for a few seconds then blew out a heavy sigh. "Okay, lay it on me."

"I need to call Jillian."

"As in your ex-wife, Jillian?"

"That's the one."

"Why the fuck are you going to call that bitch?"

I bit back a laugh. Dana made no qualms giving her opinion about someone she didn't like.

"I need Jillian to understand that we know her father may be involved in your company's losses."

"Why would that bitch care? You don't think she's involved too, do you?"

"Jillian isn't exactly the brightest bulb on the tree, Dolly."

She snorted.

"I don't think it's possible for her to even turn on a computer, much less do advanced coding in order to embezzle hundreds of thousands of dollars."

"So, you *do* think it's her father?"

"I'm not sure," I said, "but he did create your software program, and there are already allegations about his fraudulent financial activity."

"So, why are you going to contact Jillian?"

"I just want her to know that we're looking into it. And if she's involved in any way, we won't hesitate to go after her as well. There's only one thing Jillian is worried about."

"What's that? Being a skank-assed bitch?"

"No." I chuckled. "She's worried most about her financial standing in society."

"Well, then it seems like screwing her brother-in-law on your sofa would have knocked her down a peg or two."

"True. But I didn't stick around to find out. Anyway, I'm pretty sure she knows that her father is running out of money. She may do whatever she can to save herself. If her father goes to prison for embezzlement and loses his fortune, she'll be ruined, socially and financially."

"Couldn't happen to a nicer bitch." Dana howled with laughter. "I don't think I like you calling her without me around, though."

"Why?"

"You're not mean enough. Why don't you let me call the whore? I'd tell her to go suck a dick. As long as it's not yours."

I laughed.

"Seriously, I'll put the fear of God in that cow."

I shook my head and smiled, basking in the image of Dana doing just that.

"I'm not kidding, Peter. That girl fucked with the wrong person when she stepped into my life. You're mine now, and I protect what's mine."

My heart literally ached at Dana's declaration. It was comforting to know how much I meant to her and what lengths she'd go to defend me.

"I love you so much, Dana," I whispered.

"I love you too, Peter. I'm serious, though. That whore messes with me again and she's dead. She messes with you and she's MIA."

"MIA?"

"Missing in action. As in I'll bury her ass in the desert."

"Oh, okay. I'll be sure and pass on your warning." I knew my sarcastic response would go unnoticed by my Italian spitfire.

"Good." She giggled. "Promise to call me right back after you talk to her, okay?"

"I will, sweetie. I probably won't be in a good mood though."

"I know how to get you in a good mood again." She purred into the phone. Her voice was doing wicked things to my mid-section, as usual.

"Meet me at the dealership in an hour," I said.

"Why don't we say forty-five minutes? Then that will give us fifteen to play around," she exhaled in a breathy, seductive tone.

"Fifteen minutes?" I exclaimed as if I were horrified. "That's all I am to you now, fifteen minutes?"

"Oh, Peter," she moaned, "you are so much more to me than that. But with you, I'll take whatever I can get."

"I'll talk to you soon, Dolly." I needed to end this call before my dick exploded.

"Tell that douche bag ex-wife of yours that I said 'Hi,'" she said in a sweetly sickening tone. "And let her know I don't take shit off of nobody, least of all some butch-faced whore like her. If she messes with me, my dealership, or you, I'll rip her fucking head off and shit down her neck until fecal matter oozes out of her toenails."

I burst out laughing. I felt sorry for anyone who messed with our child.

"Bye, Dolly. I love you."

"I love you too, Peter. You're mine, don't forget it."

"Never," I promised. And I meant it.

CHAPTER 20

PETER

"Look, Peter," Jillian said on the other end of the phone, "I don't know what you think I can do to help you. My father isn't sabotaging your girlfriend's little company."

"She's my fiancée, Jillian."

Crap. Her silence warned me that I'd given her too much information.

"Oh," she said. "Well. Congratulations, I guess."

I didn't need her well wishes. I wanted her to call off her father's antics. If I could somehow reach Jillian, perhaps she'd give me valuable information as to whether or not her father was responsible for the dealership's losses.

"Look, Jillian, rumor is your father is in a lot of trouble, not just with business associates, but with the law." It wasn't a complete lie, I mean, there were rumors.

"There have been no charges filed, Peter."

Charges filed? So there was some truth to the rumors floating around.

"Not yet," I said.

"What does that mean?"

"It means my programmers have combed through the

accounting system *your* father's company created for Dana's business."

"Rich!" She cackled. She was mocking me, grating my last nerve.

I nearly bit through my tongue, trying not to say something I'd regret.

"Look, Peter, I wish I could help you."

No, she didn't. We both knew that.

"But Daddy doesn't talk business with me."

"Well, you give your father a message from me. You tell him that my programmers have found his deceptive coding and we're about to call the cybercrime unit for the FBI."

Okay, now that was a total lie, but I knew enough coding jargon that I was pretty sure I could scare her.

"And trust me," I continued, "once they take a look at this system, they'll figure out that your father has been skimming off the top of these accounts. And you and I both know it's not just Dana's company he's doing this to."

Again, I couldn't know this with certainty but her father had always been a bit corrupt. Even if I couldn't prove it yet, somehow my gut told me Walter Vanguard was to blame for the financial crisis behind Dana's company.

"Why don't you ask your mother for the money to save your girlfriend's precious little dealership?" Jillian said, her familiar venomous tone rearing its ugly head.

"How did you know Dana's company was a car dealership?" I asked. "I never told you that."

She remained silent, which didn't surprise me. She probably knew everything there was to know about Dana by now.

"I hear your mom is close to closing a deal to sell your father's business," she said, never answering my question.

"First of all, my family's company has nothing to do with this situation with Dana." My tone was stern but I tried to keep calm.

"Oh, but it does." Her jeering tone had the hairs on my arms standing on end. "You see, Peter, when they sell your family's company, you'll be rich."

Selling my family's company was common knowledge. According to Blake, even Walter Vanguard himself had put in a bid. No one except my family knew I held the majority of the company though, not even me.

"What makes you think I'll be rich, Jillian?" I asked.

"I heard you and your *mommy* talking about it when I went to visit her at the hospital. I know all about your majority stock in the company."

Oh, crap.

"What does any of that have to do with you?" I asked.

"Well, if my father is in as much trouble as you say he is, he'll probably need money to save himself."

"And what, you think I'm just going to give him money? You're delusional if you think I'm going to give your father one red cent, whether we sell my family's company or not."

She chuckled, and I bit back a growl.

"Tell your father he can consider himself warned."

"Is that supposed to scare me?" she asked.

"I couldn't scare you even if I wanted to, Jillian."

"Well, well, Peter, it seems as if you've grown some balls down there in Texas. That's hot." Her voice was sultry and deep.

The sound making my skin crawl. How could I have been married to this woman?

"It sounds as if your little bitch of a girlfriend has really drawn you out of your sexual shell. Hopefully, she's not as disappointed with your performance in bed as I was."

I sucked in a breath. This went beyond her father. This was personal. I had to keep it together, stay focused, for Dana. I couldn't let Jillian know how much her words were affecting me, or how infuriating her crude behavior was.

"She's my *fiancée*," I corrected through clenched teeth.

"Yes," she laughed sarcastically, "so you've already said. Hopefully you'll be able to keep this one satisfied."

I'd had her. Her baiting methods were working and I had to make my message clear and get her off the line.

"Look, Jillian, I'm not playing around here. I'm willing to go toe-to-toe with your father if he continues sabotaging Dana's company. And with you too, if need be.

"He's run his own company so far into the ground that he'll be lucky to escape this whole mess carrying the suit on his back. Hell, he'll probably end up exchanging it for a black and white striped jumpsuit courtesy of the Utah Department of Corrections. And trust me, I'll be *more* than happy to assist them."

If Jillian's father lost his company and his money, she would lose everything as well. If he went to prison, she'd be ruined, financially and socially. She was just as vested in saving his company as he was, but for completely different reasons. That was her motivation in seeking my mother out at the hospital, I was sure of it now.

Jillian was just as desperate as her father, and that made her a threat to me.

"I don't know what your father is up to," I continued, "but I know it's not legal and it's not good. If you're involved in any way, you'll go down with him."

"I have no idea what you're talking about," she said, mockery in her tone. "Good luck on your upcoming nuptials. I hope you fuck her better than you did me."

I closed my eyes, willing my insecurities away. Dana loved me. Dana was happy with me, satisfied in every way.

"Otherwise, she'll become so bored with your lack of skills she'll have to screw one of your other brothers, like I did."

A dark fog of insecurity rolled in, engulfing the self-worth I'd worked hard to regain.

"I'll tell my mother and father you said hello," she said.

Before I could respond, the line went dead. And so did my hopes of a future with Dana.

CHAPTER 21

DANA

My head was still spinning ever since my meeting with Uncle Nic and Peter a few days ago. The revelation that Peter's ex-wife and her father may have had a hand in my dealership's losses was overwhelming.

Peter's family's software company had already implemented a new accounting system. All of the dealership's access to the software had been revoked as we transferred money and set up new restrictions that would ensure we could get control of the financial hemorrhaging.

Peter hadn't wanted to share the information with anyone at the dealership except Uncle Nic. He even kept the changes from Chase, which I didn't understand, but given our current financial situation and what our company stood to lose, I allowed it.

If it were true that Jillian's father really was stealing money from our dealership, then keeping a lid on any changes would probably be best for all of us. I trusted Peter and his judgment implicitly.

I pulled into the parking lot and made my way into Sam's dorm, vowing not to let the worries of the past few days affect my time with him. I needed a break from everything—the financial problems with the dealership, Peter's ex-wife, the pending adoption, our wedding. I knew spending a day with Sam would cure what ailed me.

"Day-nah!" Sam shouted from behind the front counter. Sam loved to play receptionist and the employees at Whispering Oaks always encouraged him.

"Saammm-meee!" I drew out for effect as I rounded the counter.

He pulled me into a tight hug, shaking me side to side.

"I'm a little teapot, short and stout," he sang. "Here is my handle." He took one of my arms in his, then the other. "Here's my spout. When we get a little steamed up, hear me shout. Tip me over." He leaned me sideways.

"And pour me out!" all the residents and I shouted together.

Everyone clapped and cheered. It was a silly thing to do but for me and Sam it was tradition. We both needed stability in our lives. I loved Sam with all my heart and if anything ever happened to him, or to Peter, I knew my own life would be over.

"You ready, buddy?" I asked, releasing him.

"Cheese buh-gah, right?" he asked.

"You want bacon?" I asked, already knowing the answer.

"Bay-con, bay-con," he chanted.

"Come on, let's go, silly." I laughed, grabbing his arm. "Bye, guys." I waved to the rest of the residents.

"Bye, Dana, bye, Sam!" they all shouted.

Sam led the way to my car.

"You driving?" I asked.

"Day-nah." He laughed, bumping my shoulder. "I no drive."

"Okay," I said, acting disappointed. "Top up or down today?"

"Down, down, down!" he shouted, jumping in place.

"Okay, top down." It was hot outside, but I knew Sam loved to feel the sunshine on his face.

Sometimes I was envious of Sam and wished I had his carefree, easy-going spirit and fun-loving nature. He never worried or complained. He was just Sam.

One of the facility's vans was parked so close to my car that I knew Sam would never be able to squeeze his tall frame through. "Let me pull my car out first," I instructed. "Then you can get inside and I'll pop the top."

He smiled broadly, his expression infectious. This was what I loved about my brother. Something as simple as the promise of driving with the top down on my car was like the gift of a lifetime to him.

"I love you, Sam," I said, reaching up and hugging his neck.

"I love you too, Dana." He bent and kissed my head.

Yes, this was what I needed, a way to forget everything and everybody. Sam would do that for me. He'd always been able to take my mind off of the problems in my life.

"Get in the van," a deep voice behind me growled.

It took me a second to register that the voice wasn't Sam's.

I turned, thinking it was another resident following us. My hands flew to my chest and I gasped. "Chase, what are you doing here?"

His expression was menacing, his eyes narrowed. I'd never seen him look so…evil.

Slowly my gaze lowered and I spotted a gun in his hand. I pushed Sam behind me.

"Get in the van, Dana," Chase demanded, his eyes darting around the campus.

I stood in stunned silence, my mind racing.

"What the hell are you doing?" I asked.

"Now," he snarled through clenched teeth, jabbing the gun into my ribs.

What the fuck was happening? Should I scream? Should I get in the van? Should I run? Only one word came to mind, thanks to my martial arts training.

Fight!

I positioned myself to kick him square in the nuts but another voice stopped me mid-motion.

"Don't even think about it, bitch. I know all about your kung fu shit from Chase."

I looked over my shoulder and saw a woman crouched inside the van, holding a gun pointed at Sam.

"Get in the fucking van before I split your brother's face in two with one bullet."

I didn't know the woman but her face looked familiar.

"Are you fucking deaf?" she asked. "Chase, get her in the goddamn van."

Suddenly I recognized her. I'd only seen a few photos of her on the internet from their wedding, but it was easy to recognize those green eyes.

Jillian.

This bitch was certifiably bat shit crazy.

Chase shoved me and I stumbled into Sam.

"Day-nah," Sam cried, his chin quivering as he grabbed for me.

"No way, retard." Jillian grabbed his arm and pulled him back. "In the van, or he's dead."

The evil expression on her face and ease with which she held the gun told me she would do everything she'd just threatened.

As much as I wanted to knock the fuck out of her, I was at a disadvantage with the barrel of her gun pointing right at my brother. I cautiously lifted my foot and stepped into the van.

Jillian shoved at Sam. "Get in, retard."

"I no ree-tard," Sam said.

I turned and glanced over my shoulder.

Sam's arms were high in the air, his eyes wide with fear as he moved to step into the van.

"No way!" I shouted, holding up my hand to stop Sam. "He's not going."

Jillian laughed sardonically, wielding the gun. "You think you're calling the shots here?"

I sat stone still, feeling for the first time we were in real trouble.

"Get in, Sam," she instructed, kicking my legs to the side to make room for him to climb in.

Shit, shit, shit! I could take care of myself, of that, I was sure. Caring for Sam too would fuck with my concentration though. I had to do something.

I noticed Chase coming to stand next to Jillian at the door of the van. I knew if I could kick him, anywhere, it would jar him enough so he'd drop the gun. Fighting only one asshole with a gun might give us a chance.

I reared my legs back, staring at Chase's mid-section. Just as I was about to unleash my fury, something hard hit my head. My body recoiled, searing pain shooting from my temple to the ends of my toes. The world around me grew dim as the van door closed with a rocking thud.

"Day-nah!" Sam cried out, falling over me.

I'm okay, I wanted to say but the darkness enveloped me before the words came out.

CHAPTER 22

DANA

"WAKE UP, BITCH!" someone yelled, kicking my leg.

Pain shot through my body. Where the hell was I? I reached out but felt only cool metal underneath me. My head was throbbing. I worked to open my eyes but it felt like they'd been seared shut.

"Day-nah is no bee-yitch." I heard Sam say. "That's a bad word."

"Shut the fuck up, retard." The woman's words echoed in the space.

My stomach roiled as I realized we were moving. We were in a car.

"I not a ree-tard. You mean!" Sam yelled.

Sam. Oh, shit! Sam was here.

Jillian. Chase. Kidnapping. Memories flooded my mind. Night-marish memories.

"I'm serious, you skank." Jillian kicked my legs again. "Get up or I'm going to put one of these fucking bullets in your brother's head."

I forced my eyes open and saw Sam, lying beside me, brushing my hair back.

"Sissy, you hurt," he said, tears falling down his face. "I scare-reed."

"Don't be scared, Sam," I said softly, reaching up to touch his face but my motion was stopped. I glanced at my hands and realized my wrists were bound with duct tape. What the fuck?

Sam's gaze went from my bound hands to my eyes.

When had she tied me up?

I had to reassure him we would both survive.

"Just do everything I say to do, all right?" I said, pleading with my eyes.

He stared at me, his own eyes round as moons.

"Sissy will take care of everything, I promise." I wanted to reassure him but honestly, I wasn't completely convinced I could.

He nodded, appeased for now.

I turned my head and focused on Jillian, fighting back the nausea.

She smirked and I wanted to punch her fucking face. "That's more like it," she said.

I couldn't show emotion now. I had to play it cool. This bitch was certifiably crazy.

"Sit up," she demanded, kicking my legs again.

What the hell was she wearing, steel-toed boots? I bit back a whimper, unwilling to give her the satisfaction of knowing how excruciating the pain was.

I thought back to the self-defense classes our martial arts instructor provided twice a year. His words rang through my mind.

Only a crazy person picks a fight with a crazy person.

Well, people had always said I was crazy.

I knew my best plan of defense with this psycho was to give crazy right back, keep her pissed at me until I could get Sam to safety. Rage was the one emotion most people couldn't control, and that would make her an easier target for me. And it would keep her attention off of Sam.

"If you keep kicking me," I said, "how the fuck am I supposed to sit up, you moron?"

Her eyes narrowed and her gaze bore through me.

"You better back the fuck up," I said, "before I kick the ever-loving shit out of you, you ass-rimming shit fungus."

Her expression changed to amusement as she laughed and shook her head. "And that's the mouth you kiss my ex-husband with?"

She leaned over the front seat, raising her gun. "You even think about touching me and I'll pop a cap in your ass faster than you can drink a twelve pack of Budweiser, you trailer trash slut."

I smiled. My plan was working. The beast had been poked. "I prefer Bud Light." I laughed out, remembering the first time Peter and I had met at the concession stand.

Peter.

Oh, shit. He was going to be so worried. I had to bring down my own crazy a notch if I was going to get any answers.

"Why did you take us?" I asked, changing tactics.

Jillian turned and faced the front.

That was when I noticed Chase was driving.

I pushed up as best I could with taped wrists. "Chase, why are you doing this?"

He peered at me in the rearview mirror but remained quiet.

"Are you the one who's been stealing my company's money?"

"Afraid not, precious," Jillian answered with no hesitation, as if she'd been waiting for me to ask that exact question for days. She stared at Chase and grinned.

Had Chase done this to me? It seemed unlikely, yet here I was, duct-taped and thrown in the back of a van he was driving.

I looked out the front windshield and noticed we were on the highway, taking an exit I couldn't make out. Fuck! How long had I been out?

"Where are we headed?" I asked.

Both Chase and Jillian remained eerily silent.

"What do you want, Jillian?" I questioned her.

Glancing over my shoulder, I saw Sam huddled against the side of the van, his legs tucked up underneath his arms. He was scared, and I wanted more than anything to wrap my arms around him and assure him everything would be fine. Unfortunately, I wasn't so sure it would be anymore.

"It's okay," I mouthed to him.

He shook his head.

"I promise," I whispered, nodding my head.

He furrowed his brow and his lips pursed. He didn't believe me. And truthfully neither did I.

Raising my bound hands, I gave him the sign language symbol for 'I love you.'

He held two fingers in a 'peace' sign, our own indication that he loved me too.

I hoped my sign of affection was enough to at least keep him calm. Placing one lone finger to my lips, I signaled for him to stay silent

He nodded.

Feeling Sam was pacified for now, I turned my attention back toward Jillian.

She sat silent, facing the front, studying the road ahead of them.

The van turned into an entranceway and then jerked to a stop in front of a closed fence.

Sam and I went rolling across the floorboard. I bit my lip, fighting the need to scream out in pain. I couldn't afford for Jillian and Chase to know how weak I was.

Jillian turned and narrowed her eyes. "Stay here." She opened the door and gracefully slid out of the van.

Forcing myself up despite the pain, I wiggled closer to the front of the van.

"Chase," I said quietly, having no idea where Jillian was, "is it true? Have you been the one stealing from my dealership all this time?" I seriously couldn't believe what Jillian just said.

All this time I thought Chase cared for me, that he would never do anything to harm me, or my family.

He remained silent, hands gripping the steering wheel, staring straight ahead. His silence spoke volumes. He was involved. To what extent I didn't know, and at the moment, I didn't give a shit. He was the enemy.

"Why?"

Bam! One loud pop rang out.

We all three flinched.

"Dammit," Chase said.

I pushed up onto my knees and peered out the windshield.

Jillian turned, gun held to her side, and made her way back to the van. The fenced gate was now wide open.

Shit! Not only *could* Jillian shoot that fucking gun, she'd just proven she would if necessary.

She opened the van door. "What the fuck, Chase?" she shouted, sliding into her seat. "I thought you checked this place out for surveillance. There was a camera sitting right there on the gate post in plain sight, you moron." She wielded the gun, pointing it at the chain-link fence in front of us.

Chase remained quiet

"Pull in," she ordered.

Chase obliged, driving forward.

Jillian obviously had something over the man.

She turned in her seat, pointing the gun at us. "Sit the fuck down. The last thing I need is for you two to be able to describe this place."

Describe it? As in, 'We may get out of this,' or 'This might be a crime scene?' Fuck!

"Chase," I begged.

"Shut up, Dana," he ordered, "or I'll have Jillian gag you." His tone lacked the authority that Jillian's did. In fact, his words sounded flat. I had to believe that Chase wouldn't hurt us. That he wasn't a willing participant in this scheme. Maybe he would be our ticket out of this.

CHAPTER 23

DANA

THE VAN JERKED to a halt and Chase turned off the engine before stepping out.

Jillian turned and glared at me. "Don't move." Before I could say "fuck you" or "suck my left tit" she was out of the van as well.

I waited, wondering if this was it. Were they going to leave us in the van? It was warm outside but nothing Sam and I couldn't handle.

I startled as the van door slid open with an ominous creak.

"Get out," Jillian ordered, pointing the gun straight at me.

I motioned Sam to scoot out before me, not completely confident in my ability to move. After Sam exited, I turned my legs toward the door but gasped in pain.

Chase slid inside beside me as if to help.

I stared at him in disbelief, unable to fathom what had motivated him to act this way.

"Why, Chase?" I asked. "Why are you doing this to us?"

Chase swallowed hard but remained silent as he lifted me out of the van.

"Please, help me," I whispered.

"Shut the fuck up," Jillian said.

Chase gently placed me on the ground.

After balancing myself on weak legs I surveyed our surroundings.

We stood in front of a dilapidated metal building with no windows. I'd seen enough true-crime TV to know that wasn't a good sign.

From the looks of what I could see, we were inside an industrial park filled with metal buildings and what looked like storage units. Again, not a good sign.

I scanned the area, disappointed when I saw nothing remotely recognizable. The place was so desolate and isolated that there was no fucking way anyone was going to find us here. All my thoughts went to Peter.

Peter will find you.

"Christ, Chase," Jillian barked, "what the hell is the rental car doing beside the warehouse, you dumb ass?"

I followed her gaze and saw a blue sedan sitting next to the building. Maybe this could be our escape.

"I told you to get rid of the car when you picked up the van!" she yelled. Despite her obvious fury, she calmly walked toward the sedan. Raising her gun with a steady hand, she pointed the pistol straight at the front tire.

"Turn your back," I told Sam just before she pulled the trigger.

An ear-piercing explosion ricocheted through the buildings, leaving my ears ringing. Holy fuck.

Well, there went that idea of escaping.

"Dana," Sam cried out, clutching at me.

"Jillian," Chase yelled, "what the hell are you doing?"

"Taking care of shit you should have."

She walked around the entire car, shooting the remaining tires. With each shot that rang out, Sam and I flinched.

"It's okay," I said softly, trying to soothe him. It was difficult given that my hands were still bound at the wrist.

Think, Dana. Think.

There had to be a way out of this.

Jillian turned to me, gun hanging by her side, wearing a triumphant smile. "Don't get any bright ideas about trying to escape or I'll blow your brother's face off."

"Day-nah," Sam cried.

"Shhh," I soothed. "It's all right. Nothing will happen to you." And I meant it. I *would* figure out a way to save Sam.

Jillian pointed to the warehouse. "Open the door, Chase."

He followed her command. The screech of the metal door opened with an ominous groan. If we went inside, we were as good as dead.

I stepped in front of Sam. "No fucking way."

Jillian cocked her head, brows lifted. "What did you say?"

"I said, there's no fucking way we're going in there."

She raised the gun and pointed it at my head. "You're going in. Either on your own or I'll have Chase carry your lifeless body. Dead or alive, it doesn't matter to me, but you're going in."

"No, Day-nah!" Sam shouted, wrapping his arms around me.

I knew it was a dangerous plan but I felt my best chance with this skank was to be as obstinate and uncooperative as possible. Basically, I'd be myself.

"Fuck off, bitch!" I yelled.

Jillian walked closer.

I stiffened, my body preparing for a fight. As much as she said it didn't matter if I was alive, something inside me said it was a lie.

"What?" she asked.

"I said—Fuck. Off. Bitch. What part of that did you not understand?"

Her answer was a sharp backhand across my face.

The pain was intense but I gritted my teeth, squeezing my eyes tight. Her goal was to break me and I couldn't let that happen.

"No hurt Day-nah!" Sam shouted.

I opened my eyes and watched helplessly as Sam lunged for

Jillian. He was bigger and broader and probably could have taken her down, but Jillian was volatile. And she had a gun.

"No, Sam!" I screamed.

Jillian pointed the gun directly at him. "Don't fuck with me, retard."

He stopped, throwing both hands in the air, thankfully understanding the warning.

"Jillian, please," Chase begged, "hurting them was never part of the plan."

Plan? He and Jillian had had a plan? Of course, they did.

Jillian's green gaze cut to Chase, eyes narrowed, silently warning him to keep his mouth shut.

Chase held my gaze for a brief second before staring down at the ground.

How could I have ever considered him a loyal friend?

"Move," Jillian demanded, poking me in the back with the gun.

I searched the area, wondering how fast Jillian could run if Sam and I made a break for it.

"And if you try to take off, I will shoot your brother and drag your ass back here to watch him bleed to death. Got it?"

I fought back a tremor, not wanting to show just how scared I was.

She shoved me in the back again. "I said, got it?"

I nodded once. My options for escape were diminishing by the second. And I knew if we stepped into that warehouse, my opportunities would be next to nothing. But I couldn't lose hope. Sam needed me. I wouldn't fail him.

"You are a mean, mean lady," Sam said behind me.

I glanced over my shoulder, swallowing back the nausea from the quick movement. My head was pounding and it felt like my legs may give out at any minute. "Shhh," I mouthed.

He opened his mouth as if to speak again but I shook my head.

Suddenly a wave of dizziness hit me hard. I forced myself to focus on Sam until I righted myself.

Finally, he nodded in understanding.

"What the fuck are you saying to him?" Jillian punched me in the back again.

I stumbled forward. "I'm just telling him to be quiet."

"Like that moron could understand you." She snorted.

Anger set my entire body on fire. I hated the derogatory terms people used to describe my brother or any other person with intellectual disabilities. More than once, I'd been expelled in school for protecting Sam, usually involving physical altercation.

I drew in a deep breath, knowing now was not the time to lose it. Her time would come though.

Jillian followed behind us as I trudged into the dark warehouse.

The air inside was stale, the walls rusted and worn. It looked like an old barn from the inside.

"Did you bring the phone?" Jillian asked Chase.

He nodded, patting his back pocket.

"Battery out?" she asked.

He reached into his other back pocket and produced a black plastic block.

It didn't take a rocket scientist to know he'd removed the battery to keep from being traced on any cell tower pings.

Fuck! No one would ever find us out here in bum-fuck Egypt.

"So, what the fuck happens now?" I asked, trying to sound annoyed.

"We wait." She smiled, an evil glint in her eyes.

I couldn't believe Peter had ever been married to this skank.

"For what?" I asked.

"Your *fiancé*," she said mockingly, rolling her eyes.

"You called Peter?"

"Chase did." She nodded toward him.

I turned and stared at him. "What did you say?"

He looked at me but said nothing.

"We're gonna find out just how much you mean to your

precious little Peter." Jillian laughed, walking toward me, stopping when we were toe-to-toe.

Rearing my head back, I stared up at her. The bitch was an Amazon. She was also beautiful, I hated to admit. But her exterior hid the ugliness of her soul. She truly was evil.

"So, tell me about this wedding of yours," she said.

For once in my life, I remained silent. How the hell did she know we were engaged?

"What," she smiled, "now your smart mouth isn't working? Cat got your tongue?"

I continued to stand stock still. I needed my hands free if I was going to antagonize her more.

"You can have him," she finally said. "He was lousy in bed anyway. The idiot had no clue what to do with his dick. It was a nice-sized package, don't get me wrong," she snorted, "but still, he was as retarded with his dick as your brother back there."

That. Fucking. Bitch! She was demeaning the two men I loved most in this world.

I resisted the urge to spit in her face. Even though I wanted to knock the fuck out of this cow, I couldn't risk what she might do to Sam if I did. I drew in a deep breath and held it for several seconds before blowing out a heavy sigh. I was thankful that martial arts had also taught me self-control as well as self-defense.

I turned to Chase, figuring he may be the best person to reason with. "You've already called Peter?"

Chase remained silent, as usual. Fucking asshole.

If Peter knew we were missing, he'd be searching everywhere. This was a good sign. But Peter wasn't loaded. It wasn't like he had a shit-ton of money sitting around just waiting to hand over to this lunatic.

"You know, Peter doesn't have a lot of money," I said to no one in particular. "In case you're wanting a ransom."

"Oh," Jillian chuckled, "he has money. He's got lots of money. Trust me."

I stared at her, shocked by her statement. Maybe I didn't know as much about Peter as I thought.

"Peter holds the majority stock in his family's company, which means when he sells, he'll be rich." She stared at me, an evil smile twisting her mouth. "Trust me, if he wants to save you bad enough, he's got resources."

What could she possibly be talking about? Peter hadn't told me anything about majority stock.

Jillian took a step toward me and grabbed my chin. "We're gonna find out just how much your sweet ass is worth to him. Lord knows you don't mean shit to me." She jerked me hard. "And you'd be doing yourself a favor to remember that, sweetheart."

I pulled from her grasp. Who the fuck did this bitch think she was? "What the hell are you talking about?"

She laughed sarcastically. "So, I'm assuming you *don't* know his family is selling his father's company?"

I stood, trying not to show how fucking clueless I was. Why hadn't Peter told me?

"You really have no idea?" She stepped back, grinning.

I had no fucking clue. But I wasn't going to tell her that.

"Classic." She laughed.

Apparently, the answer had been written all over my face.

"So, let me get this straight," she said, one hand on her hip, the other still gripping the gun. "Peter keeps something this major from you and you actually think he loves you? You're even dumber than I thought."

I hated that she had the upper hand on me, but more than that, I was infuriated that Peter had kept something so important from me.

"This is rich," she said. "Maybe you don't mean as much to him as I thought."

Was she right? Maybe Peter didn't trust me as much as I trusted him.

Don't go there. You're Peter's entire world. She's trying to yank your chain. Pull yourself together and don't fall into her trap.

I squared my shoulders and raised my head as if I was the all-knowing Oz himself. "I know exactly what you're talking about, you stupid bitch. You really think I'm dumb enough to tell you?"

Jillian's brows furrowed, her triumphant grin gone.

"Peter and I share everything." Okay, that was a lie, I obviously didn't know everything, but I had to act like I did. "His family decided not to sell after all."

She jerked back in surprise.

"Peter just signed over his portion of the company to his mother yesterday. He can't stand his family and said he didn't want to have anything to do with them or their company."

"That's a lie!" she shrieked. "I heard them at the hospital. They were laughing and talking and reconciling their relationship."

"I don't know what the fuck you heard," I continued with my fabricated story, "but that's not what happened at all. They may have settled their relationship, but trust me, it's not one Peter intends to pursue. That's why he signed it all over to his mother."

Her eyes narrowed as she studied me.

I kept my face passive, trying to hide the fact that I had no clue what was going on with Peter's family.

Jillian swallowed and stared me up and down. She was doubting herself, and this was good.

"Oh," I laughed, "please don't tell me you didn't know that, Jillian?" I took a step toward her, puffing out my chest like a plumed peacock. "So, it seems your little idea of kidnapping me has backfired."

She jerked her head, glaring at Chase before turning back to me.

"Peter doesn't have shit, sweetheart, except for a busted elbow that will probably keep him from ever competing professionally again."

"That's not true," she said, her confident tone slipping.

"His sponsors are dropping him left and right." I laughed. "Didn't you know?" I cocked my head. "I guess you're even dumber than you look."

Sam snorted behind me.

She glanced over my shoulder at Sam and he immediately stopped. "I'm sure Peter will figure out a way to come up with the money once he finds out what I'm willing to do to you." Her devilish grin was back as she stared at me. "You two sit down."

I stood stock still.

"I said, sit down." She kicked at my feet.

Unable to balance with my arms still bound, I fell to the floor, straight on my ass.

"Day-nah," Sam cried out, coming to help me.

Shit, that hurt. I wasn't going to lie.

I worked to formulate a plan of escape, but my head was throbbing like a motherfucker. Peter wasn't lying to me, I was sure of it.

CHAPTER 24

DANA

JILLIAN PACED AROUND THE WAREHOUSE, chewing on her thumbnail. It was clear that my fake story had her off balance.

I needed to come up with an exit plan and fast.

"That's all right," Jillian said, coming to an abrupt halt. "You have access to the system at your dealership. Daddy told me. We'll go there and have you transfer funds yourself."

"Jillian," I said, trying to sit up straighter. "I have nothing. I don't even have access to any of the money in the dealership's bank accounts."

She laughed.

"I'm not lying." Fuck yeah, I was lying, but this bitch wasn't going to see me flinch. I was going to be Meryl Fucking Streep with my Oscar award winning performance today.

"They're transferring all the accounts to new financial holding companies thanks to your father," I continued. "No one has access for the next forty-eight hours. Chase should know that."

Lie, lie, lie.

Jillian's eyes shot wide, her long auburn hair whipping around her shoulder as she paced to the other side of the building closer to Chase.

"Does she really not have access to the money in the system?" she asked him.

He stared at me, holding my gaze. I prayed he would back me up even though he himself wasn't privy to everything going on with the accounting system right now.

"Each one of us has varying levels of access to different accounts now," he said. "But all of them require Dana and her uncle to access anything."

"What does that mean? Can she get me the two million I need or not?"

Two million! Holy fucking shit!

Chase stared at me, his internal struggle written all over his pathetic face. Should he tell Jillian the truth and save his own ass, or lie to save mine?

"She has access," he finally answered, "but she would need her uncle's rights to get to it. Peter changed all the procedures a few days ago so we could stop the financial hemorrhaging your father brought on."

Fucking Chase! Now he'd brought my Uncle Nic into this dangerous game.

Wait? Did he just say, "so *we* could stop the financial hemor-rhaging" that *her* father brought on? What game was Chase play-ing? And more importantly, whose side was he on?

"My goddamn father!" Jillian yelled, her voice echoing in the warehouse. "I have half a mind to let his ass rot in jail," she said, more to herself. "So, you can't do shit?" she questioned Chase, her deep green eyes boring straight through him.

I almost felt sorry for the poor bastard as I watched him shake his head in answer. Almost.

"Fuck!" she shouted, shaking the gun in the air.

I moved closer to Sam. This bitch was becoming more unhinged by the minute. I couldn't take any chances when it came to my brother.

Jillian turned and glared at me, daggers shooting straight through me.

A shiver ran down my spine but I straightened my back. She was not going to hurt us. Not anymore.

As if hearing my words she turned, muttering to herself.

"I understand wanting to take care of your family," I said, hoping I could reach her softer side, if there was one. "Is he in a lot of trouble? Your dad, I mean?"

"He's in a shit-ton of trouble. With the wrong kind of people. Jail would actually be a safer place for him right now," she said so quietly, I almost didn't hear her.

Okay, this was good. She was talking. And better than that, her plan was failing. And she didn't seem like the kind of person who knew how to fly on the cuff. But she was desperate so I couldn't let my guard down.

"I scared, Day-nah," Sam whispered in my ear. He clutched at my waist as if I were his security blanket.

"It's all right, Sammy," I whispered, nuzzling up against his arm.

Glancing down, I realized Sam's hands were free. Jillian had never bound them. Obviously, the bitch underestimated my baby brother's capabilities, assuming he was no threat to her.

"Sam," I whispered, "can you undo the tape around my wrist?"

"What the fuck!" Jillian strode toward me like a raging bull.

Oh, shit!

She pulled back her leg, about to kick Sam's arm.

Instinctively, I jumped on top of Sam, covering him with my body.

Before I could roll over, she kicked me square in the chest with the toe of her boot. Searing pain radiated from my core, burning through my entire body. I gasped for air but couldn't catch my breath.

"Dana!" Sam wrapped me in his arms in a protective manner, but his hold hurt me even more.

Everything around me spun, my vision a kaleidoscope of images I couldn't make out.

"Dammit, Jillian!" Chase shouted.

"Day-nah!" Sam cried.

"It's all right. I'm all right," I mumbled, pushing up on his leg.

"No more touching!" Jillian yelled. She held the gun high above her head as if to strike.

I shoved Sam's head into my body and tucked us into a ball.

She brought the gun down, intending to strike my head. I pivoted and she missed. The butt of the gun hit my hand instead.

Fuck, that hurt.

I recoiled in pain, pretty sure she'd broken at least one of my fingers, if not my whole fucking hand. I refused to give her the satisfaction of knowing just how much pain I was in.

"Jillian." Chase rushed to my side, crouching down. "Enough!"

"Get the fuck away from her," Jillian yelled at Sam, "or I'll tie up your mongoloid ass too!"

"Jillian," Chase pleaded, "you promised you wouldn't hurt her."

My entire body burned with rage when I realized Chase had been plotting with Jillian for some time. Maybe Chase didn't embezzle from my company, but he obviously had been involved in this kidnapping. My heart ached at his betrayal.

"Yeah," she said, "well, that was before I found out your dumb ass didn't have access to her company's money anymore. And before I knew Peter signed over his share of his family's business. Plans change, Chase. Get over it."

Chase stared at me, sorrow in his eyes.

I wasn't buying it. Not anymore. This man had crossed me, he'd hurt me and my brother. I would never forgive him. And I wouldn't rest until they both saw justice.

"Why the fuck didn't you know about any of this?" she asked.

I smiled to myself when I heard the desperation in her voice. She was rattled, and that was our ticket out of here.

"Hell," she continued, "you're so fucking in love with this bitch, I figured you'd have her whole goddamn life memorized."

In love with me? Chase was actually in love with me?

I stared up at Chase but he was looking away. So, it was true. Peter and Hindley had been right all along. Chase's feelings for me ran deeper than I'd imagined. But if he loved me, why would he be involved in any of this?

Sam shook against me like a frightened puppy, arms wrapped around his knees as he rocked back and forth.

I slid across the dusty floor and butted up next to him, wanting to provide reassurance that everything would be all right. I wasn't convinced myself but I didn't want him to see that.

"It's okay, Sammy," I whispered through my ragged breathing. My chest and ribs throbbed like a motherfucker. "Just do exactly what I say, when I say it, okay?"

He nodded but still remained curled in a tight ball.

"That ree-tard can't understand a fucking word you're saying," Jillian said, laughing at the two of us.

As much as I wanted to knock the fuck out of this bitch, I stifled my anger. Timing was everything. Plus, my hand and head were throbbing like a motherfucker.

"What are you going to do if you can't get the money?" I asked, knowing it was a loaded question but I had to find out what she was thinking.

"None of your fucking business." She turned and paced the warehouse, one hand on her forehead, the other still gripping the gun.

She was frazzled, worried and completely off her game. This could be my break. Before I could conjure up a way out of this hell-hole we were in, her face lit up with a wicked smirk, as if her evil plan had just been jumpstarted.

"Maybe threatening your brother's life will light a fire under your ass and get *you* to find some money for me." She smirked.

My stomach roiled at the thought of anyone hurting Sam.

Suddenly, I noticed the type of gun she was holding and cursed myself silently for not recognizing it before. It was a revolver, just like the one in my father's gun collection. Revolvers only held six bullets. She'd already shot off one at the gate and four at the car tires.

If I could just scare her, get her to shoot off that last one, then she wouldn't have anymore bullets. It would be purely hand-to-hand combat and I would win that anytime, any day. Despite my pain, there was no way I'd let her hurt Sam.

"Chase, go dial the number I gave you," she said. "You know what to do. Then go out to the van and bring me more bullets from the glove box."

Well, fuck me.

"And get your gun too," she added.

"Don't hit either of them again, Jillian," Chase said. "I mean it." He stared at me, but I turned away, disgusted by him. Even if he was trying to protect me now, it didn't matter. The bottom line was, Sam and I were in harm's way because of him.

"Don't threaten me or this all falls on your ass, Chase, remember?"

Chase remained silent.

I turned and saw him still staring at me.

"Just make the fucking call and bring me more bullets."

I watched as Chase quietly slipped through the door, head hung low. I knew I couldn't count on him for anything.

Maybe I could do something now that Jillian and I were alone. We waited in silence and I contemplated what to do next. It would be hard with my hands still bound. But for Sam, and Peter, I would do anything.

CHAPTER 25

DANA

"Shit!" she shouted.

I sat up straighter despite the pain. "What's wrong?"

"Where the fuck is he?" She was sweating now, her eyes wide. She was no longer the confident bitch from earlier.

I slid away from Sam, pressing one finger to my lips, signaling for him to remain quiet. Tucking my legs up underneath me, readying to strike, I pushed away the pain burning through my body.

Before I could make a move, she whipped around, glaring at me. "Were you going to try something, Dana?" She stalked toward me. "Legs out," she ordered. When I didn't move right away, she reared back and kicked my thigh.

My body tensed, preparing for the strike but nothing could have prepared me for the intense pain. Despite my desire to hold back my agony, I cried out. "Fuck!"

"Day-nah!" Sam shouted.

I swore to God, if this fucking bitch kicked me one more time, I was going to go ultimate fighter on her ass.

She squatted down, smiling at me. "Did you actually think you could beat me?" The question was rhetorical, but I couldn't help but answer.

"I know I can. And I will, you dumb bitch."

She backhanded me, which wasn't a surprise. But it still hurt like hell.

"Do you really think I'm gonna let you and your retarded brother make it out of this alive?"

I stiffened, every hair on my body standing straight up. Poking the beast no longer seemed like a good option. But there was no way I'd let her see the fear raging through me.

"So, what's the plan now?" I asked, trying to lure her in.

She stood and dusted off her pants.

"I mean, if you're going to kill me and Sam, why not go ahead and get it over with?"

"Because I want to see you suffer. I want to see Peter suffer, kneeling over your lifeless body." She cackled, the sound sending shivers up my spine.

"You are very, very mean," Sam said, pointing at Jillian.

She looked at him and laughed. "You have no idea."

Yeah, I was pretty sure this game had changed, and for the first time since she'd shoved us in the van, I truly feared for our lives.

"God, Dana, get a clue. I swear to God, you're just as stupid as these men."

I had no idea what she was talking about. "What men?"

"All men. Peter. Chase. My father. Men in general. I actually gave you more credit," she went on. "I'm glad to see you're just as dumb as they all are."

She was off her rocker, more than just bat-shit crazy. She was neurotic, unreachable and mentally unstable, but I had to try.

"You know you'll never get away with this," I said.

"Really?" She laughed, her hand still clutching the revolver.

"Yes, really."

"You know, it's so funny how dumb everyone seems to think I am. Actually, it's worked to my advantage in this situation." She grinned as if proud of her accomplishments. Like kidnapping and torturing people were a daily occurrence for her.

"How so?" I needed information—in particular, her weaknesses.

"Please," she laughed, pacing around us. "Men are so easily swayed by sex."

"You mean Chase?"

"Oh, God, no. I mean, yeah in the beginning that's how I lured him into my plan. Peter too, for that matter." She stared down at me and laughed. "He was lousy in bed. I'm not sure why you're staying with him."

I refused to spar with her about Peter. Just the sound of his name brought me back to reality. I knew if it were true, if she had called him for ransom, he'd find us soon. He had to.

"But poor little Chase apparently has a massive woody for you," she went on. "Kind of like your *fiancé*." She used air quotes. "They're both dopes, led around by their dicks. Luring them in to my scheme was easy. All I had to do was threaten your life and they both came running to your rescue."

Threaten my life?

"I guess your pussy's made of gold or something."

"So, what, you're jealous of me?" I asked, knowing this was a deadly game I was playing with a volatile she-beast.

"Hardly," she scoffed. "Like you could hold a candle to me."

"Then what's your game? Why are you doing this?"

"Money. Power. Plain and simple." She confessed as if it had been so obvious all along.

"For your father?"

"I guess." She shrugged.

"I mean, I know you've pretty much relied on his riches your entire life. Having your social circle of friends watch him carted off to jail, along with his fortunes, really wouldn't do much for your standing in the high society."

"Now you're getting smarter, Di Grazio." Her eyes twinkled in the dim light.

It surprised me that my sarcastic words had actually inspired her rather than provoked her.

"How are you getting out of this?" I asked. "I mean, if you kill me and Sam, you'll be following right behind your father in your own custom-fitted orange jumpsuit."

"Chase," she answered without hesitation.

"I don't get it?"

Her eyes narrowed as if she'd wised up that she was beginning to tell me her plan after all. This wasn't good. I needed to keep her talking, keep her believing that I cared.

"What does it matter if you tell me, Jillian? You've already said you're going to kill us anyway."

Still, she remained quiet.

"Does Chase know?" I asked.

"Does Chase know what?"

"That you're going to kill us. Kill Sam and me?"

"No kill! No kill!" Sam shouted.

"You better shut that fucker up," Jillian warned, glaring at me.

"It's okay, Sam." I soothed him. "We're not going to die. I promise." And I meant it. There was no fucking way I was letting this bitch be the last face I saw before meeting my maker.

Jillian walked toward the door, turning her back on me. "Chase!" she shouted.

I tucked my legs underneath me again. This was my chance.

As if hearing me, Jillian whipped back around, pointing the gun straight at me. "If you make one goddamn move, I'm going to shoot your brother dead." Her eyes were cold and unyielding. She meant it.

Fuck! I needed to calm her down, get her mind off of killing us. Talking about Chase seemed to rattle her so I thought I'd go with that.

"So, Chase does know?" I asked, ignoring her threat.

"Hell no, Chase doesn't know. He may be book smart, but his infatuation with you has muddled his mind."

Infatuation with me?

"No, Chase is my way out. Thanks to you," she added.

"Thanks to me? Why?"

"In that pea brain of his, he actually thinks if he saves you then you'll come running to him instead of my lame-dick ex-husband."

Stay calm. Breathe. She's just trying to fuck with you.

Drawing in a deep breath, I closed my eyes, pushing away the pain radiating through my chest. I was pretty sure I had a few broken ribs. I needed to keep her talking.

"Okay," I said, letting out my breath, "so how does that make Chase your way out?"

She smirked. "Wouldn't you like to know?"

"Actually, I would," I said. And I meant it. "Obviously you're smarter than all of us." Lie. Lie. Lie. The bitch was smart, but I was much more cunning.

Her devilish eyes lit up and I knew I'd set the hook. She believed me.

"As soon as your precious family figures out a way to come up with the two million dollars I need," she said, "Chase will instruct them to deposit the money into an account I created in his name."

I wanted to believe Chase was innocent but I knew from her plan he wasn't.

She walked closer. "I have the transfer number on speed dial. It will take me all of two minutes to move it out of his account and into a secured one that no one knows exists. And only I have access to."

Damn, she really did have all this shit figured out.

"But not before the cops trace it all back to Chase," she continued, as if she were reading a children's book.

I wasn't going to lie, it sounded like a semi-solid plan. "What about us?" I asked, motioning to Sam.

"Obviously, I'll kill you."

"No," Sam moaned.

I squeezed my body into him as best I could. There was no fucking way she was going to kill me or my brother.

"What happens to Chase?" I asked.

"I'll pop a cap in him after you two are done."

Sam scrunched down behind me.

"Don't worry," I whispered.

"Then I'll shoot myself in the foot, or some other innocuous appendage, to make it look like he and I struggled. I tell the cops I had no choice but to shoot him in self-defense, and boom! I'm done. Golden."

She may have thought she was golden but she'd underestimated the wonder twin powers of me and my brother.

"My father has already programmed his system to make it look like Chase was the one embezzling this entire time, so I'm free and clear. Nothing will tie me financially to your dumbass. I was an innocent captive this entire time, just like you. Or so the police will think, since you, your fucktard brother and Chase won't be alive to say otherwise."

The bitch was right. Everyone had underestimated her, me most of all.

"That's right, Dana." She laughed. "I win. Check mate!" Her head fell back and she roared with laughter.

There was only one way out of this and I was counting on my brother to help me.

Noticing her watchful gaze had been temporarily diverted by her over confidence, I stared at Sam. His eyes were wide with fear. I had to act. Now.

Bringing my bound hands up to my forehead, I tapped it several times between my eyes.

Sam smiled and nodded. Thankfully he'd recognized my signal and immediately fell down to the floor, flopping around like a fish out of water.

When Sam and I were younger, we'd come up with a signal to get us out of trouble. Anytime I tapped on my forehead, he would fake a seizure, drawing attention to himself rather than our misdeeds. It was a rotten thing to do, I knew that now as an adult, but right now I needed him. I was more than grateful today to see he still understood our childhood trick.

"Oh my God!" I screamed. "Jillian!"

She paced over to us. "What?"

I nodded to Sam. He was doing an amazing job, flopping around on the floor, hands and legs flailing. Jillian would never figure out he was faking it.

I gazed up and saw her face riddled with confusion.

"What the fuck?" She rubbed her brow. "Where the fuck is Chase?"

As she glanced over her shoulder at the door, this was my chance.

I stood and laced my fingers together, even though it hurt like hell. I quietly walked up behind her.

She turned to face me, eyes wide. And that was when I struck.

Mustering all my strength, I lifted my fisted hands and swung them up with all my might. Before she could protect herself, I clocked her under the chin.

Her head flew back, taking her body with hit. She smashed to the cement floor with a thud.

The fighter in me knew I couldn't assume I'd knocked her out. In MMA, you fought until the bell rang or your opponent tapped out. Thankfully for me, there were no referee here to stop me.

Now that she was down, I put all my jiu-jitsu training into practice. Opponents often mistook my stature as an area of weakness. Once I got them down on the mat for ground combat, I proved to them just how lethal a little pixie like me could be.

I pounced on top of Jillian, straddling her long body around her waist. Cinching my legs behind me, I pinned her thighs. She was conscious but dazed. And fuck it all if she didn't still have that gun in her hand. Thankfully my knees had trapped her arms.

I reminded myself that she only had one more bullet left. If I could get her to discharge it, I'd be home free.

Fighting instincts took over. My body was on fire, every part of me in pain. But I couldn't stop. Not until Sam and I were free. I thrust my bound hands around her throat, digging into her windpipe. "Drop the gun."

"Police!" a deep voice shouted from the other side of the warehouse. "Come out with your hands up!"

Thank fuck, the police were here. But I knew their presence would only make Jillian even more desperate. Instincts told me she still had a lot of fight in her, which meant I couldn't let up.

Pushing down harder on her windpipe, I stared down at her face.

Her eyes were wide, her pale skin tinging with blue. Normally, this would be the point in the competition when my opponent tapped out, or the referee would pull me off. I wasn't about to budge.

"I repeat, come out with your hands up!" a voice bellowed through a loud speaker outside.

"Drop the fucking gun." I shook her neck.

Despite the position she was in, she refused to surrender.

Bitch.

Movement in the corner of my eye caught my attention. I turned and saw a shoe kick Jillian's hand. A very familiar shoe.

I recognized the black suede DC brand shoes Rory had given Sam last year for his birthday. Rory was his idol. God, I loved Sam. And right now, Rory was my saving grace.

Jillian yelped but the sound was garbled since my hands were still clasped tightly around her neck.

The gun went sliding across the floor, just out of her reach.

"Get the gun, Sam!" I shouted.

"No, Day-nah. Guns bad."

"It's okay this time—" Before I could finish, something hit the side of my head. I fell off of Jillian onto the hard floor.

She'd taken advantage of my momentary distraction and turned the tables on me.

I was dazed by the blow but I had to recover quickly if Sam and I stood a chance at surviving this psycho. Jillian was a caged animal, her actions unpredictable, and Sam was refusing to take the gun.

I jumped up from the floor, assuming a fighting stance, preparing to kick this bitch's ass. Instead, I stared in confusion as her hands shot straight up in the air, her eyes wide with fear. I followed her gaze, surprised to see Sam not only holding the gun, but pointing it directly at her.

"I no ree-tard!" he shouted at her. "I no ree-tard!" Sam was so upset, his hand was shaking and I feared he might accidentally discharge the gun.

"Give me the gun, sweetie," I coaxed, trying to bring him back to me while keeping an eye on Jillian.

A huge bang echoed through the room and a clatter of voices stormed inside. "Freeze!" several people shouted.

Sam turned to look.

Jillian lunged for the gun.

I reared back my leg and kicked her arm as hard as I could.

She clutched her hand to her chest and yelped in pain.

Without hesitating, I raised one knee and twisted my hip as I gave her the best round house kick to the chest.

She fell to the floor, coughing and wheezing.

I grinned with satisfaction. Martial arts were about resolving issues peacefully and only resorting to violence when absolutely necessary. Right now, with my arms bound and body bruised, I decided it was absolutely necessary that I destroy this bitch.

I maneuvered into a fighting stance, preparing to knock this chick in the head with my heel. Suddenly strong arms wrapped around my waist, yanking me back. Kicking with all my might, I clawed at the person behind me. No one was taking me and Sam hostage again, not without a massive fight.

"Ma'am, stop," a man said in my ear.

"Fuck you!" I yelled, my legs and arms flailing.

"Ma'am, please. I'm Officer Scott Taylor with the Austin SWAT team."

"Sam!" I shouted, still struggling against the officer to break my hold. "Where's my brother?"

"Sam's safe. You're safe," he said. "Please, ma'am, quit kicking me."

"Show me your badge," I huffed, still not believing him.

He gently set me down and turned me to face him.

He was wearing dark fatigues, a gun belt and a baseball cap that said "SWAT" on it. I noticed a large rifle in one hand as his other pulled out a chained necklace that held a badge. It all looked legit.

"Where's my brother?"

"He's outside. You're safe."

I had a hard time believing what he was saying.

"Here, let's get this tape off your wrists." He pulled a knife from his belt and with one cut released me.

I rubbed my wrists, still not believing we were safe.

He held out a gray blanket. "Let's get you wrapped up and outside, okay. I know your brother wants to see you."

I nodded, fighting back tears.

As he led us out into the parking lot, I saw my brother.

"Sam!" I yelled.

His gaze found mine and I gasped. His eyes were so wide, his cheeks tear stained. I had to assure him he was safe and that this was finally over.

Sticking my good hand out of the blanket, I signaled 'I love you' in sign language.

He held up two fingers.

Tears ran down my cheeks at his silent statement. He loved me too.

The endorphins racing through my body just moments ago

began to fade and pain blanketed me. I would heal from injuries though.

Sam was safe. I was safe. And that was all that truly mattered.

CHAPTER 26

PETER

I STARED at Dana's petite body, lying motionless in the huge hospital bed. She was lost amid the blankets and sheets.

Her left hand was fitted with a brace and a bruise on her right cheek was turning purple and swelling. Underneath the pale blue hospital gown, I knew her body was littered with more bruises, abrasions and broken bones.

I gripped the bed railing, clenching my teeth. This was all my fault. I wanted to kill Jillian.

"Please, Peter," my mother whispered behind me, her hand splayed on my back. "Take a break. Go get something to eat, sweetheart. AJ and I will be here with her."

I stared at Dana, willing her to wake up so I could reassure her of my love.

"It's not your fault," my mother said.

"It is," I choked out in a raspy voice. Tears welled in my eyes. There were no words that could wash away the remorse and guilt I felt.

My mother knelt in front of me but I didn't take my eyes off Dana. "Take a break, sweetie," she said.

"I can't, Mom. I have to be here when she wakes up."

She stood and kissed me softly on the head. "All right, sweetheart."

I reached through the railing and slid my hand in hers as carefully as I could. I didn't want to hurt her anymore than she already was.

"Well, at least let us bring you something to eat, son," AJ said.

"I'm really not hungry." It wasn't a lie. The thought of food made me want to vomit.

How could this have happened, I wondered for the millionth time. I drew in a deep breath and held it for several beats. There was no answer.

I blew out a sigh, running my other hand along Dana's arm, avoiding the IV attached at the crook of her elbow. The doctors were administering pain medication and antibiotics.

My head fell onto the railing, tears running down my face. "How could I have failed her?"

"You didn't fail me, Peter."

I jerked up, stunned to see Dana's bright blue eyes staring at me.

"Oh my God, Dana!" I jumped from my chair and leaned over her bed, wiping away my tears with the back of my hand. "How are you, sweetheart?" I touched her forehead, then her cheeks. "How do you feel? Are you in pain? I can call the nurse, get you more meds." I rattled off questions like a machine gun.

She gave a small grin and reached up with her good hand to push back the hair from my face.

Even in the midst of all her pain, she was still trying to comfort me. God, I loved her.

"All I need is you." She smiled.

My heart beat wildly, threatening to break through my chest. "Oh, God, Dana, you've got me," I said, smiling, "You're stuck with me. I'll never let you go," I whispered into her hair as I gently pressed a kiss onto her head.

"Owe," she cried, pulling away from me.

"Oh, sweetheart, I'm so sorry. I completely forgot about your head." I swallowed back the familiar sting of tears. The last thing Dana needed was to see me completely break down.

"It's okay," she said. Before I could comfort her, she raised up on one arm, searching the room. "Where's Sam?"

I squeezed her shoulder, trying to comfort her. "He's fine, sweetie. He's at Whispering Oaks."

"Why?" she asked, her brows furrowed.

"We didn't think it was a good idea for him to see you like this," I said.

"It's that bad?" she asked.

I didn't want to answer, because, yes, it was that bad. "You know Sam is very protective of you," I said instead.

She nodded her head. "He probably wouldn't let anyone touch me after our ordeal."

A stab of guilt pierced my chest.

"But he's all right?" Her eyes were wide. "Nothing happened to him?"

"No, Dolly, he's fine," I reassured her. "Just worried about you. Geneva's with him. He's all right, I promise."

She fell back into the pillows, a small smile spreading across her cheeks. "Good. Geneva will take care of him."

"She will," I said. "She is."

"Can I get some water?" Dana asked softly.

My mother jumped to her feet. "Of course." She poured a glass of cold water from the pitcher and came to stand by Dana's side. "Here, darling." She held out a straw.

When I'd called my mother to tell her what Jillian had done, she and AJ had flown straight to Austin, no questions asked. She knew instinctively that Dana and I would need her. For that, I had never been more thankful.

"Are you Peter's mother?" Dana asked, staring at her.

"Yes, I'm sorry, I didn't introduce myself. I'm Barbara Fontenot, Peter's mother."

"It's nice to finally meet you," Dana said.

"Here, sweetheart, take a sip." My mother held the straw in place and I lifted Dana so she could drink.

She swallowed several times then leaned back onto the pillow. "I wish it would have been under better circumstances." She laughed but immediately grimaced with pain, clutching her ribs.

"Oh, God, Dana." I reached over the bed railing. "I'm so sorry. This is all my fault."

"Peter," she held up one hand and shook her head, "please don't do this. There's no time for guilt. None of this was your fault."

Absolutely, it was, I wanted to say.

"I need you right now," she whispered. "All of you."

She needed me? Didn't she know she had me? All of me…for life?

"No guilt." She raised her perfectly manicured brows, her blue eyes demanding. "Promise me?"

I swallowed down my emotions and nodded. She didn't need my tears, nor my remorse. She only needed me.

"Okay, Dolly." I nodded.

She grinned, those deep dimples appearing like sunshine after the rain.

I leaned down and brushed her lips in a silent gesture of love and fidelity.

"It's nice to finally meet you too, Dana," my mother said, coming to stand beside me. "Is there anything I can get you?"

"If you can convince your son that none of this was his fault that would be awesome." Dana laughed but grimaced.

"Please, Dolly," I begged.

"Peter, I'm fine." She tried to convince me with a wave. "So, what happened? With the bitch, I mean."

AJ snorted.

Dana's eyes sprang wide. "Oh, shit. I mean…" She slapped a hand over her mouth, as if that could ever silence her. I'd never seen her so flustered.

My mother giggled, actually giggled.

I couldn't help but laugh.

"I'm sorry," she said through spread fingers.

My mother grabbed Dana's good hand. "Don't be sorry, sweetheart. I think our family needs someone like you."

Dana grinned but remained silent. Her gaze lifted to mine and I knew what she was asking. She wanted answers about her and Sam's ordeal. But I wasn't prepared to share Jillian's story, not yet.

She needed to heal before she heard the truth. Actually, that wasn't the whole truth. I needed her to heal, for my own peace of mind.

I stared into her eyes. The white surrounding the blue orbs were filled with blotches of red from the beatings she'd received from Jillian.

I gritted my teeth, trying not to let my fury show. Dana and her brother had suffered tremendous trauma at the hands of a lunatic, all because of me.

"Let's talk about that later, okay," I said softly.

She held my gaze for several heartbeats before finally nodding. I laughed to myself, figuring only a concussion and painkillers could make Dana Di Grazio step down from an argument so quickly.

As I gazed over her body, unwanted tears pooled in my eyes. I remembered driving up to the emergency room entrance after receiving Nic's call. Watching the first responders pull her lifeless body from the ambulance had nearly done me in.

"Peter, please," she said.

I stared at her, swallowing my emotions. Having Dana conscious and responsive set my heart at ease.

"I'm all right," she said, clutching my hand. "Truly."

I nodded, catching my tears before they fell. I needed to be strong, for Dana, and myself.

Sensing my agony, my mother intervened. "Dana, I'm so happy about your and Peter's engagement."

Dana beamed with excitement I hadn't seen in a long time. "Thank you. I can't tell you how much it means to me that Peter gave me your mother's ring." She looked down at her finger and panic washed over her face. "Oh, shit, Peter," she shouted, "where's the ring?"

"Don't worry, Dolly," I said, trying to calm her. "It's at home, safe and sound."

"Thank God," she sighed.

"I'm so glad you accepted it." My mom smiled. "I know my mother would be ecstatic to see Peter so in love."

"Thank you," Dana sniffed, reaching out to touch my mother's hand. "That means a lot, especially coming from you."

"Well," my mother continued, "it's true."

My mother's maternal affection filled the room, and my heart swelled with joy. I was lucky to have her back in my life. There was no doubt that she would support Dana and me.

"Who's that?" Dana asked, nodding toward the corner.

"Oh, Dana," my mother's eyes twinkled, "I almost forgot to introduce you to AJ."

AJ walked toward Dana's bedside and stood next to my mother, his arm wrapped around her waist. "Hello, Dana, I'm so glad to meet you."

"Well, it's nice to meet you too, AJ." Dana grinned, knowing how special he was to both my mother and me.

I laughed inwardly as my mother's face flushed and AJ drew her in closer.

"Well, well, well." A deep, familiar voice rang through Dana's room.

My stomach churned when I recognized our newest visitor. Dr. Dick Head. What the hell was he doing here?

I stared at Dana to gauge her reaction, hoping his presence held no effect on her.

She gave a quick wink before turning to face Dr. Dick Head.

I sighed in relief. She had never *truly* wanted him, not like she wanted me.

"Dr. Moore!" she exclaimed with a smile that didn't light up her face like the ones she gave me on a daily basis. Pushing her body up in the bed, she winced in pain.

Dr. Dick Head made a move toward her but I cut him off.

"I've got her." I slipped my hands under her arms and she gripped my neck tight. After readjusting her in the bed, I fluffed up the pillows and placed a soft kiss on her lips. The gesture was more for Dr. Dick Head's benefit than Dana's.

Dana grinned up at me, obviously aware of what I was doing.

Unable to help myself, I leaned in for another kiss, this one deeper, more passionate, and solely for *my* benefit.

"What are you doing here?" she asked.

"Well," he said, chest puffed out, "I *am* an orthopedist you know."

Damn it all. I'd completely forgotten he was an orthopedic surgeon.

The smug smirk on his face made me want to punch him square on the jaw and knock out every perfect tooth in his head. Total dick head.

"When I heard you were here, I just had to take your chart and check in on you for myself to make sure you're okay."

My mother swooned.

Dana sighed.

What the hell?

He walked toward the head of the bed, hand extended as if he was going to examine her.

There was no way in hell this was going to happen. Broken hand, broken ribs, concussion, bruises, contusions, lacerations and all, I wasn't letting my future wife anywhere near this asshole.

"Actually," Dana interrupted, "another doctor stopped by earlier this morning, didn't he, Peter?" she asked, gazing up at me with a conspiratorial wink.

"Um, yes." I tried to play along.

"What was his name?" Dick Head asked, eyes narrowed.

"Oh my goodness, I don't remember now." Dana smiled innocently, pointing to her head. "Must be the blow to my noggin' I guess."

Good catch, Dolly, I thought to myself.

"Dr. Moore, I completely forgot," she said, obviously trying to change the subject, "have you met my in-laws?" She pointed toward my mother and AJ.

I smiled at her announcement.

"In-laws?" he questioned, his brow furrowed.

"Yes," she answered. "Well, actually, they'll be my in-laws soon. Peter and I are engaged."

"You're engaged?" He jerked back as if horrified.

That's right, Dr. Dip Shit, she's mine. Forever.

"Yes," she announced proudly, smiling and giving me a wink.

Yeah, she was mine.

"When's the big day?" he asked me.

Oh, crap. I didn't know, but I sure didn't want him to know that.

"Definitely sooner rather than later," Dana said, reaching across the bed to hold my hand. She stared up at me, her blue eyes bright, dimples on full display. "Very soon I think," she whispered, raising her brows.

What was she asking? We'd discussed a destination wedding, maybe Hawaii, but up until now it had just been talking, nothing set in stone. She'd always been afraid of commitment so I hadn't pushed her.

Had things changed for her? Did she truly want to get married... now? My heart pounded inside my chest and I prayed to God she was being honest.

"Really, Peter," she whispered, answering my silent question.

"Are you sure, Dolly?" I couldn't help but be concerned. I didn't want to get my hopes up for nothing if she was just putting on a display for Dr. Dick Head.

"Really." She smiled.

"Well then," Dick Head said, "congratulations are in order, I guess." He hung his head and stared at Dana's chart avoiding my gaze.

I couldn't help but feel a tiny bit sorry for the guy. I mean, Dana was a catch.

"Well, it looks like from your chart you'll be able to go home soon," he said, smiling at everyone in the room.

"Oh, that's wonderful news," my mother said, clapping her hands. "Everyone will be so thrilled."

Everyone?

"Well, congratulations again, you two."

"Thank you." Dana smiled, oblivious to the silent fight for her affection.

He grasped her foot over the sheet and squeezed. "If you ever need anything, Dana, please don't hesitate to call."

I stood tall. "She'll be fine, I'll make sure of it. But thanks for the offer." I wanted to add, Dick Head, but I knew that wouldn't be appropriate.

Dana gently squeezed my hand, and I realized this battle was over. She was mine, and she'd just announced it to everyone. I had no reason to worry.

"It was nice to meet you all," Dr. Moore said over his shoulder to my mother and AJ.

"You too," they answered.

The doctor took one last look at Dana then stared up at me. "Take care of her, Peter."

There were so many ways I could respond—tell him I was taking care of her all right, had been for a long time. Instead, I gave him a slight nod and watched him return the gesture before he left the room.

"You're so bad." Dana giggled, immediately releasing my hand and clutching her abdomen in pain.

"Oh, Dolly!" I exclaimed, crouching down beside her.

"I'm all right," she breathed heavy, trying to reassure me but I knew better.

"You're not all right."

"I am now that you're here." She reached out her hand and I bent over the railing. "Now kiss me, fiancé."

"Fiancée," I repeated. "It sounds good."

"It sounds fan-fucking-tastic." Before I could remind her that my mother was in the room, she snaked her hand around my neck and she pulled me close.

My lips brushed hers and everything inside me melted. I thanked God she was safe and secure in my arms again.

Even though this pixie creature was so unlike what I *thought* I'd wanted, Dana Di Grazio was *everything* I'd ever needed and dreamed of my entire life. And now she was going to be mine, for the rest of my life. She was right. That sounded pretty fan-fucking-tastic to me too.

CHAPTER 27

PETER

"HINDLEY, you guys are in Europe at the world championship," Dana said, resting on the sofa. "Rory needs this victory."

There was a long pause and I could hear Hindley fussing from the other end.

"There was no *way* I was going to call you," Dana said.

More silence as Dana shook her head and rolled her eyes.

"Because there was no sense in making you worry, that's why. The doctor said I would heal, there weren't any major problems, just bumps and bruises." She bit her lip and I knew she'd revealed too much. "Yes, a few broken bones, but nothing major."

She held the phone away from her ear and winced. Yeah, Hindley was pissed.

"Well, you can help take care of me when you get home, okay?" Her shoulders slumped and she sunk further into the couch.

I could hear the weariness in her voice. Hindley meant well but she was exhausting Dana. I understood her concern though. Hindley was Dana's best friend, and more than anything she wanted to be here to help.

"He what?" Dana shouted, sitting up.

I jumped at her outburst.

She winced in pain.

"Dana," I said, scooting closer.

She held up her hand. Her expression was pained more with emotions than physical distress.

"Hindley," she said, gripping the phone tighter, "I did *not* tell Leif we were engaged before I told you." Dana's eyes cut to mine, the blue orbs wide. "I'm going to kill that motherfucker," she mouthed silently, her face morphing into the deepest scowl I'd ever seen.

"Give me the phone," I demanded. She was hesitant at first, but I raised my brow and motioned my hand for her to turn it over. Finally, she agreed, tentatively holding out the phone with no words of protest. A first for Dana Di Grazio.

I took the phone and held it to my ear. "Hindley, it's Peter."

"Peter, you can try to save her, but it's not going to work. You should have called me as soon as they were taking her to the hospital."

"Hindley, Dana's right. Rory needed to stay focused for his competition, and that means that you needed to stay with him."

"That's bullshit and you know it, Peter. My best friend was kidnapped, held at gunpoint, and physically attacked, and you don't think that warrants a phone call within the first twenty-four hours? Hell, you should have called me two seconds after they loaded her in the fucking ambulance!"

I cringed at the memory of seeing Dana's unconscious body roll out of the ambulance at the hospital the day of her attack.

"You're right, Hindley," I sighed, "but please don't punish Dana. It was my decision. I know how important the world championship is to Rory and his sponsors."

"Fuck the world championship, Peter, this is my best friend. You think I give a shit about skateboarding right now?"

This was Hindley Hagen, pissed. I understood why Rory treaded lightly around her.

"You're right," I sighed. "It was a bad decision on my part, but it was all me, Hindley. Don't blame Dana. Please," I begged.

"Well, what about the engagement? Why didn't she call me about that?" Disappointment rang in her voice. She was hurt that her best friend hadn't called her first. I had to fix this, salvage the situation, and fast.

So I lied.

"She didn't tell you because I asked her not to," I said, smiling at Dana.

"Why would you do that?" She practically shrieked. I was pretty sure if she could have reached through the phone and strangled me, she would have.

"I didn't want anyone to know until I'd told my mother."

"I thought Dana said your mother gave you the ring." Crap, Dana was right. Hindley was smart, and extremely perceptive. She was not going to let me escape this easily.

"My mother did give me the ring," I said, "but I had no idea if Dana would accept it or not. I'd screwed up pretty bad with the whole Jillian thing while I was in Utah."

"Oh," Hindley said as if contemplating my explanation. This was a good sign.

"Trust me, Dana wanted to go straight to your house that evening, but she totally forgot you all were out of town." That was the truth. "I promised Dana after we told my mother she could call and share the good news with you."

"But how did Leif find out?"

God, she was *not* going to let up. This girl was an attorney, so naturally, she was tenacious.

"Leif was over for dinner and Dana just happened to have the ring on. She didn't want to lie to Leif but she made him swear not to tell you."

"I'm going to kill Leif," Dana mouthed.

"He didn't really tell me, per se," Hindley admitted. "It was kind of a slip-up on his part. I know Dana wants to kill him, doesn't she?" Hindley laughed.

Oh, thank God, finally she was beginning to calm down.

"Look, Hindley, the bottom line is Dana feels awful about this. You're her best friend and it's eating her up that she hurt you." I turned so Dana couldn't hear my next statement, pressing my mouth to the phone. "Hindley, she's in a lot of physical pain. It would mean a lot to me if you could find it in your heart to forgive her, just this once."

"I'm sorry, Peter, you're right. I'm being a bratty little kid, aren't I?"

"No," I said, "you guys have been best friends your entire lives. You've been by Dana's side during the most traumatic times of her life. You have every right to be upset. I'm just telling you that she didn't do any of this on purpose. She never meant to hurt you, but now she knows she did and she feels like shit about it."

"Peter!" Hindley exclaimed.

"What?"

"I've never heard you curse before."

"I've been hanging out with your best friend way too much, I guess."

"She's corrupting you." Hindley laughed.

"In the best of ways though." I turned back toward Dana giving her a warm smile and a wink.

"Okay, I'm over my temper tantrum. Put your *fiancée* back on the phone. I won't strangle her, I promise."

"Go easy on her, Hindley."

"I will. And thanks, Peter," she added.

"For what?"

"For making her happy. For taking care of her. For breaking down her walls."

I swallowed hard, fighting back emotions, amazed that she thought I'd had anything to do with Dana's transformation.

I stared at Dana, smiling at the woman I loved. "Actually, she's taking care of me," I said. "Breaking down *my* walls."

"Well, then I'm glad you both have each other."

"Me too, Hindley," I said. I pulled the phone away and held it toward Dana.

She paused before taking it from my hand and leaned over the couch, gently kissing my cheek. "Thank you," she whispered.

I wrapped my hand around her neck and drew her in close, my lips grazing hers. "Don't you know? You're my world. I'd do absolutely anything for you, Dana." Before she could respond, I silenced her with a kiss.

I loved this woman with everything in my being. Her injuries had almost been my undoing. In that moment I vowed to keep her safe and make her feel as special as she truly was.

CHAPTER 28

PETER

"Are you ever going to tell me what happened?" Dana asked, sitting over her bowl of chili at the dining room table. She lifted a spoonful and blew on it. Her perfectly puckered lips had my skin burning.

I shook my head to clear my sordid thoughts. "Finish dinner, then we'll talk," I said.

She dropped her spoon and it clanked against the ceramic bowl. "I'm done," she announced, crossing her arms over her chest, daring me to renege.

I'd been a fool to think she would give up so easily.

"I want to know what happened after they took me to the hospital," she said. "I'm better now, my head feels fine. Talk to me."

The dark circles under her eyes and weary expression revealed she wasn't being completely honest. We both knew you couldn't recover from a concussion after just a few days. The doctor had explained that before they released her. But Dana was a persistent vixen and I knew she was not going to stop hounding me until I gave her answers.

"I know the police are waiting to talk to me," she said, "and they've given me a few days to rest before taking my statement. I don't want to be blindsided. I want *you* to tell me, Peter."

I squirmed in my seat.

"Did Chase really plot this out with Jillian from the beginning?"

What could I say? I knew she had feelings for Chase, not the same kind he held for her, thank goodness. The truth would devastate Dana to know how involved he was. And I knew in my heart Jillian *would* have killed them, she was so desperate. The thought nearly brought me to my knees.

"Do you think Jillian *really* would have killed us?"

My hands shook and my stomach clenched thinking about what could have happened to her and Sam. That was why I hadn't told her everything. She was right, though. She needed to hear the truth from me, not some detective at the police station.

"Peter, just answer me."

"Let's go sit down on the couch, Dana." I walked around the table and helped her up. We walked into the living room and I positioned her on the sofa so she was as comfortable as possible.

"You're stalling," she said.

I raised my gaze from the pillows I was plumping. She was right.

"Just tell me."

I sat beside her and swallowed. "Yes and no."

She drew in a deep breath and held it as her eyelids fluttered closed. After several seconds, she exhaled and opened her eyes, her gaze meeting mine.

"Start with the yes," she said.

"Chase actually used to work for Jillian's father, Walter, several years ago."

Dana straightened. "Are you serious?"

"Yes."

"So, he knew Jillian?"

"He knew *of* her."

Her brows furrowed. "What does that mean?"

"Jillian had a way of making herself known around her father's company. I have no doubt that Chase knew her, I'm just not sure to what extent."

"Do you think they were involved?" she asked.

I shrugged, having no clue, and not really caring.

"Did he know her while you guys were married?" she asked.

"No. Chase worked for Walter after Jillian and I broke up." I didn't want to continue this story, not now, but I knew I had to.

"What?" she whispered, reaching out to touch my leg.

I drew in a deep breath and exhaled. "Chase fell in love with you, Dana. He admitted it to the police."

Her gaze fell to her lap. "I know. I'm sorry."

"Why are you sorry, Dolly? You did nothing wrong."

She raised her head, her blue eyes trained on mine for a long beat. "Go on."

"He was basically obsessed with you. When I came into the picture and started making changes to your company, he wasn't happy, especially when he realized I'd actually been married to Jillian."

She scooted closer. "So, what happened? How did he and Jillian get together?"

"Jillian wanted one thing. Money. Not only to help her dad's company stay afloat and ensure he wouldn't go to jail, but to help her keep her cushy lifestyle and prominent place in high society."

"Bitch," Dana swore under her breath.

"Yeah, she was."

"Is," she corrected.

"Anyway," I continued, "somehow, she heard through the business world in Utah that my family was going to sell our company. When she found out my mom was sick, and in the hospital, I guess she thought she'd take the opportunity to get back into her good graces. Hell, I don't know, Dana."

"Peter," she called softly. "I love you. You know that."

I swallowed back my emotions. I did know. And it was her love that made me strong. "I love you too, Dolly." I reached out and slipped my fingers around her neck, my thumb stroking her soft cheek.

She smiled, her dimples on display. I hadn't seen something so welcoming in days.

"Tell me more."

I let my hand fall and continued. She was strong enough. "In addition to finding my mother at the hospital, she also found me."

"So, she didn't purposely seek you out?"

"No." I shook my head. "Me being at the hospital was a complete surprise to her. She spotted my bag at the nurses' station when she arrived and recognized it was mine."

Dana frowned. "How did she know it was yours? You two haven't been together in several years."

"It's a Utah Jazz basketball duffle bag I won when I was a senior in high school. Jillian used to give me a hard time about the bag."

"How?"

"She always wanted me to buy new luggage, saying I looked like white trash and I embarrassed her when I carried it."

"What a bitch."

"It was a huge bone of contention between us." Jillian had always been more concerned about what *others* thought of her, especially the snooty socialites she ran with. I laughed at the memory.

"What's funny?" she asked.

"I bet Jillian would love to have that duffle bag now as opposed to the orange jumpsuit she'll be wearing for years to come."

Dana giggled and my heart filled with joy.

"So, anyway," I said, "once Jillian realized I was back in Utah, I guess she changed her strategy. Somehow, she convinced the nurse that she was my wife and they handed my bag over to her, no questions asked."

"That was dumb."

"Totally inappropriate. Anyway, she heard my phone ringing inside the bag, dug it out and answered it before she reached my mother's room."

"That's when she talked to me, isn't it?"

"Yep," I said, gritting my teeth.

"So, you guys were really never together while you were in Utah?"

"Dana, I told you that."

"I know," she slumped, "it's just…"

I reached for her hand. "What?"

"I was hurt and confused, and my head was all over the place. She told me she was your wife and I freaked out." She dropped her head, closing her eyes.

She was obviously tired and I was only upsetting her more. I needed to end this story.

"Apparently, Jillian overheard AJ and my mother tell me that I actually owned almost half of my family's company. But nothing could be done, as far as the sale of it went, without my approval."

"Hold it right there, Peter." Her eyes narrowed. "I got in a shit-ton of trouble with Jillian when she found out I had no clue about your family's company, its potential sale, or your stake in it. Why didn't you tell me?"

"Dolly, it wasn't like that, I swear. You were sick and had a lot going on with the dealership. To be honest, my head was focused on that, not my family's business. I'm so sorry, it wasn't intentional."

"Well, lucky for you I'm a good actress because I told her you signed your shares over to your mom and wouldn't receive any money from the sale. And I told her you didn't have access to any of the funds."

"Dana, that was brilliant. And she bought it?"

She shrugged one shoulder and smiled. "I'm very convincing when I want to be."

I laughed. "Yes, yes, you are."

"So, then what happened?" She yawned and I knew we should stop.

"Maybe we should finish this story tomorrow, after you've gotten some sleep."

"No way, Fontenot." She held up a finger and poked me in the shoulder. "You are finishing this story. Tonight."

I shook my head and smiled. "Bossy much?"

Her blue eyes twinkled with a devilish promise. "You have no idea."

I swallowed hard. This girl was dangerous. And I loved her more than life itself.

"Go on." She rolled her wrist in an effort to prod me on.

"After Jillian called you on my phone at the hospital, she realized who you were and that you owned a dealership. Somehow, she discovered your company used her father's software. She assumed you were one of the many whom her father had syphoned money from."

"How?" Dana asked.

"I don't know. No one seems to right now."

"And?"

"And, I guess she figured skimming more off the top of your company would be an easy enough task. Once she dug further, she discovered Chase was working for you as your CFO. I think that's when her game plan changed."

"How so?"

"I think she decided to get her money *and* destroy me. Through you."

Dana tilted her head. "I don't understand. Why didn't Chase just go to the police when Jillian contacted him? Or at least come to me or Uncle Nic and tell us?"

The pain in her expression was palpable. It killed me to know someone she trusted so vehemently had betrayed her.

"I don't know, sweetheart." I rubbed her thigh, trying to bring her solace.

She grabbed my hand and squeezed it.

Glancing down I saw the brace on her other hand. I shuddered at the memory of what Jillian had done to her. Dana was hurting, mentally and physically, but I knew she'd never rest until I finished the story. Against my better judgment, I continued.

"Once Jillian realized just how much you meant to Chase, she used his affections to blackmail him."

"How?"

"She threatened to hurt you and pin the embezzlement scheme on him if he went to the cops. At least that's the story he's telling the police. Jillian isn't talking."

"Holy shit!" Dana exclaimed. "That's a lot of bat-shit crazy right there."

I fought to bury the images of Jillian actually killing Dana and Sam. If Sam hadn't been brave enough to fight back, I knew Dana wouldn't be sitting here in front of me today.

"Peter," Dana said, squeezing my hand.

My gaze found hers.

"This wasn't your fault," she said. "None of it. You were trying to protect me this entire time. Please, stop blaming yourself. I'm here, Sam's here, and we're safe. That's all that matters. Okay?"

I glanced over her shoulder, staring at the wall of glass behind her. Would I ever stop blaming myself?

"Please, Peter. I need you."

I returned my attention to her.

"I need all of you," she said on a breathy sigh.

I nodded. She was right. Her recovery depended on me letting the "what-ifs" go. Dana and Sam were here, they were safe, and she was mine. That was what I had to concentrate on now. That was all that really mattered.

"So, you said yes and no that Chase was involved," she said. "What's the no?"

"Well, technically Chase didn't plan any of this. He told the police Jillian blackmailed him. He thought by going along with the kidnapping, he was actually protecting you, if you can believe that bullshit."

"What a crock," she said with a laugh, wincing.

I shuddered at her pain but continued. "The bottom line is, he had a chance to call the police from the very beginning and he didn't."

"Isn't he the one who called the police in the end, I mean?"

All I could do was nod. I didn't want to give this asshole any credit, but the truth was Chase had called the police, and for that I was thankful. Even though I wanted to kill the bastard with my bare hands.

"Did Chase ever hit you?" I asked. If that asshole had laid one finger on her, not even jail would keep him safe from my wrath.

"No."

"Thank God."

"Actually," she continued, "he tried to stop Jillian. Most of the time he wasn't even near me when she was attacking me."

I closed my eyes and grimaced at the image.

"Peter," she called out.

I opened my eyes and stared at her.

"I'm here. I'm safe. I know Chase could have done better, but honestly, he did protect me, somewhat." She paused as if trying to justify a way to explain her bizarre thinking. "I could tell the whole time that Chase wasn't completely involved in this, like he was being forced to go along with Jillian's plan."

"It doesn't change anything, Dana," I said, my voice growing louder. I was tired of her giving this asshole a free pass just because she'd cared about him at one point in the past.

"Will he be charged?" she asked.

I couldn't believe she was still worried about this guy. "Why are you so concerned about Chase, Dana?" I demanded. Her blindness toward Chase and his involvement in her attack was pissing me off.

"Calm down, Peter. I'm not concerned about him. I just feel...." She struggled to find the right words. "I'm just heartbroken, I guess.

I trusted Chase, with my life. It hurts to know he could do this to me." She stared down at her lap for a long moment before returning her gaze to me. "In the end, I guess he did help me though."

"Helped you?" I sneered. "This guy could have stopped this before it ever escalated to a kidnapping. All these injuries you've sustained," I waved my hand up and down her body, "are a direct result of him allowing Jillian to intimidate him. I'm not going to sit here and listen to you defend him anymore." I jumped up and started to walk away.

Her small hand grabbed my wrist and tugged me back but I kept walking. She yelped in pain and I turned and sunk down to my knees.

"Dana, I'm so sorry, I didn't mean to hurt you."

"It's all right," she exhaled through gritted teeth. "You're right. Chase could have and should have stood up to Jillian and stopped her. Or at the very least gone to the police, or me as soon as he found out what she was up to."

I pressed a kiss to her hand, knowing this was hard for her to accept. The betrayal of an employee and a friend weighed heavy on her heart.

"It's obvious that his 'love' for me," she mocked with air quotes, "was warped, at best." Drawing in a deep breath, she worked to calm herself, pain etched in her face.

"Dana, just rest, sweetheart. None of this is important right now. All that matters is you're safe, you're here with me, and those assholes won't ever hurt you or Sam again."

I slipped my hands around her face and my thumbs traced the dark circles under her eyes. I wanted so much to take away her pain and suffering. Chase had wounded her in more ways than even *I* could understand.

"Are you still hungry?" I asked, trying to change the subject. "You didn't eat all your dinner."

"Actually, I'm really tired." She blew out a breath. "Would you mind taking me to bed?"

I smiled and scooped her in my arms. "May I join you?"

"Peter," she said in a husky tone, "we've been joined together since the day I doused you with beer."

I laughed at the image in my head—Dana's shirt completely soaked, her nipples puckered and pointed toward the heavens. I'd never seen such an arousing sight in all my life. My body hummed with desire but I worked to tamp down my lust.

She reached up and stroked my face. "When I hurt, you hurt."

I nodded in agreement.

"And whenever I'm content, whenever I'm happy, it's *because* of you."

I lowered my head and pressed a soft kiss to her mouth. "Same, Dolly. When you're happy, I'm happy."

"It's funny," she said as I carried her down the hall.

"What's that?" I asked, walking into the bedroom. I reached down and pulled the covers back, trying not to jostle her.

"Since my parents died and my boyfriend walked out on me, I pretty much closed myself off to love, of any kind. I mean, there was Hindley and Sam, of course, they were unconditional loves for me, but that's different."

I watched as she struggled for words, possibly a first for Dana Di Grazio.

She drew in a breath and held it for a long moment before sagging into my arms with a sigh. Her blue eyes met mine. "When my parents died and my boyfriend left me, my walls went up. Months turned into years and eventually my walls became like a cement fortress around my heart, so high and so strong that I couldn't even feel the beat of it anymore."

I sat down beside her, my throat constricting at her raw honesty.

"You're the first person I've ever loved with my whole heart, Peter."

Her gaze held mine and my eyes burned.

"To be honest," she continued, "I didn't even know if I could love again. Then one day I looked up into these mesmerizing, mix-matched eyes and that was when I felt it. That was the moment I found myself, in your eyes, Peter. My heart began to beat again, my *whole* heart, maybe for the first time ever."

"Dana, that's—" I swallowed hard, not knowing how to express the depths of my love for this sprite of a woman.

"I meant what I said at the hospital, Peter. I want to marry you." There was a long pause. "Now," she added.

My eyes searched hers, looking for any hesitation. Were her words real or was she delirious from the pain meds?

"I don't want to wait until Hawaii," she said. "I mean, I want to go and have a ceremony there too, but I want to marry you here. Now. I don't want to wait."

I sat dumfounded by her request.

"I don't want to waste another day not being yours, completely. What happened to Sam and me opened my eyes. The kidnapping made me realize, for the second time, just how precious life is. Over the years since my cancer diagnosis, I'd forgotten that fact. I'd become terribly self-absorbed."

"Are you sure, Dana?" I asked. "I mean, we can wait."

She grinned, her deep dimples revealing her complete and utter honesty. "I'm sure, Peter."

My heart filled with so much joy I thought I might actually explode.

"Now, come to bed with me," she said in that smooth, sultry voice. "I know I can't fuck you fifty ways to Sunday but I can at least hold on to you. I can rest my head on your chest and listen to your heartbeat."

I couldn't believe her words of love and adoration, her confession of commitment toward me. God, this woman was amazing.

"My heart beats your name, Dana."

She stared at me in disbelief.

"Always," I added.

Switching off the light on her nightstand, I walked around the bed and pulled the covers back, sliding in next to her, cautious not to move the bed too much for fear of hurting her.

From the glow of the downtown lights outside I could see her smiling.

I snaked my arm under her neck and drew her in close to my chest.

"I love you, Peter," she said softly.

I pressed a kiss to her head. "I love you more."

Her breathing evened out and within a few seconds, she was asleep.

I squeezed her tighter, thanking God she and Sam were safe. Right here, in my arms, was the only place I wanted Dana to be.

Her walls had finally fallen. Now it was up to me to protect her and her heart, for the rest of our lives.

CHAPTER 29

PETER

THE DOORBELL CHIMED with an ominous tone. My body trembled, knowing who stood on the other side, and the power she held.

"Are you sure you want me to stay, darling?" my mother asked Dana as I walked toward the door.

"You have to," Dana said, beseeching her. "If the adoption agency says no, if she says no kid wants someone like me to be their mother, maybe you can convince them."

I paused and glanced over my shoulder. It was unlike her to be filled with so much self-doubt.

"I just love him so much, Barbara," she whispered, assuming I couldn't hear their private conversation. "I can't give him his own children, so I have to give him this. I just have to," she whimpered, her words so sorrowful it literally made my heart ache.

"Dana," I called.

She whipped around to face me, unaware that I'd heard her pleas, her expression graver than I'd ever seen.

Forgetting the ring of the bell, I stalked back toward her, taking her face firmly in my hands. "You've given me *everything* I've ever wanted. You've given me *yourself*, your whole heart, remember?"

She nodded her head and I wiped away a tear.

"And you've promised me your life. Whatever happens, we're in this together. I'm not leaving you. You're not leaving me. Children or not. Got it?"

Her eyes darted between mine, and for a minute, I was actually worried she'd lost it. Finally, she collapsed in my arms, wrapping her tiny hands around my waist.

"I just love you so much, Peter." She breathed into my chest.

"I love you too, Dolly," I whispered in her hair. "Now come on." I tugged on her good hand, staring down at the brace on the other, images of her kidnapping threatening to ruin this moment. I quickly wiped them away, remembering how lucky I was to have Dana here with me. "Let's answer the door and find out what Jane has to say. No past, no future, just today, Dana," I stated flatly.

Her expression slayed me. She looked so weak and vulnerable.

I wiped away the smudge marks of mascara under her eyes. "There," I said, placing a soft kiss on her forehead. "Better?"

She gave a small nod. We walked together toward the door and I gave her hand a slight squeeze.

"Together, no matter what?" I asked, raising a brow.

"No matter what," she said, smiling.

I opened the door and stared at the woman before me. "Good afternoon, Jane," I said. "Please, won't you come in?"

Her gaze traveled from me to Dana and her smile fell.

I squeezed Dana's hand, trying to remind her she had to pull herself together.

"Hey, Jane, it's great to see you again. Please, come in." Dana smiled, and just like that, my girl was back.

We stepped back, allowing Jane to enter.

"Would you like something to drink?" Dana asked, her voice void of any anxiety or nervousness. God, I loved this woman.

"No, but thank you," she answered softly.

"Jane, this is Peter's mother, Barbara Fontenot." Dana held out her hand, motioning toward my mother. "And this is AJ Rhyne, her..." She was at a loss as to how to introduce AJ and honestly, so was I.

"Yes, this is my boyfriend," my mother said with all the confidence in the world.

My stomach twisted in knots. I was happy for her, I really was, but I had to keep all my wits about me right now.

A satisfied gleam flashed in AJ's eyes at my mother's admission. They both smiled at one another and shared the same look that Dana and I did. I couldn't help but be happy for both of them in that moment.

"Nice to meet you both," Jane said. She turned to Dana. "Are you feeling better? I heard about your attack."

I winced at the reminder.

Dana's body tensed and I gave her another reassuring squeeze.

"I'm much better, thank you for asking," she said. She glanced up at me. "I've had a good caretaker."

"She hasn't been the best patient." I laughed, giving Jane a knowing wink. Her returning smirk revealed she knew exactly what I meant. "But yes, she's healing nicely, thank you for asking, Jane."

"May I speak freely in front of them?" Jane asked, looking from me over to my mother and AJ.

"Please," Dana said before I could. "They're family."

Family.

My heart swelled at the admission.

My mother beamed with joy.

"Please, have a seat," I offered, motioning to a chair.

Dana and I sat on the sofa as Jane took the chair opposite us. She sat her briefcase on the floor near her feet. I couldn't help but wonder what answers lied within the leather bag.

"Well." Jane drew in a deep breath and exhaled. This couldn't be good. "I have good news and I have bad news."

"Oh, God," Dana whimpered.

I tucked her into my side, trying to quell my own fears.

"The good news is, you've been approved, not only for foster care but for adoption as well."

"Are you serious?" Dana asked, her hands covering her mouth.

Jane nodded. "Yes, I'm sure."

"Oh, thank God!" Dana shouted, throwing her hands up in the air. "Peter," she cried, glancing up at me, "we're going to be parents."

I grinned from ear to ear. Parents.

"I'm sorry," Jane said. "I should have told you sooner."

"How did it happen so quickly?" Dana asked the question I was wondering as well. "I thought you said it may take months to be approved."

"Well, that's where the bad news comes in."

"Oh, no," Dana sighed.

"It's only bad news depending on how you look at it," Jane explained, the tilt of her head and the gleam in her eye an indicator that she was about to ask us for something she usually didn't.

My body froze. What would she ask us to do? It didn't matter. We just wanted a child, any child.

"I know you all were looking for a younger child."

"Yes," Dana answered.

"Well, we have one. A girl, two-and-a-half years old," she said with an expression of uncertainty that made my stomach clench. There was more here that she wasn't telling us.

"Peter!" Dana squealed, her eyes welling up with tears. "She and Abbi could be best friends." Her smile lit up the room, and I couldn't remember a time I loved her more.

"That's not all," Jane interrupted our celebration.

Dana and I stilled as our eyes instantly fixated on Jane, our bodies hanging on her next words as if our lives depended on them. Actually, our lives did depend on Jane's words.

"The girl has two brothers," she said.

"They're going to be separated?" Dana asked, her brow furrowing.

"We don't want them to be," Jane said, staring between us.

"So, wait," Dana said, sitting up straighter. "You want us to adopt all *three* kids?"

Jane nodded her head. "That's why I put your application on the fast track, to get it approved so quickly."

Dana jerked her head and stared up at me, her face cautiously optimistic. "Peter?" she whispered, her eyes full of anxiety and excitement. She was silently asking for permission that she feared I'd deny, but the truth was, I'd always wanted a large family. I never dreamed I'd get it instantly though.

"There's more," Jane interrupted.

"More kids?" Dana half shouted, jerking around so fast, her raven-colored curls swatted me in the face.

"No," Jane laughed, "there's more to their story."

"Abuse?" Dana whispered.

"No. This is something entirely different." Jane stared at Dana. "I thought, given your background and family history, Dana, these children might be a good fit for you and Peter."

"So, what's the more?" I asked.

"The girl, Lillian," Jane began, "has Down syndrome."

A collective gasp escaped from all of us in the room, everyone except Dana. Instead, her face erupted into an angelic smile, as if she'd been given the most precious gift imaginable.

Jane went on, ignoring our obvious surprise. "I just thought if there was ever a better person to be Lilly's mother, it would be you, Dana," Jane explained. "Given your brother's situation and your experience with him, that is."

"Oh, God," Dana whispered, her hands covering her mouth.

"You'll need time to talk about this, I'm sure," Jane said. "I've brought all three of their files." She reached into her bag and pulled out several manila folders, laying them on the coffee table.

Attached to each folder was a black and white photo stapled to the outside with the children's names on the top. All three had the same last name, *Avelar*.

I scanned each file.

Lucas – age 10

Levi – age 6

Lillian – age 2

"Peter, look," Dana whispered, running her fingers over the photos. "They're beautiful."

I studied the pictures over her shoulder and observed they were of Hispanic descent, each having jet-black hair just like Dana and me. Even though the photos were in black and white, it was clear to see that Lilly's eyes were light, like Dana's, and her hair wavy like both of ours.

"I'll leave these files here for you to look through," Jane said. "I'll give you a call tomorrow afternoon after you've had some time to talk it over."

"How long have they been in the foster care system?" Dana asked.

"Only for a few months. Their mother left them shortly after Lilly was born. They've been in the care of their maternal grandmother for the past two years, but she just had a stroke and can no longer care for them. There is no other family willing to take them in. I suspect because of Lilly," she said, her voice full of the pain we all felt.

"Are you serious?" Dana jerked up, her tone clipped and snarky.

"Raising a special needs child is very challenging, Dana," Jane explained with no apologies. "You of all people should know that."

"I also know it's one of the most rewarding and amazing opportunities of your life if you're graced with the presence of a special needs person," Dana replied. Her words were harsh and defensive, a reprimand of sorts, and I feared Jane may be taken aback by Dana's outburst. "They bless you in ways you never dreamed imaginable.

It's been *my* honor and *my* privilege to have my brother in my life, not a challenge."

Jane smiled. "That's exactly why I thought you would be a good match for them."

"Why?" she asked.

"You're fearless in your convictions, Dana. That's something these children will need from their mother."

Dana's chin quivered and she bit her lip to keep from crying. "You think I'll be a good mother?" There was such doubt in her voice that it surprised me.

Jane walked over to sit beside Dana, gently placing her hand on Dana's thigh.

"Dana, you'll make an amazing mother. Whether it's to these children or to others we have in the system, whomever you and Peter choose will be blessed to have you."

Dana fell into Jane's embrace, her shoulders shaking with sobs.

I sat back, knowing this was the kind of comfort only Jane could offer her.

Jane rubbed her back and after a few moments, Dana leaned back, wiping at her eyes with her sleeves.

AJ reached over and handed her tissues, winking at Dana and offering his own type of reassurance.

"Well," Jane sighed, "take a look at their folders and think about it." She stood and walked toward her briefcase. "I'll call you tomorrow afternoon and you can let me know what you've decided."

"We want them!" Dana shouted.

Jane stopped mid-motion as Dana spun around to face me, her eyes pleading for an answer as if she were a small child begging Santa Claus to grant her one wish. I'd told her before I'd give her anything she wanted, and this request was no different.

I knew in my gut that Lilly needed Dana. They all needed us, as much as we needed them. Together we would be a family. Our decision was clear and required no more time to make.

I nodded once.

An expression of sheer joy lit up her face and she wrapped her arms around me. "Thank you," she whispered.

"But you haven't even looked at their files or read over their history," Jane questioned, her brows furrowed.

"It doesn't matter," I said. Dana released me and stood by my side, wrapping an arm around my waist. "They need us, we need them. What do we need to do to make this happen?"

Dana hugged me tight, glancing up at me. Her deep dimples were on display. "I love you," she mouthed.

I kissed her head. "I love you too, Dolly," I whispered in her ear.

"Well, um," Jane stumbled, "we'll need to complete more paperwork. We'll need to schedule a home visit with the children, so they can meet you. And I'll need your bank statements showing your joint financial relationship."

Dana released her hold and stared up at me, her eyes wide. We'd been so preoccupied with the events over the last week that we'd completely forgotten to open a joint bank account.

"I don't want to take your money, Peter," she said.

I stared at her in confusion. "What are you talking about?"

"From the sale of your family's company," she explained. "I don't want you to think I am trying to get your money. If we get married, this is a community property state. Whatever is yours is mine, no matter if you acquired it before or after we get married."

"Dolly," I said, grasping her face, "what in the hell are you talking about? I couldn't care less about the money. All I want is you." I pressed a soft kiss to her lips.

"Peter," she sighed, wrapping her arms around me. Suddenly she released me and whipped around to face Jane. "What if we're married? Didn't you say that would give us a better standing in court?"

"Well, yes," Jane said, "but I don't think adopting these children is a good reason to get married if you weren't already planning to."

"We were," Dana explained. "I just told Peter a few days ago that I want to get married now, not wait for our plans in Hawaii, didn't I, Peter?" She looked up at me, begging for my confirmation.

"Dolly," I whispered, pulling her closer, "I don't want to rush you just so we can adopt these children." I meant it. I knew getting her to agree to Hawaii next month had been huge.

"Peter, I love you," she declared. "I want to be with you. Forever. I told you that the other night and I don't want to wait. You have my heart. Why can't our forever start sooner rather than later?"

My breath caught at the expression in her bright blue eyes. She really did want this.

"Dana," Jane called, reaching out to touch her arm, "I know you love Peter and you two were already planning to marry soon, but are you sure this is a good idea?"

Dana glanced up at me, her eyes holding me captive. "Do you love me?"

Why did she need to ask me? I thought I'd already made it abundantly clear to her with my actions and words. "More than anything. You know that."

"Do you want to marry me?"

"More than anything in this world."

She smiled and turned to face Jane. "You see, this isn't about the children. I understand better than anyone how precious life is, especially now after my kidnapping."

I shuddered at the thought of what might have happened to her.

"I don't want to waste another minute to start my life with Peter. And now, you've shown us these children, and well, we're willing to start sooner rather than later." She looked up to me for confirmation.

I nodded my head and smiled.

"So, what do we need to do to get these kids?"

Jane chuckled and leaned toward her bag, unloading a massive pile of papers. "All right then."

"Holy shit!" Dana exclaimed. "Oh, I'm sorry." She slapped a

hand over her mouth as she realized her offense. "I guess I better start learning to watch my tongue." Her laughter was infectious.

For the first time in hours, I saw the tension ease from Dana's body. Her joy made my heart swell. This was it, the day all my dreams were finally coming true. The day the woman I loved agreed to be mine, forever, and the moment our children were born. Born from our hearts and our combined love and desire to give them a better life. I truly was the luckiest man alive.

CHAPTER 30

DANA

WE WALKED IN THE DOOR, just now returning from dropping Sam back off to Whispering Oaks. Peter was busy in the kitchen preparing dinner so I made my way to the shower.

Sam had spent the night with us. We'd had a marathon of his favorite show, *The Three Stooges*. I needed to reassure myself that Sam was all right after being kidnapped and witnessing my attack. And he needed to see that his sister was on the mend, physically and emotionally.

After undressing, I stepped into the shower. The water cascading over my body felt like heaven, a soothing balm for all that ailed me. The pain in my ribs was diminishing, and the constant throbbing in my head from my concussion was all but gone. Even my hand was feeling remarkably better. I attributed the speedy recover to my gorgeous nurse.

Reaching up to grab the shampoo I noticed a dull ache in my chest. I cringed at the memory of Jillian's boot connecting with my body multiple times during her attack. I'd had a few nightmares over the last week. Peter was worried about the long-term effects the kidnapping would have on Sam and me, but I assured him we would both be fine in time. I just hoped it was true.

Peter and I had sat Sam down and told him about adopting the kids. He instantly fell in love with all three, especially Lilly, as I knew he would. He wasn't quite sure of the concept of an instant family, but he was more than excited about being an uncle. He loved Uncle Nic, and when I told him that was what he'd be to our children, his face lit up like Christmas.

Thoughts of Peter, me, and our children running around a huge yard with a dog and a white picket fence danced through my mind as I lathered the suds in my hair. Never before had I allowed myself to dream of a family. It hurt too much. Now that I had Peter, that possibility was no longer a dream. It was becoming a reality for us.

I turned my back toward the spray of water surging from the showerhead above, closing my eyes as I let the rippling droplets wash away the foaming bubbles from my hair while visions of Peter flashed through my mind. God, I loved him.

Suddenly, a blast of cold air drifted over my body. I shivered, wondering if perhaps I'd run out of hot water. Before I could open my eyes, the shower door clicked closed and warm lips covered one breast as a large hand massaged my other. I moaned and pushed my chest into Peter's delicious hold.

"I see you made it," I joked.

He bit my nipple and sucked hard.

"Oh, God," I groaned. The man's mouth was lethal. My arms fell to his shoulders, now slick with water. Grabbing his face, I pulled it away from my breasts, no longer able to keep my lips off from his. "I thought you didn't want to shower with me. You said I smelled."

He grinned, a devilish smirk I'd never seen before. "I figured I should help you get clean since you're obviously so dirty." His gaze traveled the length of me before he winked. I nearly came on the spot. This man would be the death of me. And I couldn't wait.

"What about dinner?" I asked.

"Dinner can wait," he replied, his deep voice sending shock

waves of desire through my entire body. "This can't." His lips came crashing down on mine, his tongue licking along my bottom lip.

I opened my mouth and allowed him entry. This man could kiss like a sailor home on leave. God, it was so good, more potent than any liquor I'd ever consumed. My body melted into his as his erection rested along my stomach, causing me to draw in a quick breath.

My good hand slid down between our bodies and wrapped around his length.

He moaned into my mouth and deepened the kiss. Slowly his hands drifted down to my hips. With a firm grasp he flipped me around.

I gasped and was choked by the water pelting on my face.

He reached above me and adjusted the showerhead. I pushed the hair from my face as the water ran down my back like a warm massage.

"I don't want to hurt you," he whispered in my ear. His voice sounded so anguished it broke my heart. He was still consumed with worry over my physical well-being.

I turned and face him. "I'm better, Peter. You're not hurting me. The only way you will is if you stop touching me."

He chuckled and the sound went all the way down to my center.

"Put your good hand on the wall, Dolly," he instructed, his voice a low growl.

My eyes widened in anticipation. This was not a persona Peter usually donned but I found myself wildly aroused. I pressed my hand against the tile and smiled, anxiously awaiting his next move.

One hand slid along my back, coming to rest between my shoulders as the other still held my hips firm.

I held my breath, anticipating what would come next.

Slowly he pressed me down until my back was parallel to the shower floor and my ass pressed up against his impressive package. Holy fuck, this was hot.

His hand moved up into my long, wet hair. He fisted a hand full and twisted it around his fingers, giving it a slight tug that was just this side of painful.

My legs shook with anticipation, I was so close to release.

He leaned over me. "Are you okay?"

I could hear the controlled desire in his voice. I wanted him, but I needed him to know I was getting better every day, with him.

"I'm fine, Peter. Please," I urged, "don't stop."

With no other words he surged inside me.

I moaned at the fullness of him.

His grip tightened and the heat of his fingers seared me. He was perfect. This moment was perfect. I knew I would do anything to make Peter happy. The last of my walls crumbled with each deep thrust. Suddenly I realized, I had given myself to him completely a long time ago.

I turned and glanced over my shoulder. "I love you."

He grinned and lifted my hips, pushing in deeper.

I braced myself on the shower wall. "Oh, fuck, Peter!" I screamed, my words echoing as I adjusted to his new angle.

He slowed his pace. "Oh, God, Dana, are you all right?"

"Peter," I moaned, pushing against him, "don't stop. It feels so fucking good."

One hand clutched my waist, securing my body as he pumped into me harder. His other slipped between my thighs, playing my body like a finely-tuned instrument.

My insides clenched around him. I was so close.

He leaned over me, his chest on my back. "Dana," he moaned in my ear. "God, you're beautiful." With each word he pushed deeper, our climax near.

I turned and saw our reflection in the glass shower wall. Our bodies working together, in and out, was the most erotic thing I'd ever seen. The image sent me spiraling out of control.

"Shit, Dana," he groaned.

Peter rarely cursed, especially during sex, and for some reason his expletives made me smile.

"Yes!" I yelled as my climax rolled over me. "Oh, Peter, yes! Harder."

He thrust two more times and he stilled inside me, both our bodies shaking through our release.

We stood for several minutes, my body still slumped against the wall, both of us gasping for air.

"I'm sorry, Dolly," he whispered as he pulled me tighter into his body, molding us together.

"Why?"

"I was rough with you. I hurt you."

I couldn't believe what he was saying. Peter thought he'd physically harmed me. I had to reassure him that nothing could be further from the truth.

I turned to face him and smiled. "Peter, I loved every minute of this...." What could I call our lovemaking? There were no words to describe what we'd just experienced together.

"I didn't hurt you?" he asked, brows raised.

"Oh, Peter," I whispered, stroking his strong, stubble-covered jaw. "You didn't hurt me at all. I wanted this. I wanted you," I professed. "That was the most erotic, sensual thing I've ever done. Being with you is always amazing."

He bent down and lifted me in the air. I straddled his waist and my good hand snaked around his neck, grabbing a fistful of wet hair.

"I love you," I said.

He grinned, small dimples bracketing his full lips. Leaning down he kissed me softly.

Being in Peter's arms, pressed close to his body, my head fell into the crook of his neck. After years of searching, I'd finally found home.

CHAPTER 31

PETER

THE OVEN TIMER buzzed and I opened the door and pulled out the cookie sheet containing the snack-sized pizza I'd put in earlier in anticipation of our guests. I set them on the island to let them cool. Glancing across the room, I watched as Dana fluffed the pillows on the couch for what seemed like the hundredth time. My heart seized with worry for her. She was so nervous for this meeting and so was I.

Suddenly the doorbell rang.

Dana stood ramrod straight, her gaze locking on mine, eyes wide. My usually fearless, pint-sized dynamo was scared.

"It will be okay, Dolly," I said, walking toward the front entrance. I held out my hand and smiled. "Come on. Let's not keep them waiting."

She slowly made her way to me and took my hand. She stared up at me, her face pale. "But, Peter, what if—"

I leaned down and kissed the words from her mouth. Pulling back, I stared down into the most beautiful blue eyes I'd ever seen. Her silent gaze begged me for the assurance she needed.

"They will love you. Just like me," I added, placing a soft kiss on her head. I motioned toward the door and she nodded. I turned the handle and swung open the door. "Hey, Jane," I said.

"Hi, Peter." Her gaze swung to Dana. "Hey, Dana."

Dana stood mute.

I squeezed her hand.

"Oh, sorry," Dana said. "Hi, Jane." All of her attention was trained on the boys behind her.

Jane stepped back and waved toward the boys. "Lucas, Levi," she called. "Come meet Mr. and Mrs. Fontenot."

Mr. and Mrs. Fontenot. It had a good ring.

Jane's eyes went wide. "Oh, I'm sorry, you two haven't—"

"Soon," Dana and I spoke in unison. We both laughed and suddenly some of the tension was broken.

Slowly, two boys stepped around Jane. "This is Peter and this is Dana," she said, waving her hand toward us.

I studied the two boys standing before me. They were shocked and scared, like animals you'd find in the pound. The younger of the two, Levi, seemed to still have a sense of innocent bewilderment. As if he wanted to believe this place was safe, but history had given him a reason to be skeptical.

Lucas, the oldest, stood a head taller than Levi and his scowl was much more menacing. He wore the face of a brave warrior, someone preparing to do battle. The dark smudges underneath his eyes made me wonder how many sleepless evenings he'd spent watching over his brother and sister to keep them safe.

"Hey, guys," Dana said, smiling. I knew if anything would work on these boys it would be Dana's dimples. And hopefully my pizza rolls.

Both boys stood stock-still, afraid to move, as if their very lives depended on them keeping up their walls. It was a defense mechanism and I'd seen it in Dana when I first moved in. I'd broken down her walls and I knew, given enough time, I would with these children as well. Much like Dana, it would take time, a lot of time, but I had that. And I had more than enough love to share.

"Would you guys like a popsicle?" Dana asked in a voice about two octaves higher than her normal gruff tone.

Again, the boys stood like statues, their eyes downcast. This was not going well, but I knew Dana was determined to break through.

"I bought the tropical fruit flavored pack," she continued, unfazed by their silence.

In sync, both boys' eyes shot up to Dana's. Had she hooked them?

"I've got pineapple, peach and mango," she said.

The younger one, Levi, squirmed in place like an animal eager to seek the affections of his owner. It was obvious both boys wanted a popsicle, but feared what we may do, expecting us to reprimand them for asking for something so simple as a treat.

"Wath mango?" Levi finally spoke, his voice hinting at a small lisp.

Dana's face lit up as she and I both realized this was her chance to at least chip away at their walls.

"Oh, mango is *so* good," she said. "It's a fruit, like apples or bananas, but so much better." She smiled, her dimples deeper than I'd ever seen them. "Do you want to try one?"

Levi's eyes darted toward his brother, silently asking for permission, but Lucas's eyes stayed locked on mine. This was my reminder that *he* was in charge of his brother and sister. This was going to take time, a lot of time.

"Peter made pizza rolls too," she said.

Lucas's gaze darted to Dana. Maybe my pizza rolls would be his hook.

"Oh," Levi said, "Lucas lovth pitha rolls." He gazed back at his brother. "Come on." Unwilling to wait, Levi took hold of Dana's outstretched hand.

She glanced up at me, the brightest smile adorning her face. Levi was already hers.

"What happened to your hand?" he asked, pointing to Dana's brace.

"I, uh." She glanced up at me.

My body stiffened at the reminder of her attack.

"I just hit it on something," she finally said.

"What did you bang it on?" This kid was relentless. Like the woman holding his hand.

Dana stared back at me again.

I shrugged, having no clue how this parenting thing worked. Did you lie to protect them?

"It was this big metal thing," she answered. "A girl was swinging it around and it hit my hand."

"Wath it a athident?" he asked, the lisp in his voice more pronounced as he warmed up to her.

"Yes." Dana smiled lovingly. "It was an accident." I noticed her voice was strained but controlled.

His brows furrowed. "You thould be more careful next time." God, this little boy was adorable, worrying about Dana's well-being.

Dana glanced over her shoulder as she tugged Levi into the kitchen, giving me a small wink. He followed her, asking more questions. Like most men, Levi was already a goner for Dana.

I looked back at Lucas, knowing it would take much more than a popsicle and pizza rolls to win him over.

I shoved my hands in my pockets, unsure of what to say next. "Do you want some pizza rolls?" I asked, nodding to the kitchen.

He just stared at me, his lips pressed in a firm line.

Well, crap.

"So, um, Lucas," I stumbled, not really knowing where I was going. "What grade are you in?"

His gaze roamed up and down my body, assessing me.

"You're what, ten, right?"

Still, he stood unmoving, silent.

"So, what, that's like third grade, right?" I asked.

Still nothing.

"Lucas," Jane prompted, placing her hand on his back. "Mr.

Fontenot has asked you several questions. It's not polite to ignore him."

"It's all right, Jane." The last thing I wanted to do was get him in trouble. "I'm not really a big talker either." I smiled nervously at Lucas.

Sports, I thought. Maybe he was into sports.

"Do you like to ride bicycles?" I asked.

His eyes widened fractionally and I thought I might actually have an in with this kid.

"I don't have one," he answered.

Well, hell.

"I have a friend and he lets me borrow his," he said, staring down at his shoes.

"I don't have one either," I said. "Well, I mean here in Austin."

"You have another bike somewhere else?" he asked.

"Yeah, in Utah. That's where I'm from."

He stared at me, a blank look on his face again. I was losing him.

"I need to buy one because Austin has some cool places to ride."

"I only ride in my neighborhood," he said.

"The bicycle shop down the street has some really cool attachments for your car," I said, trying to keep the conversation going. "You can carry like three or four bicycles and take them anywhere."

Lucas stepped closer. "Really?"

I knew I couldn't get too excited or I'd spook him.

This young boy had been abandoned by his mother, never knew his father, and now his grandmother was clinging to life.

According to Jane, they'd already been in three foster care homes in the last few months, none of the caregivers able to handle their sister Lillian's special needs. This boy was not going to throw down roots until *we* proved ourselves to *him*. Lucas was the gatekeeper to his family and Dana and I were just outsiders looking in. For now.

"I like bicycles, but motorcycles are more my thing," I said.

"You ride motorcycles?" he asked, moving one step closer toward me. It was the first time I'd heard any real emotion from him.

"Yeah," I answered, walking toward the mantel. I pulled down one of the photos Dana had taken of me a few days after we met, just before my fall. Walking back, I held the picture out so Lucas could see.

Cautiously, he wrapped his fingers around the wooden frame and stared down at it. His eyes widened in amazement, his mouth hanging lax in what I hoped was admiration. Maybe this would be *my* in. Dana had popsicles, I had motorcycles.

"This is really you?" he asked in shock, glancing up at me.

"Oh, yeah. I have the scars to prove it." I laughed.

He cut his eyes up to mine, his face contorted with an adult-like expression of confusion.

"Right after Dana took this photo, I fell. Busted my elbow," I said, rubbing my right elbow. "I'm right-handed so it was pretty brutal for a while. I couldn't even brush my teeth with my left hand." I laughed, remembering what a complete spaz I'd been.

"I'm left-handed," he admitted, staring down at the photo again.

"My sister's left-handed too."

"Really?" he asked.

"Yeah. That's why I could never teach her to ride a motorcycle." I chuckled.

"Why?" he asked, brows wrinkled.

"Well, first off," I laughed, "she's not very coordinated." I thought about how Victoria could trip just walking down the hall. "Plus, she's left-handed so everything is backward for her."

"Why does that matter?" he asked.

I smiled. Finally, I'd gained his attention. "Well, on motorcycles, the right hand is responsible for a lot."

"Like what?"

"Like the throttle, brake, shifting. Trying to get my sister to do more than one thing with her right hand was like teaching a one-legged man to play soccer." I laughed at my analogy but noticed the confused expression on Lucas's face. "Let's just say, it was difficult."

"I only write with my left hand," he said, staring down at the picture. "Everything else I do with my right."

"Like baseball?"

He glanced up. "Yeah, I swing with both hands, but I throw with my right. Weird, huh?" he asked, not really needing an answer from me. This was going well. Lucas was starting to open up.

"Do you like baseball?" I asked.

"I used to." His smile faded and his shoulders slumped.

"Why don't you like it anymore?"

"We've moved a lot lately," he explained, turning to stare behind me.

I followed his gaze. The look of disappointment on Jane's face told me everything Lucas couldn't. He was a foster child. For him, nothing was permanent.

"Well, they've got a great park not far from here," I said. "And several sports stores around the corner. Maybe we could pick up some gloves and balls and a bat or two and go play."

Lucas's head whipped around so fast it made me dizzy. He stared up at me, eyes wide. "Really?" he asked. He didn't believe me. Trust for him was no longer a luxury he could afford to extend and I understood that. My actions would have to show him what my words couldn't.

"Hey, Dana!" I shouted over my shoulder toward the kitchen.

"Yeah, babe?" she answered, covering Levi's popsicle stick with a paper towel before handing it to him. She gently rubbed his back as they walked toward us. She was glowing in her newfound role of mother and I couldn't help but smile.

In that moment I knew, with her single act of kindness, my family had just been born.

"What street is that sporting goods store on, the one downtown?" I asked. "You know, that small one where I got the shin guards?"

"You mean Murphy's?" she asked, her face just as confused as Lucas's. "It's on the corner of Congress and Fourth Street. Why?"

"I thought maybe later I'd take the boys down there and look at some baseball stuff. Lucas here likes to play. He's left-handed though," I teased.

"Oh, you'll love it," she said, smiling. "They've got *everything* there." She gently brushed back a piece of Levi's dark hair that had fallen across his forehead. She was born to love these boys, and my heart skipped a beat.

The doorbell rang, shattering our moment.

"She's here!" Jane exclaimed, rushing to the front door. She glanced over her shoulder. "Do you mind if I open it?"

Dana and I both shook our heads, instinctively knowing who the "she" Jane referred to was.

Jane swung the door wide and smiled.

Just beyond the threshold stood another woman holding the most beautiful little girl I'd ever seen.

There was no mistaking from her facial features that she had Down syndrome, but it wasn't the first thing you noticed. It was her eyes. They were light brown, like melted caramel, and seemed larger from the magnification of the glasses she wore.

Lillian's hair hung to her shoulders in dark waves and tiny curls that looked so much like Dana's it was uncanny. She wore small, hot-pink framed glasses secured to her face with a purple, curly, elastic band that ran around the back of her head. Her frilly, pale-yellow dress was littered with flowers and butterflies, two of Dana's favorite things.

I smiled, realizing Lillian was destined to be Dana's. I glanced at Dana, trying to gauge her reaction to meeting Lillian for the first time.

She stood stock-still, one hand covering her open mouth.

"She's very outgoing," the woman holding her said. "But she can be a little shy at first."

"Oh, sorry," Jane said. "Dana and Peter, this is Erica. She's another caseworker helping me."

"It taketh a while to get to know her," Levi explained, walking up beside us.

Dana's lips spread wide in amusement as she gazed down at him, rubbing his back. "Thanks for the warning, buddy." She winked.

"Lillian," Jane said to the little girl, "this is Dana."

Dana took a few tentative steps toward Lillian. Their eyes locked and I held my breath.

"Hi, Lillian." Dana smiled. Her words sounded unsure, something completely opposite of what I knew her to be. She was obviously scared.

"You can call her Lilly," Lucas said.

We all turned and stared at him in disbelief. His concession was huge, and its meaning wasn't lost on Dana or me. Lucas was allowing Dana to use his sister's nickname, something I sensed he allowed few to do.

Dana nodded. "Thank you, Lucas."

He nodded and shrugged as if it were nothing but everyone in the room knew it was much more.

"Hi, Lilly. I'm Dana," she said, stepping closer. She pointed to me. "That's Peter."

Lilly's gaze wandered from Dana's to me. She smiled wide and I gasped in shock. Two huge dimples appeared on Lilly's plump cheeks. It was official. This little girl had instantly captured my heart.

Dana turned toward Lilly and stared at her with such love and adoration, already. "She has dimples," she said softly.

I watched the two in amazement.

Dana reached out and ran her fingers softly over Lilly's face, gently caressing her cheeks. "I have dimples too," she announced, pointing to her own smiling face.

Lilly's small hand reached down and softly grazed Dana's face, similar to what Dana had done.

Dana beamed, leaning into Lilly's touch.

I knew from what Dana had told me about Sam and the other residents at Whispering Oaks, that some people with Down syndrome had an aversion to touch. This act of affection from Lilly spoke volumes to her instant connection with Dana.

I placed a hand on my chest, swallowing back the tears threatening. These children were so much like Dana and me—both physically and emotionally—it was frightening. We'd all been left by those we loved. The five of us belonged together. I felt it to my bones. I knew if given the chance, Dana and I would love these children for the rest of our loves. Together we would ensure that they would never be alone again.

Dana raised her arms out toward Lilly, coaxing the child to come to her. Without a second thought, Lilly reached out and fell into Dana's arms.

I thought of Dana's broken hand and worried it might hurt her. That fear was quickly gone when I saw Dana's eyes light up with joy. There was no way Dana was going to deny this little girl anything, no matter what physical pain it might cause her.

"Look," Levi said, "thee like-th you."

"It looks like it." Dana grinned as she admired the front of Lilly's outfit. "I love your dress, Lilly. Butterflies are my favorite things in the whole world. And yellow is my favorite color."

"Mine too!" Levi shouted as if he'd just heard the best news ever.

"What's your favorite color, Lucas?" Dana asked as she bounced Lilly on her hip. She stroked the ringlet strands of Lilly's jet-black hair like she'd been Lilly's mother her entire life.

Lucas stood still, lips pressed together. He would be difficult to break down his walls. But I had done it with Dana. I was prepared.

"Hith favorite color ith red," Levi answered for him.

"Peter likes red, don't you, Peter?" Dana winked at me.

"I used to have a red motorcycle."

"Do you still have it?" Lucas asked, his eyes cautiously warming to me.

"I have several motorcycles." I gazed down at him, taking a step closer. "But if you want to see a lot of bikes, you have to go to Dana's company."

"You have a whole company?" Lucas asked.

"I have a dealership," she said. "A car dealership."

Lucas's brows furrowed.

"We sell cars. And motorcycles."

Lucas stood straighter, his eyes wide. "For real? You sell motorcycles."

"Dude, Dana's got tons of motorcycles," I answered. "She actually let me pick one out the other day and take it for a ride."

His mouth fell open and he stared at me in disbelief. "Seriously?"

"Oh, yeah, Dana has lots of cool stuff," I said.

Lucas's gaze moved from me to his brother then over to Dana. Anyone could tell from his body language that his resolve was wavering. He wanted to trust us, but his life had been filled with disappointments.

"Maybe we could try out bicycles first," I said.

"Where's the bicycle shop?" Lucas asked.

And just like that, I knew he wanted to stay. It would take Lucas a long time to relinquish control of his family and learn to let Dana and I care for him, but I was a patient man and I knew in my heart this was where he belonged, with me and with Dana.

I'd waited my entire life for the woman of my dreams but I'd finally found her. And now, looking at these three amazing children, it was spectacularly clear to me, I'd finally found the family I'd always longed for.

CHAPTER 32

PETER

"Can I take this thing off my eyes yet?" Dana reached behind her head at the scarf I'd tied around her face.

I turned my gaze from the road and stared over at her. "No." I reached over and swatted her hand away.

"Owe," she cried, shaking her uninjured hand. "Dammit, Peter, that hurt."

"I didn't even hit you that hard so quit crying, you baby."

She pouted and it took everything inside me not to lean over and kiss her. But this was important.

"Don't touch it again," I said, pointing at her as if she could see me.

She folded her arms across her chest. "Or what?"

"Or you won't get your surprise." As we drew closer to our destination I prayed for her restraint.

She drew in a long breath and sighed. No one would ever accuse Dana Di Grazio of being patient. The thought made me smile.

"It's important to me, Dolly," I said, squeezing her leg. "Can you wait a few more minutes?"

She turned and smiled, those deep dimples appearing like a long lost friend. "I'd wait a lifetime for you, Peter, you know that."

I grabbed her hand and brought it up to my lips. I brushed a light kiss over her knuckles. "Me too," I whispered.

I slowed the car and turned onto the dirt driveway. Stopping in front of the makeshift gate, I put the car in park and turned to face her. "We're here."

"Oh, thank God," she said, throwing her hands in the air. "Can I *please* pull this damn thing off now?"

I chuckled, reaching to untie the scarf. The material fell away and I watched as she blinked several times, adjusting to the light of the afternoon sky.

"This is my parents' property," she said, turning to face me. Her brows were knit together and her expression seemed pained. "Why are we here?"

I swallowed back my fear. In my heart I knew this was right. Hopefully I could make Dana see that too. I pointed to the gate. "Can you let us in?"

"Why?" Her curt tone reminded me that this could be a mistake. But like with most things in life, I trusted my gut.

I smiled, hoping she wouldn't see my apprehension. "I have a surprise for you."

"What kind of surprise?" she asked, her face twisting into a scowl.

I lifted her hand to my lips and kissed her knuckles again. I needed to reassure her that I only had good intentions in my heart. "Please, sweetie."

She studied me for several heartbeats but finally opened the door.

I watched as she made her way to the entrance and undid the lock. Slowly she drew the gate back and stood as I drove into the property. In the rearview mirror I stared as she secured everything and stalked back to the car.

She opened the door and sat down but kept one foot on the ground.

"Are you going to shut the door?" I asked

"Are you going to tell me why we're here?" Her tone was flat, so much different than her normally vivacious lilt.

I gripped the steering wheel, assuring myself that this was right, this was for our future.

"Shut the door, Dolly," I demanded.

She cut her eyes at me, a look of surprise on her face. I was usually never this stern.

"Please," I added. "I'll tell you soon, I promise."

She nodded once and pulled the door closed but remained silent, staring straight ahead.

This land was sacred to her, I needed to remember that. I had just entered hallowed ground.

I maneuvered the car around the dirt path until we came to the spot I'd surveyed earlier in the week. I'd actually been on the property several times without Dana, but now wasn't the time to disclose that to her. She was already on edge, and I needed her approval if we were going to go forward with my plans.

I put the car in park, and stepped out. Making my way to the passenger side, I opened the door and held out my hand.

"Peter, what's going on?" she asked, her face marred with confusion.

"Do you trust me?"

She nodded. "You know I do."

"Then take my hand."

She stared down at my outstretched palm for several seconds before finally slipping her hand into mine. She stepped out of the car and I shut the door.

Leaning down I pressed a soft kiss on her lips. "Come with me," I whispered. I led her toward the area I'd mapped out earlier in the week.

"What are these stakes?" she asked.

I glanced at the wooden sticks tied with orange ribbons scattered around the area. "They're survey markers."

She dropped my hand and stared up at me, her blue eyes frozen like a block of ice. "Who's been on the property?"

"It's okay, Dolly," I assured her. "It was just me."

"Why were you here?" Her hands were fisted and propped on her hips.

I swallowed back my anxiety, praying she would understand.

"I had an idea."

She raised one perfectly arched brow.

I held up one hand, palm facing her. "Hear me out, okay?" I pleaded.

"Let's hear it." She crossed her hands over her chest. This wasn't going to be easy.

"Your parents always intended to move here when they retired, right?"

"Yes."

"Did you know they'd already contracted with an architect who'd drawn up plans?"

Dana's head reared back and she stared up at me, a frown on her face. "How did you know that?"

"I talked to your uncle. He told me."

She still seemed annoyed, but appeased, so I continued.

"I contacted the architect last week once you told me you wanted to marry me sooner rather than later. The firm still had your parents' original blueprints and allowed me to look at them."

"So, you saw the plans?"

I walked back to the car and popped open the trunk. Slowly I pulled out a smaller version of the architect's rendition of the home. "I actually have them," I said, kneeling down beside Dana. I slowly and reverently unrolled the papers on the rocky ground at her feet.

"These are my parents' plans?" she whispered.

"Yeah." I nodded. "The design is really spectacular." At her silence, I gazed up.

She stood motionless, staring down at the papers, a hand covering her mouth.

"Come, look." I nodded toward the plans.

She knelt beside me, her eyes riveted to the blueprints.

"It's a master home," I said, "almost four thousand square feet, five bedrooms, four baths. The architect said he'd always wondered why a soon-to-be retiring couple like your parents would want such a large home."

She glanced up at me. "What did my parents say?"

I hesitated, wondering if the excuse would upset her. "The architect said your parents wanted to build it to fill the space with their grandchildren."

Her blue eyes filled with unshed tears. Her parents had passed away before she'd been diagnosed with cancer. I knew my revelation brought her grief, knowing her illness meant she would never be able to give them what they desired. I had other plans though, plans to give her parents their dying wish.

"Let's fill it," I said, smiling. "With their grandchildren and great-grandchildren."

"What are you saying?"

"I'm saying these are amazing plans, Dana. Your parents had a beautiful vision for you and Sam, and your futures. Let's build that future, here, for *our* family."

"I don't understand." She stood and shook her head.

"These stakes are from the surveying company," I explained, rising to my feet. "The surveyors and architects have already looked at the land. We're actually in the master bedroom, right here." I extended my arm and waved my hand out over the area.

"You want to build a house, my parents' house, on their land?" she asked, her tone still questioning, but hopeful.

I nodded. "Yes, Dolly, I want to build this house, for you, and for our children. And for Sam," I added.

Huge tears welled in her eyes.

I held my breath.

What if she hated the idea? I'd never let my thoughts go in that direction. I'd just always assumed she'd love the idea of building this house. What if I'd been wrong? What if she saw my plans as an invasion into her past?

"So," I said hesitantly, "what do you think?"

She took a step back and studied the area, hands firmly planted on her hips.

I waited for what felt like a lifetime while she remained silent.

"Dana," I called out.

She still didn't answer. Closing her eyes, she tilted her head back, the sunshine washing over her face. I realized in that moment she was in the presence of her parents, silently talking to them, perhaps even asking for their advice and approval.

Slowly, her head lowered and she opened her eyes. "Whose room is this?"

I reached for the plans and held them close. "That's actually the kitchen. See." I raised my hand, pointing past her. "The sink will face the cliffs so you'll always have the best view when you're washing the dishes. Well," I snorted, "I guess *I'll* have the best view since cooking and cleaning aren't your finer attributes."

She laughed and I released a sigh of relief. "My mother loved to cook," she confessed, smiling fondly as she reminisced. "I would expect her to want the most dramatic view to be from her kitchen window."

My heart ached for her tragic loss.

"Where would the kids' rooms be?" she asked, turning to face me.

"Well, that depends." I walked toward her, floor plans in my grasp.

"On what?"

"On if you want a one story or a two story."

"What were my parents' plans originally?"

"One story," I said.

She smiled and nodded. "I want a one story then."

At her declaration and approval, my body sagged in relief.

"All right then." I grasped her hand and led her around the land.

"This is one of the guest bedrooms," I said, stopping at one spot as I looked down at the prints. "And that's another one right there, with a bathroom in between."

"So, where was the master bedroom?" she asked, her eyes dancing.

I smiled, my own thoughts thinking of our future. I'd always dreamt of this moment, picturing nights spent alone with my wife, our bodies pressed against one another while our children slept safely down the hall.

"It's on the other side of the kitchen," I answered, "where we were first standing."

"That's too far." She shook her head. "Lilly needs to be closer to us."

"Well, I thought these two bedrooms could be for the boys." I pulled her back toward the master bedroom. "And this room," I announced, stopping just shy of where we'd started, "this could be Lilly's. It's only a few feet down the hall from the master, and she has her own ensuite bathroom."

Dana dropped my hand and surveyed the area.

"I talked to the architect and explained our circumstances. He said he could customize Lilly's room, actually the entire house, to fit our needs, to fit Lilly's needs."

She stared up at me, her expression blank.

"We can wire it with special cables for video equipment so we can monitor her twenty-four-seven. I'm also having him design a special playroom, just for Lilly, full of all the most advanced sensory equipment she'll need to keep up with her therapy."

She stood silent, just looking at me.

"What?" I asked.

"You've already thought about all of this? Planned it all out?" she asked, disbelief in her words.

"Of course, I did, Dolly. I would never bring you here without knowing exactly what I wanted to give you."

Her chin trembled and she bit her bottom lip. I knew Dana was fighting back her emotions.

"And you already took the children's needs into consideration," she whispered, more of a statement than a question.

"Always," I said, wrapping my arms around her tiny waist. The blueprints dropped to the ground. "I'll always take you and the children into consideration." I paused to study her face. Her beauty was profound and everlasting. She literally took my breath away.

"Peter," she sighed.

"My one and only desire now is to protect you and the children," I said, "provide and ensure your safety, and supply all your needs." I leaned down and gently brushed my lips against hers. "Always, Dolly."

"I can't believe you did all of this." Her gaze traveled over the area.

"There's more," I said. Releasing my hold, I grasped her hand and walked toward the other side of the house.

"What next? A stable?" She laughed.

"Do you want a stable?"

"God, no," she gasped in horror. "I can't stand horses. They scare the shit out of me." She sucked in a deep breath, covering her mouth. "Oh, shit, I mean. . ." She fumbled, trying to correct her words.

I laughed. A censored Dana was about as impossible as a frog sprouting wings to fly.

"Don't worry, sweetheart." I kissed her forehead. "When the kids get here, you'll be fine."

"I sure as shit hope so. Oh no," she gasped. "I did it again."

I laughed. What else was there to do. Clearing my throat, I gathered my courage to continue. "I know you want me to compete again."

"Peter, you have to, it's your passion. I can handle the children while you're away, I promise. I have Geneva and Hindley, and Leif too. Plus, your mom and AJ. They all said they'd help me—"

I pressed my finger to her soft lips. "First of all, I've already told you. *You* are my passion."

She smiled, her dimples deep.

"Creating a family with *you* is my passion," I continued. "Remember?"

She was hesitant but nodded her head.

"I love riding, Dana, more than anything, except you and the kids. I really do."

"I know, but—"

I pinched her lips together to silence her. "Listen," I said.

She laughed and swatted my hand away. "I'm listening."

"Thank you." I leaned down and kissed her lightly. "Dana, you are my dream come to life. I love to ride, you know that."

She swallowed and remained silent.

"Riding freestyle motocross is another one of my passions in life, and I'm so blessed that you understand that and support me. But to be honest, I've never enjoyed competing."

"Really?"

"Really," I said. "I hate being on the road so much. It's lonely. And now, with all the media hype and the way that the extreme sports world has catapulted into mainstream society it's getting more dangerous."

She bit her lip and nodded. I knew she was thinking of my fall.

"The sport is so competitive that often the joy of the ride is overshadowed by the need to gain one more point, risk serious injury for one more thrill or one more endorsement. Hell, even the X Games has permanently cancelled some of the more dangerous events because guys were risking their lives to do bigger, better, more dangerous tricks."

I drew in a deep breath, knowing my next words may scare her more.

"I want to open up a motocross course here." I waved my hand out over the vast area of land behind me. "I'll have various courses. I can teach kids and pros who want to come here. I can train them,

I'm good at that. Maybe we could even have camps during the summer, bring out some of Rory's kids if they're interested in learning how to ride."

I studied her, trying to gauge her reaction, but her attention was focused on the land ahead of us, as if she weren't even hearing me.

"I thought over there," I pointed in the opposite direction, "we could have a garage. We could teach kids and adults how to work on bikes, how to customize them. A lot of the pros don't even know what the hell they're doing sometimes. If kids and newbies had a place to learn, learn new tricks, learn about safety, how to fix bikes, maybe I could give them options in their life, a new career or something, ya know?"

She covered her brows with her hand to shield the sun as she stared off in the distance. I didn't know how to explain myself, how to make her understand how excited I was about all of this.

But this was her parents' land, not mine. I feared she'd be upset that I'd planned my future on a spot that was sacred to her.

She finally turned to face me. "I want to make your passion mine, Peter." Her eyes were bright, her smile huge. "You've already given me so much."

"Not really."

"I want you to be happy, Peter." She took both my hands in hers. "If this is what you want, what you've dreamed about, then I want it too." Even though she was smiling, I could hear the hesitancy in her voice.

"But?" I asked.

"But, you know I'm selling the dealership to my uncle. Hindley and Luis have already started drafting the contract."

"I know."

"And, I'm not taking any money from the sale of the company. I'm practically just giving it to Uncle Nic."

"And?"

"And, my finances will be much more limited," she explained with caution. "I have the trust and that gives Sam and me a nice yearly allowance, but to build something this elaborate, I don't think I'll be able to afford it. I mean, I don't want finances to stop us."

What was she talking about?

"We could always try to get a business loan," she went on, hands raised in the air. "I mean, hell, you have an MBA, for Christ's sake, and I've been semi-running a corporation for almost a decade. There's no reason they'd turn us down. We'll make it work, Peter, I promise," she vowed. "We'll figure it out. This is your vision. There are no buts. I want to make all your dreams come true, because that's what you've done for me."

I frowned in confusion as I looked at her, surveying the land surrounding us.

"What?" she asked.

Suddenly, it hit me like a hammer. Dana actually thought I was expecting *her* to foot the bill for this entire plan. I couldn't help but laugh, my deep rumblings echoing across the cliffs.

"What's so funny?" she asked in the pouty way only Dana could.

"Did you forget we're selling my family's business?"

She stared at me, head tilted. Obviously, she had.

"I own forty percent of the company, Dolly, remember? As it stands today, my father's business is worth just over eighty-five million dollars, not including pending patents which have the potential to double that."

Her blue eyes shot wide.

"Did you really think I was counting on *your* money to do all this?" I asked.

"Well, yeah, I guess I just assumed." She shrugged and I loved her even more. "I don't mind at all. You know, what's mine is yours."

"And what's mine is yours too, Dolly." I tucked my arm around her waist and pulled her toward me. "Especially my heart."

Dana grinned, her face bright with love, for me.

"These are *my* dreams," I said. "I would never ask you to fund them."

She abruptly shoved off of me as if insulted by my words.

"They're *our* dreams, Peter. Your dreams are *my* dreams." She thumped her chest with the palm of her hand. "I'll do whatever I can to make them come true."

I grabbed her back to me, brushing a stray lock of curly black hair behind her ear. "I don't know how I became lucky enough to deserve you, Dana Adele Di Grazio," I whispered, "but I promise I'll spend the rest of my life making all *your* dreams come true."

"You already have," she whispered just as my lips covered hers.

CHAPTER 33

PETER

"Remind me again why we're doing this?" I asked Dana as I plugged my cell phone into the wall charger in Leif's spare bedroom.

"Because you can't see me on the day of our wedding until I walk down the aisle." Her tone was matter-of-fact but I could hear the joy in her voice. All I ever wanted to do was make Dana happy, and if staying away from her for one night did it, I'd begrudgingly oblige her.

"But you're not coming down an aisle," I teased. "We'll be at the courthouse in the judge's chambers."

"Still." She laughed.

"So, now I'm stuck here at Leif's house sleeping all alone the night before I'm supposed to marry you?"

"That's tradition. This is the one and only time I plan on getting married," she said, "and I don't want to take any chances tempting the fate of luck."

"It's not luck, Dolly. It's love. I love you, and that will last a lifetime. Even though I can't hold you and make love to you tonight."

Her laughter had my jeans pulling painfully tight. One night away from her was driving me insane and I couldn't believe I'd been dumb enough to let her talk me into this.

"Well, still. One night won't kill you."

"Want to make a bet?" I asked, adjusting myself. "Maybe you should talk dirty to me," I whispered. "Help me relieve some of the pressure in my pants."

"Peter!" she gasped.

"What are you wearing, Dolly?" My voice dropped deeper, surprising myself, as I tried to sound as seductive and sexy as she did naturally.

"Oh, fuck," she moaned. I laughed, knowing I affected her just as much as she did me. "I'm completely naked, lying in front of a roaring fire, my legs spread open, taking in the heat from the flames," she whispered.

"What?" I shouted, my dick now engorged to a point that was actually painful, as I pictured her sumptuous body splayed out for anyone's perusal.

"I'm kidding." She giggled. "I'm wearing jeans and a tank top. Hindley and Geneva are stopping by in a few minutes to take me to dinner. My last meal as a single lady. Then we're stopping by Sam's. They moved Bingo to tonight so he didn't want to miss it, not with Tanya calling. I'll pick him up afterward so he can spend the night with me. I'm sure we'll have a marathon evening watching *The Three Stooges*, so you're safe."

"Where are you guys going to dinner? It better not be a strip club."

"It's called Beef Eaters, if you must know. All the waiters walk around butt-naked with hard-ons the size of Montana."

"What?" I yelled into the phone. I hated being away from her, not able to gauge her truthfulness by examining her animated expressions.

"Calm down, Romeo, I'm just teasing. We're going out for Chinese." She laughed. I felt bad for actually feeling relieved. I mean, I knew she'd never do anything, but still, I already missed her and vowed to never spend another night away from her again if I could help it.

"What about you?" she asked.

"What am *I* wearing?" I whispered seductively.

"No." She laughed. "What do Leif and Rory have planned for you? Hit up the local titty bars?"

"Actually, I think everyone's coming over here to play some poker and then the strippers are coming by around midnight, right after we finish with the porn videos."

"What?" she shouted.

"Yeah, we're going to swing by the bank here in a second and try to break all these twenty-dollar bills I have into singles so I can fill up their G-strings. Wait, what if they're all naked? Where do I put the money then?"

"What the fuck, Peter?" she growled.

"Sounds like two can play your game, Miss Di Grazio," I teased, chuckling under my breath. I knew better than to poke the lioness, but I couldn't help it. It was her decision to spend the night apart so I was going to make her suffer.

"Just wait, Mr. Fontenot, you just wait," she seethed in mock anger. "I may not put out tomorrow after the ceremony, even though it's your wedding night."

"You wouldn't?" I snarled.

"Oh, I would." She laughed.

"No, you wouldn't. You're the biggest horn dog I know. You'll probably even break out one of your vibrators tonight."

"Oh my God!" She shrieked in such a high-pitched tone, I had to pull the phone away from my face for fear of her bursting my eardrum. "How do you know about my vibrators?" She cried. Her surprise had me laughing out loud.

"I was looking for more towels in the bathroom last week and ran across your, um...*collection*." I smirked.

"Are you serious?" she screamed in panic.

"Yeah, I'm serious. That's some crazy stuff you got in there, Miss Di Grazio."

"Oh my God, Peter, I'm so embarrassed."

"Why?"

"I don't know, it's just…."

"What if I said I want to try some out? On you?" I asked.

"Are you shitting me?"

"I shit you not."

"Oh my God," she gasped.

"What?"

"I think I just came right here on the couch."

"Good night, Dolly. I love you. I'll see you at the courthouse bright and early."

"All right, lover boy. I'll see you tomorrow. I love you too, Peter," she declared with all the sincerity I'd ever wanted.

I smiled to myself at her words of affection.

"Oh, and, Peter," she breathed out, her raspy, provocative voice nearly sending me over the edge as my body ached for her touch.

"Yes?" I whimpered, knowing what came out of her mouth next may very well be my undoing.

"When I'm lying naked across my bed tonight, my legs spread open wide, I'll be screaming out your name in ecstasy when that big, purple vibrator rubs against me and makes me come so hard all I'll be able to think about is your dick so far up inside me it hurts," she whimpered, lost in her own sexual fantasies.

I choked, unable to speak, nearly passing out from the blood loss as every ounce of it pooled in my mid-section. Visualizing her sensual body, completely naked, splayed across the bed with one of those play toys had my entire body quivering with desire.

"Don't fuck with me, Peter, or I'll keep going until you come right there in your pants," she taunted.

I chuckled in amusement, knowing she could, and *would* do just that if I didn't end this call soon.

"Good night, lover boy," she howled. Without another word the phone went dead and I made my way toward the bathroom for a very cold shower. Tomorrow couldn't come fast enough.

CHAPTER 34

PETER

THE LIGHT from the early morning sky shone brightly through the judge's chambers, illuminating Dana's crystal blue eyes. The sequins on her wedding dress sparkled, making her appear other-worldly.

"Are you ready?" I whispered.

She nodded and smiled.

"I love you," I mouthed.

"I love you too," she echoed silently.

Together we turned and faced the judge.

"The coming together of a man and a woman isn't the difficult part," the judge said. "The laws of attraction demand that people of similar wants and desires should gravitate to one another."

I tried to pry my eyes off of Dana, to focus on the judge as he proclaimed these prophetic words, but it was too difficult. I'd waited my entire life for this day, the day I would be joined together with my soul mate. Now that I had her here in front of me, safe and sound, I just couldn't let my gaze fall anywhere else but her loving face.

"What *is* difficult," the judge continued, "is the marriage—the weeks, the months, and the years that follow your wedding day."

There was a momentary silence and I realized the judge was waiting for my full and undivided attention. As much as it pained me to do so, I tore my gaze from Dana and stared at the tall man before us, adorned in a black robe with a white shirt and pale green tie.

"A marriage isn't about the vows you give and receive today," he went on, his gaze going back and forth between Dana and me. "Marriage is a journey, full of hills and valleys, peaks and bases, and a multitude of emotions and events in between. As you two stand here today, pledging your lives to one another, it's important that you remember you are on this journey *together*."

I thought it interesting he put such emphasis on the word *together*. My eyes cut to Dana's, surprised to see them completely fixated on the judge, as if she'd never heard these words before.

"Some days you'll feel the type of attraction that brought you together from the very first moment you saw one another," the judge spoke, as if he had inside access to our first meeting.

Dana muffled a laugh under her breath but I kept my gaze firmly on the judge, fighting back a grin. I knew we were both recalling the same image—the memory of her dousing both of us with her beer and me gawking at her breasts like a pervert.

The judge cleared his throat and we squeezed one another's hands.

"Other days," he said, "you will ask yourself where that loving person went, the one you connected with and were so attracted to from the beginning. In the midst of arguments and misunderstandings, you'll wonder if it's all been worth it, the sacrifices you've made to live with another human being."

I stood stock-still, my mind riveted by the judge's words of wisdom.

"I believe it is in *those* moments," he continued, "during the inevitable struggles and fights you'll have as husband and wife, where you will become strong, unified and strengthened. Two beings molded into one, a fortress that won't be easily broken."

I'd never thought about fighting making our bond stronger.

"The hard times will be like a furnace to iron," he said, "preparing you to be strengthened into a stronger, more vibrant couple where *true* intimacy lies. Never question your love for one another during the hard times, for it is in *those* times you will truly become one."

My eyes burned with unshed tears. Never had I heard marriage explained or defined so honestly and reverently. My hands tightened around Dana's as I allowed the judge's words to become seared to my heart. That was Dana, my Dolly. A fortress who hadn't been easily broken despite what life had given her.

"Dana and Peter, having just shared your vows with one another and these witnesses," he paused as Dana and I gazed over our shoulders, surveying the group behind us.

In attendance to watch the ceremony were all those we loved, our family and friends. Those people who had molded us and made us into the people we were today. And those who would always be there when we needed them in the years to come.

"By the power vested in me by the state of Texas," the judge's voice thundered, "it is now my privilege and my honor to pronounce you husband and wife."

I stared down at Dana, still surprised she'd said yes, to join her life with mine.

Her blue eyes were filled with unshed tears and I prayed to God they were happy ones.

"Peter," the judge called, snapping me back to attention.

I turned and stared at him.

"You may kiss your forever bride."

My forever bride. I liked that.

My gaze traveled down the length of Dana. I wanted this moment to be etched in my mind forever.

She was gorgeous in a strapless ivory dress with a corseted bodice that pushed her breasts up high. The silk skirt accentuated every sensual curve God had graced her with. The sparkly high heels she balanced on made her taller, but I still had to bend quite a bit to reach her pouty, pink lips.

I slipped my arm around her waist, drawing her closer.

Her raven black hair was twisted in an elaborate updo, giving me access to her delectable neck and shoulders. The diamond earrings I'd given her this morning sparkled in the sun and the small pearl choker my mother had given her earlier brought attention to the divot between her collarbone. All I could think about was how much I wanted to taste her in that very spot.

How had I ever captured this dynamo and convinced her to be mine forever?

"Peter," she whispered, her eyes searching mine. "The kiss?"

The kiss? Our first kiss as husband and wife. How could I forget?

I wanted to flip her over parallel to the floor and kiss her long and hard like they did in the movies, but I knew her ribs were still tender and any sudden movement could cause her more pain, something I'd vowed never to do again. Instead, I let my free hand slide around the back of her neck, tilting her face up toward mine as my eyes searched the depths of her soul, reaching for her kindred spirit.

Instantly, my mind was transported back to the first time we met, the second I'd realized her eyes carried something in them, something that struck a chord with me and I'd wanted to consume her, even back then.

We'd been soul mates from the beginning, but we'd both been too stubborn to admit it to one another, no matter how much our hearts had tried to convince us from the start. Now, as I gazed down at my beautiful wife, I knew I was the luckiest man alive. All my dreams were coming true. She was alive and she was mine, forever.

I lowered my head, closing the small distance between us as my lips lightly brushed against hers, knowing I had to keep this kiss tame for the sake of our friends and family who were present in the judge's chambers.

Apparently, Dana had different plans. Her hands tangled in my hair, pulling me hard against her. She opened her mouth, her tongue coaxing until I had no choice but to reciprocate. With Dana, a little taste was never enough and she knew it.

I would love her forever, of that there was no doubt. I'd always known it, but standing here with her in my arms, our bodies connected in an intimate way as husband and wife, it was palpable, tangible, and I never wanted to break our bond.

"Get a room!" someone shouted behind us, but it did nothing to break our connection. If anything, Dana and I pulled even closer together, our mouths and tongues and teeth determined to solidify our union.

The judge was right. I knew throughout our married years we'd have good times and bad, we'd fight and make up. Hell, I knew with Dana, at times she may even run away from me. But I knew her soul. I was part of her now, and in the end, it was inevitable that she would always come back. She was my dream girl, my fantasy come to life, and I couldn't wait to start living the rest of it with her.

EPILOGUE
DANA

THREE MONTHS LATER

I STOOD at the sink of our new house, washing the last of our lunch bowls. Well, it wasn't the new house, just the mobile home we'd moved on the land to watch as they built our forever home.

We'd enjoyed my famous macaroni and cheese with hot dogs earlier, which, thankfully, was a dish the kids loved.

"Peter!" I yelled, trying to shout over the noise of the video game he and the boys were playing.

He remained still, completely engrossed in the game.

I couldn't help but smile. He was such a wonderful father, and a not-so-bad husband too.

Looking past the boys, I glanced out the windows of our new living room which overlooked my family's land and smiled.

Unbeknownst to me, Peter had purchased a mobile home and placed it on the land while we waited for our custom home to be built. He said he wanted me and the children to be close to my parents. I'd bawled like a baby when he opened the front door and carried me over the threshold. Being here, on this land, brought me a peace I hadn't felt since before their deaths.

"Yes!" Lucas exclaimed. Obviously, he'd beaten Peter and his brother. It was so nice to see him drop his guard every now and then and just be a kid.

Sam sat beside Lucas, cheering him and Levi on. The entire moment was surreal and I wondered if I would wake up at any minute and find out it had all been a dream—the house, my husband, my children.

My children.

We'd completed all the necessary training for foster care and the children were in our custody. Now it was just a wait for the final adoption. My once hardened heart thrummed at the thought of these kids being mine, legally.

"Peter!" I yelled again.

"What, Dolly?" he called out, never once turning around to look at me. When he and the boys were engrossed in one of their video games, it was nearly impossible to drag them away.

Realizing the fight was futile, I turned toward the dining room table. Lilly sat in her high chair, pushing macaroni noodles and hot dogs on her plate. She glanced over the edge of the tray, watching the food as it fell on to floor. Judging by the mess on her tray, I assumed very little had made it into her mouth.

"Lilly," I scolded, walking around the counter toward her. "What did I tell you?"

Her gaze met mine and she smiled, batting her caramel-colored eyes at me. This girl was good.

I shook my head in amusement, knowing full well there was absolutely no way I could be mad at this adorable little girl. "Are you going to eat your lunch, young lady?" I asked, even though it was obvious she was having much more fun playing than eating.

She stared at me as her hands moved the food around her tray.

I tilted my head and returned her gaze. "You know I have ice cream?" I hoped the reward would coax her into shoving in a few more bites. She was small and needed to put on weight.

Her eyes went wide and her mouth formed a small "o."

"Just two more bites and you can have a bowl."

"No," she pouted, covering her mouth with her chubby hands. I knew Lilly, and if she didn't eat her lunch, she'd be cranky and never lie down for a nap. Today, that wasn't an option. I needed the extra time this afternoon, so I had no choice but to pull out my big guns.

"Sam!" I hollered over the noise of the television and his cheers for Levi. He jerked his head up, unlike my husband.

Husband. I smiled. It still felt strange that Peter was my husband, but also so right.

"Yes?" Sam answered.

"Will you *please* get Lilly to finish her lunch?"

Without a moment's hesitation, Sam stood and marched toward Lilly.

"Sah-mee!" Lilly exclaimed, her hands banging on the tray so hard I thought she would actually break it.

"Lilly," Sam scolded, one hand on his hip as the other pointed at her.

Her smile disappeared. Without another word from Sam, her little fingers picked up the noodles and shoved them into her mouth.

I laughed. This little girl loved her Uncle Sam and would do anything to make him happy.

"Good girl," Sam dragged out the words in praise. He sat next to Lilly and picked up a piece of hot dog and held it out.

I stared in fascination as she grabbed the food, no goading needed, and popped it into her mouth. She chewed for several seconds, swallowed, then opened her mouth wide, sticking her tongue out as if to prove she'd done his silent bidding.

Sam leaned over her tray, pressing his forehead to hers. They both shook their heads then broke out into contagious laughter.

It had really been no surprise to me how quickly Sam and Lilly took to one another. They were alike, in so many ways. Even though their cognitive diagnoses were completely different, they bonded over the simple fact that, for them, life would be a constant challenge, but in a good way.

If I ever needed Lilly to do anything, take a nap, finish her food, stop throwing a temper tantrum, all I had to do was ask Sam for help. If he wasn't at our house, I would simply call him at Whispering Oaks and give Lilly the phone. It never ceased to amaze me how he could coax her into doing anything he wanted. She loved her Uncle Sam, and he absolutely adored Lilly and the boys.

"I-keem!" Lilly yelled.

I sat down beside her and took the wet rag, wiping away the cheesy mess that covered her face and hands.

"It's *ice cream*, Lilly," I corrected, trying to enunciate every syllable.

Speech delays were not uncommon with cognitive disorders like Down syndrome and cerebral palsy. I was used to it with Sam and worked hard with him when we were younger to develop his vocabulary.

The social workers told us that Lilly never received any type of specialized therapy before she was in foster care. I knew from past experience with Sam, it could make all the difference for a person with special needs.

Not only did Lilly now have a physical and occupational therapist, she also had a speech therapist and was becoming more verbal every day. The therapist was also helping Levi with his prominent lisp. Therapy had become a family affair for us. The boys, Peter and I all actively worked with Lilly's group of specialized professionals to help her gain more independence in her life.

"Say it, Lilly," I encouraged. "Ice," I repeated.

Her eyes cut to Sam.

He smiled at her and nodded. "Ice," he said, echoing me.

"Ice," Lilly said clearly.

"Good girl, Lilly!" I exclaimed, kissing her hand. "Cream," I enunciated.

Not surprising, her gaze fell on Sam, waiting for his instruction. I wondered if this little girl would *ever* do something just for me.

Sam's brows knitted and I knew he was concentrating. His own speech was difficult at times due to the cerebral palsy. "Cah," he said slowly.

"Cah," Lilly repeated.

I waited patiently for Sam to continue, not wanting to break his own self-therapy. God, he was amazing.

"Ream," Sam whispered.

"Ream!" Lilly shouted, banging her hands on the tray.

Sam and I looked at one another and tried to smother our laughing.

"I-keem!" she yelled.

I stared at Lilly, at her beautiful, perfect face. This would all take time, just like with the boys.

We were all learning how to live with one another, learning how to be parents and children existing together. Learning how to trust one another. It hadn't always been easy, and we'd each had our moments and meltdowns, but today had been a good day.

I was happy with Lilly's accomplishment and wouldn't push her further. With cognitive recovery, it was all about baby steps.

"Chocolate or vanilla?" I asked, standing and heading to the kitchen.

"Chocolate," she said clearly.

I stared at her wordless, surprised at her diction.

"Chocolate," she repeated.

"Dat's good, Lilly," Sam said, trying to concentrate as much as Lilly had. This was difficult for him too.

I nodded. "Chocolate it is." I opened the freezer and hid behind the door. My eyes stung with tears and I worked to control myself. It wasn't good for Lilly to see me cry, even if they were happy tears.

In the smallest of ways—everyday—it was evident to me that these children were exactly where they needed to be. With Peter and me.

"You all right, Dolly?" Peter's deep voice rumbled behind me, nuzzling my neck as his lips grazed the sensitive skin. A tingle of desire ran down my spine.

"Having the kids makes spontaneity a little more difficult." He smiled against my skin. "But trust me, Dolly, it will be worth the wait tonight."

Ah, hell. My knees grew weak and I closed my eyes, imagining Peter completely naked underneath me as I rode him like a—

"Ice cream!" Lilly screamed, bringing me back from my lust-filled fantasies.

"Oh my God!" I shouted.

"What?" Peter released me and stepped back.

"She said it."

"Said what?"

"Ice cream," I whispered. "She said ice cream."

"I scream, you scream. We all scream for ice cream." Peter chuckled, totally ruining my moment.

"Scoop her out a bowl," I said and left him in the kitchen and raced to the table. "Lilly, that is so good, Mommy—" I stopped mid-sentence. She wasn't mine. Yet.

"Where i-keem?" Lilly asked, holding out her hands.

I couldn't contain my laughter. "Peter is bringing it."

She nodded and turned her attention back to Sam. Apparently, I was just her meal ticket. And that was fine by me.

I played with her dark hair, trying not to think of losing these kids. We still had weeks, maybe even months to go until the children could officially be adopted, and that was *if* the kids agreed.

So far, Levi and Lillian seemed completely on board. It was Lucas who was having a more difficult time. Peter and I just couldn't seem to reach him. Suddenly, I realized, I hadn't seen him since before lunch.

"Where's Lucas?" I asked to no one in particular. I glanced into the living room. Levi was still busy playing video games. "Have you seen him, Peter?" I asked, glancing over my shoulder.

"He's probably in his room reading a Sci-Fi book or watching another *Star Wars* movie." Peter laughed.

I smiled at the reminder of just how much Lucas loved *Star Wars*. I told him it was fitting, seeing as it was written and directed by a man whose last name was Lucas.

I stood. "I'm going to go look for him. Can you finish up with Lilly and try to get her down for a nap?"

Hearing no response, I turned and saw Peter leaning over Lilly, spoon-feeding her the chocolate ice cream.

I wanted to tell him he shouldn't do things for her, she needed to learn on her own. But I appreciated the moment for what it was. This wasn't about a man helping a child with special needs. This was about a father spoiling his daughter. It was a sight I'd only dreamt of just a few short months ago. After having my hysterectomy at such a young age, I'd never really allowed myself to imagine having a family of my own.

I drew in a deep breath, completely enthralled by the two of them, committing it to memory for the rest of my life. I'd gone through some major shit in my life, but this scene, the sight of my husband feeding my soon-to-be daughter with my brother excitedly watching their interactions, was worth every sacrifice I'd ever made.

"Levi!" I yelled over the noise of the television.

"Huh?" he answered, never taking his attention away from the TV.

Not bothering to ask again, I wandered through the house, peering into every bedroom and bathroom. I couldn't find Lucas anywhere. My heart rate revved up with worry.

Racing back to the dining room, I worked to catch my breath. "He's not in his room or in the playroom."

"Try outside," Peter suggested, his gaze trained on Lilly.

She smiled at him, her own eyes glued to Peter's as her adorable mouth opened wide for another bite. The picture was so heartwarming.

Lucas, I reminded myself. I was searching for Lucas.

I stepped across piles of pillows littering the living room floor and opened one of the French doors. Stepping out onto the deck, I made my way to the railing and surveyed the area. Not far away was the construction site of our new home. Lucas loved to run around the cement foundation, which had just been poured a few weeks before.

So far, the contractor was on schedule, and for that I was thankful. I loved the mobile home, but I couldn't wait to have a permanent place to call our own. Barring any problems with the weather, we hoped to be moved in by Christmas.

When I realized Lucas was nowhere to be found, a ball of fear burned in my gut. What should I do? Call the police? File a missing persons report? I was at a complete loss. That was when I understood this was the life of a parent—worry, anxiety. and fear.

Thankfully I spotted him off in the distance before my mind thought of other possibilities.

Lucas sat several yards away on the bench Peter had given me as a wedding present. The seat sat under a large oak tree that we'd purposely asked the construction crew to preserve when they cleared land for the house. They estimated the tree was over two hundred years old. The massive oak was situated on the perfect spot on our plot of land, a place where you could watch both the rising and the setting of the sun. And the tree offered the perfect amount of shade as you gazed down at the river below.

I came up behind Lucas, afraid to say anything, fearing I might actually frighten him.

"Hey," he spoke softly, obviously hearing my approach despite my sleuth-like tactics.

"Hey, yourself." I walked around the bench and sat beside him. "I was worried about you."

He gazed up at me, a look of confusion marring his young face. "Why?"

I knew he'd lived with his grandmother for the past few years.

She'd cared for them as best she could, but it dawned on me that perhaps the roles between grandmother and grandchild had been reversed. Perhaps it was Lucas who had taken care of and worried about his grandmother, along with his brother and sister.

"I couldn't find you anywhere," I answered.

"I'm sorry." He turned his attention back to the lake.

"You don't have to be sorry," I said. "Just tell me the next time you leave the house so I don't worry. Okay?"

He nodded but remained quiet.

"Hey," I said, nudging his arm. "Is everything okay? You seem a little down today. Don't you want to go to Hawaii?" I smiled, thinking that anyone in his or her right mind would be ecstatic to go.

Instead of a wedding, we decided to have a vow renewal ceremony. Peter thought it would give all three of the kids a sense of just how committed we were, not only to one another, but especially to them.

"I guess," he sighed, his confession nothing like I thought a ten-year-old's would be. In reality, he wasn't ten, emotionally or psychologically. He'd had to assume more responsibilities than someone three times his age, and sitting here next to him it was clear to see just how much of a toll it had taken on his body. My heart ached for him.

"When we get back from Hawaii," I said, "why don't we go visit your grandmother?" Lucas cared for her greatly. Her condition wasn't improving and I knew Lucas was well aware of that fact, even though he kept a brave face.

He stared up at me in surprise. "Really?"

"Of course, Lucas. Anytime you want to go see her, all you have to do is ask."

He tilted his head and studied me, as if he wasn't quite sure if I was telling the truth.

I reached over and straightened the collar of his shirt, studying his small face, so innocent and yet so worn.

Lucas had experienced so much loss and rejection in his life. Raising his hopes about anything was a luxury he couldn't, or wouldn't afford himself.

"Lucas, I don't want to replace your grandmother or deny her position in your life. She's your family," I said. "She always will be. All I'm asking for is a chance to share a place in your heart with her."

He stared at me, his face a mask, but I saw something in his eyes, a small spark of vulnerability. I recognized it in myself. He was starting to believe me.

"Did I ever tell you my parents died when I was nineteen?" I asked.

He shook his head.

"I was in college at the time, not much responsibility really, just studying and partying."

I laughed, realizing that fact probably wasn't the *best* thing to admit to a ten-year-old. But I wanted Lucas to get a real sense of what my life had been like before.

"I miss my parents so much. Especially my mom." I sighed, thinking of all the things she'd given me over my nineteen years—encouragement, stability and love—all the things I wanted to give these children.

"I don't miss my mom," Lucas said through gritted teeth. I stared down and saw his hands balled into fists.

"Can I ask you what happened?" I spoke softly, knowing I was treading on shaky ground.

He remained quiet, his hands flexing and unflexing.

I decided the best thing to do was continue with my own story.

"My mom cared for Sam full time while my dad worked at the dealership." My head fell back and I stared up at the tree, wondering what it would say if it could talk with its two hundred years of history and memories.

"How did they die?" Lucas asked, his voice filled with curiosity and concern.

"Car wreck," I answered flatly. "Freak accident, no one at fault. Which actually made it even harder for me."

"Why?"

"I had no one to blame. I had all this anger inside, anger that they'd left me, anger that I had all this responsibility that I didn't want. There was no one I could hit or punch or cuss out," I admitted quietly. Staring down at Lucas, I wasn't surprised to see him nodding his head in understanding.

"So, anyway, here I was at nineteen, all alone with Sam to care for. You know what I'm talking about," I added, knocking his shoulder with my arm. "Caring for your sibling who has special needs?"

"Yep," Lucas answered quietly.

"I had Sam, and I had a multi-million-dollar company all counting on me. I had no earthly idea what the hell to do. I didn't know jack shit about business or about how to care for Sam."

Lucas's eyes widened and a small smile spread across his face.

"What?"

"You said a bad word." He laughed.

"I did? Oh, shit!" I slapped my hands over my mouth, hoping that would stop the flow of curse words.

Lucas's laughter grew louder.

"I didn't even realize it. What did I say?"

His eyes shot wide.

"Never mind." I shook my head. "You probably shouldn't say it. I guess I owe the Cuss Bucket another dollar."

Peter and the kids had come up with a way to help me tone down my vocabulary. It was actually an idea that Hindley told them about, a way to curb Rory's filthy mouth from Abbi.

For every curse word I said, I had to add a dollar to a bucket. At the end of the week, if it had more than ten dollars, I had to double it and split the money between the boys.

I think the bucket had an adverse effect though because the boys were actually *encouraging* me to say bad words, hoping to receive

more money each week. The bucket was quickly beginning to bankrupt me, and I feared I might have to take on a part-time job to keep
up with my debt.

"I won't tell if you won't." Lucas smiled and the expression
warmed my heart. One thought came to mind as I looked down at
his innocent face. Kindred spirits.

"Deal," I agreed with a conspiratorial, shit-eating grin.

"So, what happened," he asked, "I mean with the dealership and
with Sam? He lives in that place now, right?"

"Well, I knew I couldn't take care of Sam as well as my mom
had. Not at nineteen anyway." I tried not to sound as guilty as I felt,
but I was failing miserably. "I kind of had no choice."

"Why?"

I didn't want to drown Lucas with my own failings after my
parents' deaths. What could I say though? "Sam needed a chance to
learn more, to live with people who understood what he was going
through."

"So, you just left him?"

Had I? I sat in silence, thinking about his question.

"No, I didn't just leave him. I found a place where he's happy, a
place he can truly be a part of."

Lucas nodded but said nothing.

"And you know I visit him all the time. And he comes to see
me for overnight trips, like he did today." Shit, I was rambling. It
seemed no matter what I said, I couldn't wash away the shame of
having left my brother, as Lucas said. I hung my head, remembering how difficult it had been to make the decision to place
Sam at Whispering Oaks, to realize I couldn't do it all for my
brother.

"Sometimes it hurts doing the right thing," Lucas said.

I turned toward him, not shocked to see him staring at the
ground, hands folded in his lap.

I wrapped an arm around his shoulder and squeezed. Lucas and
I were warriors. Even though his battle had been more brutal than

mine, and he'd entered into his own war at a much younger age, we both had scars to prove how deadly our combat with life had been.

"So, what's been the hardest for you?" I asked.

"Leaving my grandma," he admitted without hesitation.

"Why?"

"I'd always helped take care of her. I mean, she took care of us as best she could, but she was older, you know?"

I nodded even though I sensed he wasn't really looking for an answer. "So, you were upset," I said, "after her stroke? Upset that you couldn't stay and take care of her?"

"Kind of."

"What else?"

"I was also upset that we had to go to a foster home. That our mom didn't even care enough about us to come take us and at least *try* to care for her own mom."

He glanced up at me, his eyes holding no emotion, like he was numb to everything. My heart ached for him, for the little boy who'd been forced to harden himself at such a young age just to survive. As much as I wanted to comfort him, I knew I should keep quiet.

He turned and stared out over the cliff. "My mom never took good care of us. Even though we lived with her, she neglected us. At least that was what the social workers called it. All I knew was, she was a horrible mom."

My heart squeezed in agony but I remained silent.

"It was really me who fed us and made sure Levi and me had clothes to wear to school, stuff like that. My grandma came over sometimes, but for the most part, it was just me and Levi, on our own."

Oh, God, what all these kids had been forced to endure because of their mother's selfishness broke my heart.

"Then, my sister was born," he began again as if unable to close the dam of his memories. "I blamed my mom for what happened to Lilly. I know she was doing drugs while she was pregnant."

His voice broke with emotion and I slid closer, surprised when he didn't pull away. I gave a sigh of thanks.

He bit his lower lip and fumbled with his hands before going on. "I don't know if my mom left because Lilly had Down syndrome or just because she couldn't handle another kid. I don't really care though." His words were flat and void of any emotion, but I knew he was torn apart inside, like any child would be if their mother had abandoned them. Especially a ten-year-old who'd been left with the burden of raising his siblings.

"That must have been really hard, Lucas," I said quietly. "Your mom choosing something else over you and Levi and Lilly."

"I guess." He shrugged.

"After my parents died, I kind of did the opposite of you," I said.

"How?"

"Well, you went into parent mode, even before your mom left. Then you had to take care of your grandmother and Lilly."

He nodded. "Yeah."

"I just handed my dad's dealership over to my uncle and put Sam in a new home and went along with my life."

I didn't tell him about the cancer and the treatments that had made it virtually impossible for me to care for anyone else. He didn't need to know that right now. And he certainly didn't need the added stress of worrying about me like I knew he would.

"My parents had been my *whole* world," I said, trying to swallow down my emotions. "I had a purpose in my life when they were alive. I wanted to please them and make them happy and proud of me. I wanted to live the best life I could, for me and for Sam. Then they died and my dreams died with them. I felt alone and helpless."

"I know how you feel," he said.

His statement surprised me. I drew in a deep breath, wanting to share with him just how much he, Levi, and Lilly already meant to me. I hoped maybe if he knew, Lucas would slowly begin to let down his guard and allow me in.

I turned to face him, my hand resting on his shoulder. "When Jane first showed us your files and I saw the pictures of you, Levi and Lilly, something changed inside me, Lucas. For the first time since my parents died, I felt like I had a purpose, something, or someone to live for. Does that make sense?"

His brows knitted together and I knew he didn't understand.

"I've wanted a family my entire life," I said. "Even though I lived my life like I didn't after my parents died."

"What do you mean?" he asked. I was reluctant to share with him everything, but knew I needed to be honest.

"I partied a lot, basically gave up caring about anything, including myself. Then I met Peter and slowly my life changed. He gave me a reason to change."

We sat in comfortable silence for a while as he let my words wash over him.

"Peter's wanted a family his whole life," I said. "It's been his dream. Even more than motocross riding."

"Really?" Lucas's head jerked up.

I nodded. "Really. I couldn't give him that, though." I breathed deeply to keep the tears at bay. "I can't have children, and I was scared shitless to tell him."

Lucas laughed and I immediately realized my words.

"Three dollars now, right?" I grinned, nudging him with my shoulder.

He smiled, the expression warming his brown eyes. "No, I promise not to tell."

Instincts told me he wouldn't. I could sense Lucas and I were beginning to bond and the thought warmed my soul.

"So, what did Peter say when you told him you couldn't have babies?"

How could I answer? Tell Lucas that Peter had run out on me? No, I couldn't say that because technically it wasn't true.

"After some time," I said, "he realized that what he wanted was a life with me. He told me we could adopt or we could spend our lives together, just the two of us, it didn't matter, as long as we were together."

"That was nice."

"Very," I agreed.

"So, you decided on fostering?"

"No," I corrected immediately. "We decided on adoption."

He stared at me, blinking rapidly.

Didn't he know?

"Lucas, Peter and I want to adopt you, all three of you. They're making us foster you first, but our ultimate goal is to keep you, forever. If that's what you want," I added, knowing if we were ever going to adopt them, it would be because Lucas allowed it, not the agency.

The small beginnings of a smile tugged at his mouth and I finally had hope that perhaps this young man would let me into his heart.

"But what about Lilly?" he asked with genuine concern.

"What about her?"

"You really want to take care of her? Forever?"

"You guys wouldn't be here if I didn't."

"Oh," he said softly.

"Lucas, I've been around special needs kids my whole life. Sam is my brother, my twin brother."

He stared at me, a blank look on his face.

Suddenly I realized I'd never told him Sam and I were twins. "I know what it will take to raise Lilly, the commitment and strength required. I know how to love her and care for her. I've done it with Sam my whole life."

"But you let Sam go." His words cut me like a razor blade and he knew it instantly. "I'm sorry, I didn't mean it like that."

"Are you afraid that once I adopt you guys, I'll give Lilly away, turn her over to some institution or something?"

"Sort of, I guess."

"Lucas, look at me," I demanded in a tone that was sterner than I'd intended.

His eyes cut to mine, glued for the duration, giving me his undivided attention.

"I'm in this for the long haul, for forever. I want to take care of you, take the burden off you, let you be a kid again. That doesn't just go for you, that goes for Levi and Lilly as well."

His eyes widened and I knew this was what he needed. The truth.

"I'm not going to lie or sugarcoat this," I warned. "There may come a time as Lilly progresses into adulthood when a place like Whispering Oaks will be a better fit for her than here with us. But I *promise* you this, Lucas." I stared intently into his dark brown eyes. "I will *never* make that decision on my own. I will *always* involve you in her care. Do you understand that?" I meant every word I said. I couldn't imagine someone coming into my life and making decisions for Sam unilaterally without my consent.

Lucas sat quietly, absorbing my words, but I barreled on, knowing I needed to make him understand.

"Right now, you know Lilly better than any of us. I will count on you a lot during these early months, to guide me and direct me. But I need you to start letting go of some of the guilt and the burden that's weighing you down. As much as you will be a part of Lilly's life, I don't want you to feel solely responsible for her anymore. You need to share it with me and with Peter, okay?"

Tears welled up in his eyes and I didn't know whether to pull him in for a hug or let him process what I was saying. Instead, I opted to continue.

"I truly believe that I can't have children because I was destined to care for you, Levi, and Lilly. I believe that you three belong here, with me and Peter. If you don't feel the same way, I understand, but you have to believe me when I tell you this."

He stared up at me, anxiously awaiting my words.

"I've loved you since the moment I saw your black and white photo on my coffee table when Jane brought your files to my condo. I didn't need to take even one second to decide you three belonged to me. It was at that very moment that I finally understood what it must feel like for a doctor to put a newborn baby in his mother's arms for the first time."

His chin quivered and his eyes narrowed.

I scooted closer, slipping one arm around his shoulders.

"You've never really had that before, Lucas, and I understand. You've never been wrapped up in the arms of a mother, surrounded by her unconditional love, but that's what I want to do, that's what I want to give you. That's what I want to give myself. To love my own child as much as he loves me."

He blinked rapidly, tears welling in his eyes.

"I know you don't trust me, not yet," I said, "and I completely understand why. But I'm not leaving you, and neither is Peter. You've given my life purpose and meaning. You are the reason I'm here on this earth, to love and protect you, not just foster you, but to adopt you and make you my own, forever, like you were born to be."

He sat stark still, his chest rising and falling in a quickened pace.

"I honestly believe I was created so that I could be your mother one day," I said, choking on the words. "All the things I've gone through—good or bad, happy or sad, and everything in between—have prepared me for this moment. I felt it deep within my soul, the joy and the purpose of my life finally revealed to me the instant I saw your beautiful face in that photo. I had the same feeling when I met Peter."

Tears welled in his eyes and I knew I was breaking through his tough exterior, reaching to the heart of him.

"You were born to be my son, Lucas, and I was created to be your mom."

Before I realized it, tears were pouring down his face. Without another thought, I scooped him into my arms, tucking him underneath my protective wing like only a mother could.

His small arms slipped around my waist and held me tight.

I kissed his head, knowing finally I was home.

I drew in a deep breath, overwhelmed by the familiar scent of my father's cologne and my mother's floral perfume. They were here with me, guiding me and directing me, and for one of the first times since they'd passed, I truly felt alive and confident. I could do this. I *could* be their mother. Actually, I already *was* their mother, and somehow, I knew Lucas felt it too.

"There you two are," Peter called behind us.

As much as I fought it, trying to keep Lucas firmly in my motherly arms, I had no choice when he quickly pushed away from me. I knew what he was doing. He had to be strong in front of Peter, but I knew in time, Lucas would learn to relinquish his role as a caregiver to everyone and allow Peter and me to take that burden for him. Before he could break our connection, I grabbed his wrist trying to gain his attention.

"Are you okay with that?" I asked, hoping he'd understand. "For now, I mean? Letting me take care of you, Levi and Lilly?"

A smile spread across his face and small dimples curved around the corner of his lips as his dark eyes sparkled with a small sheen of unshed tears.

I knew he rarely showed this side of himself to anyone and I was more than grateful he trusted me. I was actually honored.

He nodded his head. "For now," he whispered quietly.

For now. That was enough.

"Do you have *any* of your bags packed, Lucas?" Peter hollered behind us.

Lucas scooted to the other end of the bench.

"You better go get packed, dude," I said, sensing he needed to be alone to process our conversation. I didn't want him to feel like he'd *always* be alone though.

"And only *one* Star Wars guy, got it?" I laughed, knowing he'd try to pack his whole damn collection if we let him.

"Three?" he asked softly.

I arched a brow in warning, knowing full well he could bring as many of those fucking dolls as he wanted, but I couldn't back down now. It was one of the first lessons Hindley had taught me about parenting–consistency and follow-through.

"Three dollars?" he reminded me, his brows waggling in amusement. The little shit was threatening me, and I loved that part of his personality, loved that he was feeling comfortable enough to tease with me.

"You can bring three," Peter said, making his way around the bench, holding Lilly.

Lucas stood, his face lighting up with a childlike joy I'd never seen before. Before he walked away he turned and stared at me, brows raised.

I knew he was asking for my permission and my heart warmed. I gave him a single wink and a nod of my head in confirmation, and gratitude for seeking out my consent and approval.

"You better go, though," I said. "We leave early in the morning and I know you're like me, you like to sleep in."

Lucas laughed and I hoped he would see it for what I'd intended. A reminder to him that although we weren't biologically connected, there would still be physical attributes we shared, things that made us family.

Lucas walked past Peter and his hand grazed Lilly's outstretched arm as he brushed past.

"Loo-coo!" Lilly shouted after him.

"Lee-lee." He smiled, his expression one of brotherly affection as he brought his hand up to his mouth, blowing her a kiss.

She brought her small hand to her lips, slobbering on her palm before rearing back and throwing it toward him like a football.

I laughed with amusement when Lucas raised up his hand, catching the invisible kiss in mid-air, his face animated and bright as he stuffed the unseen sign of Lilly's affection into his pocket. He loved his little sister more than words could express.

"Only three action figures!" I shouted after him, knowing he wouldn't want to keep this scene sappy for long. That wasn't Lucas's way, and I had to respect that about his personality.

"Three dollars!" he yelled back with a light-hearted laugh, warning me that he held more power over me than I wanted him to. I would have paid a million dollars to that fucking Cuss Bucket just to see the smirk tugging at the corners of his mouth.

Peter sat beside me, Lilly in his lap. "What was that all about?"

Lilly rested her head on Peter's chest.

I scooted closer, thinking there was no better place for either one of us to be.

He draped his free arm around my shoulders.

"It's a private joke." I laughed, knowing Lucas and I were bonding, hoping beyond hope, he'd let me in completely one day.

Lilly reached out and stroked my hair.

I sighed in true contentment.

"We came out here to show you something," Peter said, pushing me to a sitting position.

I held out my hands to Lilly. "Come here, sweetie." She literally fell into my arms and I laughed, her hands still toying with my hair.

"Lilly," Peter called, smiling while he tried to get her attention.

She stared up at Peter and smiled. I laughed to myself. Peter had that effect on girls.

"Who am I?" he asked her.

"Pee-pah," she answered without hesitation.

"It's Pee-ter, sweetie," I enunciated, knowing we needed to give her consistent guidance as she built her vocabulary.

"That's not what she's saying, Dana," Peter corrected me.

"She's trying to say your name," I said.

He shook his head. "No."

I stared at him in confusion.

"Who is this?" Peter asked, pointing to me.

Her wide eyes met mine and she stared at me for the longest time. It pained me to think she still didn't know who I was after being with us for over a month.

Lilly dropped the piece of hair she'd been holding and spread her fingers wide, placing her hand on my cheek, gently caressing my face with her palm. Besides Peter's touch, it was the most heavenly sensation I'd ever experienced. Our souls were connected in a way I hadn't felt since my own mother was alive.

I could feel my mother's presence with us, delighted to meet her granddaughter for the first time.

"Mah-mah," Lilly finally said.

My jaw went lax and tears sprang to my eyes. Maybe I misunderstood her. She was probably saying Dana and just got confused.

"Who is she?" Peter asked again, pointing at me.

"Mah-mah," Lilly repeated, patting my cheek with her small hand. "Mah-mah."

She smiled wide and the expression stopped my heart, robbing me of breath.

"That's what I used to call *my* mother," I whispered as tears rolled down my cheeks. "Is that what she's calling me?" I looked up at Peter. "Is she calling me Momma?"

He smiled and nodded his head. "Sam's been working with her, helping her learn more words. But that one Lilly mastered all on her own."

"Was she calling you Peter or Poppa?" I asked, understanding what her term of endearment would mean not only to Peter and me, but also to the boys.

"I'd like to think it's Poppa," he admitted.

"Mah-mah, no cry," Lilly demanded, wiping my cheeks with both her hands.

I pulled her to me, kissing her head as I sat in stunned silence. This was the most surreal moment of my life. I'd always dreamed of being a mother, dreamed of loving my own child. Sitting here with this little girl on my lap, her words and her actions warming my heart, I knew my childhood dreams could never compare to this moment.

"Look," Lilly said clearly, pulling away and pointing to my shoulder.

I turned and drew in a sharp breath. A butterfly sat on my shoulder, its yellow and black spotted wings open for the world to admire.

Lilly stared in amazement.

I took her finger and licked the tip, like my mother had shown me many times before, and held her hand out toward my shoulder. All three of us sat stock-still, knowing any movement may scare off the creature.

The butterfly flapped its wings several times before lifting off my shoulder and hovering quietly above Lilly's finger.

I stared at Lilly.

Her eyes were wide and a small smile adorned her face. I reveled in the marvel of this little girl. She remained surprisingly still, instinctively knowing it was the only way the butterfly would come to her.

The symbolism wasn't lost on me. I knew a relationship with these children would have to be forged through trust and time. But I had time. Peter and I both did. And just like Lilly with the butterfly, I was patient. I would wait forever for them to finally trust us.

Cautiously, the butterfly hovered near the tip of Lilly's finger before slowly landing.

Lilly stayed still, her expression one of pure astonishment.

I couldn't help but believe this butterfly was my own mother, coming to bring comfort to me and security to Lilly, in the form she knew was the most special to me. A butterfly.

I slowly released Lilly's arm and let her balance the creature on her own.

She held her hand still, inspecting the insect resting on her finger. Her gaze cut to mine, her eyes wide, her smile even broader.

Time stood still for me in that moment. The last puzzle piece of my once shattered life had just clicked into place. All the walls surrounding my hardened heart fell away.

I had a purpose. I had a husband. I had a family. And even if it was just a fleeting moment, I had my parents as well.

Lilly brought her finger to her lips and puckered. The butterfly flew away and the look on her face heartbreaking.

"They'll be more, sweetie," I said. "Butterflies always live together."

She pouted and I kissed the top of her head, rubbing her back. I wanted to give her the kind of comfort my mother used to give me and Sam.

"Day-nah!" Sam shouted from the deck.

I shot straight up, clutching Lilly to my chest. I stood and made my way toward my brother, heart racing. "Sam, what's wrong?"

"Isn't it right, you build a pool?" he asked.

"What?" I asked, still reeling from the heart attack he'd just given me.

"You and Pete-tah, build a pool here?" He pointed toward the foundation of the house not far from the mobile home.

"I think so, why?"

Sam loved the pool at Whispering Oaks, but given the fact I couldn't swim, I'd never been a real fan of the idea of building one in our new home. It was one of Peter's wishes, especially with the kids coming, so I'd reluctantly given in.

Sam turned and faced Levi and Lucas who were standing close by. "I told you."

"What's going on?" I asked.

"Levi can't swim," Lucas said.

I turned and stared at Levi.

His face was ashen and his hands were trembling by his sides.

I passed off Lilly to Sam and knelt down in front of Levi.

He stared down at the ground.

I placed a finger under his chin and lifted his face. "Hey."

His gaze lifted but his head still hung low.

"I can't swim either," I confessed.

He snapped his head up and stared at me, eyes wide. "Really?"

"Really." I smiled. "I damn near drowned the first night Peter and I were together." I snorted at the memory, glancing over my shoulder at Peter.

Peter's brows furrowed.

"What?" I asked.

"Four dollars." Lucas laughed.

"Oh, shit!" I exclaimed.

Everyone burst into fits of laughter. I wondered where in the hell I was going to come up with enough money to fill that fucking Cuss Bucket.

"Five dollars." Lucas chuckled.

I studied the people standing around me. My family. Joy filled me so completely it stole my breath. This was what I'd wanted since the night I'd discovered my parents had been killed in a car accident.

After the laughter died down, Peter turned to Levi and Lucas. "Boys, you better get inside and finish packing," he said, as if sensing my need for need to be alone and process everything. "Sam, will you try to get Lilly down for a nap? Dana and I will be in in just a minute."

Two small hands wrapped around my legs.

I looked down to find Levi's body pressed tightly against mine.

I knelt and wrapped my arms around him. He was mine, and I was his.

"I'm afraid," he whispered.

My heart ached for this little boy. "We'll both take swimming lessons together," I said. "Okay?"

He nodded but didn't let go. Swimming wasn't the only thing he was afraid of.

I pulled back and cupped his face. "I won't let anything happen to you, Levi. I promise."

Relief washed over his face and I nearly lost it. Just as quickly as it appeared, his expression fell, and our moment was gone. He was assured though, and that was all that mattered.

He raced to catch up with the others, turning back once to wave at me.

"Well," Peter said.

I turned to face him.

A huge grin spread wide across his face. "It would appear that you've bonded with all *three* of our children today, Mrs. Fontenot."

I loved it when he called them 'our children,' Almost as much as I loved being reminded that I was his wife.

"It would appear so, Mr. Fontenot." I slid my arms around his waist and snuggled into his chest. We stared out over the railing at the land I knew my parents had once dreamt of living near. Closing my eyes, I drew in a long, deep breath, feeling their presence all around us. "You know my parents are here," I said. "I can feel them."

"I can too."

I raised my head and stared up at him. "Really?"

He nodded.

"How?"

"Dolly," he chuckled, "they're a part of you. Anything that's a part of you is a part of me too."

Good God, I didn't think it was possible to love this man more, but with his declaration my adoration grew.

"You know, you were really *never* alone, right?" Peter asked.

I nodded, afraid I may start to cry if I spoke.

"And you'll *never* be alone," he added.

I squeezed him tighter.

"You can quit worrying, Dana. I'm not going anywhere."

"I thought that about my parents," I whispered into his chest.

"And your parents never left you either." He waved his arm toward the cliffs in front of us.

He was right. In my heart, I knew I'd never *truly* been alone all these years. No matter what happened in my life, whoever came in or out of it, I would always be surrounded by people who loved me unconditionally.

"Thank you," I whispered, placing a kiss on his chest.

"For what?"

"For giving me everything I never dreamed I'd have."

"I'll always give you that and more, Dolly." He bent down and placed a soft kiss against my lips. "I've waited a lifetime for you," he confessed, his tone deep and serious.

"Was I worth the wait?" I laughed nervously, tilting my head, trying to be sexy and coy.

His mismatched eyes shimmered in the afternoon sun. "What do you *think*, Dolly?" Peter asked, peering down at me, a small smile lighting up his beautiful face.

I suddenly remembered the first time I'd seen Peter, standing in line at the concession stand. The feeling I had now was exactly the same. Our journey had been long and trying at times, but there was no denying the fact that we belonged together.

"What do I think?" I laughed.

He raised a curious brow.

"I think you're pretty fan-fucking-tastic, Mr. Fontenot, that's what I think."

"I think you're pretty fan-fucking-tastic too, Mrs. Fontenot." He laughed, leaning down, gently rubbing my nose with his.

I laughed out loud at his expletive. "I'm a bad influence on you."

His expression grew serious and he tugged me close.

I feared I'd upset him in some unknown way.

"You've been the best influence of my life, Dolly," he said. "And I thank God every day that you doused me with beer."

I slumped in relief.

"What?"

"Nothing." I sighed against his chest.

"Oh, yeah, I forgot to tell you," he added.

"What?" My heart raced with concern.

Peter leaned in closer, his lips caressing my ear. His warm breath wafted over my skin as he spoke. "I'm going to fuck you forty ways to Sunday in Hawaii."

I covered my mouth, eyes wide. "Holy shit, Peter." I couldn't believe how brazen my husband was becoming. I really was a bad influence.

"What?" he asked, his brows furrowed. "Doesn't that sound like fun to you?"

I shook my head, staring into those mesmerizing eyes that had captured my heart long ago. "Not fun. It sounds amazing, Peter."

"Fan-fucking-tastic?" he asked.

I snorted. "Yeah," I stuttered out through my laughter, "it sounds pretty fan-fucking-tastic."

He grasped me around the waist and led us back toward the house.

"And by the way," I said, "you owe the bucket two dollars."

Peter laughed as we stepped through the sliding glass door, into our future.

Yeah, my life was pretty fan-fucking-tastic for sure. Cuss Bucket be damned.

Thank you for reading
Extreme Trust

Be sure to turn the page for a sneak peek at
Geneva and Berk's love story
Extreme Attraction

Geneva Barton was a bitch—until the threat of criminal charges and the loss of her family forced her to confront the demons from her past. Two years later she's worked hard to overcome her vindictive ways. Will attending her best friend's destination wedding be her chance to prove to everyone she's changed?

After suffering heart-breaking loss, Berk Rigby left his career as a professional snowboarder and returned to his native island home in Kauai, Hawaii. The last thing he deserves is absolution from the ghosts that haunt him. When a beautiful guest at his family's island resort attracts his attention and forces him to confront his past, he's suddenly dreaming of the future again—a future with her. But all they have is seven days. Right?

A chance encounter.
A leap of faith.
A vacation that could last a lifetime.

Extreme Attraction
Available now

CAN'T GET ENOUGH OF DANA?

Neither could I, so I wrote a bonus chapter, an entry from Dana's secret diary the night before she and her family leave for their destination wedding in Hawaii.

This link is exclusive to readers who have purchased *Extreme Trust*.

www.kaymanis.com/pages/dana-s-secret-diary

WANT TO RECEIVE A FREE EBOOK?

Join my email list and I'll send you *Extreme Beginning*, the X-Treme Love Prequel for free. It's the story of Caroline Hagen and Paul Barton. Just visit the website below and join today.

I also give away free things all the time, including ebooks and signed paperbacks (my own and from best-selling authors) and more.

You'll also receive exclusive sneak peeks and teasers of upcoming books in my series.

Visit my website to join now and receive your free ebook today!

www.kaymanis.com

IF YOU ENJOYED THIS BOOK

Please:

    1. Write a review. It's so important to my work.

    2. Tell your family and friends about my books.

    3. Visit my website and sign up for my newsletter. You can also send me an email. I love to hear from my readers.

    www.kaymanis.com

    4. Follow me on social media.

    Facebook: www.facebook.com/kaymanisauthor2

    Twitter: www.twitter.com/kaymanis

    Instagram: www.instagram.com/kaymanis

JOIN MY PRIVATE FACEBOOK GROUP

THE MANIS MOB SQUAD

We support and enable those diagnosed with **MOB Disease (Mania of Books) -** a rare and debilitating disease that causes sufferers to become unable and/or unwilling to stop reading and obsessing over all things book related.

Are you a book-aholic? Do you have a One-Click addiction? Then come join this support group. We're all about fun in here, no judgment.

ALSO AVAILABLE BY KAY MANIS

X-Treme Love Series

Extreme Risk (Hindley and Rory)

Extreme Devotion (Hindley and Rory)

Extreme Sacrifice (Dana and Peter)

Extreme Trust (Dana and Peter)

Extreme Attraction (Geneva and Berk)

Extreme Courage (Geneva and Berk)

Extreme Promise (Hindley and Rory)

Extreme Gift: The New Arrival (Hindley and Rory)

Extreme Beginning: The Prequel (Caroline and Paul)

Baxter Bay

You Could Be Mine (Aiden and Olivia)

Sumner Brothers Series

Born to Be My Baby (Ben and Maggie)

Never Say Goodbye (Emmett and Elle)

Thank You for Loving Me (Max and Devlin)

With These Two Hands (Aaron and Kayleigh)

I'll Be There for You (Jake and Lina)

If That's What It Takes (Grant and Sophie)

Now and Forever (Max and Devlin)

Season of Love Short Story Series

Second Chance Heart

Dance with Me
Fall for Me

EXTREME ATTRACTION EXCERPT

X-TREME LOVE SERIES BOOK 5

GENEVA

The sun's rays cast a welcome blanket of warmth over my exposed skin. The smell of salt air and the calming lull of the waves transported my mind to a distant place where worries no longer existed, and my past was completely absolved. My only desire was to stay locked in this Hawaiian bubble forever. But Dana's cutting words disintegrated the moment like a nuclear bomb.

"Holy motherfucker, guys!"

"What?" Hindley asked.

Even with my eyes closed and covered by dark sunglasses, I could still picture Hindley sitting straight up on her lounger, her face contorted in fear as she scanned the pristine Hawaiian beach, searching for any lurking child predators. I quietly chuckled at what a protective mother she'd become—fierce and strong.

"This time tomorrow I'll be married!" Dana shouted, loud enough for people inside the resort to hear.

"You're just now realizing that?" I laughed, never once opening my eyes or turning to face her.

"Yeah," she answered, as if astonished by her own words, "I guess I am."

"Technically, you're already married," Hindley corrected.

Dana and her husband, Peter, had already married in a small ceremony back in Austin where we were from. This destination wedding in Hawaii was a bonus.

"Well, yeah," Dana agreed. "But this is different. I mean, the kids will be there."

Dana and Peter were currently fostering three children they hoped to adopt soon. Since she was unable to carry a child, she and her husband had decided to adopt. Thankfully for them, the adoption had come more quickly than expected. I delighted in seeing my friend in her new role as wife and mother.

Hearing a slight quiver in her voice made me realize my friend needed more than just a snarky comeback from me.

I sat up on my lounge chair on the beach, pushing my shades up high on my head. "What's wrong, Dana? Peter loves you. The kids adore you. Tomorrow will be perfect." I reached beside my lounger, grasping for the plastic glass. "Drink this." I held the fruity cocktail out to her.

She took it willingly, chugging the remainder of my pina colada as if she were a college student in a fraternity drinking contest.

"It's just…" Dana stumbled with her words.

"You feel like this is your last night of freedom?" Hindley asked.

"Yeah, I guess," Dana sighed. "Something like that."

"So *now* you want a bachelorette party?" I half yelled, glaring at her. "I offered to throw you one for the last three weeks." I held up three fingers for emphasis. "Now, here we sit on the tropical shores of Kauai, thousands of miles away from the friends I know would want to attend." Her destination wedding was a small affair, just family and close friends. How the hell was I supposed to pull something together?

"But you were sick," Dana pouted.

"It was just a stomach bug," I said. "We still could have gone out."

"It wasn't *just* a stomach bug, Geneva. You were puking up your toenails for over a week," Hindley said.

"You were so sick, I wasn't even sure if you were going to be able to come to Hawaii," Dana said. Her concern for me wasn't surprising, but I still didn't feel worthy of it.

"I would have given you a party back home if that's what you wanted, no matter how sick I was."

"I don't want a party," Dana said with a coy smile.

"Cut the shit, Di Grazio," I said. "Your demure expression does nothing for your face."

"Fuck you, Geneva." She laughed, wadding up the damp napkin under her glass and tossing it in my direction.

"You'd like to." I smirked, snagging the napkin mid-air.

"Actually, no. I think you'd like to fuck *him*." Dana nodded toward something, or rather someone, out in the water.

Curious, Hindley and I followed her gaze and stared, jaws lax, as a man emerged casually out of the water carrying a bright yellow surfboard under one arm. His other hand pushed back long, jet-black hair from his face.

I thumbed through the massive bank of adjectives floating around in my mind but discovered there truly were no words you could use to describe this man.

He wasn't your typical beau-hunk, romance hero, the ones authors wrote about. The kind you fantasize over for days after reading all of their steamy sex scenes with the virginal heroine. At least not the ones I read.

I gazed down at the semi-pornographic cover of the novel sitting beside me on my beach bag. No, the man sauntering toward us looked *nothing* like the blond fox posing semi-naked on the front of my book, but it didn't make this ball-of-hotness walking toward us any less cover model worthy. The man, who had all three of us speechless, was a Greek God, Poseidon, rising from the waters of his home deep within the ocean.

His body was ripped like a Calvin Klein underwear model, his chest hard and dark, in grave contrast to the neon yellow and green board shorts hanging low on his hips. A tingle erupted between my legs and I had to cross my ankles and rub my thighs together for relief.

What the hell was that?

I didn't have to ask. I knew what it was—sexual desire for a complete stranger. Something I was used to, something I would have acted on in my old days. Thankfully these days I was a new girl.

"Holy fuck!" Dana bellowed.

I'm sure her outburst caught the demi-god by surprise, as well as the other guests lounging nearby.

I slammed my eyes shut, denying myself the pleasure of gawking. He was probably used to women ogling his gorgeous body. I pictured his delicious lips curving up into a seductive smile, his long mane of hair dancing in the island breeze—*Stop, Geneva. Stop it.*

I couldn't help it. I hadn't experienced this instant connection, this burning desire for a man, in years. I didn't need that type of relationship, though. Not now.

These types of feelings always ended the same. They started with a tiny spark, but quickly turned into a raging inferno that would destroy everything in its path. Especially me.

I'd survived many sordid relationships before I was married. But after my divorce, I'd closed myself off to those carnal feelings, choosing instead to concentrate on my studies and my new career as a teacher.

I slid my shades down over my eyes and drilled them shut before sinking back in my chair.

"Are you ladies busy this afternoon?"

I shuddered slightly from the sounds of the deep voice above the roar of the waves, his words gliding over my skin like suntan oil. His masculine vibrato was laced with the hint of an island accent, and I didn't have to open my eyes to know it was Poseidon. Instantly, my stomach twisted in knots.

Don't look, don't look.

"Whatcha got in mind, sailor?" Dana giggled.

I'm sure the dude was lost in her hypnotic blue eyes and deep dimples.

Don't look, don't look. It's like the sun. If you look at him, it could blind you.

I couldn't stand the suspense. Against my better judgment, I slowly lifted my lids.

Damn!

Drawing in a deep breath, I tried to appear as unaffected as possible. I didn't want him to see the goose bumps prickling over my skin. Even though they were probably visible from the space station and dotting every surface of my body, despite the warm sun.

"I was wondering if you all might be interested in some surfing lessons today." He was staring straight at me.

I squirmed in discomfort, afraid I might scream from my spontaneous orgasm about to erupt from the rich tenor of his voice. Thinking about straddling a surfboard, my legs gaping wide open with Poseidon poised behind me, his massive erection poking in my back…*Stop!*

I jumped up from my seat, gathered my towel and cover-up, and nervously shoved them both into my beach bag. I had to get the hell out of here or this guy was gonna end up underneath me on this lounge chair, screaming out my name in a chant of pure ecstasy, begging for mercy. Yeah, I was that good, and I knew it. Unfortunately, so did half the men in Texas.

"Well, I'm getting married tomorrow," Dana answered, "and I don't want to walk down the aisle with a broken leg. And this one here," she said, motioning her thumb toward Hindley, "she's preggers, so that's a no go."

I knew what Dana was doing. She was setting up Poseidon to put all his surf lesson sales efforts on me. I cut my eyes toward the surfer, surveying his perfect form. When our eyes finally met, I wasn't surprised to find his focus squarely on me. It was as if he hadn't even noticed Dana and Hindley at all.

"What about you?"

His quiet voice had my body humming. This was bad, *really* bad. If I accepted his invitation, it would be over. I would throw him down and fuck him senseless right here on the beach.

It's only a week. What could it hurt?

True. No commitment, no strings. Maybe Poseidon was just what I needed.

"What about me?" I asked.

"Would you like to learn how to ride?"

Dana giggled at the innuendo, always turning the most mundane things into something sexual. My eyes drank him in from top to bottom like the sexual predator I used to be.

His deep, rich tan was not a product of hours in the sun, but God-given, his heritage as a native islander. Jet-black hair hung past his shoulders and moved with the light breeze.

I swallowed the lump in my throat, watching helplessly as he dug his massive hand deep into his scalp. Threading his fingers through the strands of his silky mass, he pulled back the hair that had blown across his face. His face.

Holy fuck!

"Wow." Dana laughed. "That's an offer *any* chick would have to be completely insane or half dead to turn down."

She was right. A woman would have to be a gold-star lesbian not to be affected by this man's sultry invitation.

One problem, though. I was a creature of habit. The turbulent wakes I'd created in my past were constant reminders to stay alert to my natural tendencies. I couldn't afford to surrender now.

Something about Poseidon warned me that if I let him lead me into the ocean and put his body anywhere close to mine, even for something as simple as a surfing lesson, I'd never return. I didn't want a man to have that kind of power over me. I never had. I existed in a bubble for a reason.

"Maybe some other time," I answered nonchalantly, as if his invitation hadn't affected me.

Throwing my bag over my shoulder, I stalked through the sand toward my private cabana, never once looking back at the mythical god of the sea standing behind me. I knew if I did, I'd regret it. But now, walking away from him, I already felt like it was the biggest mistake of my life.

~

To read more of Geneva and Berk's love story purchase
Extreme Attraction
X-Treme Love Series, Book 5
Available now

ACKNOWLEDGMENTS

I found out when you write a book, there are *a lot* of people to thank along the way. So here goes…

Kimberly, my daughter (a girl who's more like me than she'll ever admit) — You were the first person to believe in my abilities as a writer. My intense, late night therapy sessions with you really are the reason I'm still writing. I can't thank you enough for making me believe in myself. I love you, shoogie and wish you much success in your own life. I hope I can be there for you as much and as often as you have for me.

Tony, my husband — You've been my best friend since we met, and one of my biggest supporters throughout this process. Your belief in me boosted my confidence and made me take this crazy-ass journey into the unknown world called writing. Your support has allowed me the freedom to pursue a dream I never even knew existed. I love you.

Lorrie Anson, my editor — You've made me a better writer in spite of myself. You've also become one of my best friends. Words can't express how much your friendship means to me. I truly am blessed to know you. And equally as blessed that you put up with all my psycho bullshit.

Julie, Melody, Christina C. Stacy, Christina B., Jessica, Elisabeth and Jane, my Beautiful Beta Bitches — You girls helped me find the voice within me that I never knew existed. Thank you for giving up your spare time to help me make my series the best it could be.

ABOUT THE AUTHOR

Kay Manis is a funny chick who's sprinkled with a little crazy on top. Okay, let's be honest. . . there's ALOTTA crazy up there.

She writes books filled with passion, promise and purpose (with laughter and a few tears, but always an HEA).

She is a native Texan and lives with her family in Florida. When not reading or writing, you'll find Kay eating out with friends or napping with her favorite pillow (stolen from an Inn in Vermont - true story).

Please feel free to contact her at: **www.kaymanis.com**

facebook.com/kaymanisauthor2
x.com/kaymanis
instagram.com/kaymanis